VAST. EPIC. INTERSTELLAR.

FEDERATIONS

OTHER BOOKS BY

JOHN JOSEPH ADAMS

By Blood We Live
The Improbable Adventures of Sherlock Holmes
The Living Dead
The Living Dead 2
Seeds of Change
Wastelands

VAST. EPIC. INTERSTELLAR.

FEDERATIONS

EDITED BY

JOHN JOSEPH ADAMS

PRIME BOOKS

FEDERATIONS

Cover art by Sergoe.
Backcover art by James Thew.
Cover design by Stephen H. Segal.
Interior layout & design by Garry Nurrish.

Prime Books
www.prime-books.com

For more information, contact Prime Books.

ISBN: 978-1-60701-201-6

PERMISSIONS

"Mazer in Prison" by Orson Scott Card. © 2005 Orson Scott Card. Originally published in *Intergalactic Medicine Show*, October 2005. Reprinted by permission of the author.

"Carthago Delenda Est" by Genevieve Valentine. © 2009 Genevieve Valentine.

"Life-Suspension" by L. E. Modesitt, Jr. © 2009 L. E. Modesitt, Jr.

"Terra-Exulta" by S. L. Gilbow. © 2009 S. L. Gilbow.

"Aftermaths" by Lois McMaster Bujold. © 1986 Lois McMaster Bujold. Originally published in *Far Frontiers,* Volume V, Spring 1986. Reprinted by permission of the author.

"Someone is Stealing the Great Throne Rooms of the Galaxy" by Harry Turtledove. © 2006 Harry Turtledove. Originally published in *Space Cadets.* Reprinted by permission of the author.

"Prisons" by Kevin J. Anderson and Doug Beason. © 1992 Kevin J. Anderson and Doug Beason. Originally published in *Amazing Stories.* Reprinted by permission of the authors.

"Different Day" by K. Tempest Bradford. © 2009 K. Tempest Bradford.

"Twilight of the Gods" by John C. Wright. © 2009 John C. Wright.

"Warship" by George R. R. Martin and George Guthridge. © 1979 George R. R. Martin and George Guthridge. Originally published in *The Magazine of Fantasy & Science Fiction*. Reprinted by permission of the authors.

"Swanwatch" by Yoon Ha Lee. ©2009 Yoon Ha Lee.

"Spirey and the Queen" by Alastair Reynolds. © 1996 Alastair Reynolds. Originally published in *Interzone.* Reprinted by permission of the author.

"Pardon Our Conquest" by Alan Dean Foster. © 2009 Thranx, Inc.

"Symbiont" by Robert Silverberg. © 1985 Agberg, Ltd. Originally published in *Playboy.* Reprinted by permission of the author.

"The Ship Who Returned" by Anne McCaffrey. © 1999 Anne McCaffrey. First appeared in *Far Horizons.* Reprinted by permission of the author and the Virginia Kidd Agency, Inc.

CONTENTS

INTRODUCTION

JOHN JOSEPH ADAMS

It's safe to say that without *Star Wars* and *Star Trek*, I might have never become a science fiction fan. When I was a kid, it was those movies and television shows that first interested me in the genre. And when I tested the waters of science fiction reading, some of the first books I bought with my own money were *Star Trek* and *Star Wars* novels. In a sense, these properties and their tie-in novels acted as a kind of gateway drug to the wider genre of science fiction for me. Since reading those first books, I have expanded my tastes and interests, but my fondness for the *Trek*-type of narrative has remained, and so to me, the idea of doing an anthology that builds on those same tropes and traditions held great appeal. That, more than anything, is the reason this book exists.

But of course it is not just *Star Trek* and *Star Wars* that explore the vastness of interstellar, galaxy-spanning societies—of governments, not of countries, but of *worlds*, or *entire groups of worlds*. SF literature has a great many examples of it as well. There are classics like Isaac Asimov's *Foundation*, Ursula K. Le Guin's Hainish cycle, and Frank Herbert's *Dune* series; in fact, the tradition in print SF goes back long before *Star Trek* and *Star Wars*, all the way back to the days of the pulps, when writers like E. E. "Doc" Smith was writing his *Lensman* novels.

These classic federations have revealed and shaped much of American life. But with this anthology, we look to see what comes next. What will the interstellar federations of the future look like now that our society accepts (for the most part) racial and gender equality? President Barack Obama himself was a *Trek* fan as a child. Now, he is the first African-American president, something that even optimists like Gene Roddenberry might have had a hard time imagining. There will always be federations on the horizon, in our future, describing who we wish we were, or might become.

Over the decades, writers have continued to develop new and exciting takes on this theme—indeed, contemporary writers like Alastair Reynolds and Lois McMaster Bujold have crafted some of the finest examples of interstellar science fiction of all time, work that will likely be considered classic in the future. Writers like them, and the others in this book, are keeping the tradition alive, building on what the generations before have laid out, innovating to keep the sub-genre fresh and vital.

In the pages that follow, you will find a mix of all-new, original fiction, alongside selected reprints from authors whose work exemplifies what interstellar science fiction is capable of.

MAZER IN PRISON

ORSON SCOTT CARD

Orson Scott Card is the best-selling author of more than forty novels, including *Ender's Game*, which was a winner of both the Hugo and Nebula Awards. The sequel, *Speaker for the Dead*, also won both awards, making Card the only author to have captured science fiction's two most coveted prizes in consecutive years. His most recent book is another entry in the Enderverse, *Ender in Exile*.

"Mazer in Prison," which first appeared in Card's webzine, *Intergalactic Medicine Show*, takes place prior to the events in *Ender's Game* and follows Mazer Rackham, a war hero in the First Formic War, as he travels alone through space experiencing relativistic travel. Those familiar with the series will recognize several characters and will come to have a deeper understanding of how Battle School came to be. For newcomers, this story is a glimpse into military bureaucracy and one man's sacrifice for the human race.

MAZER IN PRISON

Being the last best hope of humanity was a lousy job.

Sure, the pay was great, but it had to pile up in a bank back on Earth, because there was no place out here to shop.

There was no place to *walk*. When your official exercise program consisted of having your muscles electrically stimulated while you slept, then getting spun around in a centrifuge so your bones wouldn't dissolve, there wasn't much to look forward to in an average day.

To Mazer Rackham, it felt as though he was being punished for having won the last war.

After the defeat of the invading Formics—or "Buggers," as they were commonly called—the International Fleet learned everything they could from the alien technology. Then, as fast as they could build the newly designed starships, the IF launched them toward the Formic home world, and the other planets that had been identified as Formic colonies.

But they hadn't sent Mazer out with any of *those* ships. If they had, then he wouldn't be completely alone. There'd be other people to talk to—fighter pilots, crew. Primates with faces and hands and voices and *smells*, was that asking so much?

No, he had a much more important mission. He was supposed to command *all* the fleets in their attacks on all the Formic worlds. That meant he would need to be back in the Solar system, communicating with all the fleets by ansible.

Great. A cushy desk job. He was old enough to relish that.

Except for one hitch.

Since space travel could only approach but never quite reach three hundred million meters per second, it would take many years for the fleets to reach their target worlds. During those years of waiting back at

International Fleet headquarters—IF-COM—Mazer would grow old and frail, physically *and* mentally.

So to keep him young enough to be useful, they shut him up in a near-lightspeed courier ship and launched him on a completely meaningless outbound journey. At some arbitrary point in space, they decreed, he would decelerate, turn around, and then return to Earth at the same speed, arriving home only a few years before the fleets arrived and all hell broke loose. He would have aged no more than five years during the voyage, even though decades would have passed on Earth.

A lot of good he'd do them as a commander, if he lost his mind during the voyage.

Sure, he had plenty of books in the onboard database. Millions of them. And announcements of new books were sent to him by ansible; any he wanted, he could ask for and have them in moments.

What he couldn't have was a conversation.

He had tried. After all, how different was the ansible from regular email over the nets? The problem was the time differential. To him, it seemed he sent out a message and it was answered immediately. But to the person on the other end, Mazer's message was spread out over days, coming in a bit at a time. Once his whole message had been received and assembled, the person could write an answer immediately. But to be received by the ansible on Mazer's little boat, the answer would be spaced out a bit at a time, as well.

The result was that for the person Mazer was conversing with, many days intervened between the parts of the conversation. It had to be like talking with somebody with such an incredible stammer that you could walk away, live your life for a week, and then come back before he had finally spit out whatever it was he had to say.

A few people had tried, but by now, with Mazer nearing the point where he would decelerate to turn the ship around, his communications with IF-COM on the asteroid Eros were mostly limited to book and holo and movie requests, plus his daily blip—the message he sent just to assure the IF that he wasn't dead.

He could even have automated the daily blip—it's not as if Mazer didn't know how to get around their firewalls and reprogram the shipboard computer. But he dutifully composed a new and unique message every day that he knew would barely be glanced at back at IF-COM. As far as anyone there cared, he might as well be dead; they would all have retired or even died before he got back.

The problem of loneliness wasn't a surprise, of course. They had even suggested sending someone with him. Mazer himself had vetoed the idea, because it seemed to him to be stupid and cruel to tell a person that he was so completely useless to the fleet, to the whole war effort, that he could be sent out on Mazer's aimless voyage just to hold his hand. "What will your recruiting poster be next year?" Mazer had asked. "'Join the Fleet and spend a couple of years as a paid companion to an aging space captain!'?"

To Mazer it was only going to *be* a few years. He was a private person who didn't mind being alone. He was sure he could handle it.

What he hadn't taken into account was how long two years of solitary confinement would *be*. They do this, he realized, to prisoners who've misbehaved, as the worst punishment they could give. Think of that—to be completely alone for long periods of time is *worse* than having to keep company with the vilest, stupidest felons known to man.

We evolved to be social creatures; the Formics, by their hivemind nature, are never alone. They can travel this way with impunity. To a lone human, it's torture.

And of course there was the tiny matter of leaving his family behind. But he wouldn't think about that. He was making no greater sacrifice than any of the other warriors who took off in the fleets sent to destroy the enemy. Win or lose, none of *them* would see their families again. In this, at least, he was one with the men he would be commanding.

The real problem was one that only he recognized: He didn't have a clue how to save the human race, once he got back.

That was the part that nobody seemed to understand. He explained it to them, that he was not a particularly good commander, that he had won that crucial battle on a fluke, that there was no reason to think he could do such a thing again. His superior officers agreed that he might be right. They promised to recruit and train new officers while Mazer was gone, trying to find a better commander. But in case they didn't find one, Mazer *was* the guy who fired the single missile that ended the previous war. People believed in him. Even if he didn't believe in himself.

Of course, knowing the military mind, Mazer knew that they would completely screw up the search for a new commander. The only way they would take the search seriously was if they did *not* believe they had Mazer Rackham as their ace-in-the-hole.

Mazer sat in the confined space behind the pilot seat and extended his left leg, stretching it up, then bringing it behind his head. Not every man his age could do this. Definitely not every *Maori*, not those with the traditional bulk of the fully adult male. Of course, he was only half-Maori, but it wasn't as if people of European blood were known for their extraordinary physical flexibility.

The console speaker said, "Incoming message."

"I'm listening," said Mazer. "Make it voice and read it now."

"Male or female?" asked the computer.

"Who cares?" said Mazer.

"Male or female?" the computer repeated.

"Random," said Mazer.

So the message was read out to him in a female voice.

"Admiral Rackham, my name is Hyrum Graff. I've been assigned to head recruitment for Battle School, the first step in our training program for gifted young officers. My job is to scour the Earth looking for someone to head our forces during the coming conflict—instead of you. I was told by everyone who bothered to answer me at all that the criterion was simple: Find someone just like Mazer Rackham."

Mazer found himself interested in what this guy was saying. They were actually looking for his replacement. This man was in charge of the search. To listen to him in a voice of a different gender seemed mocking and disrespectful.

"Male voice," said Mazer.

Immediately the voice changed to a robust baritone. "The trouble I'm having, Admiral, is that when I ask them specifically what *traits* of yours I should try to identify for my recruits, everything becomes quite vague. The only conclusion I can reach is this: The attribute of yours that they want the new commander to have is 'victorious.' In vain do I point out that I need better guidelines than that.

"So I have turned to you for help. You know as well as I do that there was a certain component of luck involved in your victory. At the same time, you saw what no one else could see, and you acted—against orders—at exactly the right moment for your thrust to be unnoticed by the Hive Queen. Boldness, courage, iconoclasm—maybe we can identify those traits. But how do we test for vision?

"There's a social component, too. The men in your crew trusted you enough to obey your disobedient orders and put their careers, if not their lives, in your hands.

"Your record of reprimands for insubordination suggests, also, that you are an experienced critic of incompetent commanders. So you must also have very clear ideas of what your future replacement should *not* be.

"Therefore I have obtained permission to use the ansible to query you about the attributes we need to look for—or avoid—in the recruits we find. In the hope that you will find this project more interesting than whatever it is you're doing out there in space, I eagerly await your reply."

Mazer sighed. This Graff sounded like exactly the kind of officer who should be put in charge of finding Mazer's replacement. But Mazer also knew enough about military bureaucracy to know that Graff would be chewed up and spit out the first time he actually tried to accomplish something. Getting permission to communicate by ansible with an old geezer who was effectively dead was easy enough.

"What was the sender's rank?" Mazer asked the console.

"Lieutenant."

Poor Lieutenant Graff had obviously underestimated the terror that incompetent officers feel in the presence of young, intelligent, energetic *replacements.*

At least it would be a conversation.

"Take down this answer, please," said Mazer. "Dear Lieutenant Graff, I'm sorry for the time you have to waste waiting for this message . . . no, scratch that, why *increase* the wasted time by sending a message stuffed with useless chat?" Then again, doing a whole bunch of editing would delay the message just as long.

Mazer sighed, unwound himself from his stretch, and went to the console. "I'll type it in myself," said Mazer. "It'll go faster that way."

He found the words he had just dictated waiting for him on the screen of his message console, with the edge of Graff's message just behind it. He flipped that message to the front, read it again, and then picked up his own message where he had left off.

"I am not an expert in identifying the traits of leadership. Your message reveals that you have already thought more about it than I have. Much as

I might hope your endeavor is successful, since it would relieve me of the burden of command upon my return, I cannot help you."

He toyed with adding "God could not help you," but decided to let the boy find out how the world worked without dire and useless warnings from Mazer.

Instead he said "Send" and the console replied, "Message sent by ansible."

And that, thought Mazer, is the end of that.

• • •

The answer did not come for more than three hours. What was that, a month back on Earth?

"Who is it from?" asked Mazer, knowing perfectly well who it would turn out to be. So the boy had taken his time before pushing the matters. Time enough to learn how impossible his task was? Probably not.

Mazer was sitting on the toilet—which, thanks to the Formics' gravitic technology, was a standard gravity-dependent chemical model. Mazer was one of the few still in the service who remembered the days of air-suction toilets in weightless spaceships, which worked about half the time. That was the era when ship captains would sometimes be cashiered for wasting fuel by accelerating their ships just so they could take a dump that would actually get pulled away from their backside by something like gravity.

"Lieutenant Hyrum Graff."

And now he had the pestiferous Hyrum Graff, who would probably be even more annoying than null-g toilets.

"Erase it."

"I am not allowed to erase ansible communications," said the female voice blandly. It was always bland, of course, but it *felt* particularly bland when saying irritating things.

I could make you erase it, if I wanted to go to the trouble of reprogramming you. But Mazer didn't say it, in case it might alert the program safeguards in some way. "Read it."

"Male voice?"

"Female," snapped Mazer.

"Admiral Rackham, I'm not sure you understood the gravity of our situation. We have two possibilities: Either we will identify the best possible commanders for our war against the Formics, or we will have you as our commander. So either you will help us identify the traits that are most likely to be present in the ideal commander, or you will *be* the commander on whom all the responsibility rests."

"I understand that, you little twit," said Mazer. "I understood it before you were born."

"Would you like me to take down your remarks as a reply?" asked the computer.

"Just read it and ignore my carping."

The computer returned to the message from Lieutenant Graff. "I have located your wife and children. They are all in good health, and it may be that some or all of them might be glad of an opportunity to converse with you by ansible, if you so desire. I offer this, not as bribe for your cooperation, but as a reminder, perhaps, that more is at stake here than the importunities of an upstart lieutenant pestering an admiral and a war hero on a voyage into the future."

Mazer roared out his answer. "As if I had need of reminders from *you!*"

"Would you like me to take down your remarks as—"

"I'd like you to shut yourself down and leave me in—"

"A reply?" finished the computer, ignoring his carping.

"Peace!" Mazer sighed. "Take down *this* answer: I'm divorced, and my ex-wife and children have made their lives without me. To them I'm dead. It's despicable for you to attempt to raise me from the grave to burden their lives. When I tell you that I have nothing to tell you about command it's because I truly do not know any answers that you could possibly implement.

"I'm desperate for you to find a replacement for me, but in all my experience in the military, I saw no example of the kind of commander that we need. So figure it out for yourself—I haven't any idea."

For a moment he allowed his anger to flare. "And leave my family out of it, you contemptible . . . "

Then he decided not to flame the poor git. "Delete everything after 'leave my family out of it.'"

"Do you wish me to read it back to you?"

"I'm on the toilet!"

Since his answer was nonresponsive, the computer repeated the question verbatim.

"No. Just send it. I don't want to have the zealous Lieutenant Graff wait an extra hour or day just so I can turn my letter into a prize-winning school essay."

• • •

But Graff's question nagged at him. What *should* they look for in a commander?

What did it matter? As soon as they developed a list of desirable traits, all the bureaucratic buttsniffs would immediately figure out how to fake having them, and they'd be right back where they started, with the best bureaucrats at the top of every military hierarchy, and all the genuinely brilliant leaders either discharged or demoralized.

The way I was demoralized, piloting a barely-armed supply ship in the rear echelons of our formation.

Which was in itself a mark of the stupidity of our commanders—the fact that they thought there could *be* such a thing as a "rear echelon" during a war in three-dimensional space.

There might have been dozens of men who could have seen what I saw—the point of vulnerability in the Formics' formation—but they had long since left the service. The only reason *I* was there was because I couldn't afford to quit before vesting in my pension. So I put up with spiteful commanders who would punish me for being a better officer than they would ever be. I took the abuse, the contempt, and so there I was piloting a ship with only two weapons—slow missiles at that.

Turned out I only needed one.

But who could have predicted that I'd be there, that I'd see what I saw, and that I'd commit career suicide by firing my missiles against orders—and then I'd turn out to be right? What process can test for *that?* Might as well resort to prayer—either God is looking out for the human race or he doesn't care. If he cares, then we'll go on surviving despite our stupidity. If he doesn't, then we won't.

In a universe that works like *that*, any attempt to identify in advance the traits of great commanders is utterly wasted.

"Incoming visuals," said the computer.

Mazer looked down at his desk screen, where he had jotted:

Desperation

Intuition (test for *that*, sucker!)

Tolerance for the orders of fools.

~~Borderline~~-insane sense of personal mission.

Yeah, *that's* the list Graff's hoping I'll send him.

And now the boy was sending him visuals. Who approved *that?*

But the head that flickered in the holospace above his desk wasn't an eagerbeaver young lieutenant. It was a young woman with light-colored hair like her mother's and only a few traces of her father's part-Maori appearance. But the traces *were* there, and she was beautiful.

"Stop," said Mazer.

"I am required to show you—"

"This is personal. This is an *intrusion*."

"—all ansible communications."

"Later."

"This is a visual and therefore has high priority. Sufficient ansible bandwidth for full motion visuals will only be used for communications of the—"

Mazer gave up. "Just play it."

"Father," said the young woman in the holospace.

Mazer looked away from her, reflexively hiding his face, though of course she couldn't see him anyway. His daughter Pai Mahutanga. When he last saw her, she was a tree-climbing five-year-old. She used to have nightmares, but with her father always on duty with the fleet, there was no one to drive away the bad dreams.

"I brought your grandchildren with me," she was saying. "Pahu Rangi hasn't found a woman yet who will let him reproduce." She grinned wickedly at someone out of frame. Her brother. Mazer's son. Just a baby, conceived on his last leave before the final battle.

"We've told the children all about you. I know you can't see them all at once, but if they each come into frame with me for just a few moments—it's so generous of them to let me—

"But he said that you might not be happy to see me. Even if that's true, Father, I know you'll want to see your grandchildren. They'll still be alive when you return. *I* might even be. Please don't hide from us. We know that when you divorced Mother it was for her sake, and ours. We know that you never stopped loving us. See? Here's Kahui Kura. And Pao Pao Te

Rangi. They also have English names, Mirth and Glad, but they're proud to be children of the Maori. Through you. But your grandson Mazer Taka Aho Howarth insists on using the name you went . . . *go* by. And as for baby Struan Maeroero, he'll make the choice when he gets older." She sighed. "I suppose he's our last child, if the New Zealand courts uphold the Hegemony's new population rules."

As each of the children stepped into frame, shyly or boldly, depending on their personality, Mazer tried to feel something toward them. Two daughters first, shy, lovely. The little boy named for him. Finally the baby that someone held into the frame.

They were strangers, and before he ever met them they would be parents themselves. Perhaps grandparents. What was the *point?* I told your mother that we had to be dead to each other. She had to think of me as a casualty of war, even if the paperwork said Divorce Decree instead of Killed in Action.

She was so angry she told me that she would rather I had died. She was going to tell our children that I was dead. Or that I just left them, without giving them any reason, so they'd hate me.

Now it turns out she turned my departure into a sentimental memory of sacrifice for God and country. Or at least for planet and species.

Mazer forced himself not to wonder if this meant that she had forgiven him. She was the one with children to raise—what she decided to tell them was none of his business. Whatever helped her raise the children without a father.

He didn't marry and have children until he was already middle-aged—he'd been afraid to start a family when he knew he'd be gone on voyages lasting years at a time. Then he met Kim, and all that rational process went out the window. He wanted—his DNA wanted—their children to exist, even if he couldn't be there to raise them. Pai Mahutanga and Pahu Rangi—he wanted the children's lives to be stable and good, rich with opportunity, so he stayed in the service in order to earn the separation bonuses that would pay to put them through college.

Then he fought in the war to keep them safe. But he was going to retire when the war ended and go home to them at last, while they were still young enough to welcome a father. And then he got *this* assignment.

Why couldn't you just *decide*, you bastards? Decide you were going to replace me, and then let me go home and have my hero's welcome and then retire to Christchurch and listen to the ringing of the bells to tell me God's in his heaven and all's right with the world. You could have left me home with my family, to raise my children, to be there so I could talk Pai out of naming her firstborn son after me.

I could have given all the advice and training you wanted—more than you'd ever use, that's for sure—and then *left* the fleet and had some kind of life. But no, I had to leave everything and come out here in this miserable box while you dither.

Mazer noticed that Pai's face was frozen and she was making no sound. "You stopped the playback," said Mazer.

"You weren't paying attention," said the computer. "This is a *visual* ansible transmission, and you are required to—"

"I'm watching *now,*" said Mazer.

Pai's voice came again, and the visual moved again. "They're going to slow this down to transmit it to you. But you know all about time dilation. The bandwidth is expensive, too, so I guess I'm done with the visual part of this. I've written you a letter, and so have the kids. And Pahu swears that someday he'll learn to read and write." She laughed again, looking at someone out of frame. It had to be his son, the baby he had never seen. Tantalizingly close, but not coming into frame. Someone was controlling that. Someone decided not to let him see his son. Graff? How closely was he manipulating this? Or was it Kim who decided? Or Pahu himself?

"Mother has written to you, too. Actually, quite a few letters. She wouldn't come, though. She doesn't want you to see her looking so old. But she's still beautiful, Father. More beautiful than ever, with white hair and—she still loves you. She wants you to remember her younger. She told me once, 'I was never *beautiful*, and when I met a man who thought I was, I married him over his most heartfelt objections.'"

Her imitation of her mother was so accurate that it stopped Mazer's breath for a moment. Could it truly be that Kim had refused to come because of some foolish vanity about how she looked? As if he would care!

But he *would* care. Because she would be old, and that would prove that it was true, that she would surely be dead before he made it back to Earth. And because of that, it would not be *home* he came back to. There was no such place.

"I love you, Father," Pai was saying. "Not just because you saved the world. We honor you for that, of course. But we love you because you made Mother so happy. She would tell us stories about you. It's as if we knew you. And your old mates would visit sometimes, and then we knew that Mother wasn't exaggerating about you. Either that or they *all* were." She laughed. "You *have* been part of our lives. We may be strangers to you, but you're not a stranger to us."

The image flickered, and when it came back, she was not in quite the same position. There had been an edit. Perhaps because she didn't want him to see her cry. But he knew she had been about to, because her face still worked before weeping the same way as when she was little. It had not been so very long, for him, since she was small. He remembered very well.

"You don't have to answer this," she said. "Lieutenant Graff told us that you might not welcome this transmission. Might even refuse to watch it. We don't want to make your voyage harder. But Father, when you come home—when you come back to us—you *have* a home. In our hearts. Even if I'm gone, even if only *our* children are here to meet you, our arms are open. Not to greet the conquering hero. But to welcome home our papa and grandpa, however old we are. I love you. We *all* do. *All.*"

And then, almost as an afterthought: "Please read our letters."

"I have letters for you," said the computer, as the holospace went empty.

"Save them," said Mazer. "I'll get to them."

"You are authorized to send a visual reply," said the computer.

"That will not happen," said Mazer. But even as he said it, he was wondering what he could possibly say, if he changed his mind and did send them his image. Some heroic speech about the nobility of sacrifice? Or an apology for accepting the assignment?

He would never show his face to them. Would never let Kim see that he was *not* changed.

He would read the letters. He would answer them. There were duties you owed to family, even if the reason they got involved was because of some meddling jerk of a lieutenant.

"My first letter," said Mazer, "will be to that git, Graff. It's very brief. 'Bugger off, gitling.' Sign it 'respectfully yours.'"

"'Bugger' is a noun. 'Git' is a substandard verb, and 'gitling' is not in any of my wordbases. I cannot spell or parse the message properly without explanation . . . Do you mean 'Leave this place, alien enemy'?"

"I made gitling up, but it's an excellent word, so use it. And I can't believe they programmed you without 'bugger off' in the wordbase."

"I detect stress," said the computer. "Will you accept mild sedation?"

"The stress is being caused by your forcing me to view a message I did not want to see. *You* are causing my stress. So give me some time to myself to calm down."

"Incoming message."

Mazer felt his stress levels rising even higher. So he sighed and sat back and said, "Read it. It's from Graff, right? Always use a male voice for the gitling."

"Admiral Rackham, I apologize for the intrusion," the computer baritoned. "Once I broached the possibility of letting your family contact you, my superiors would not give up on the idea, even though I warned them it would be more likely to be counterproductive if you hadn't agreed in advance. Still, it was my idea and I take full responsibility for that, but it was also clumsily handled without waiting for your permission, and that was not my responsibility. Though it was completely predictable, because this is the military. There is no idea so stupid that it won't be seized upon and made the basis of policy, and no idea so wise that it won't be perceived as threatening by some paper pusher, who'll kill it if he can, or claim complete credit for it if it works. Am I describing the military you know?"

Clever boy, thought Mazer. Deflect my anger to the IF. Make me *his* friend.

"However, the decision was made to send you only those letters that you would find encouraging. You're being 'handled,' Admiral Rackham. But if you want *all* the letters, I'll make sure you get the whole picture. It won't make you happier, but at least you'll know I'm not trying to manipulate you."

"Oh, right," said Mazer.

"Or at least I'm not trying to trick you," said the computer. "I'm trying to persuade you by winning your trust, if I can, and then your cooperation. I will not lie to you or leave out information in order to deceive you. Tell me if you want all the letters or are content with the comfortable version of your family's life."

Mazer knew then that Graff had won—Mazer would have no choice but to answer, and no choice but to request the omitted letters. Then he would be beholden to the gitling. Angry, but in debt.

The real question was this: Was Graff staging the whole thing? Was *he* the one who withheld the *un*comfortable letters, only so he could gain points with Mazer for then releasing them?

Or was Graff taking some kind of risk, scamming the system in order to send him the full set of letters?

Or did Graff, a mere lieutenant, have a degree of power that allowed him to openly flout the orders of his superiors with impunity?

"Don't send the bugger-off letter," said Mazer.

"I already sent it and receipt has been confirmed."

"I'm actually quite happy that you did that," said Mazer. "So here's my next message: Send the letters, gitling."

Within a few minutes, the reply came, and this time the number of letters was much higher.

And with nothing else to do, Mazer opened them and began to read them silently, in the order they were sent. Which means that the first hundred were all from Kim.

The progression of the early letters was predictable, but no less painful to read. She was hurt, angry, grief-stricken, resentful, filled with longing. She tried to hurt him with invective, or with guilt, or by tormenting him with sexually charged memories. Maybe she was tormenting herself.

Her letters, even the angry ones, were reminders of what he had lost, of the life he once had. It's not as if she invented her temper for this occasion. She had it all along, and he had been lashed by it before, and bore a few old scars. But now it all combined to make him miss her.

Her words hurt him, tantalized him, made him grieve, and often he had to stop reading and listen to something—music, poetry, or the drones and clicks of subtle machinery in the seemingly motionless craft that was hurtling through space in, the physicists assured him, a wavelike way, though he could not detect any lack of solidity in any of the objects inside the ship. Except, of course, himself. He could dissolve at a word, if it was from her, and then be remade by another.

I was right to marry her, he thought again and again as he read. And wrong to leave her. I cheated her and myself and my children, and for what? So I could be trapped here in space while she grows old and dies, and then come back and watch some clever young lad take his rightful place as commander of all the fleets, while I hover behind him, a relic of an old war, who lived out the wrong cliche. Instead of coming home in a bag for his family to bury, it was his family who grew old and died while he came back still . . . still young. Young and utterly alone, purposeless except for the little matter of saving the human race, which wouldn't even be in his hands.

Her letters calmed down after a while. They became monthly reports on the family. As if he had become a sort of diary for her. A place where she could wonder if she was doing the right thing in her raising of the children—too stern, too strict, too indulgent. If her decisions could have a wrong outcome or a wrong motive, then she wondered constantly if she should have done it differently. That, too, was the woman he had known and loved and reassured endlessly.

How did she hold together without him? Apparently she remembered the conversations they used to have, or imagined new ones. She inserted his side of the conversation into the letters. "I know you'd tell me that I did the right thing . . . that I had no choice . . . of course you'd say . . . you always told me . . . I'm still doing the same old . . . "

The things that a widow would tell herself about her dead husband.

But widows could still love their husbands. She *has* forgiven me.

And finally, in a letter written not so long ago—last week; half a year ago—she said it outright. "I hope you have forgiven me for being so angry with you when you divorced me. I know you had no choice but to go, and you were trying to be kind by cutting all ties so I could go on with life. And I *have* gone on, exactly as you said I should. Let us please forgive one another."

The words hit him like three-g acceleration. He gasped and wept and the computer became concerned. "What's wrong?" the computer asked. "Sedation seems necessary."

"I'm reading a letter from my wife," he said. "I'm fine. No sedation."

But he wasn't fine. Because he knew what Graff and the IF could not have known when they let this message go through. Graff *had* lied to him. He *had* withheld information.

For what Mazer had told his wife was that she should go on with life *and marry again.*

That's what she was telling him. Somebody had forbidden them to say or write anything that would tell him that Kim had married another man and probably had more children—but he knew, because that's the only thing she could mean when she said, "I *have* gone on, exactly as you said I should." That had been the crux of the argument. She insisting that divorce only made sense if she intended to remarry, him saying that of course she didn't think of remarrying *now*, but later, when she finally realized that he would never come back as long as she lived, she wouldn't have to write and ask him for a divorce, it would already be done and she could go ahead, knowing that she had his blessing—and she had slapped him and burst into tears because he thought so little of her and her love for him that he thought she could *forget* and marry someone else . . .

But she had, and it was breaking his heart, because even though he had been noble about insisting on the divorce, he had believed her when she said she could never love any other man.

She did love another man. He was gone only a year, and she . . .

No, he had been gone three decades now. Maybe it took her ten years before she found another man. Maybe . . .

"I will have to report this physical response," said the computer.

"You do whatever you have to," said Mazer. "What are they going to do, send me to the hospital? Or—I know—they could cancel the mission!"

He calmed down, though—barking at the computer made him feel marginally better. Even though his thoughts raced far beyond the words he was reading, he did read all the other letters, and now he could see hints and overtones. A lot of unexplained references to "we" and "us" in the letters. She wanted him to know.

"Send this to Graff. Tell him I know he broke his word almost as soon as he gave it."

The answer came back in a moment. "Do you think I don't know exactly what I sent?"

Did he know? Or had he only just now realized that Kim had slipped a message through, and now Graff was pretending that he knew it all along . . .

Another message from Graff: "Just heard from your computer that you have had a strong emotional response to the letters. I'm deeply sorry for that. It must be a challenge, to live in the presence of a computer that reports everything you do to us, and then a team of shrinks try to figure out how to respond in order to get the desired result. My own feeling is that if we intend to trust the future of the human race to this man, maybe we ought to tell him everything we know and converse with him like an adult. But my own letters have to be passed through the same panel of shrinks. For instance, they're letting me tell you about them because they hope that you will come to trust me more by knowing that I don't like what they do. They're even letting me tell you *this* as a further attempt to allow the building of trust through recursive confession of trickery and deception. I bet it's working, too. You can't possibly read any secret meanings into *this* letter."

What game is he playing? Which parts of his letters are true? The panel of shrinks made sense. The military mind: Find a way to negate your own assets so they fail even before you begin to use them. But if Graff really did let Kim's admission that she had remarried sneak through, knowing that the shrinks would miss it, then did that mean he was on Mazer's side? Or that he was merely *better* than the shrinks at figuring out how to manipulate him?

"You can't possibly read any secret meanings into *this* letter," Graff had said. Did that mean that there *was* a secret meaning? Mazer read it over again, and now what he said in the third sentence took on another possible meaning. "To live in the presence of a computer that reports everything you do to us." At first he had read it as if it meant "reports *to us* everything you do." But what if he literally meant that the computer would report everything Mazer *did to them*.

That would mean they had detected his undetectable reprogramming of the computer.

Which would explain the panel of shrinks and the sudden new urgency about finding a replacement for Mazer as commander.

So the cat was out of the bag. But they weren't going to tell him they *knew* what he had done, because he was the volatile one who had done something insane and so they couldn't believe he had a rational purpose and speak to him openly.

He had to let them see him and realize that he was not insane. He had to get control of this situation. And in order to accomplish that, he had to trust Graff to be what he so obviously wanted Mazer to think he was: An ally in the effort to find the best possible commander for the IF when the final campaign finally began.

Mazer looked in the mirror and debated whether to clean up his appearance. There were plenty of insane people who tried, pathetically, to look saner by dressing like regular people. Then again, he *had* let himself get awfully tangle-haired and he *was* naked all the time. At least he could wash and dress and try to look like the kind of person that military people could regard with respect.

When he was ready, he rotated into position and told the computer to begin recording his visual for later transmission. He suspected, though, that there would be no point in editing it—the raw recording was what the computer would transmit, since it had obviously reported his earlier reprogramming.

"I have reason to believe that you already know of the change I made in the onboard computer's programming. Apparently I could take the computer's navigational system out of your control, but couldn't keep it from reporting the fact to you. Which suggests that you *meant* this box to be a prison, but you weren't very good at it.

"So I will now tell you exactly what you need to know. You—or, by now, your predecessors—refused to believe me when I told them that I was not the right man to command the International Fleet during the final campaign. I was told that there would be a search for an adequate replacement, but I knew better.

"I knew that any 'search' would be perfunctory or illusory. You were betting everything on me. However, I also know how the military works. Those who made the decision to rely on me would be long since retired before I came back. And the closer we got to the time of my return, the more the new bureaucracy would dread my arrival. When I got there, I would find myself at the head of a completely unfit military organization whose primary purpose was to prevent me from doing anything that might cost somebody his job. Thus I would be powerless, even if I was retained as a figurehead. And all the pilots who gave up everything they knew and loved on Earth in order to go out and confront the Formics in their own space would be under the actual command of the usual gang of bureaucratic climbers.

"It always takes six months of war and a few dreadful defeats to clear out the deadwood. But we don't have time for that in this war, any more than we did in the last one. My insubordination fortunately ended things abruptly. This time, though, if we lose *any* battle then we have lost the war. We will have no second chance. We have no margin of error. We can't afford to waste time getting rid of you—you, the idiots who are watching me right now, the idiots who are going to let the human race be destroyed in order to preserve your pathetic bureaucratic jobs.

"So I reprogrammed my ship's navigational program so that I have complete control over it. You can't override my decision. And my decision is this: I am not coming back. I will not decelerate and turn around. I will keep going on and on.

"My plan was simple. Without me to count on as your future commander, you would have no choice but to search for a new one. Not go through the motions, but really search.

"And I think you must have guessed that this was my plan, because you started letting me get messages from Lieutenant Graff.

"So now I have the problem of trying to make sense of what you're doing. My guess is that Graff is trained as a shrink. Perhaps he works as an intelligence analyst. My guess is that he is actually very bright and innovative and has got spectacular results at . . . at something. So you decided to see if he could get me back on track. Only he is exactly the kind of wild man that terrifies you. He's smarter than you, and so you have to make sure you keep him from getting the power to do anything that looks to you like it might be dangerous. And since everything remotely effective will frighten you, his main project has been figuring out how to get around you in order to establish honest communication between him and me.

"So here we are, at something of an impasse. And all the power is in your hands at this moment. So let me tell you your choices. There are only two of them.

"The first choice is the hard one. It will make your skin crawl. Some of you will go home and sleep for three days in fetal position with your thumbs in your mouths. But there's no negotiation. This is what you'll do:

"You'll give Lieutenant Graff real power. Don't give him a high rank and a desk and a bureaucracy. Give him genuine authority. Everything he wants, he gets. Because the whole reason he is alive will be this: To find the best possible commander for the fleets that will decide the future of the human race.

"To do this he first has to find out how to identify those with the best potential. You'll give him all the help he asks for. All the *people* he asks for, regardless of their rank, training, or how much some idiot admiral hates or loves them.

"Then Graff will figure out how to *train* the candidates he identifies. Again, you'll do whatever he wants. Nothing is too expensive. Nothing is too difficult. Nothing requires a single committee meeting to agree. Everybody in the IF and everybody in the government is Graff's servant, and all they should ever ask him is to clarify his instructions.

"What I require of Graff is that he work on nothing but the identification and training of my replacement as battle commander of the International Fleet. If he starts bureaucratic kingdom building—in other words, if he turns out to be just another idiot—I'll know it, and I'll stop talking to him.

"In exchange for your giving Graff this authority is that once I'm satisfied he *has* it and is using it correctly, then I'll turn this ship around immediately. I'll get home a few years earlier than the original plan. I'll be part of training whatever commander you have. I'll evaluate Graff's work. I'll help choose among the candidates for the job, if you have more than one that might potentially do the job.

"And all along the way, Graff will communicate with me constantly by ansible, so that everything he does will be done with my counsel and approval. Thus, through Graff, I am taking command of the search for our war leader *now.*

"But if you act like the idiots who led the fleet during the war *I* won, and try to obfuscate and prevaricate and procrastinate and misdirect and manipulate and lie your way out of letting Graff and me control the choice and training of the battle commander, then I won't turn this ship around, ever.

"I'll just sail on out into oblivion. Our campaign will fail. The Buggers will come back to Earth and they'll finish the job this time. And I, in this ship, will be the last living human being. But it won't be my fault. It will be yours, because you did not have the decency and intelligence to step aside and let the people who know how to do the job of saving the human race *do* it.

"Think about it as long as you want. I've got all the time in the world. But keep this in mind: Whoever tries to take control of this situation and set up committees to study your response to this vid—*those* are the people you need to assign to remote desk jobs and get them out of the IF right now. They are the allies of the Buggers—they're the ones who will end up getting us all killed. I have already designated the only possible leader for this program: Lieutenant Graff. There's no compromise. No maneuvering. Make him a captain, give him more actual authority than any other living human, stand ready to do whatever he tells you to do, and let him and me get to work.

"Do I believe you'll actually do this? No. That's why I reprogrammed my ship. Just remember that I *am* the guy who saved the human race, and I did it because I was able to see exactly how the Buggers' military system worked and find its weak spot. I have also seen how the human military system works, and I know the weak spot, and I know how to fix it. I've just told you how. Either you'll do it or you won't. Now make your decisions and don't bother me again unless you've made the right one."

Mazer turned back to the desk and selected save and send.

When he was sure the message was sent, he returned to his sleeping space and let himself think again about Kim and Pai and Pahu, about his grandchildren, about his wife's new husband and what children they might have. What he did not let himself think about was the possibility of returning to Earth to meet these babies as adults and try to find a place among them as if he were still alive, as if there were anyone left on Earth for him to know and love.

• • •

The answer did not come for a full twelve hours. Mazer imagined with amusement the struggles that must be going on. People fighting for their jobs. Filing reports proving that Mazer was insane and therefore should not be listened to. Struggling to neutralize Graff—or suck up to him, or get themselves assigned as his immediate supervisor. Trying to figure out a way to fool Mazer into thinking they had complied without actually having to do it.

The answer, when it came, was from Graff. It was a visual. Mazer was pleased to see that while Graff was, in fact, young, he wore the uniform in a slovenly way that suggested that looking like an officer wasn't a particularly high priority for him.

He wore a captain's insignia and a serious expression that was only a split second away from a smile.

"Once again, Admiral Rackham, with only one weapon in your arsenal, you knew right where to aim it."

"I had two missiles the first time," said Mazer.

"Do you wish me to record—" began the computer.

"Shut up and continue the message," growled Mazer.

"You should know that your former wife, Kim Arnsbrach Rackham Summers—and yes, she does keep your name as part of her legal name—was instrumental in making this happen. Because whenever somebody came up with a plan for how to fool you and me into thinking they were in compliance with your orders, I would bring her to the meeting. Whenever they said, 'We'll get Admiral Rackham to believe' some lie or other, she would laugh. And the discussion would pretty much end there.

"I can't tell you how long it will last, but at this point, the IF seems to be ready to comply fully. You should know that has involved about two hundred early retirements and nearly a thousand reassignments, including forty officers of flag rank. You still know how to blow things up.

"There are things I already know about selection and training, and over the next few years we'll talk constantly. But I can't wait to take actions until you and I have conferred on everything, simply because there's no time to waste and time dilation adds weeks to all our conversations.

"However, if I do something wrong, tell me and I'll change it. I'll never tell you that we've already done this or that as if that were a reason *not* to do it the right way after all. I will show you that you have not made a mistake in trusting this to me.

"The thing that puzzles me, though, is how you decided to trust me. My communications to you were full of lies or I couldn't have written to you at all. I didn't know you and had no clue how to tell you the truth in a way that would get past the committees that had to approve everything. The worst thing is that in fact I'm very good at the bureaucratic game or I couldn't have got to the position to communicate directly with you in the first place.

"So let me tell you—now that no one will be censoring my messages—that yes, I think the highest priority is finding the right replacement for you as battle commander of the International Fleet. But once we've done that—and I know that's a big if—I have plans of my own.

"Because winning this particular war against this particular enemy is important, of course. But I want to win all future wars the only way we can—by getting the human race off this one planet and out of this one star system. The Formics already figured it out—you have to disperse. You have to spread out until you're unkillable.

"I hope they turn out to have failed. I hope we can destroy them so thoroughly they can't challenge us for a thousand years.

"But by the end of that thousand years, when another Bugger fleet comes back for vengeance, I want them to discover that humans have spread to a thousand worlds and there is no hope of finding us all.

"I guess I'm just a big-picture guy, Admiral Rackham. But whatever my long-range goals are, this much is certain: If we don't have the right commander and win this war, it won't matter what other plans anybody has.

"And *you* are that commander, sir. Not the battle commander, but the commander who found a way to get the military to reshape itself in order to find the right battle commander without wasting the lives of countless soldiers in meaningless defeats in order to find him.

"Sir, I will not address this topic again. But I have come to know your family in the past few weeks. I know now something of what you gave up in order to be in the position you're in now. And I promise you, sir, that I will do everything in my power to make your sacrifices and theirs worth the cost."

Graff saluted, and then disappeared from the holospace.

And even though he could not be seen by anybody, Mazer Rackham saluted him back.

CARTHAGO DELENDA EST

GENEVIEVE VALENTINE

Genevieve Valentine's fiction has appeared in or is forthcoming in *Strange Horizons, Journal of Mythic Arts, Fantasy Magazine, Farrago's Wainscot, Diet Soap, Shimmer, Sybil's Garage,* and *Escape Pod.* She is a columnist for Tor.com and *Fantasy Magazine.* Her appetite for good costumes and bad movies is insatiable, obsessions she tracks on her blog glvalentine.livejournal.com.

Valentine says that her favorite parts of old war movies are the nights before or the moments between battles, when tension is building and character is revealed in the short silences between engagements. This story sprang from the concept of this overnight waiting presented on a galactic scale; what happens after hundreds of years of waiting for something, based on a beautiful promise?

CARTHAGO DELENDA EST

Wren Hex-Yemenni woke early. They had to teach her everything from scratch, and there wasn't time for her to learn anything new before she hit fifty and had to be expired.

"Watch it," the other techs told me when I was starting out. "You don't want a Hex on your hands."

By then we were monitoring Wren Hepta-Yemenni. She fell into bed with Dorado ambassador 214, though I don't know what he did to deserve it and she didn't even seem sad when he expired. When they torched him she went over with the rest of the delegates, and they bowed or closed their eyes or pressed their tentacles to the floors of their glass cases, and afterwards they toasted him with champagne or liquid nitrogen.

Before we expired Hepta, later that year, she smiled at me. "Make sure Octa's not ugly, okay? Just in case—for 215."

Wren Octa-Yemenni hates him, so it's not like it matters.

• • •

It's worse early on. Octa and Dorado 215 stop short of declaring war—no warring country is allowed to meet the being from Carthage when it arrives, those are the rules—but it comes close. Every time she goes over to the Dorado ship she comes back madder. Once she got him halfway into an airlock before security arrived.

We reported it as a chem malfunction; I took the blame for improper embryonic processes (a lie—they were perfect), and the Dorado accepted the apology, no questions. Dorado 208 killed himself, way back; they know how mistakes can happen.

Octa spends nights in the tech room, scanning through footage of

Hepta-Yemmeni and Dorado 214 like she's looking for something, like she's trying to remember what Hepta felt.

I don't know why she tries. She can't; none of them can. They don't hold on to anything. That's the whole point.

• • •

The astronomers at the Institute named the planet Carthage when they discovered it floating in the Oort cloud like a wheel of garbage. They thought it was already dead.

But the message came from there. It's how they knew to look in the cloud to begin with; there was a message there, in every language, singing along the light like a phone call from home.

It was a message of peace, they say. It's confidential; most people never get to hear it. I wouldn't even believe it's real except that all the planets heard it, and agreed—every last one of them threw a ship into the sky to meet the ship from Carthage when it came.

• • •

Every year they show us the video of Wren Alpha-Yemenni—the human, the original—taking the oath. Stretched out behind her are the ten thousand civilians who signed up to go into space and not come back, to cultivate a meeting they'd never see.

"I, Wren Alpha-Yemenni, delegate of Earth, do solemnly swear to speak wisely, feel deeply, and uphold the highest values of the human race as Earth greets the ambassador of Carthage." At the end she smiles, and her eyes go bright with tears.

The speech goes on, but I just watch her face.

There's something about Alpha that's . . . more alive than the copies. They designated her with a letter just to keep track, but it suits her anyway—the Alpha, the leader, the strong first. Octa has a little of that, sometimes, but she'll probably be expired by the time Carthage comes, and who knows if it will ever manifest again.

Octa would never be Alpha, anyway. There's something in Alpha's eyes that's never been repeated—something bright and determined; excited; happy.

It makes sense, I guess. She's the only one of the Yemennis who chose to go.

• • •

Everybody sent ships. Everybody. We'd never heard of half the planets that showed up. You wonder how amazing the message must be, to get them all up off their asses.

Dorado was in place right away (that whole planet is kiss-asses), which is why they were already on iteration 200 when we got there. Doradoan machines have to pop out a new one every twenty years. (My ancestors did better work on our machines; they generate a perfect Yemenni every fifty years on the dot—except for poor Hex. There's always one dud.) Dorado spends their time trying to scrounge up faster tech or better blueprints, and we give our information away, because those were the rules in the message, but they just take—they haven't given us anything since their dictionary.

WX-16 from Sextans-A sent their royal house: an expendable younger son and his wife and a collection of nobles, to keep the bloodline active until the messenger arrived. We don't deal with them—they think it's coarse to clone.

NGC 2808 (we can't pronounce it, and sometimes it's better not to try) came out of Canis Major and surprised everyone, since we didn't even think there was life out there. They've only been around a few years; Hepta never met them. Their delegate is in stasis. Whenever that poor sucker wakes up he's going to have some unimpressed ambassadors waiting to meet him. They should never have come with only one.

Xpelhi, who booked it all the way from Cygnus, keep to themselves; their atmosphere is too heavy for people with spines. They look like jellyfish, no mouths, and it took us a hundred and ten years to figure out their language; the dictionary they sent us was just an anatomical sketch. Hepta cracked it because of something Tetra-Yemenni had recorded about the webs of their veins shifting when they were upset. The Xpelhi think we're a bunch of idiots for taking so long. Which is fine; I think they're a bunch of mouthless creeps. It evens out.

Neptune sent a think-tank themselves, like they were a real planet and not an Earth colony. They've never said how they keep things going on that tiny ship, if it's cloning or bio-reproduction or what; every generation they elect someone for the job, and I guess whenever Carthage shows up they'll put forward the elected person and hope for the best. Brave bunch, Neptune. Better them than us.

Centauri was the smartest planet. They sent an AI. You know the AI isn't sitting up nights worrying itself into early expiration. It's not bothered by a damn thing.

• • •

Octa makes rounds to all the ships. She's the only one of them who does it, and it works. Canis Major sent us help once, when we had the ventilation problem on the storage levels. She didn't ask for help; they're not obligated to share anything but information. But when she came back, an engineer was with her.

"Trust me, I know everything about refrigeration," he said, and after the computer had translated the joke everybody laughed and shook his hand.

Octa stood beside him like a mother until they had taken him into the tunnels, and then she tucked her helmet under her arm like she was satisfied.

"They're good people," she said to the shuttle pilot, who was making a face. "With no ambassador to keep them going, they must feel so alone. Give them a chance to do good."

"I've got the scan ready," I said. (I scan her every time she comes back from somewhere else. It's a precaution. You never know what's going on outside your own ship.)

"Let's be quick, then," she said, already walking down the corridor. "I have to make some notes, and then I need to talk to Centauri."

(Centauri's AI is Octa's favorite ship; she's there far more often than she needs to be. "Easier to come to decisions when it's just a matter of facts," she said.)

Octa did a lot of planning, early on, like she had a special purpose beyond what Alpha had promised—like time was short.

Of all the copies, she was the only one who ever seemed to worry that her clock was ticking down.

• • •

All the Yemennis have been different, which is unavoidable. Even though each one has all the aggregated information of previous iterations without the emotional hangover, it can get messy, like Hepta and Dorado 214. Human error in every copy. It's the reason her machines all have parameters instead of specs; some things you never can tell. (Poor Hex.)

It's hard on them, of course—after fifty years it all starts to fall apart no matter what you do, and you have to shut one down and start again—but it's the best way we have to give her a lifetime of knowledge in a few minutes, and we don't want Carthage to come when we're unprepared.

I don't know what's in the memories, what they show her each time she wakes. That's for government guys; techs mind their own business.

• • •

There's a documentary about how they picked Alpha for the job, four hundred years back. One man went on and on about "the human aesthetic," and put up a photo of what a woman would look like if every race had an influence in the facial features.

"Almost perfect. It's like they chose her for her looks!" he says, laughing.

Like Carthage is going to know if she's pretty. Carthage is probably full of big amoebas, and when they meet her they'll just think she's nasty and fragile and full of teeth.

They have a picture of Alpha up in the lab anyway, for reference. No one looks at it any more—nobody needs to. When I look in the mirror, I see a Yemenni first, and then my own face. I have my priorities straight.

Wren Yemenni is why we're here, and the reason none of us have complained in four hundred years is because she knows what she owes us. She's seen the video, too, with those ten thousand people who gave up everything because someone told them the message was beautiful.

No matter what her failings are, she tries to learn everything she can each time, to move diplomacy forward, to be kind (except to Dorado 215, but we all hate those ass-kissers so it doesn't matter). She knows what she's here to do. It's coded deeper than her IQ, than her memories, somewhere inside her we can't even reach; duty is built into their bones. Alpha passed down something wonderful, to all of them.

Octa doesn't look like Alpha. Not at all.

• • •

Just before Dorado 215 hits his twenty-year expiration, he messages a request that Octa accompany him on an official visit to the Xpelhi. There's something he wants to show them; he thinks they'll be interested.

Everyone asks her to go when they have to talk to Xpelhi. We gave everyone the code once we cracked it (we promised to exchange information, fair and square), but no one else is good at it and they need the help. The Yemmenis have a knack for language.

"I hate him," she says as I strap her into her suit. (It's new—our engineers made it to withstand the pressure in the Xpelhi ship. It's the most amazing human tech we've ever produced. Earth will be proud when they get the message.)

"If peace didn't require me to go. . ." she says, frowns. "I hope they see that what he's offering won't help anyone. It never does."

She sounds tired. I wonder if she's been up nights with the playback again.

"It's okay," I say. "You can hate him if you want. No one expected you to love him like the last one did. It's better not to carry the old feelings around. You live longer."

"He's different," she says. "It's terrible how it's changed him."

"All clones feel that way sometimes," I say. "Peril of the job. Here's your helmet."

She takes it and smiles at me, a thank-you, before she pops it over her head and activates the seal.

"I feel like a snowman," she says, which is what Hepta used to say. I wonder if anyone told Octa, of if she just remembered it from somewhere.

I stay near the bio-med readout while she's on the Xpelhi ship; if anything starts to fail, the suit tells us. If her lungs have collapsed from the pressure there's not much we can do, but at least we'll know, and we can wake up the next one.

Her heart rate speeds up, quick sharp spikes on the readout like she's having a panic attack, but that happens whenever Dorado 215 says something stupid. After a while it's just a little agitation, and soon she's safely back home.

She stands on the shuttle platform for a long time without moving, and only after I start toward her does she wake up enough to switch off the pressure in the suit and haul her helmet off.

I stop where I am. I don't want to touch her; I've worked too hard on them to handle them. "Everything all right?"

She's frowning into middle space, not really seeing me. "There's nothing on the ship we could use as a weapon?"

Strange question. "I guess we could crash the shuttle into someone," I say. "I can ask the engineers."

"No," she says. "No need."

It was part of the message, the first rule: no war before Carthage comes. We don't even have armed security– just guys who train with their hands, ready in case Octa tries to shove any more people in airlocks.

She hasn't done that in a while. She's getting worn down. It happens to them all, nearer the end.

"There's been no war for four hundred years," she says as we walk, shaking her head. "Have we ever gone that long before without fighting? Any of us?"

"Nope." I grin. "Carthage is the best thing that hasn't happened to us yet."

Her helmet is tucked under one arm, and she looks down at it like it will answer her.

• • •

The Delegate Meeting happens every decade. It wasn't mandated by Carthage; Wren Tetra-Yemenni began it as a way for delegates to have a base of reference, and to meet; no one has even seen the new Neptunian Elect since they picked her two years back, and they have to introduce Dorado 216.

We're not allowed to hear what they talk about—it's none of our business, it's government stuff—but we hang around in the hallways just to watch them filing in, the humanoids and the Xpelhis puttering past in their cases. The Centauri AI has a hologram that looks like a stick insect with wings, and it blinks in and out as the signal from his ship gets spotty. I cover my smile, though—that computer sees everything.

On the way in, Dorado 216 leans over to Octa. "You won't say anything, will you? It would be war."

"No," she says, "I won't say anything."

"It's just in case," he goes on, like she didn't already give him an answer. "There's no plan to use them. We're not like that—it's not like that. You never know what Carthage's plans are, is all." Then, more quietly, "I trusted you."

"215 trusted me," she says. "You want someone to trust you, try the next Yemenni."

"Watch it," he says. A warning.

After a second she frowns at him. "How can you want war, after all this effort?"

He makes a suspicious face before he turns and walks into the reception room with the rest of them.

Octa stands in the hall for a second before she follows him, shoulders back and head high. Yemmenis know their duties.

• • •

After the Delegate Meeting, Octa takes a trip to the Centauri AI. She's back in a few hours. She didn't tell anyone why she was going, just looks sad to have come back.

(Sometimes I think Octa's mind is more like a computer than any of them, even more than Alpha. I wonder if I made her that way by accident, wishing better for them, wishing for more.)

In the mess, the pilots grumble that it was a waste of shuttle fuel.

"That program shows up anywhere they need it to," one of them says. "Why did we have to drive her around like she's one of the queens on Sextan? They should expire these copies before they go crazy, man."

"Maybe she was trying to give us break from your ugly face," I say, and there's a little standoff at the table between the pilots and the techs until one of the language ops guys smoothes things over.

I stay angry for a long time. The pilots don't know what they're talking about.

Yemennis do nothing by mistake.

• • •

Alpha was the most skilled diplomat on the planet.

They don't say so in the documentary; they talk about how kind she is and how smart she is and how she looks like a mix of everyone, and if you just listened to what they were saying you'd think she hardly deserved to go. There were a lot of people in line; astronauts and prime ministers and bishops all clamoring for the privilege.

And she got herself picked—she got picked above every one of them; she was the most skilled diplomat who ever lived. She could work out anything, I bet.

• • •

There's an engineer down five levels who looks good to me, is smart enough, and we get married. We have two kids. (Someone will have to watch over the Yemennis when I'm gone, someone with my grandfathers' talents for calibrating a needle; we've been six generations at Wren Yemmeni's side.)

We celebrate four hundred years of peace. All the delegates put a message together, to be played in every ship, for the civilians. For some of them, it's the first they've heard of the other languages. Everyone on the ship, twelve thousand strong, watches raptly from the big hangar and the gymnasium level, from the tech room and the bridge.

They go one by one, and I recognize our reception room as the camera pans from one face to another. They talk about peace, about their home planets, about how much they look forward to all of us knowing the message, when Carthage comes.

Wren Octa-Yemenni goes last.

"I hope that, as we today are wiser today than we were, so tomorrow we will be wiser than we are," she says. Dorado 216 looks like he wants to slap her.

She says, "I hope that when our time comes to meet Carthage, we may say that we have fulfilled the letter and spirit of its great message, and we stand ready for a bright new age."

Everyone in the tech room roars applause (Yemennis know how to talk to a crowd). Just before the video shuts off, it shows all the delegates side by side; Octa is looking out the window, towards something none of us can see.

• • •

One night, a year before she's due to be expired, I find Octa in the development room. She's watching the tube where Ennea is gestating. Ennea's almost grown, and it looks like Octa's staring at her own reflection.

"Four hundred years without a war," she says. "All of us at a truce, talking and learning. Waiting for Carthage."

"Carthage will come," I promise, glancing at Ennea's pH readout.

"I hope we don't see it," she says, frowns into the glass. "I hope, when it comes, all of us are long dead, and better ones have taken their places. Some people twist on themselves if you give them any time at all."

Deka and Hendeka are in tubes behind us, smaller and reserved, eyes closed; they're not ready. We won't even need them until I'm dead. Though it shouldn't matter, I care less for them than I do for Ennea, less than I do for Octa, who's watching me.

Octa, who seems to think none of them are worthy of Carthage at all. She's been losing faith for years.

None of these copies are like Alpha. They all do their duty, but she *believed.*

• • •

At the fifty-year mark, Octa comes in to be expired.

She hands over the recording device, and the government guys disappear to their level to put together the memory flux for Ennea, who will wake up tonight and need to know.

"You shouldn't keep doing this," she tells me as we help her onto the table and adjust the IV.

There are no restraints. The Yemennis don't balk at what they have to do; duty is in their bones. But Octa looks sad, even sadder than when she found out that the one before her had loved someone who was already dead.

"It's fine," I say. "It's the best way—one session of information, and she's ready to face Carthage."

"But she won't remember something if I don't record it? She won't know?"

Octa's always been a little edgy—I try to sound reassuring. "No, she won't feel a thing. Forget Dorado. There's nothing to worry about."

Octa looks like she's going to cry. "What if there's something she needs to know?"

"I'll get you a recorder," I say, and start to hold up my hand for the sound tech, but she shakes her head and grabs my sleeve.

I drop my arm, surprised. No one else has even noticed; they're already starting the machines to wake up the next one, and Octa and I might as well be alone in the room.

After a second she frowns, drops my hand, makes fists at her sides like she's holding back.

The IV drips steadily, and around us everyone is laughing and talking, excited. They seem miles away.

Octa hasn't stopped watching me; her eyes are bright, her mouth drawn.

"Have you seen the message?"

She must know I haven't. I shake my head; I hold my breath, wondering if she's going to tell me. I've dreamed about it my whole life, wondering what Alpha knew that made her cry with joy, four hundred years ago.

"It's beautiful," she says, and her eyes are mostly closed, and I can't tell if she's talking to me or just talking. The IV is working; sometimes they say things.

She says, "I don't know how anyone could take up a weapon again, after seeing the message."

Without thinking, I put my hand over her hand.

She sighs. Then, so quietly that no one else hears, Octa says, "I hope that ship never comes."

Her face gets tight and determined—she looks like Alpha, exactly like, and I almost call out for them to stop—it's so uncanny, something must be wrong.

But nothing is wrong. She closes her eyes, and the bio-feed flatlines; the tech across the room turns off the alarm on the main bank, and it's over.

We flip on the antigrav, and one of the techs takes her down to the incinerator. He comes back, says the other delegates have lined up in the little audience hall outside the incinerator, waiting to clap and drink champagne.

It's always a long night after an expiration, but it's what we're here to do, and it's good solid work, moving and monitoring and setting up the influx for Yemenni's first night. Nobody wants a delay between delegates. You never know when the Carthage is going to show up. We think another four hundred years, but it could be tomorrow. Stranger things have happened.

Wren Ennea-Yemenni needs to be awake, just in case; she'll have things to do, when Carthage comes.

LIFE-SUSPENSION

L. E. MODESITT, JR.

L. E. Modesitt is the bestselling author of the Saga of Recluse, the Spellsong Cycle, the Corean Chronicles, and several other series, as well as a number of standalone novels, such as *The Eternity Artifact, The Elysium Commission*, and a new book, *Haze*, that's due out in June. His short fiction has appeared in a number of anthologies, and was recently collected in *Viewpoints Critical.*

"Life-Suspension" is set in a future where interstellar travel is possible, but where there is warfare over who controls the lines of interstellar communication. "It's a story that shows how thin the lines between all human passions are, especially in war," Modesitt said. "I was a military pilot, and I've tried to capture the feel of those situations, and the contrast between the times of action and the quiet civility of officers in between action."

LIFE-SUSPENSION

I

The *S.R.S. Amaterasu* had left Kunitsu Orbit Station 2 less than three hours earlier, and Flight Captain Ghenji Yamato was more than ready to eat when the junior officers' wardroom opened at 1600 KMT. He wasn't the first entering—that would have been most impolite—but he was far from the last when he took his seat halfway down the second table.

He'd barely seated himself when his eyes registered a flash of white, and he glanced up.

The officer who had just entered the mess caught his eyes immediately, not because she was full-figured, which she was not, boyish as her frame was, but because her short-cut hair was pure white, and her pale white face was almost unearthly in its beauty. He almost laughed at the thought. Unearthly? None of them would ever see Earth—and probably not even Kunitsu—again for years. Objective years, not subjective, he reminded himself. He found himself still looking at her. For all the white hair, she was probably younger than he was. He couldn't help but stare before he looked down abruptly.

She was ship's crew—that was certain—and not one of the attack pilots for the mission ahead, because he knew most of them, except for the transfers and replacements, although her hair was cut every bit as short as that of the women pilots in his squadron. Yet . . . for all that he knew he had never seen her before; there was something about her. He just didn't know what it was. He ate almost mechanically, although he did enjoy the black tea, probably a variant from the Nintoku Islands.

As he left the mess after the meal, he glanced back, but he didn't see the white-haired captain. As he looked to the corridor ahead, leading to the attack operations spaces—there she was, waiting and looking at him. Her eyebrows were also white, as were her eyelashes, but she had deep black eyes and red lips.

"Hello," he offered. "I'm Ghenji Yamato, Flight Captain."

"I know. Your name, that is, and your reputation as 'the monk.'"

"The monk?" Ghenji knew the allusion, but wasn't about to admit it.

"The flight captain utterly devoted to his duties once he's shipside." She smiled. "I'm Rokujo. Rokujo Yukionna." She smiled. "I'm in life-support."

He thought he ought to recognize her name, but he hadn't checked the roster of ship's officers. He'd also never paid that much attention to names or where they came from. His educational background had been engineering, but he'd been fortunate, if one could call it that, to have been accepted by the service for training as an attack needle pilot. The current tour was his fourth, and, afterwards, he'd be eligible for promotion to major—and squadron commander, or the equivalent. With the time-dilation effect, even with military pay discounting, he'd even be able to retire, not that he'd ever considered that.

Ghenji glanced at her green skinsuit—medical—and the senior captain's insignia on the collars of her shipvest. "Doctor or technical?"

"Does it matter?" She laughed ruefully. "At least you asked. Most of the pilots just assume tech because I look so young."

"You're in charge of . . . ?" He thought he'd recovered as gracefully as possible.

"Very good. I'm a recovery specialist, but I'm chief of the suspension and support."

"A most necessary specialty, especially for attack pilots," he said with a smile. He couldn't have met her before, but the sense of familiarity remained. "You didn't study at Edo Institute, did you?"

"No. Fumitomo, then Heian for my residency."

"Why did you decide on the service?"

"I like the specialty. It fits me, and where else would I get this kind of experience? All planetside suspension facilities are either geriatric wards for the wealthy or holding pens for clone-replacement therapy, and there aren't many of the latter."

Ghenji nodded. "In a way, it's like attack flying. If you want to pilot anything outside the service, all you are is a tram driver . . . "

All in all, they talked for close to two stans before he had to leave to stand an ops-watch, not that doing so meant more than watching the system indicators.

Ghenji didn't see Rokujo the next day, but when he woke the following morning and rolled out of his cubicle, he decided that he would make an effort to encounter her, while he had time to get to know her . . . even though that was unlike him. But she did fascinate him, perhaps because of the calm, almost unblinking, way she viewed him, as if she were focused on him and him alone.

Still, the *Amaterasu* would enter deep jump in three days, and in two Ghenji Yamato would climb into a cocoon and be hibernated until the ship re-entered normspace, not that he knew that destination, only that it was in the area disputed by the Mogulate and the Republic. After that, his real tasks would begin.

For all his engineering background, he still found it hard to understand a universe where instantaneous—or near-instantaneous—interstellar communications were possible, but where interstellar travel was far slower. It did make for an interesting galaxy—and one that required the space service . . . and one Ghenji Yamato—or other pilots like him.

Despite his interest in Rokujo, with his own duties and schedule, it was just before the evening meal when he saw her standing just outside the officers' lounge adjoining the junior officers' wardroom.

"Good afternoon, Rokujo."

"Good afternoon."

"I was looking for you earlier, at lunch."

"We were running tests, and I didn't get away . . . "

Since seating was not strictly by rank except at the formal mess dinners, they sat together and talked.

"You know your names are almost contradictions of who you are," she said, taking a quick mouthful of rice.

"I hadn't thought about it. I'm an engineer."

"Yamato was an emperor, filled with courage, and willing to commit the most treacherous acts possible in search of honor. Ghenji was a schemer and a lover and the first non-divine Shinto romantic hero—as depicted by a woman. You certainly have courage, but your honor is that of a monk's, and I doubt you could betray anyone."

"That's a fault?"

"I didn't say that it was, so long as honor doesn't preclude love."

"What about you?"

"Let us just say that I have two natures, hot and cold, and I'm always seeking balance while believing in absolutes . . . "

After spending the meal mainly listening and just watching her, Ghenji realized that it was one of the more enjoyable he had spent in a service wardroom in years, if ever.

Unfortunately, afterwards, Rokujo hurried off to deal with some sort of system glitch in the suspension diagnostics, but that, as Ghenji knew all too well, was more than typical for anyone who had to deal with systems. His turn would come once they entered the combat zone.

He turned, debating whether to stay and play speed-chess, when another pilot approached.

"I saw you with Captain Yukionna," offered Hotaru, the flight captain in charge of Kama-three.

"What about her?" asked Ghenji cautiously.

"Oh . . . nothing."

"What you're not telling me isn't nothing," replied Ghenji with a grin.

"Well . . . if you want to be with her . . . don't even think about being with anyone else."

"Oh . . . ?" For Ghenji, the implications were appealing. He'd never liked it when women, especially officers, played off men against each other. "Is that a return flight?"

"If you're hers, she's yours, and no one else's. I'll see you later."

Ghenji stood, watching. He thought he heard Hotaru murmur something else but he wasn't certain. What was certain was that Hotaru could have said more. There was also no doubt he had no intention of doing so.

• • •

On threeday, after his shift on the combat simulator, Ghenji cleaned up and made his way down to the life-support deck, with the rows and rows of cocoons. He found Rokujo system-linked, and sat down on the deck, cross-legged—monk-fashion, he supposed—to wait.

"How long have you been here?" she asked, as she finished de-linking from the system.

"Not long." He stood and gestured toward the console. "What were you doing?"

"I was checking diagnostics on the medical suspension cocoons."

"There's not a problem, is there?"

"No. That's why now is a good time to check everything in detail. After you and the other pilots start flying missions, we'll need them—that isn't the time to find out something's wrong."

"That makes sense." He paused. "Would you like to join me for some tea, if you can . . . and, if . . . ?" How could he ask what he really wanted to know?

She smiled, amusedly. "Are you trying to find out if I'm committed to someone in some way? I'm not. And yes, I'd love some tea, even what passes for it in the wardroom. Then, we'll see . . . "

Ghenji hadn't made that offer, although it was what he had in mind.

II

The space service was practical, but not given to more than acknowledging that humans, particularly with mixed crews, did require a certain privacy. Cubicles for one officer would fit two, but not with all that much room to spare.

Rokujo, lying in Ghenji's arms, or on his right arm, looked up. "Officers' cubes have a cross-section that's almost bell-shaped."

"It helps get rid of excess heat," he replied languidly.

"Or traps it . . . my not-so-monkish lover."

He stroked her short, silky, brilliant white hair.

"I need to go," she said. "I do have the med-section mid-watch."

"You didn't . . . "

"I wasn't about to. Your monkish concern with duty would have had you protesting that you didn't want to interfere with mine." Almost absently, she licked her lips, before smiling at him. "This way, you'll get a good night's sleep."

He had to admire the seemingly boneless way in which she slithered into her uniform skin-suit and shipvest before leaving him and the cubicle.

He lay back, amazed at what had happened. In a way, she had almost coiled around him, he reflected, yet cool as she seemed, and as cool as her touch was, she also radiated warmth. How could anyone look so cool, even feel so cool, and then pour forth such heat? But then she *had* said that her nature was both hot and cold.

Later, alone in his small cubicle, he finally drifted into an uneasy sleep, knowing that before long he'd be in suspension in transit to the combat zone, even if he had no idea where it was or exactly what the mission would be.

He dreamed, and the dream was like all the others. He was awake and trapped in his cocoon, and, just as the shakes and shivers began to subside, the temperature began to plunge once more. He could not move, and at that moment, the face of a woman with flowing white hair and skin as white as porcelain, and lips like cherries appeared above him, and bestowed a loving kiss upon him—and the ice encased him with whiteness.

He woke, not sweating, but chill. The face in his dream had been that of Rokujo. The chill in his soul intensified as he realized that it had been her face all along. Every dream about life-suspension he'd ever had was exactly the same—and it had always been her face. He just hadn't known it.

Surely, he was just back-projecting. He had to have been. He'd never met Rokujo Yukionna before embarking on the *Amaterasu*.

III

Ghenji didn't know whether to be relieved or disappointed when the cocoon opened and a thin techie glanced down at him. "Signs are green, Flight Captain. You know the drill, ser."

"Thank you."

Ghenji eased his way out of the cocoon and sat on the stool, sipping the special post-suspension "tea," waiting until the monitors showed that he was clear to resume duty.

After the evening spent with Rokujo, he hadn't seen her again before he'd entered suspension, not because he hadn't looked, but because their work and watch schedules had simply not coincided in any practical fashion.

He checked the ship-link—three point four standard years since they'd pushed off from Kunitsu orbit station two, and who knew how many more before they returned? *If* they returned.

Four stans later, he was in the squadron ready room with the other flight captains, listening to Operations Commander Togata.

" . . . In less than forty hours, we'll begin the attack on the first Mogul station. Flight Captain Nokamura will lead Kama-one . . . . Flight Captain

Yamato will lead Kama-four . . . . Full briefings are on all consoles." Togata gave a brisk nod to the flight captains, releasing them to study the attack profiles.

The briefing consoles were enclosed booths set against the bulkhead on the starboard side of the flight operations center. Ghenji sat down in the not-totally-comfortable padded seat and lowered the hood, waiting while the ops system verified his identity and then began the briefing.

The mission itself was simple. The Mogulate had already begun to change the planetary dynamics of the uninhabited system into whose outer reaches the *Amaterasu* had recently emerged. If the Parthindians completed the re-engineering, they would disrupt the clear-link-comm line used by the Republic that connected the upper galactic "west" section to the "east" section of the inhabited Republic solar systems.

The *Amaterasu*'s needles were "just" to take out the two central engineering installations in the system. At the very least, that would cost the Mogulate another ten years of investment and resources. At best, the Parthindians would abandon the project and attempt some other form of havoc. The mission required two separate attacks, roughly one to two days apart.

In the centuries since the Diaspora, warfare, like everything else, had changed, and with information and knowledge as the basis for technological societies, inter-system communications had become more and more paramount, for a system that lacked that connection could falter technologically and become vulnerable. So warfare involved attacks on the link-lines as much as attacks on systems and planets—and had also become rooted more and more in convictions of "rightness." Not that righteousness and "truth" hadn't been prime motivations behind battle from the first knapped flint spear.

Afterward, Ghenji went to the wardroom and had a large mug of green tea. He'd always felt cold, inside and out, after a console briefing.

Then he went back to the ops center and began to study the possible attack vectors from the drop spot, and particularly the last-instant options. Before he finished it was time to eat, but he was late and didn't see Rokujo until she was already seated between several others members of the ship's crew.

As soon as he could, he hurried to meet her before she escaped to the med-center . . . or wherever.

She stood waiting, smiling.

"I'd almost hoped to see you when I came out of suspension," he confessed.

"You don't want that," she replied with a laugh. "I'm only there when there's trouble, the snow-maiden-woman, if you will." Her voice dropped. "Except I'm no maiden . . . as you well know."

Ghenji blushed.

She took his hand.

Everything would have been perfect, except after she left his cubicle, he dreamed the suspension dream again—and the face was indeed that of Rokujo, and she was trying to tell him something . . . something urgent.

IV

Ghenji had run through the checklist, and waited in his needle, monitoring the operations net, with his armor tight and restrainers locked, as the *Amaterasu* began to spew forth the attack needles.

Kay-one, stand by for release.

Standing by, Sunbase control.

Launch one!

Kay-one is clear. Flight kay-two to position . . .

Before long, the four needles of Kama-four were in position in the mass-drivers.

Launch four!

The brutal jolt of acceleration pinned Ghenji and his armor into the needle's couch as the *Amaterasu*'s mass drivers hurled the four needles of his flight "downward" toward the solar engineering facility orbiting the F2 star that the Mogulate was working to turn into a facsimile of a nova.

Kay-four, release on schedule.

Affirm, kay-four on line and alpha victor, Ghenji beamed back, concentrating on the mental display fed to him by the needle AI, showing his four needles on courseline aimed directly at the Mogulate installation. They were traveling energy-blanked, hurled out by the sun-like power of the *Amaterasu*. Without energy emissions the Mogulate EDIs would detect nothing until the needles were within enhanced visual range, and by then, effective reaction would be difficult. Not impossible, because nothing could conceal that a ship had entered the system and that it had released a single blast of energy. But the defenders could only estimate what sort of attack might be coming, on what vectors, and when. There was always the possibility that the launch blast had been a decoy, designed to lure defenders into position, wasting time and energy, and even putting them in the wrong location.

Even so, Ghenji kept checking the EDI and detectors for any signs of defender vessels.

Fourteen and a half minutes later, he had visual on the Mogulate installation—as well as EDI on more than a dozen hot-scouts—the high-powered and heavily-shielded Mogulate defenders. The Kama-four needles had certain advantages—far higher down-system absolute velocity than the defenders could ever match, greater numbers, and, until they began to use their drives to maneuver, virtual invisibility. The disadvantages were that the defenders knew where the Kama needles had to go in order to plant their torps and that the defenders individually had greater firepower.

Seconds later, his sensors could pick out a gap between two of the hot-scouts not linked by defense screens. Too obvious. He tweaked the drives and angled for a narrower space "above" and to the right of the central hexagonal energy net maintained by the Parthindian defenders.

Almost as soon as he'd committed, he was through the gap and releasing his four torps. The rear screen display, only "rear" in the sense that his mind identified it as such, showed the fading energy flares that had been Republic attack needles. Initially, he could see that three of the four needles in his flight had survived the defense barrage.

Torp energy lines, seemingly from everywhere, converged on the hollowed-out nickel-iron asteroid that would have been one of two energy fulcrums used to change the stellar dynamics of the F2 sun that dominated one quadrant of his EDI. Then, the entire EDI "screen" flared, before blanking to avoid overloading both the nanotronics of the needle and the brain cells of the pilot.

Ghenji checked his departure vector against the projected track of the *Amaterasu*. If the giant needle-carrier followed the projected track . . . if . . . then he was home free.

That was all there was to it, in a sense—an approach in which the less maneuvering required, the greater the possibility of success and survival; a window of between nanoseconds and seconds in which to launch torps; and the selection and execution of an escape vector that would take the pilot back to the needle-carrier that had launched him or her. In the end, nanoseconds were all that separated success and failure.

Kay-four lead, kay-four-delta . . . massive damage . . . vectoring on you, open slave link . . .

Within his armor, Ghenji winced, but immediately activated his slave acquisition system. Then he checked the inputs from the damaged needle. The drives had kicked the needle onto the departure vector before fusing, but outside of the separate slave transmitter, the delta needle was half-junk, and habitability was nil. He could only hope that Kashiwagi's emergency life-suspension system had functioned as designed.

Ghenji used his steering drives to link with the damaged needle but, even hull-to-hull, could get no feedback.

Another seventeen minutes passed before Ghenji had lock-on with the *Amaterasu.*

Sunbase control, kay-four lead, approaching from your eight-seven, amber level.

Kay-four lead, interrogative status.

Kay-four lead and beta green, kay-four gamma strike at target. Kay-four delta on slave-link and tow. Status unknown.

Standing by for link-recovery for delta. Couplers ready. Suggest decel in ten.

Sunbase control, affirm decel in ten.

Operations control took Kashiwagi's needle first, and then the two remaining Kama-four needles, with Ghenji last.

Before he powered down and left the cradle, he linked to ops. *Interrogative status, kay-four delta.*

Recovery successful, pilot in suspension.

Thank you, Sunbase ops.

He finished the shutdown checklist and then eased himself out of the restrainers and then out of the needle through the flexible umbilical tube.

Later, there would be a complete debrief, after operations correlated all the information, but, once he finished the post-flight and mech report, he checked the mission status. Out of sixty needles launched, seven had been lost, and four had returned with various stages of damage to the needles and their pilots. He nodded—the stats were close to operational norms.

He still had time before the flight leader debrief, and he needed to check on Lieutenant Kashiwagi. The lieutenant was one of his pilots. Tired as Ghenji was, he headed up to the medical section. As he neared the two technicians stationed at the master suspension consoles, he couldn't help but overhear the quiet words between them.

"Snow-woman got him . . . but he should make it . . . bring 'em back from a block of ice . . . not medically possible . . . she can . . . "

Snow-woman? Ghenji stepped forward. "Can you tell me about Lieutenant Kashiwagi?"

"Ser!" Both stiffened. Neither spoke for a moment.

Then one finally said, "Dr. Yukionna could best tell you, and it will be a while."

"I'll wait."

He stood there, pacing back and forth, for close to a stan before he saw a flash of short brilliant white hair.

"You're here because of one of your pilots?" Rokujo's words were barely a question.

"Kashiwagi . . . Kama-four-delta. Will he make it?"

She offered a faint smile. "It's likely. He did suffer explosive decompression before life-suspension fully kicked in. That's in addition to major organ failures. We don't have the facilities to rebuild him here, but there's a good chance that we can keep him alive in suspension until we return to Kunitsu . . . "

"Likely?" That didn't sound good.

"Most of those who are likely to survive do, and if they survive, the med-systems at Kunitsu orbit station can return almost all to full function."

That was the best Ghenji could hope for. He nodded.

"Later?" he asked.

"It might be much later, but . . . yes." The quick smile that burst through the formal frosty exterior was gone almost as soon as it had appeared . . . but Ghenji had seen it.

V

Immediately after the needle recovery, the *Amaterasu* withdrew and began the maneuvers to move into position for the second attack.

Ghenji had appreciated Rokujo's company the evening after the first attack . . . but he did not see her again until the evening meal the following ship-day. She was looking for him, though, as she entered the wardroom.

"How is Kashiwagi?" he asked.

"He's under suspension. There's no way to tell now, not until they bring him out when we return. How are you?"

"Concerned. Now that I've thought about it, there should have been more defenders at the last installation."

They settled near the end of the second table.

"You think there'll be more at the next?"

"Maybe they thought we'd attack it first." He shook his head. "Enough of that. Do you prefer the art of calligraphy, representation, or actuality?" That should spark some discussion, since it had been more than a little controversial on Kunitsu just before they had left, in part because one of the "art-monks" had used a molecular shredder to destroy an entire actuality exhibit at the national museum at Oharano, claiming that the actuality school did not practice art, but merely plagiarized reality.

"I tend toward representation." She smiled. "Especially when embellished by calligraphy . . . "

As she talked, occasionally gesturing, turning her hand, in the indirect light of the mess, Ghenji thought he saw the faintest pattern of white on her white skin. White on white, almost diamond-like, or . . . he wasn't quite certain. He thought there might be the same pattern on her neck as well, but then again . . .

Much, much later, as they lay there together in Ghenji's cubicle, he did not wish to think about the next day. He'd never really worried about missions and duty, not before he'd met Rokujo. So he tried to think of something, anything, that would divert her . . . and him.

"You said you were the snow-woman . . . and so did one of the techs . . . " Ghenji didn't want to turn his statement into a question.

"That's because of my billet, and my name. The name is the same as one from an old legend, and . . . you know what I do . . . I'm responsible for bringing people out of suspension, out of the cold . . . or putting them into it, if necessary." She absently licked her lips, red, but thin, and, as he had discovered, more than mobile.

Ghenji couldn't help watching closely. They were very close, and when she'd done that, it had looked to him almost as though she'd flicked her tongue—a rather pointed tongue. He wanted to shake his head. That wasn't possible. "And the white hair?"

She just shrugged in that incredibly sinuous and sensual fashion that fascinated him. "The hair goes a long ways back, to Old Earth at least. It's always run in my family. I've been told the women are an odd mixture."

"What else runs in your family?" Ghenji tried to keep his tone light. "Besides passion?" He grinned.

"Jealousy." She bent forward and nibbled his ear. "We don't share. Ever."

That was fine with Ghenji. Then he thought. "What about duty? You do have to share me with duty."

"You're fortunate. One of my ancestors didn't understand that. I do . . . mostly." She wrapped her arms around him, coiling herself about him.

At that moment, Ghenji had no more interest in biographical questions.

When he woke, she was gone.

VII

Once more, Flight Captain Ghenji Yamato waited in his needle, monitoring the net. Within his armor, he felt hot and clammy, yet cold and chill. Why? What had happened to the warrior-monk?

Kay-four, stand by for release.

Standing by, Sunbase control, he pulsed back.

Launch four!

The sudden acceleration slammed Ghenji and his armor into the needle's couch as the *Amaterasu*'s mass drivers hurled his needle out and away. He and the remaining two needles of his flight slashed "upward" at an angle toward the second component of the Mogulate solar engineering facility. Ghenji checked vectors and relative speeds. *Sunbase control, affirm, kay-four on-line.*

He forced himself to concentrate on the mental display, while he kept checking the EDI and detectors for the first signs of the Parthindian defenders. Less than twelve minutes later, he had both visual and full EDI on the Mogulate defenses—and he didn't like what he saw. There were close to forty hot-scouts comprising a defense net with four energy-screen hexagons, and all were lined up almost perfectly to block the *Amaterasu*'s needles.

He mentally checked the options, scanned the offshoots, and pulsed to his flight, *Kay-four, course change follows . . . Execute . . . NOW!*

The two quick heading changes would do nothing to the flight's projected target release point, but they would change the angle of penetration of the defense screen—enough, Ghenji hoped, to allow a successful torp release. He wasn't so sure about whether they could correct enough afterwards, assuming they did penetrate, to regain a departure vector that would allow successful recovery.

There were no real gaps in the defense screens, not given the speeds and vectors involved, and Ghenji angled his needle toward the lowest energy concentration level in the screens with the least course deviation possible. Then, just in the nanosecond when the needle impacted the screens, the system shifted all power to ablation and defense.

The needle was through the Mogulate defenses, and nothing lay between it and the second hollowed-out asteroid.

Ghenji released all four torps.

In his mental display, ahead of him, his screens showed far fewer energy lines impacting the Parthindian installation than during the first mission and, behind him, far greater numbers of energy flares that had once been Republic attack needles.

At that instant, the EDI screen blanked in overload protection. Nearly simultaneously, the needle bucked and shuddered—and the diversion screens crumbled. That was trouble. At the velocities his needle carried, anything at all that struck the needle could now turn it into a mass of scrap composite and metal.

A second shudder rattled the needle, and Ghenji couldn't help but wince as fire shot through his back and down both legs. Then . . . he felt nothing below his waist. Nothing, not heat or chill.

Ignoring what he couldn't do anything about, Ghenji forced himself to study the needle's diagnostics. The shield generators had already gone red. The converter blinked amber, then red, and stored power reserves running down, barely enough for a return to the *Amaterasu* on residual velocity.

He funneled almost all the remaining power into the steering drives, trying to get the needle back at least close to the departure vector for rendezvous with the *Amaterasu*. If he didn't get close enough, then injuries and habitability didn't matter.

The fading screens did show him that the mission had been successful—where the second installation had been was a rapidly expanding mass of energy and mass. Then, needle system after system began to shut down.

Ghenji quickly cross-checked his departure vector against the projected track of the *Amaterasu*. Close . . . but was it close enough?

There were no other needles from flight four that had made it through, and the close-screens didn't show any needle nearby enough to slave to. On his courseline and velocity, ETA with the *Amaterasu* was a good forty-three minutes away. And something like forty would be without power.

He triggered a burst comm. *Sunbase control, kay-four lead, all systems red, on track for pick up. ETA plus forty-three. Will activate beacon. Mission accomplished.*

Within less than five minutes, he could feel the chill beginning to creep above his waist, a sure sign of far greater damage to his needle and armor—and himself—than he'd realized. He hated the idea, but there was no help for it. He triggered the emergency suspension system.

As the cold rose around him, the shakes and shivers began, if only in his upper body, and he could not move. Somewhere in the mist beyond, there was the face of a woman with flowing white hair and skin as white as porcelain, and lips like cherries appeared above him.

"Speak of this to no one else, and you will be spared eternal winter," she said, and bestowed a chilling kiss upon him—and the ice encased him with whiteness.

VIII

Ghenji blinked as the cocoon opened, and Rokujo smiled at him, bending down and brushing his lips with hers—warm and merely apple-red, rather than chill and cherry red.

"You gave even me quite a bit of trouble," she murmured, "but you'll be fine."

"You're not . . . " He remembered the words of the snow-woman in white—so like, if not identical to Rokujo—and he forced a smile.

"I am what I am, and you have a very good memory, for which I'm grateful." She kissed him gently once more. "Besides, you really don't believe in those ancient legends, do you?" Her white eyebrows arched, just slightly, but sinuously.

This time, after her kiss, his body and blood did not turn to ice.

TERRA-EXULTA

S. L. GILBOW

S. L. Gilbow is a relatively new writer, with three stories published to date, all in *The Magazine of Fantasy & Science Fiction*. He debuted in the February 2007 issue with "Red Card," a dystopian SF story in the vein of Shirley Jackson's "The Lottery."

Gilbow taught college English for a few years in the early nineties, but claims that he hasn't had much training in writing fiction. He says he's currently writing the great American novel. He's only got one line so far, but says to trust him, it's definitely going to be great, and it's definitely going to be American.

This story is about language and how words can be created and used. It was inspired by the word "grimpting," which was made up in junior high by Gilbow's wife, her sister, and a childhood friend. Gilbow says he and his wife use it to describe those things that are so bad you can't think of another word for them.

So add that one to your vocabulary, just don't use it in reference to any of these stories.

TERRA-EXULTA

I submit the following translation to the Galactic Society of Ancient Languages in response to the absurd assertion made at our last conference. Although we all agree that Archaic Planetary English can be translated into our Galactic Standard, some still hold that the process cannot be effectively reversed. Therefore, I submit the following sample of my work as evidence that such a translation is indeed possible.

I have selected a transmission at random from my files so that none can accuse me of selecting text based solely on its simplicity. I have chosen to retain some words in Galactic Standard, but only those few which cannot be logically translated. However, rest assured, the text below, and even this introduction written in that ancient language, could have been understood on Earth so very long ago. I hope, once and for all, this puts this issue to rest.

Doctor Galwot Kradame
Linguist

• • •

My Good Doctor Kradame,

May this transmission find you safe, warm, and well. It is difficult to believe seventeen years have passed since last we met. Where does time flow? I plan to return to the old system within the half-year and hope to see you once again. I will soon complete my latest project and begin the long journey home, to Earth—that place I left so very long ago. I have been gone far too long. It is now time to return.

I read your recent article in *Interstellar Linguistics* with great enthusiasm. Your proposal to translate our language into Archaic

Planetary English fascinates me. If you want for material, I welcome you to use one of my works to complete your exercise. I recommend two of my articles for your consideration: "Terrology Made Simple" and "My Vision, My Worlds." I await with great curiosity to see if such a translation—as academic as it may be—can actually be accomplished.

I also enjoyed your superb study of languages in this part—let us call it "my part"—of the Galaxy. Your analysis was brilliant, as always, and I delighted in seeing the information I provided you regarding dead languages proved helpful. I appreciate the eloquent way you put it: "Experience is surpassed only by more experience."

In your previous transmission you asked me to identify all the words I have coined that are now a permanent—if anything is permanent—part of our wonderful language. As you know well, my career has been long and my writings voluminous, so attempting to track down every word I have created—intentionally or unintentionally—would prove futile. Nevertheless, as a lover of language, like you, I treasure the opportunity to highlight a few words which come to mind.

Certainly the word I must first mention is "grimpting." To define "grimpting" would, of course, be ludicrous. It is so common now, I might as well define "planet," "terraship," or "lubradroid." Nevertheless, it is the word for which I am best known, so, with your kind indulgence, I will tell you how this word first came to be. It is a story I seldom relate.

Truth is truth, so I must admit that I was not the first to use the word; although, to the best of my knowledge, I was the first to form it into writing. I initially heard the word "grimpting" from a young worker of mine while I headed the Kolome Project. Although you are, by decades, younger than I, I am sure you have heard stories of what a difficult project that turned out to be. I can assure you there is much truth in those stories—and many lies. What a troubling project. What a troubling time.

Kolome provided some unique challenges we had not previously encountered. This was long ago, back when we were still working out many of the protocols for terraforming planets and our Federation was still young—when the various species scattered across the galaxy were just learning to work with one another.

In my defense, I arrived on the project quite late, well after things had grown complicated. But I can assure you we began making steady progress soon after my arrival.

One day—with day being relative of course—I was leading a meeting on a capital-class terrology station orbiting Kolome. This was no ordinary gathering of petty busicrats. No faclicants or holo-reps were allowed. Only those who had proven themselves worthy were invited, and all the representatives, each carefully selected, had traveled very far. Some came from our most newly developed planets. The rest came all the way from Earth, such was their profound commitment to this project.

I held the meeting in the station's main conference room where a long table stood before an enormous window looking out over Kolome, a beautiful red drop in the distance. Outside the window six Klarmond ships, even now considered the finest terraships ever built, were lined abreast in construction formation. Have you ever seen a Klarmond ship, Doctor Kradame? Nothing else made by man possesses such power. Two Klarmond ships can transform a small planet in a half-year. They can level mountains or empty seas, move continents or cleanse a chlorine atmosphere. Initially I ordered the Klarmond ships to Kolome merely to illustrate my resolution. Initially, I had no intention of actually using them.

The meeting turned out to be quite a challenge. Five senior leaders, seven adjuncts, a full team of my engineers and I were struggling with some delicate issues, but things were going very well and some wonderful ideas were being tossed about. Just as I made an excellent point, a point—you must understand—with which almost everyone agreed, one of the engineers sitting next to me slammed her hand down on the conference table making a sound as deafening as a continental Klarmond shot. I assure you, I have been in many meetings in my life, and that is the only time I have ever witnessed such uncivilized behavior. But she did. She hammered the table with the blunt of her hand and shouted, much to my embarrassment, "This is the most grimpting thing I have ever heard in my life."

I stopped. I stopped talking. I stopped listening. For a few seconds, I stopped breathing. I think my heart was even still. The fruitful discussion we had been having and the excellent progress we had been making immediately ceased. We all just stared at her, not really sure how to react. I sensed that I could lose control of the meeting if I did not act quickly. This was not just a disruption; this was a challenge, a challenge to my very authority. The senior leaders, all wise and gerbunctious, looked at me; after all, she was *my* employee and it was *my* meeting. I could have had her ejected immediately, but I did no such thing. I just looked as her and thought for a moment, and then I said, as calmly as I could, "What do you mean?"

"What do I mean?" she asked. She did not look well. She was pale and trembled like a baby limik. Even now I attribute her behavior to some undetected illness, the Regulian flu perhaps. "Just look," she whispered, "just look at what you are proposing. Just stop for a second and look at it."

"No," I said. Obviously the young woman had completely missed my point. Another sign of her illness, I assume. "What do you mean by 'grimpting?'" I asked. Her eyes widened and she stared at me as if I had spoken in a language she could not comprehend. Two of the leaders at the table smiled at me and one of the adjuncts even laughed, so I seized the opportunity. I leaned towards her, moving as close as I could without leaving my seat. Her breath was hot on my face. "Are you making up words?" I asked. A few more joined the adjunct in laughter. "Are you sure you're well?" I added.

The young woman turned as red as a glamik and explained that she and her sister had made up "grimpting" as children and that to define it would be difficult. They had, in fact, never defined it; they had merely used it. She looked down at her hands and then she looked at mine. Finally she said, quite seriously I believe, "But whatever the hell it means, I am sure it is entirely appropriate." The young woman rose from her seat and ran from the room. After the laughter had faded, we composed ourselves and continued our excellent progress.

I must admit, I owe much to that young woman. I cannot remember her name and really do not know whatever happened to her. She was off the station within two hours, and I can assure you she is no longer a terrologist. But that young woman made me keenly aware of language. She made me aware of how easily words can be created, how they can be crafted and used. I have uttered the word "grimpting" (or one of its various forms—grimpts, grimpter, grimptel, grimpted) almost every day since I last saw that young woman. What wonderful words they all are.

• • •

As I look back on the Kolome Project, I realize that it provided many fine words to our language. To avoid wandering into a topic that cannot be easily covered in one short transmission, please allow me to limit my discussion to the words that emerged from my work with that single planet.

I am not sure of how familiar you are with Kolome. I certainly do not remember it coming up in any of our conversations. So please indulge me while I recount a little history. If you need more information, I encourage you to read my early work on the subject: *Kolome—When Rumors Meet Truth*.

Kolome was the eighth planet outside our solar system we had attempted to settle. A remote planet, Kolome is best remembered for being the first planet we colonized with indigenous life already on it. By the time I was brought onto the project, humans had been living on Kolome for almost two years. Initially there was no plan to terraform Kolome at all. The atmosphere was breathable, and the temperature, although frodeling, was warm enough to sustain human life. Water was scarce, but enough could be extracted from minerals to negate the need to import more. All in all, it was a decently hospitable planet.

The first colonists established one settlement in the north and one far to the south—with "north" and "south" being relative of course. The equatorial region, warm and lush, could have much more easily sustained human life, but the first settlers avoided the region in order not to conflict with the numerous life forms that already thrived there.

For almost two years the colonies survived without any problem, at least nothing more than the usual challenges of settling an alien world. The northern settlement grew to more than seven-thousand inhabitants and showed signs of economic potential. The southern colony, although not quite as prosperous, began to expand to the north. Things seemed to be going very well. Very well indeed, until, inexplicably, one of the indigenous species started to migrate toward the southern pole.

The migrating species was red and long but no wider than the tip of your little finger. They looked like quick ribbons fluttering about close to the ground. Their migration started slowly, no more than a few kilometers a week, but by the time I was summoned the creatures had come within fifty kilometers of the southern settlement's primary base. They did not seem particularly aggressive, and the colonists initially assessed them to be quite harmless. Unfortunately, initial assessments are frequently wrong.

As the creatures neared one of our outposts, many colonists there grew ill. It started with a few isolated cases of fever and hallucinations. The doctors on Kolome initially thought they could contain the disease, but it rapidly spread into an epidemic, incapacitating the entire southern settlement. Most patients recovered after a few days. For some the illness lingered for weeks. For a few, but far, far too many, the disease proved fatal.

At first the colonists did not draw a connection between the illness and the migrating species. They initially thought the symptoms might be a delayed reaction to one of the native plant-like species the colonists fed upon. The food had been thoroughly tested years before but was studied again and found to be quite harmless, as initially assessed. The finest physicians in that part of the galaxy were brought in, but none of them could cure the disease or even determine its cause. In the end we could only assume the illness had something to do with the migration of the little red creatures. By the time I arrived, almost two-hundred colonists in the south had perished. There was talk of abandoning the settlement. Some even proposed leaving Kolome altogether.

I will not go into the details of how we resolved the problem, for that is not my purpose here. I fear I have already digressed. I will try to restrict myself to the subject at hand, the words which arose from my work on the Kolome Project.

I must admit that I saw the little creatures only once, and that was during a brief excursion to Kolome's surface. I had traveled over a hundred kilometers north of the southern settlement. Some of the colonists had encouraged me to take a faclicant to help me properly assess the situation. As it is, on this excursion, I preferred to travel as one, trusting my instincts. An ancient philosopher once said, "When a man is alone, he is alone."

Truth is truth, and I must admit I have never felt so isolated, even with the settlement only ten minutes away by galaride. While I surveyed what I can only describe as a hopelessly barren landscape, one of the creatures came flitting by, alternately displaying its crimson back and its underside flecked with orange and yellow. As the creature passed within half-a-ten meters, I heard it make a high-pitched singing sound. The first colonists, understandably entranced with the creatures, had named them "trillbrights."

As I watched the trillbright dance over that desolate landscape, I realized the challenge I faced, the problems that lay before me. The creature was, as I had feared, quite beautiful, more beautiful than the holopics could ever portray.

As the trillbright twisted its way into the distance, I knew what I would have to do. I knew I would have to change the trillbright's name. After days of deliberation, I decided upon "slaggerbug." Truth is truth, so I must admit the creatures actually had very little in common with insects, except size. But it was not the accuracy of the word that was important to me. With a little coaxing, "slaggerbug" became the accepted term among the colonists and scientists in the region. I correctly assumed that if I could change the word used by the local population, the rest of the galaxy would follow their lead.

Soon afterwards, I wrote an article for *Galactic Science* in which I coined another word—"delinction." "Delinction" was, I proposed, the methodical elimination of a harmful or useless species. We had to acknowledge, I argued, that we no longer had life on a single planet to contend with—or even a handful of planets for that matter. We had an entire galaxy potentially teeming with life. We had to recognize that just because something "did exist," it did not necessarily mean it "should exist." The article, I am proud to say, was well received in this part of the galaxy.

Of course, language rarely resolves problems by itself. It is only one of many tools used to address difficult issues. And I used all my tools to help persuade others to see the logic in my argument. But it is language I am addressing here, so I will try to restrict myself to that topic.

Of course things are never as simple as they first appear. Many believe that terraforming is merely using powerful equipment to shape, reform and refine a planet. In reality, terraforming is about managing cause and effect, about judging consequences. When you are working on a planetary scale, every action will have a dramatic reaction, often one you did not predict. It is the terrologist's job to assess those reactions and respond accordingly. Kolome is an excellent case in point.

Once the slaggerbugs were gone, the small gray plantlike organism which had sustained the colonists began to perish. It was not completely unexpected but many busicrats grew angry when what we had already identified as a possibility actually occurred.

I took, however, another approach. The organism had originally been named "calobush," so I merely asserted that if we were going to use plant analogies, referring to the organism as a "bush" was not entirely accurate. I rationally recommended changing the organism's name to "caloweed." I also pointed out that although the caloweed was capable of sustaining life, much more flavorful and nutritious food could be grown on Kolome. I argued that since the caloweed was already perishing and could be replaced it would be logical to speed up the process.

Once the caloweed was gone, the remaining species declined as well. The "glushworm" and "testimite" were gone within a year. The "cessfish" hung on a little longer.

This brings us to the word "retoration." "Retoration" would be, I asserted, simply the removal of all life from a planet in order to repopulate it with other life forms to create a more balanced ecology.

But of all the words which arose from the Kolome Project, I believe my personal favorite is "Terra-Exulta." During the first year of the transformation, things were extremely difficult. The planet had to be temporarily abandoned while the Klarmond ships did their work. Many argued not to return to Kolome at all. I countered by saying that although things were difficult, in the end the result would be "Terra-Exulta," a perfect world, an ideally-constructed planet.

In the end, I worked on the Kolome project for over five years. After four years, Kolome was once again a viable planet. But you should see it now. It has little resemblance to the frigid wasteland I visited long ago. The entire planet thrives, full of life and features you would quickly recognize. Even though it was one of my early works, I am especially proud of it.

Since that time I have worked on many planets, and with each project came new challenges and new words. The Walgard Project brought us anaclam, fecateria, glomoration, reimmolate, and elimitest. The Glaman Project itself spawned seventeen new nouns, six verbs and one of my favorite words, "ecoviserate."

Oh, how I could go on, for the list is almost endless. I have, as it is, written far more than I intended. I hope you find this information useful as you continue your studies. Please let me know if you need any more information, for I do so enjoy reminiscing.

As I said at the beginning of this transmission, I will soon be returning to the old system. I am excited about once again seeing the places I left behind so very long ago. I have heard that Mars grows greener with each passing day and the Moon's rivers run deep and clean. It warms my heart to see the positive changes my profession can make. Such works bring tears to the eyes of even the most seasoned terrologist.

But what I have heard of Earth is quite disheartening. The air is thin and the seas are thick and hot. I have also heard the population has become quite grimpting. Unfortunately, as most of our human race grows strong, there are, regrettably, some few who do not. Earth's viability falls with each passing day and there is some talk out here of redoing it. For it is out here, among the various scattered species of the galaxy, among those new planets that we have marked with the gifts of my profession, that we have truly perfected the art of terraforming.

I have made some proposals, modest ones I assure you, for improving Earth and anxiously await a response. For is it not obvious that when a planet fails some form of dilinction is in order? Can we not see what a positive influence a retoration can have on even the most ancient of our treasured worlds? Should we not work to ecoviserate those few who are not functioning as they should and replace them with the stronger species that have grown, even flourished, out here on the fringes of civilization?

Will we not take the effort to turn the birthplace of what is now a well-traveled species—a galactic species—into a true Terra-Exulta?

I have already taken the liberty of ordering eight Klarmond ships to head toward Earth. It will be my gift to humanity—using those talents I have developed out here, so very far from Sol—to turn our ancestral home into the Terra-Exulta it deserves to be. What a wonderful opportunity. Who knows what new words will spring from this new project?

Give my love to the family.

Humbly Yours,
Harald K. Jeribob
Terrologist

AFTERMATHS

LOIS McMASTER BUJOLD

Lois McMaster Bujold is a five-time winner of the Hugo Award and the winner of three Nebula Awards. She has published nearly two dozen novels, including several in her popular Barrayar series, which mostly feature aristocrat and interstellar spy Miles Vorkosigan. The first of these, T*he Warrior's Apprentice*, appeared in 1986, but she made her debut a few years earlier in 1984 when she sold a short story to *Twilight Zone Magazine*. Over the years, she hasn't written much other short fiction, so this one is a rare treat.

Although Bujold's career started off in science fiction, lately, she's turned her hand to fantasy, writing first the Chalion series, then moving onto *The Sharing Knife*; volume four of that series, *Horizon*, came out in February. Learn more about her and her work at www.dendarii.com.

This story, which takes place in her Barrayar milieu, takes a rather grim look at some of the professions that will arise in the wake of interstellar war.

AFTERMATHS

The shattered ship hung in space, a black bulk in the darkness. It still turned, imperceptibly slowly; one edge eclipsed and swallowed the bright point of a star. The lights of the salvage crew arced over the skeleton. *Ants, ripping up a dead moth,* Ferrell thought. *Scavengers . . .*

He sighed dismay into his forward observation screen, picturing the ship as it had been scant weeks before. The wreckage untwisted in his mind—a cruiser, alive with the patterns of gaudy lights that always made him think of a party seen across night waters. Responsive as a mirror to the mind under its pilot's headset, where man and machine penetrated the interface and became one. Swift, gleaming, functional . . . no more. He glanced to his right and self-consciously cleared his throat.

"Well, Medtech," he spoke to the woman who stood beside his station, staring into the screen as silently and long as he had. "There's our starting point. Might as well go ahead and begin the pattern sweep now, I suppose."

"Yes, please do, Pilot Officer." She had a gravelly alto voice, suitable for her age, which Ferrell judged to be about forty-five. The collection of thin silver five-year service chevrons on her left sleeve made an impressive glitter against the dark red uniform of the Escobaran military medical service. Dark hair shot with gray, cut short for ease of maintenance, not style; a matronly heaviness to her hips. A veteran, it appeared. Ferrell's sleeve had yet to sprout even his first-year stripe, and his hips, and the rest of his body, still maintained an unfilled adolescent stringiness.

But she was only a tech, he reminded himself, not even a physician. He was a full-fledged Pilot Officer. His neurological implants and biofeedback training were all complete. He was certified, licensed, and graduated—just three frustrating days too late to participate in what was now being dubbed the Hundred and Twenty Day War. Although in fact it had only been 118 days and part of an hour between the time the spearhead of the Barrayaran invasion fleet penetrated Escobaran local space, and the time the last survivors fled the counterattack, piling through the wormhole exit for home as though scuttling for a burrow.

"Do you wish to stand by?" he asked her.

She shook her head. "Not yet. This inner area has been pretty well worked over in the last three weeks. I wouldn't expect to find anything on the first four turns, although it's good to be thorough. I've a few things to arrange yet in my work area, and then I think I'll get a catnap. My department has been awfully busy the last few months," she added apologetically. "Understaffed, you know. Please call me if you do spot anything, though—I prefer to handle the tractor myself, whenever possible."

"Fine by me." He swung about in his chair to his comconsole. "What minimum mass do you want a bleep for? About forty kilos, say?"

"One kilo is the standard I prefer."

"One kilo!" He stared. "Are you joking?"

"Joking?" She stared back, then seemed to arrive at enlightenment. "Oh, I see. You were thinking in terms of whole—I can make positive identification with quite small pieces, you see. I wouldn't even mind picking up smaller bits than that, but if you go much under a kilo you spend too much time on false alarms from micrometeors and other rubbish. One kilo seems to be the best practical compromise."

"Bleh." But he obediently set his probes for a mass of one kilo, minimum, and finished programming the search sweep.

She gave him a brief nod and withdrew from the closet-sized Navigation and Control Room. The obsolete courier ship had been pulled from junkyard orbit and hastily overhauled with some notion first of converting it into a personnel carrier for middle brass—top brass in a hurry having a monopoly on the new ships—but like Ferrell himself, it had graduated too late to participate. So they both had been re-routed together, he and his first command, to the dull duties he privately thought on a par with sanitation engineering, or worse.

He gazed one last moment at the relic of battle in the forward screen, its structural girdering poking up like bones through sloughing skin, and shook his head at the waste of it all. Then, with a little sigh of pleasure, he pulled his headset down into contact with the silvery circles on his temples and mid-forehead, closed his eyes, and slid into control of his own ship.

Space seemed to spread itself all around him, buoyant as a sea. He was the ship, he was a fish, he was a merman; unbreathing, limitless, and without pain. He fired his engines as though flame leapt from his fingertips, and began the slow rolling spiral of the search pattern.

• • •

"Medtech Boni?" he said, keying the intercom to her cabin. "I believe I have something for you here."

She rubbed sleep from her face, framed in the intercom screen. "Already? What time—oh. I must have been tireder than I realized. I'll be right up, Pilot Officer."

Ferrell stretched, and began an automatic series of isometrics in his chair. It had been a long and uneventful watch. He would have been hungry, but what he contemplated now through the viewscreens subdued his appetite.

Boni appeared promptly, sliding into the seat beside him. "Oh, quite right, Pilot Officer." She unshipped the controls to the exterior tractor beam, and flexed her fingers before taking a delicate hold.

"Yeah, there wasn't much doubt about that one," he agreed, leaning back and watching her work. "Why so tender with the tractors?" he asked curiously, noting the low power level she was using.

"Well, they're frozen right through, you know," she replied, not taking her eyes from her readouts. "Brittle. If you play hot-shot and bang them around, they can shatter. Let's stop that nasty spin, first," she added, half to herself. "A slow spin is all right. Seemly. But that fast spinning you get sometimes—it must be very unrestful for them, don't you think?"

His attention was pulled from the thing in the screen, and he stared at her. "They're *dead,* lady!"

She smiled slowly as the corpse, bloated from decompression, limbs twisted as though frozen in a strobe-flash of convulsion, was drawn gently toward the cargo bay. "Well, that's not their fault, is it?—one of our fellows, I see by the uniform."

"Bleh!" he repeated himself, then gave vent to an embarrassed laugh. "You act like you enjoy it."

"Enjoy? No . . . But I've been in Personnel Retrieval and Identification for nine years, now. I don't mind. And of course, vacuum work is always a little nicer than planetary work."

"Nicer? With that godawful decompression?"

"Yes, but there are the temperature effects to consider. No decomposition."

He took a breath, then let it out carefully. "I see. I guess you would get—pretty hardened, after a while. Is it true you guys call them corpse-sicles?"

"Some do," she admitted. "I don't."

She maneuvered the twisted thing carefully through the cargo bay doors and keyed them shut. "Temperature set for a slow thaw, and he'll be ready to handle in a few hours," she murmured.

"What do you call them?" he asked as she rose.

"People."

She awarded his bewilderment a small smile, like a salute, and withdrew to the temporary mortuary set up next to the cargo bay.

• • •

On his next scheduled break he went down himself, drawn by morbid curiosity. He poked his nose around the doorframe. She was seated at her desk. The table in the center of the room was as yet unoccupied.

"Uh—hello."

She looked up with her quick smile. "Hello, Pilot Officer. Come on in."

"Uh, thank you. You know, you don't really have to be so formal. Call me Falco, if you want," he said, entering.

"Certainly, if you wish. My first name is Tersa."

"Oh, yeah? I have a cousin named Tersa."

"It's a popular name. There were always at least three in my classes at school." She rose and checked a gauge by the door to the cargo bay. "He should be just about ready to take care of, now. Pulled to shore, so to speak."

Ferrell sniffed and cleared his throat, wondering whether to stay or excuse himself. "Grotesque sort of fishing." *Excuse myself, I think.*

She picked up the control lead to the float pallet and trailed it after her into the cargo bay. There were some thumping noises, and she returned, the pallet drifting behind her. The corpse was in the dark blue of a deck officer, and covered thickly with frost, which flaked and dripped upon the floor as the medtech slid it onto the examining table. Ferrell shivered with disgust.

Definitely excuse myself. But he lingered, leaning against the doorframe at a safe distance.

She pulled an instrument, trailing its lead to the computers, from the crowded rack above the table. It was the size of a pencil, and emitted a thin blue beam of light when aligned with the corpse's eyes.

"Retinal identification," Tersa explained. She pulled down a pad-like object, similarly connected, and pressed it to each of the monstrosity's hands. "And fingerprints," she went on. "I always do both, and cross-match. The eyes can get awfully distorted. Errors in identification can be brutal for the families. Hm. Hm." She checked her readout screen. "Lieutenant Marco Deleo. Age twenty-nine. Well, Lieutenant," she went on chattily, "let's see what I can do for you."

She applied an instrument to its joints, which loosened them, and began removing its clothes.

"Do you often talk to—them?" inquired Ferrell, unnerved.

"Always. It's a courtesy, you see. Some of the things I have to do for them are rather undignified, but they can still be done with courtesy."

Ferrell shook his head. "I think it's obscene, myself."

"Obscene?"

"All this horsing around with dead bodies. All the trouble and expense we go to, collecting them. I mean, what do they care? Fifty or a hundred kilos of rotting meat. It'd be cleaner to leave them in space."

She shrugged, unoffended, undiverted from her task. She folded the clothes and inventoried the pockets, laying out their contents in a row.

"I rather like going through the pockets," she remarked. "It reminds me of when I was a little girl, visiting in someone else's home. When I went upstairs by myself, to go to the bathroom or whatever, it was always a kind of pleasure to peek into the other rooms and see what kind of things they had, and how they kept them. If they were very neat, I was always very impressed—I've never been able to keep my own things neat. If it was a mess, I felt I'd found a secret kindred spirit. A person's things can be a kind of exterior morphology of their mind—like a snail's shell, or something. I like to imagine what kind of person they were, from what's in the pockets. Neat, or messy. Very regulation, or full of personal things . . . Take Lieutenant Deleo, here. He must have been very conscientious. Everything regulation, except this little vid disc from home. From his wife, I'd imagine. I think he must have been a very nice person to know."

She placed the collection of objects carefully into its labeled bag.

"Aren't you going to listen to it?" asked Ferrell.

"Oh, no. That would be prying."

He barked a laugh. "I fail to see the distinction."

"Ah." She completed the medical examination, readied the plastic body bag, and began to wash the corpse. When she worked her way down to the careful cleaning around the genital area, necessary because of sphincter relaxation, Ferrell fled at last.

That woman is nuts. I wonder if it's the cause of her choice of work, or the effect?

• • •

It was another full day before they hooked their next fish. Ferrell had a dream, during his sleep cycle, about being on a deep-sea boat and hauling up nets full of corpses to be dumped, wet and shining as though with iridescent scales, in a huge pile in the hold. He awoke from it sweating, but with very cold feet. It was with profound relief that he returned to the pilot's station and slid into the skin of his ship. The ship was clean, mechanical and pure, immortal as a god; one could forget one had ever owned a sphincter muscle.

"Odd trajectory," he remarked, as the medtech again took her place at the tractor controls.

"Yes . . . Oh, I see. He's a Barrayaran. He's a long way from home."

"Oh, bleh. Throw him back."

"Oh, no. We have identification files for all their missing. Part of the peace settlement, you know, along with prisoner exchange."

"Considering what they did to our people as prisoners, I don't think we owe them a thing."

She shrugged.

The Barrayaran officer had been a tall, broad-shouldered man, a commander by the rank on his collar tabs. The medtech treated him with the same care she had expended on Lieutenant Deleo, and more. She went to considerable trouble to smooth and straighten him, massaging the mottled face back into some semblance of manhood with her fingertips, a process Ferrell watched with a rising gorge.

"I wish his lips wouldn't curl back *quite* so much," she remarked, while at this task. "Gives him what I imagine to be an uncharacteristically snarly look. I think he must have been rather handsome."

One of the objects in his pockets was a little locket. It held a tiny glass bubble filled with a clear liquid. The inside of its gold cover was densely engraved with the elaborate curlicues of the Barrayaran alphabet.

"What is it?" asked Ferrell in curiosity.

She held it pensively to the light. "It's a sort of charm, or memento. I've learned a lot about the Barrayarans in the last three months. Turn ten of them upside down and you'll find some kind of good luck charm or amulet or medallion or something in the pockets of nine of them. The high-ranking officers are just as bad as the enlisted people."

"Silly superstition."

"I'm not sure if it's superstition or just custom. We treated an injured prisoner once—he claimed it was just custom. That people give them to the soldiers as presents, and nobody really believes in them. But when we took his away from him, when we were undressing him for surgery, he tried to fight us for it. It took three of us to hold him down for the anesthetic. I thought it a rather remarkable performance for a man whose legs had been blown away. He wept . . . Of course, he was in shock."

Ferrell dangled the locket on the end of its short chain, intrigued in spite of himself. It hung with a companion piece, a curl of hair embedded in a plastic pendant.

"Some sort of holy water, is it?" he inquired.

"Almost. It's a very common design. It's called a mother's tears charm. Let me see if I can make out—he's had it a while, it seems. From the inscription—I think that says 'ensign,' and the date—it must have been given him on the occasion of his commission."

"It's not really his mother's tears, is it?"

"Oh, yes. That's what's supposed to make it work, as a protection."

"Doesn't seem to be very effective."

"No, well . . . no."

Ferrell snorted his irony. "I hate those guys—but I do guess I feel sort of sorry for his mother."

Boni retrieved the chain and its pendants, holding the curl in plastic to the light and reading its inscription. "No, not at all. She's a fortunate woman."

"How so?"

"This is her death lock. She died three years ago, by this."

"Is that supposed to be lucky, too?"

"No, not necessarily. Just a remembrance, as far as I know. Kind of a nice one, really. The nastiest charm I ever ran across, and the most unique, was this little leather bag hung around a fellow's neck. It was filled with dirt and leaves, and what I took at first to be some sort of little frog-like animal skeleton about ten centimeters long. But when I looked at it more closely, it turned out to be the skeleton of a human fetus. Very strange. I suppose it was some sort of black magic. Seemed an odd thing to find on an engineering officer."

"Doesn't seem to work for any of them, does it?"

She smiled wryly. "Well, if there are any that work, I wouldn't see them, would I?"

She took the processing one step further by cleaning the Barrayaran's clothes and carefully re-dressing him, before bagging him and returning him to the freeze.

"The Barrayarans are all so army-mad," she explained. "I always like to put them back in their uniforms. They mean so much to them, I'm sure they're more comfortable with them on."

Ferrell frowned uneasily. "I still think he ought to be dumped with the rest of the garbage."

"Not at all," said the medtech. "Think of all the work he represents on somebody's part. Nine months of pregnancy, childbirth, two years of diapering, and that's just the beginning. Tens of thousands of meals, thousands of bedtime stories, years of school. Dozens of teachers. And all that military training, too. A lot of people went into making him."

She smoothed a strand of the corpse's hair into place. "That head held the universe, once. He had a good rank for his age," she added, rechecking her monitor. "Thirty-two. Commander Aristede Vorkalloner. It has a kind of nice ethnic ring. Very Barrayaranish, that name. Vor, too, one of those warrior-class fellows."

"Homicidal-class loonies. Or worse," Ferrell said automatically. But his vehemence had lost momentum, somehow.

Boni shrugged. "Well, he's joined the great democracy now. And he had nice pockets."

• • •

Three full days went by with no further alarms but a rare scattering of mechanical debris. Ferrell began to hope the Barrayaran was the last pickup they would have to make. They were nearing the end of their search pattern. Besides, he thought resentfully, this duty was sabotaging the efficiency of his sleep cycle. But the medtech made a request.

"If you don't mind, Falco," she said, "I'd greatly appreciate it if we could run the pattern out just a few extra turns. The original orders are based on this average estimated trajectory speed, you see, and if someone just happened to get a bit of extra kick when the ship split, they could well be beyond it by now."

Ferrell was less than thrilled, but the prospect of an extra day of piloting had its attractions, and he gave a grudging consent. Her reasoning proved itself; before the day was half done, they turned up another gruesome relic.

"Oh," muttered Ferrell, when they got a close look. It had been a female officer. Boni reeled her in with enormous tenderness. He didn't really want to go watch, this time, but the medtech seemed to have come to expect him.

"I—don't really want to look at a woman blown up," he tried to excuse himself.

"Mm," said Tersa. "Is it fair, though, to reject a person just because they're dead? You wouldn't have minded her body a bit when she was alive."

He vented a little macabre laugh. "Equal rights for the dead?"

Her smile twisted. "Why not? Some of my best friends are corpses."

He snorted.

She grew more serious. "I'd sort of like the company, on this one." So he took up his usual station by the door.

The medtech laid out the thing that had been a woman upon her table, undressed, inventoried, washed, and straightened it. When she finished, she kissed the dead lips.

"Oh, God," cried Ferrell, shocked and nauseated. "You *are* crazy! You're a damn, damn necrophiliac! A *lesbian* necrophiliac, at that!" He turned to go.

"Is that what it looks like, to you?" Her voice was soft, and still unoffended. It stopped him, and he looked over his shoulder. She was looking at him as gently as if he had been one of her precious corpses. "What a strange world you must live in, inside your head."

She opened a suitcase, and shook out a dress, fine underwear, and a pair of white embroidered slippers. A wedding dress, Ferrell realized. This woman was a bona fide *psychopath* . . .

She dressed the corpse and arranged its soft dark hair with great delicacy, before bagging it.

"I believe I shall place her next to that nice tall Barrayaran," she said. "I think they would have liked each other very well, if they could have met in another place and time. And Lieutenant Deleo was married, after all."

She completed the label. Ferrell's battered mind was sending him little subliminal messages; he struggled to overcome his shock and bemusement, and pay attention. It tumbled into the open day of his consciousness with a start.

She had not run an identification check on this one.

Out the door, he told himself, *is the way you want to walk. I guarantee it.* Instead, timorously, he went over to the corpse and checked its label. *Ensign Sylva Boni,* it said. *Age twenty.* His own age . . .

He was trembling, as if with cold. It *was* cold, in that room. Tersa Boni finished packing up the suitcase, and turned back with the float pallet.

"Daughter?" he asked. It was all he could ask.

She pursed her lips and nodded.

"It's—a helluva coincidence."

"No coincidence at all. I asked for this sector."

"Oh." He swallowed, turned away, turned back, face flaming. "I'm sorry I said—"

She smiled her slow sad smile. "Never mind."

• • •

They found yet one more bit of mechanical debris, so agreed to run another cycle of the search spiral, to be sure that all possible trajectories had been outdistanced. And yes, they found another; a nasty one, spinning fiercely, guts split open from some great blow and hanging out in a frozen cascade.

The acolyte of death did her dirty work without once so much as wrinkling her nose. When it came to the washing, the least technical of the tasks, Ferrell said suddenly, "May I help?"

"Certainly," said the medtech, moving aside. "An honor is not diminished for being shared."

And so he did, as shy as an apprentice saint washing his first leper.

"Don't be afraid," she said. "The dead cannot hurt you. They give you no pain, except that of seeing your own death in their faces. And one can face that, I find."

Yes, he thought, the good face pain. But the great—they embrace it.

SOMEONE IS STEALING THE GREAT THRONE ROOMS OF THE GALAXY

HARRY TURTLEDOVE

Harry Turtledove—who is often referred to as the "master of alternate history"—is the Hugo Award-winning author of more than eighty novels and a hundred short stories. His most recent novels are T*he Man With the Iron Heart, After the Downfall,* and *Give Me Back My Legions!* In addition to his SF, fantasy, and alternate history works, he's also published several straight historical novels under the name H. N. Turteltaub. Turtledove obtained a Ph.D. in Byzantine history from UCLA in 1977.

Given the seriousness of much of Turtledove's work, it might surprise people what a great sense of humor he has. In his career, he's written several humorous works, such as this one, which explores the adventures of a space cadet, who happens to be a hamster and the galaxy's last, best hope. Warning: It contains fowl language. Er, actually, it contains rodent language. What I mean to say is, it's full of puns. But it's funny anyway, I promise. If you disagree, I give you permission to call it grimpting.

SOMEONE IS STEALING THE GREAT THRONE ROOMS OF THE GALAXY

When thieves paralyzed the people—well, the saurian humanoids—inside the palace on the main continent of Gould IV and made off with the famous throne room (and the somewhat less famous antechamber), it made a tremendous stir all over the continent.

When pirates paralyzed the people—well, the ammonia/ice blobs—inside the palace on the chief glacier of Amana XI and made off with the magnificent throne room (and the somewhat less magnificent antechamber), it raised a tremendous stink all over the planet.

When robbers paralyzed the people—well, the highly evolved and sagacious kumquats—inside the palace on the grandest orchard of Alpharalpha B and made off with the precociously planted throne room (and the somewhat less precocious antechamber), it caused a sour taste in mouths all over the sector.

And when brigands paralyzed the people—well, the French—inside the palace of Versailles in a third-rate country on a second-rate continent with a splendid future behind it and made off with the baroque throne room (and the somewhat less baroque antechamber), it caused shock waves all over the Galaxy.

As Earth has always been, it remains the sleazy-media center of the Galactic Empire. Anything that happens there gets more attention than it deserves, just because it happens there. And so there was an enormous hue and cry.

Something Must Be Done!

Who got to do it?

Why, the Space Patrol, of course. Specifically, Space Cadet Rufus Q.

Shupilluliumash, a Bon of Bons, a noble of nobles . . . a fat overgrown hamster with delusions of gender. And when Cadet Rufus Q. Shupilluliumash (last name best sung to the tune of "Fascinatin' Rhythm") got the call, he was, as fate and the omniscient narrator would have it, massively hung over from a surfeit of fermented starflower seeds.

The hero who gave him the call, Space Patrol Captain Erasmus Z. Utnapishtim (last name best sung to the tune of "On, Wisconsin"), was a member of the same species, and so understood his debility. This is not to say the illustrious Space Patrol captain—another fat overgrown hamster—sympathized. Oh, no. "You're a disgrace to your whiskers, Shupilluliumash," he cheebled furiously.

"Sorry, sir," Rufus Q. Shupilluliumash answered. At that particular moment, he rather hoped his whiskers, and the rest of his pelt, would fall out.

Captain Utnapishtim knew there was only one way to get to the bottom of things: the right way, the proper way, the regulation way, the Space Patrol way. "Go find out who is stealing the great throne rooms of the Galaxy," he ordered. "Find out why. Arrest the worthless miscreants and make the mischief stop."

"Right . . . sir," Cadet Shupilluliumash said miserably, wishing Utnapishtim were dead or he himself were dead or the omniscient narrator were dead (no such luck, Shup baby)—any way at all to escape from this silly story and the pain in his pelt. "Where do I start . . . sir?"

"Start on Earth," Captain Utnapishtim told him. "Earth is the least consequential planet in the Galaxy, and all the inhabitants talk too bloody much. If you can't find a clue there, you're not worth your own tail."

"Like you, sir, I am a fat overgrown hamster," the space cadet replied with dignity. "I have no tail."

"Well, if I remember my briefings, neither do Earthmen," the Space Patrol officer said. "Now get your wheel rolling."

"Yes, sir," Shupilluliumash said resignedly, and headed off to check out a Patrol speedster, the P.S. *Habitrail.*

Now you should know that there are many kinds of space drives to span the parsecs of the Galaxy. You should, yes, but since you don't—you can't fool the omniscient narrator (otherwise he wouldn't be omniscient)—you have to sit through this expository lump. There is the hyperspace drive: traditional, but effective. There is the hop-skip-and-a-jump drive: wearing, but quick. There is the overdrive. There is the underdrive. There is the orthodontic drive, which corrects both overdrive and underdrive but is hellishly expensive. There are any number of others—oh, not *any* number, but, say, forty-two. And, particularly for fat overgrown hamsters, there is the wheel drive.

The wheel drive translates rotary motion into straight-ahead FTL by a clever mechanism with whose workings the omniscient narrator won't bore you (the O.N. knows you have a low boredom threshold, and you won't sit still for two expository lumps in a row). Suffice to say that Space Cadet Shupilluliumash jumped in his wheel, ran like hell, and almost before he'd sweated out the last of his hangover he found himself landing outside of Paris—sort of like Lindbergh long before, but much fuzzier.

He got full cooperation from the French authorities. Once local Galactic officials secured his release from jail, he went to Versailles to view the scene of the crime. "This is a very ugly building," he said with the diplomacy for which his race was so often praised.

After local Galactic officials secured his release from jail again—it took longer this time—they told him, "The French tend to be emotional."

"So do I," Rufus Q. Shupilluliumash said. "Especially about the food in there—it's terrible."

"And such small portions," the Galactic officials chorused.

"How did you know?" Shup asked in genuine surprise. "Or do they bust everybody?"

"Never mind," the officials said, not quite in harmony. "Go back to Versailles. Observe. Take notes. For God's sake, don't talk."

"Oh, all right," the hamster space cadet grumbled.

Go back he did. Observe he did. Take notes he did. Talk he didn't, for God's sake. Except for two missing rooms and an enormous RD spray-painted on the side of the palace, nothing seemed out of the ordinary.

Frustrated, Rufus Q. Shupilluliumash hopped into his wheel and departed for Alpharalpha B, home of the sagacious kumquats. "So what kind of jam are you in?" he asked them.

After local Galactic officials secured his release from the thornbush, he proceeded with his investigation. "You see what they have done!" a sagacious kumquat cried, showing him the ruins of the royal palace.

"Looks like the throne room and the antechamber are gone, all right,"

Shup agreed . . . sagaciously. “What are those big squiggles on the wall there?”

“They stand for the characters you would call RD,” the kumquat replied.

“They do, do they? Looks like it might be a clue.” Rufus Q. Shupilluliumash’s sagacity score went right off the charts with that observation—in which direction, it is better to specu late than never. The Space Patrol didn’t raise any dummies, but sometimes it found one and took him in and made him its own.

“What will you do? You must get the sacred structures back!” the kumquat keened. “How will our sovereign root in peace without them?”

“Somebody did something pretty seedy to you, all right,” the space cadet said.

After local Galactic officials secured his release from the thornbush again—it took longer this time—they told him, “Perhaps it would be better if you pursued your investigations somewhere else. Otherwise, the kumquats warn, they will soon be pursuing you.”

“Some people—well, highly evolved and sagacious kumquats—are just naturally sour,” Rufus Q. Shupilluliumash complained. Neverthenonetheless, and entirely undisirregardless of the slavering mob of fruit salad at his furry heels, he made it into the Patrol speedster and got the hatch shut just in the proverbial Nicholas of time.

Even with the wheel drive, it’s a long, long way from Alpharalpha B to Amana XI. Our intrepid space cadet put the time to good use, but after a while even porn began to pall and he decided to do some research instead. He Googled RD. How he could get online while far beyond the normal limits of space and time may well be known to the omniscient narrator (I mean, after all, what isn’t?), but he ain’t talking. What the space cadet found . . . you’ll see. Eventually. Keep your shirt on.

Before climbing out of the airlock on Amana XI, Rufus Q. climbed into his coldsuit. Otherwise, all he would have needed was a stick shoved up the wazoo to become the Galaxy’s first Hamstersicle. But he would have been too damn frozen to shove a stick where it needed to go, so it’s just as well he remembered the suit.

“Tell me,” he said to one of the ammonia/ice blobs awaiting his arrival at the spaceport, “are your females frigid?”

Once local Galactic officials had secured his release from the hotbox . . .

the space cadet was rather vexed at them. The ammonia/ice blobs of Amana XI tormented convicts by subjecting them to heat well above the freezing point of water, and were also inblobane enough to make them endure an oxygen-enhanced atmosphere. Some of the munchies were stale, but it was the best digs ol' Rufus Q. could've found on the whole planet.

He got back into his coldsuit for a whirlwind tour of the devastated palace. Once the whirlwind subsided, he saw on the icy wall now exposed to the elements—and compounds—some writing in an alien script he couldn't begin to read. "What's that say?" he asked.

"In your symbology, it would stand for RD," the nearest ammonia/ice blob answered.

"Probably doesn't mean *Research and Development*, then," Rufus Q. Shupilluliumash sighed. "That'll teach me to hit the *I Feel Lucky* button, even if I did."

"What are you going to do?" the blob demanded. "Do you not see the magnificence despoiled?"

"Reminds me more of the inside of a root freezer without the goddamn roots," the forthright space cadet replied. He was, by then, quite looking forward to seeing the inside of the hotbox once more. The ammonia/ice blobs appeared overjoyed to oblige him, too. His only real complaint was that the seeds they fed him still weren't of the freshest. He stuffed his cheek pouches full even so.

Once local Galactic officials had secured his release from the hotbox again, they gently suggested his investigation might proceed more promisingly elsewhere. He was inclined to agree with them; he'd discovered that spitting seed casings inside a coldsuit was an exercise in sloppy futility.

Thus it was that Cadet Rufus Q. Shupilluliumash reboarded the redoubtable *Habitrail*, spun the wheel up to translight speed, and sped off to Gould IV and its saurian humanoids. Past walking on their hind legs, they didn't particularly remind him of Frenchmen. Of course, they were even less hamsteroid, which might have colored his opinion. As far as he was concerned, anything with a long scaly tail at one end and a big mouth full of sharp teeth at the other was not to be trusted.

One of the saurians at the spaceport eyed him and remarked, "You look like you'd go down well with drawn butter."

Shup drew not butter but his trusty blaster. "You look like you'd look good on my wall," he replied cheerfully. "In this Galaxy, nothing is certain but death and taxidermy."

He belonged to the Patrol. He had the right to carry any weapon he chose. If he killed, he was assumed to know what he was doing. The Galaxy, as you will have figured out, was in deep kimchi, but this isn't that kind of story. This is the kind of story where the saurians would have jugged him not for toting lethal hardware but as punpunishment. And since it is that kind of story, you may rest assured they did.

Once local Galactic officials had pulled the cork from the jug, a somewhat chaster (he was alone, after all, and not even bull-hamster horniness could make the saurians sexy) but unchastened Rufus Q. Shupilluliumash emerged. He didn't even have to draw his blaster again—which was just as well, since he was no artist—to get the saurians to take him to their royal palace so he could view the missing throne room and antechamber (or rather, view that they were missing—he couldn't very well *view* them *while* they were missing, could he?) and what he was coming to think of as the inevitable graffiti.

There seemed to be rather more of them this time. "What do they say?" he inquired of his guide, a stalwart, shamrock-green Gouldian named Albert O'Saurus.

Albert seemed to have inherited a full set of teeth from each parent, and a set from each grandparent, too, maybe for luck. "'Royal Drive,'" he answered. "'Next stop—Galactic Central!'"

Sinister organ chords rang out in the background, or at least in the space cadet's perfervid imagination. "A clue!" quoth he.

"Faith, what a brilliant deduction," Albert O'Saurus said—the Gouldians didn't find sarcasm illegal, immoral, or fattening. "And how did you come up with it, now?"

Rufus Q. Shupilluliumash eyed the saurian. "Well, it's not exactly a cloaca-and-dagger operation," he replied.

Once local Galactic officials had pulled the cork from the jug again—it took longer this time, as second offenses, and offensive offenses, were commonly punpunished by devourment—they encouraged him to spread his talents widely across the sea of stars. "If you stay here any longer," one of them said, "the Gouldians *will* eat you. With mustard."

The hamster space cadet made a horrible, incisor-filled face. "Can't stand mustard," he said. "Ta-ta! I'm off! Me and the baked beans."

"Where will you go?" the official inquired.

"Galactic Central, I do believe," Rufus Q. Shupilluliumash answered.

Ah, Galactic Central! I could go on for pages, or even reams—the disadvantage of being an omniscient narrator. But this isn't *that* kind of story, either, and I will pause while you thank your local deity or demon that it isn't. . . . There. Are you finished now? Good. We can go on.

What you do need to know about the fabulous Galactic Central, and what you will most likely (probability, 87.13%—how's that for omniscient?) have figured out for yourself, is that it boasts the grandest and spiffiest palace in all the Galaxy, that being where the Galactic Emperor and Empress hang out. Said palace boasts the most garish and over-the-top—excuse me, most colorful and extravagant—throne room in all the Galaxy, and also the most likewise and likewise—excuse me, most likewise and likewise—antechamber in all the et cetera.

"I bet the bad guys are going to try and steal them for the Royal Drive," Shup said as he powered up the *Habitrail*'s wheel. Then he said, "What the hell *is* the Royal Drive?" Except for the graffiti on Gould IV, he'd never heard of it.

Google had never heard of it, either. Rufus Q. Shupilluliumash wondered whether he was accessing the Chinese system. But no. It was—cue the portentous music again—Something New.

Though his electronic aids failed him, the dedicated space cadet persevered. He had one major advantage over the others whom Erasmus Z. Utnapishtim (remember him?) might have chosen to save the Galaxy . . . or at least its throne rooms and antechambers. Not only was he a hamster, he was a punster as well, as he had proved to the dismay and discomfiture of ammonia/ice blobs and shamrock-green saurian humanoids alike.

And as he neared Galactic Central, he suddenly slowed on the wheel in astonishment—and almost pitched the P.S. *Habitrail* back into normal space in an abnormal place. That wouldn't have been good—so he didn't actually *do* it.

What he did do was cry out, "Eureka!" Why the name of a not very large city in northern California should have become the cry for discovering something, Rufus Q. Shupilluliumash did not know, but it had. The Patrol could be a tradition-bound—even a tradition-gagged—outfit sometimes.

He spun the wheel up to an almost blistering pace. Then, when his feet and little front paws started to hurt, he slowed down again—but not so much, this time, as to endanger his speedster. He thought furiously, which was odd, because he wasn't particularly furious.

"It must work that way," he said. "This story won't run long enough for a lot of wrong guesses." If he'd guessed wrong there, he might have found himself trapped in a novel, but the speedster wasn't a Fforde, so he escaped that fate, anyhow. He shook his head and snuffled his whiskers at the iniquity of the throne-room (and antechamber) thieves. "I must foil them," he declared, and checked his supplies of aluminum, tin, and silver.

He was so transfixed by his fit of analytical brilliance that he almost wheeled right past Galactic Central and back out into the Galactic Boonies. But he didn't—this story won't run long enough for a lot of mistakes, either.

Being a space cadet helped him get through the entry formalities in jig time—which, since he didn't dance, was more than a little challenging. A day and a half later, the freedom of Galactic Central was his, as long as the GPS and radiological tracking devices surgically implanted near his wazoo gave answers the powers that be approved of. Otherwise, the tiny nuke implanted near that very same sensitive place would sadly spoil our upcoming dénouement, to say nothing of half a city block. So we won't.

He hopped on the closest available public transport, discovered it was going the wrong way (see?—we did have room for a mistake after all), hopped off, and got on, this time, as luck (and the necessities of plotting) would have it, going toward the sublime (or something) residence of the beloved (or something) Galactic Emperor and Empress.

No sooner had he arrived—talk about timing! I mean, really!—than a giant chainsaw suddenly appeared in the sky and started carving away at (are you surprised?) the throne room . . . and the antechamber. People screamed. People ran. People coughed from flying sawdust. People of several different flavors got turned into hamburger of several different flavors. People inside the palace, caught by the paralyzer ray that went with the saw, didn't do much of anything.

Guards outside the palace started shooting at the parts of the chainsaw crunching through the walls. Quick-thinking Rufus Q. Shupilluliumash fired at the power button instead: a dot a centimeter wide three kilometers up in the air. Being a Patrol-trained markshamster and luckier than Lucky Pierre, he hit it dead on, the very first try.

The chainsaw stopped chainsawing. It fell out of the sky and smashed one of the ritziest neighborhoods—actually, several of the ritziest neighborhoods, because that was a big mother of a chainsaw—of Galactic Central to cottage cheese. Our bold space cadet cared nothing for that, though. He was doing his duty, and he was damned if he'd let common sense stand in his way.

Dashing toward the chainsaw's survival capsule (How did he know where it was? He just knew. This is that kind of story.), he was Rufus Q. Shupilluliumash on the spot when a saurian humanoid, an ammonia/ice blob in a hotsuit, a kumquat, and a Frenchman came staggering out.

"You're under arrest!" he shouted, covering them with his ever-reliable blaster. "Suspicion of firing a chainsaw without a license and operating an unauthorized space drive within city limits. Don't nobody move!"

Nobody didn't move . . . or something like that. "What do you know about the Royal Drive?" the Frenchman sneered. "How do you know it's unauthorized?"

"It must be unauthorized, because I couldn't Google it. And I know the Royal Drive uses the hellacious energy output from mixing"—our space cadet paused to build the moment, for he was indeed punster as well as hamster—"chamber and antechamber to propel your spacecraft across the Galaxy in pursuance of your nefarious ends. But now you're busted, space scum!"

The Frenchman, the kumquat, and the saurian humanoid blanched. Rufus Q. Shupilluliumash presumed the ammonia/ice blob did, too—it is, after all, what self-respecting villains do under such circumstances—but the hotsuit kept him from being sure. Palace guards came up behind him. "What do we do with them, sir?" they asked respectfully.

"Take them away," the hamster replied grandly. "They will trouble the spaceways no more."

Your omniscient narrator also has the pleasure to report that, shortly thereafter, Space Cadet Rufus Q. Shupilluliumash became Ensign Rufus Q. Shupilluliumash, with all the rights and privileges appertaining thereto. (Of course, he knew that wouldn't happen. Didn't you?) Our space cadet's actions in this case were deemed to be in the highest tradition of the Space Patrol.

PRISONS

KEVIN J. ANDERSON and DOUG BEASON

Bestselling author Kevin J. Anderson has written nearly a hundred novels, many of them co-written (as this story is) with Doug Beason, with his wife, Rebecca Moesta, or with Brian Herbert, with whom he continues Frank Herbert's Dune saga. Anderson has written several media tie-ins, for such properties as Star Wars and The X-Files. His most recent original project is the Saga of Seven Suns series, which concluded with last year's *The Ashes of Worlds,* and his nautical fantasy epic *Terra Incognita.*

Doug Beason is a physicist and a retired Air Force Colonel. He is currently works at the Los Alamos National Laboratory, where he is responsible for programs that reduce the global threat of weapons of mass destruction. He has published fourteen books, eight of them in collaboration with Anderson. The writing team's novel *Assemblers of Infinity* was a finalist for the Nebula Award.

"Prisons," first published in *Amazing Stories,* explores the repercussions of a revolt on a prison planet and shows how one person's existence influences the decisions of those in power. It examines black market trade, brainwashing, and how far some will go for revenge.

PRISONS

I am still called the Warden. The prisoners consider it an ironic jest.

Barely a meter square, the forcewalls form the boundaries of my holographic body. Once this felt like a throne, an isolated position from which I could control the workings of Bastille. Now, though, I must look out and watch my former prisoners laughing at me.

This projection has been an image of authority to them. Since living on this prison world was too great a punishment to inflict upon any real warden or guards, my Artificial Personality was entrusted to watch over this compound. I am based on a real person—a great man, I think—a proud man with many accomplishments. But I have failed here.

Amu led the prisoners in their revolt; he convinced them that Bastille is a self-sufficient planet after all their forced terraforming work for the Federation. They have survived all Federation attempts to reoccupy the world, keeping the invaders out with the same systems once intended to keep the prisoners in. Besides the prisoners, I am the only one left.

Once, I ran the environmental systems here, the production accounting, the resources inventory. I monitored the automated digging and processing machinery outside. I controlled the fleet of tiny piranha interceptors in orbit that would destroy any ship trying to escape. But now I am powerless.

Amu's lover Theowane comes to taunt me every day, to gloat over her triumph. She paces up and down the corridor outside the forcewalls. To me, she is flaunting her freedom to go where she wishes. I do not think it is unintentional.

At the time of the revolt, Theowane used her computer skills to introduce a worm program that rewrote the control links around my Personality, leaving me isolated and helpless. If I attempt to regain control, the worm will delete my existence. I feel as if I have a knife at my throat, and I am too afraid to act.

At moments such as this, I can appreciate the sophistication of my Personality, which allows me to feel the full range of human emotions.

It allows me to hate Theowane and what she has done to me.

• • •

Theowane makes herself smile, but the Warden refuses to look at her. It annoys her when he broods like this.

"I am busy," he says.

Leaving him to dwell on his fate, Theowane crosses to the panorama window. Huge, remotely driven excavators and haulers churn the ground, rearing up, crunching rock and digesting it for usable minerals. *At least,* she thinks, *Bastille's resources are put to our own use, not exported for someone else.*

Lavender streaks mottle the indigo sky, blotting out all but the brightest stars. A dime-sized glare shows the distant sun, too far away to heat the planet to any comfortable temperature; but overhead, dominating the sky, rides the cinnamon-colored moon Antoinette, so close to Bastille and so nearly the same size that it keeps the planet heated by tidal flexing.

On some of the nearby rocks, patches of algae and lichen have taken hold. These have been genetically engineered to survive in Bastille's environment, to begin the long-term conversion of the surface, of the atmosphere. On a human timescale, though, they are making little progress.

Farther below, Theowane sees the oily surface of the deadly sea, where clumps of the *ubermindist* weed drift. A few floating harvesters ride the waves, but the corrosive water and the sulfuric-acid vapor in the air cause too much damage to send them out often. That does not matter, since they no longer need the drug as a bargaining chip. Amu has refused to continue exporting *ubermindist* extract, despite a black market clamoring for it.

Theowane finds it bitterly ironic that she and so many others sentenced here for drug crimes had been forced by the Federation to process *ubermindist*. The Federation supports its own black market trade, keeping the drug illegal and selling it at the same time. After taking over the prison planet, Amu cut off the supply, using the piranha interceptors to destroy an outgoing robot ship laden with *ubermindist*. The Federation has gone without their precious addictive drug since the prison revolt.

When the intruder alarms suddenly kick in, they take Theowane by surprise. She whirls and places both hands on her hips. Her close-cropped reddish hair remains perfectly in place.

"What is it?" she demands of the Warden.

He is required to answer. "One ship, unidentified, has just snapped out of hyperspace. It is on approach." The Warden's image straightens as he speaks, lifting his head and reciting the words in an inflectionless voice.

"Activate the piranha swarm," she says.

The Warden turns to her. "Let me contact the ship first. We must see who they are."

"No!" Bastille has been quarantined by the rest of the Federation. Any approaching ship can only mean trouble.

Shortly after the prison revolt, the Praesidentrix had tried to negotiate with Bastille. Then she sent laughable threats by subspace radio, demanding that Amu surrender under threat of "severe punishment." The threats grew more strident over the weeks, then months.

Finally, after the sudden death of her consort in some unrelated accident, the Praesidentrix became brutal and unforgiving. The man's death had apparently shocked her to the core. The negotiator turned dictator against the upstart prisoners.

She sent an armada of warships to retake Bastille. Theowane had been astonished, not thinking this hellhole worth such a massed effort. Amu had turned loose the defenses of the prison planet. The piranha swarm—so effective at keeping the prisoners trapped inside—proved just as efficient at keeping the armada out. The piranhas destroyed twelve gunships that attempted to make a landing; two others fled to high orbit, then out through the hyperspace node.

But Amu is certain that the Praesidentrix, especially in her grieving, unstable state, will never give up so easily.

"Piranha defenses armed and unleashed," the Warden says.

Five of the fingerprint-smeared screens beside the Warden's projection tank crackle and wink on. Viewing through the eyes of the closest piranha interceptors, Theowane sees different views of the approaching ship, sleek yet clunky-looking, a paradox of smooth angles and bulky protuberances.

"Incoming audio," the Warden says. "Transmission locked. Video in phase and verified."

The largest screen swirls, belches static, then congeals into a garish projection of the ship's command chamber. The captain falls out of focus, sitting too close to the bridge projection cameras.

"—in peace, for PEACE, we bring our message of happiness and hope to Bastille. We come to help. We come to offer you the answers."

Theowane recognizes the metallic embroidered chasuble on the captain's shoulders, the pseudo-robe uniforms of the other crew visible in the background. She snorts at the acronym.

PEACE—Passive Earth Assembly for Cosmic Enlightenment, a devout group that combines quantum physics and Eastern philosophy into, from what Theowane has heard, an incomprehensible but pleasant-sounding mishmash of ideas. It has appealed to many dissatisfied scientists, ones who gave up trying to understand the universe. PEACE has grown because of their willingness to settle raw worlds, places with such great hardship that no one in his right mind would live there voluntarily.

Theowane sees it already: upon hearing of the prisoners' revolt, some PEACE ship conveniently located on a hyperspace path to Bastille has rushed here, hoping to convert the prisoners, to gain a foothold on the new world and claim it for their own. They must hope the Praesidentrix will not retaliate.

"Allow me to stop the piranhas," the Warden says. "This is not an attack."

"Summon Amu," she says. "But do not call off the defense." Theowane lowers her voice. "This could be as great a threat as anything the Praesidentrix might send."

She hunkers close to the screens and watches the lumbering PEACE ship against a background of stars. The deadly pinpoints of piranha interceptors hurtle toward it on a collision course.

• • •

The First Secretary enlarges the display on his terminal so he can read it better with his weakened eyesight. Across from him, the Praesidentrix sits ramrod straight in her chair.

She waits, a scowl chiselled into her face. The Praesidentrix looks as if she has aged a decade since the death of her consort, but still she insists on keeping her family matters and all details of her personal life private.

The way her policies have suddenly changed, though, tells the First Secretary just how much she had loved the man.

The First Secretary avoids her cold gaze as he calls up his figures. "Here it is," he says. "I want you to know that your attempts to retake Bastille have already cost half of what we have invested in Bastille itself. On the diagram here,"—he punches a section on the keypad—"you'll see that we have thirteen equivalent planets in the initial stages of terraforming, most of them under development by the penal service, two by private corporations. Several dozen more have gone beyond that stage and now have their first generation of colonists."

Overhead, the Praesidentrix chooses the skylight panels to project a sweeping ochre-colored sky from a desert planet. The vastness overwhelms the First Secretary. His skin is pale and soft from living under domes and inside prefabricated buildings all his life. He doesn't like outside; he prefers the cozy, sheltered environment of the catacombs and offices. He is a born bureaucrat.

"So?" the Praesidentrix asks.

The First Secretary flinches. "So is it worth continuing?" *Especially,* he thinks, *with more important things to worry about, such as raising the welfare dole, or gearing up for the next election six years from now.*

"Yes, it's worth continuing," she says without hesitating, then changes the subject. Her dark eyes stare up at the artificial desert sky. "Have you learned how one prisoner managed to take over the Warden system? He has a very shrewd Simulated Personality—how did they bypass him? I thought computer criminals were never assigned to self-sufficient penal colonies for just that reason."

The First Secretary shrugs, thinks about going through an entire chain of who was to blame for what, but then decides that this is not what the Praesidentrix wants. "That's the problem with computer criminals. Theowane was caught and convicted on charges of drug smuggling although all of her prior criminal activity seems to have involved computer espionage and embezzlement."

"Why was this not noticed? Aren't the records clear?"

"No," the First Secretary says, raising his voice a bit. "She . . . altered them all. We didn't know her background."

"Nobody checked?"

"Nobody could!" The First Secretary draws a deep breath to calm himself. "But I think you are following a false trail, Madame. Theowane only implemented the takeover on Bastille. Amu is the mind behind all this. He's the one who convinced the prisoners to revolt. He's the one who refuses to negotiate."

She turns, making sure she holds his gaze. "I have already set a plan in motion that will take care of him once and for all. And it will get Bastille back for us." The Praesidentrix leans back in her purple chair as it tries to conform to her body. Her gray-threaded hair spreads out behind her. *She was a beautiful woman once*, the First Secretary thinks. The rumors have not died about her dead consort . . .

The First Secretary makes a petulant scowl. "It's obvious you don't trust me with your plans, Madame. But will you at least explain to me why you are doing this? It goes beyond reason and financial responsibility." He purses his lips. "Is it because the prisoners are in the *ubermindist* loop? I find that hard to believe. It's just another illegal drug. Cutting off the supply will upset a few addicts—"

"More than that!"

"And cause some unrest," he continues, "as well as some reshuffling on the black market, but they'll adjust. Within a few years we'll have an equivalent drug from some other place, perhaps even a synthetic. Why is Bastille so important to you?"

The coldness in her gaze is worse than anything he could have imagined from her two months before.

"The *ubermindist* is only one reason." the Praesidentrix says. "The other is revenge."

• • •

I feel as if I am watching my own hand plunge a sword into the chest of a helpless victim. The piranha interceptors are part of me, controlled by my external systems—but I cannot stop them now. Theowane has given the order.

I watch through the eyes of five interceptors as they home in for the kill, using their propellant to increase velocity toward impact. With their kinetic energy, they will destroy the vessel.

I receive alarm signals from the PEACE ship, but I ignore them, am forced to watch the target grow and grow as the first interceptor collides with a section amidships. I see the hull plate, pitted with micrometeor scars, swell up, huge, and then wink out a fraction of a second before the interceptor crashes, rupturing the hull and exposing the inner environment to space.

Another interceptor smashes just below the bridge. I hear a transmitted outcry from the captain, begging us to stop the attack. Two more interceptors strike, one a glancing blow alongside the hull; the shrapnel tears open a wider gash. The PEACE ship continues its own destruction as air pressure bursts through the breaches in the hull, as moisture freezes and glass shatters. The fifth interceptor strikes the chemical fuel tanks, and the entire ship erupts in a tiny nova.

From the debris, a small target streaks away. I recognize it as a single escape pod. I detect one life form aboard. Of all the people on the ship . . . only one.

The escape pod descends, but then my own reflexes betray me as another interceptor also detects the pod, aligns its tracking, and streaks after it. Both enter the atmosphere of Bastille.

Now Amu arrives in the control center. I can tell he is upset by his expression, by his elevated body temperature. His head is shaved smooth, but his generous silvery beard, and eyebrows, and eyes give him a charismatic appearance. He is raising his voice to Theowane, but I cannot pay attention to their conversation.

The PEACE escape pod heats up, leaving an orange trail behind it as it burrows deeper into the atmosphere. It seems to have evasive capabilities, and it knows the piranha is behind it.

The interceptor also picks up speed, bearing down on the escape pod. But their velocities are so well matched that the piranha causes no damage when it bumps its target.

A few moments later, the interceptor—with no shielding to protect it from a screaming entry into the atmosphere—breaks into flying chunks of molten slag.

Amu seems mollified when Theowane explains to him that the intruder was a PEACE ship. I know Amu wants nothing to do with religious fanatics; he has had enough of them in his past.

I pinpoint the splashdown target for the escape pod. Without waiting for an order, I dispatch one of the floating *ubermindist* harvesters across the oceans of Bastille. No matter how great a hold Theowane has over my

Simulated Personality, she can do nothing against my life-preservation overrides, except when the security of the colony is at stake.

Ostensibly to allow it greater speed, but actually just out of spite, I tell the harvester to dump its cargo of *ubermindist* before it churns off across the sea to reach the pod.

• • •

Amu stands in the holding bay of the cliffside tunnels. His bald head glistens in the glare of glowtablets recessed in the ceiling. His eyes flash.

A second rinse sprays the outside of the escape pod. Black streaks stain the hull from its burning descent, but the craft appears otherwise undamaged. After its dunking in the corrosive seas, Amu waits for purified water to purge the acidity.

Theowane follows him into the chamber. Amu listens to the last trickles of water come out of the spray heads; drips run through a grate on the floor where the rinse water will be detoxified and reused.

For the hours it has taken the floating harvester to retrieve the escape pod, Amu has waited in silence with Theowane. He keeps his anger toward her in check.

Sensing his displeasure, she twice tries to divert his thoughts. Normally he would acquiesce just to please her. She has been his lover since before the revolt. But he doesn't like her making such important decisions on her own. It sets a bad example for the rest of the prisoners.

On the other hand, Amu knows that Theowane tried to keep Bastille free of the PEACE ships. And he approves.

Both of Amu's parents had been involved in a violent, fanatical sect and had raised him under their repressive teachings, grooming him to be a propagator of the faith. He had absorbed their training, but eventually his own wishes had broken through. He fled, later to use those same charismatic and mob-focusing skills to whip up a workers' revolt on his home planet. If the revolt had succeeded, Amu would have been called a king, a savior. But instead Amu had ended up here, on Bastille.

He wants nothing more to do with religious fanatics. Now this one PEACE survivor presents him with an unpleasant problem.

Theowane runs her fingers over the access controls. "Ready," she says. She keeps her voice low and her eyes averted.

Amu stands to his full height in front of the escape pod. "Open it."

As the hatch cracks, a hiss of air floods in, equalizing the two pressures. Then comes a cough, then sputtering, annoying words. A young boy wrestles himself into a sitting position and snaps his arms out, flexing them and shaking his cramped hands. "What took you so long? You're as bad as PEACE."

Theowane steps back. Amu blinks, but remains in place. The boy is thin, with dark shadows around his eyes. His body appears bruised, his hands raw, as if he has been trying to claw his way out of the escape pod.

Amu can't stop himself from bursting out with a loud laugh. The boy whirls to him, outraged, but after a brief pause he too cracks a grin that contains immense relief and exhaustion. With this one response, he proves to Amu that he is no PEACE convert.

"Why didn't you let yourself out?" Theowane asks. "Isn't there an emergency release inside?"

The boy turns a look of scorn to her. "I know what's in the air on Bastille, and in the water. I couldn't see where I was. It might be bad to be cramped in this coffin for hours—but it would be plenty worse to take a shower in sulfuric acid." He pauses for just a moment. "And speaking of showers, can I get out of here and take one?"

• • •

After the boy has cleaned and rested himself, Amu summons him for dinner. The other prisoners on Bastille have expressed their curiosity, but they will have to wait until Amu decides to make a statement.

"Dybathia," the boy says when Amu asks his name. "I know it sounds noble and high-born. My parents had high expectations of me." He stops just long enough for Amu to absorb that, but not long enough for him to ask any further questions.

"I ran away from home," Dybathia says. "It took me a week to make it to the spaceport. When I got there, I slipped onto the first open ship and hid in their cargo bay. I didn't care where it was going, and I didn't plan to show myself until we were on our way into hyperspace. I figured anyplace was better than home, right?" He snickers.

"It turned out to be a PEACE ship. They wouldn't let me off. They kept me around, constantly quoting tracts at me, trying to make me convert. Do my eyes look glazed? Am I brain-damaged?"

Amu allows a smile to form, but he does not answer.

Dybathia says, "They shut off their servo-maintenance drones and made me do the cleaning, scrubbing down decks and walls with a solvent that should have been labeled as toxic waste. Look at my hands! The captain said monotonous work allows one to clear the mind and become at peace with the universe."

Theowane breaks into the conversation, "Why were you the only one who got to an escape pod?" Amu looks up at her sharply, but she doesn't withdraw the question.

Dybathia shrugs. "I was the only one who bothered. The rest of them just sat there and accepted their fate."

This rings so true with Amu from his memories of his parents that he finds himself nodding.

• • •

Dybathia looks at the mind-scanning apparatus; this will be the most dangerous moment for him. The device is left over from the first days of Bastille, when human supervisory crews had established the colony. That month had been the only time when non-prisoners and prisoners cohabited the planet; as a precaution they had used intensive search devices and mental scanners, which had remained unused since those other humans had turned Bastille over to the Warden.

"You do understand why we have to do this?" Amu asks.

Dybathia sees more concern on the face of the leader than he expects. This is going better than he had hoped. "Yes, I understand perfectly." He flicks his gaze toward Theowane, then back to Amu. "It's because she's paranoid."

Theowane bristles, as he expects her to. She makes each word of her answer clipped and hard. "Your story is too convenient. How do we know you're not an . . . assassin? What if you've been drugged or hypnotized? We can't know what the Praesidentrix might do."

Knowing it is imperative for him to allay their suspicions, Dybathia submits to an intensive physical search that scans every square centimeter of his body, probes all orifices, uses a sonogram to detect any subcutaneous needles, poison-gas capsules, perhaps a timed-release biological plague.

They find nothing, because there is nothing to find.

"The psyche assessor won't hurt you," Amu says. "Just stick your head within its receiving range."

"How does it work?" Dybathia asks. He frowns skeptically. "How do I know this isn't one of those machines to condition prisoners? I don't want to end up like a PEACE convert."

"Explain it to him, Theowane." Amu smiles at her, as if he knows how it will rankle her.

Theowane blows air from her lips. "Everyone has a basic mental pattern, like a normal position that can never change. However, certain training—brainwashing, you'd call it—can superimpose another set of reactions on top of it. If you've been brainwashed or specially trained to do anything to Amu, or Bastille, it will show up here." She adjusts her apparatus.

Dybathia rolls his eyes. Amu smiles at that. Dybathia knows he is easing past the leader's defenses. "Let's just get this over with."

Without a word, the boy leans into the psyche assessor's range. Theowane makes no other comment as she works with the apparatus and takes her reading. She asks him a series of questions designed to break down mind-blanking techniques.

Dybathia answers them all without resisting.

Finally, Theowane shrugs. "It's clear," she says. "No one's been messing with his mind. He has no special training. He hasn't been brainwashed."

"I could have saved you trouble if you had just listened to me in the first place."

Amu claps a hand on the boy's shoulder. "I'll let you know when I've thought of a suitable way for Theowane to apologize."

• • •

When the survivor of the PEACE ship comes through with Theowane and Amu, I receive the unmistakable impression of tourist and tourguides. No, that is not quite correct . . . more like a visiting dignitary being shown points of interest.

Inside the forcewalls I watch them. True, I have a million different eyes around Bastille, optics to observe through, from monitoring cameras around the corridors, to the remote sensors of automatic digging machines. But my real eyes are here.

Purposely, I think, Amu ignores me as he brings the boy down the corridor. He points to the auxiliary control systems, explaining them with deceptive ease, making them sound simpler than they are. The three keep their backs pointedly turned and walk to the viewing window, outside of which the diggers continue their relentless excavations. The sky swirls with dark, oily colors over the hostile sea.

"It's going to be generations before anybody can bask under the Bastille sun, but at least it is now ours," Amu says, then lowers his voice. "And we aren't going to give it back when this world becomes habitable."

"Is it going to be worth the wait?" the boy asks, pushing his face close to the thick glass. I flick my concentration to one of the digger machines outside, looking through a different set of eyes, but the coarse optics and the glass distort the boy's face through the window.

Amu shrugs and rubs a hand on his silvery beard. "Theowane spends hours down here staring out the window. Actually, I think she just likes to taunt the Warden."

Finally, they turn toward me. I am too familiar with Theowane's close-cropped reddish hair and her narrow, hard eyes. Amu carries much more capacity within him—an extraordinary person, with charisma and intelligence and compassion that allows him to do virtually anything he wants to. But he has chosen a path that society deems unacceptable.

The boy is the last to turn away from the sprawling view. He looks at me directly. I see him.

I know him.

He has counted on me recognizing him.

Instantly, I flash through a handful of buried newsclips, quick photographs shaded by the promise of anonymity, but it is enough. It augments my suspicions. I can remember few details of the person on whom I myself have been based, but some things are impossible to erase.

I remember.

I wonder what he is up to. Why is he here, and what am I supposed to do about it?

The three visitors say no word to me as they continue their tour. I am left with the absolute conviction that the fate of Bastille, and perhaps the Praesidentrix's Federation, depends upon me recognizing this boy, understanding what he wants, and acting accordingly.

I can no longer avoid the risk to myself. I must save my son.

• • •

Amu sits across from Dybathia for another meal. The boy fascinates him. He reminds Amu of himself as a young boy, or what Amu wanted to be—scrappy, irreverent, and intelligent.

Amu serves the two plates himself. Prisoners in the kitchen have prepared a tough pancake-like dish from cultured algae and protein synthesizers. They are trying to develop a pseudo-steak, but they are several years from perfecting it. No matter. Amu is used to it and it is, after all, nutritious. What more can they ask for, with their limited supplies?

"It's tough. You might need to use your knife to cut it," he says. Dybathia frowns at the crude knife in his hand, but Amu continues. "It is easy to get mush from the hydroponics tunnels, but we keep striving for something with a firm texture. It's only been in the last month or two that we've been able to have something tough enough to cut."

Dybathia works at the food on his plate. "I was looking at the knife." The blunt instrument is barely serviceable.

Amu smiles; it is the "winning" smile he uses when making converts to his various causes. "A holdover from prison life."

"That was long ago," Dybathia says.

"Yes, and things have changed now."

Dybathia lifts an eyebrow.

"We're here alone, with no non-prisoners for us to worry about. Knives are no longer any threat. And the Warden is nicely contained. But we like to remember what we are and where we are. We manufacture these knives, and they serve the purpose." Amu lowers his voice. "Maybe if the meat gets a little more meat-like, we'll need better ones."

Amu looks across the table at Dybathia. The boy seems fascinated with everything about Bastille, and Amu waits for him to ask the obvious question. But over several days it has not been forthcoming. Finally Amu breaks down and answers it anyway. "I grew up on New Kansas and left my parents, and their religious sect—" he burns inside, thinking of the PEACE converts.

Dybathia smiles. Amu dims the lights, bathing the room in a softer glow. It is storytime.

"New Kansas was a young planet, the soil somewhat unstable. We had planted grassland across entire continents. Wheat, alfalfa and prairie grass, with some used as rangeland for imported animals. But three-quarters of what we grew, the landholders exported offplanet. They were a handful of people who had financed the first colony ships and therefore claimed to own all of New Kansas. We were forbidden to leave our holdings.

"But I had learned how to whip my followers into a frenzy of religious devotion. We fought for our freedom. The colonists had come to New Kansas to start a fresh life. They felt that the Federation owed them at least a chance at autonomy. I knew how to galvanize them.

"They burned their fields. The fires swept across the plains for dozens of kilometers, pouring smoke into the sky that you could see from landholding to landholding. The others rose up."

Amu speaks with a sense of wonder, paying little attention to the boy. "My people were ready to die for me. Can you imagine that? Holding people so much in the palm of your hand—" Amu extends his fist across the table, opening it so that Dybathia can see the callouses from his hard life—"they were ready to *die* for me. And we almost succeeded."

Amu lowers his eyes and pushes his plate away from him. "Almost."

"I've had enough," Dybathia says. He has eaten most of his pseudo-steak, but Amu stares at the wall, seeing in his memories the visions of burning grass and the bodies of his followers after the landholders had called in Federation reinforcements.

He doesn't notice as Dybathia stands and slips toward the door. "I'm going to sleep," the boy says. "I'll see you in the morning."

Amu nods and blinks his eyes. But they are filled with water and sting as if from smoke.

• • •

Theowane enters the control center alone. She moves with precise steps, as if stalking. She wants to know what is going on. She will catch the Warden. She will get the information together, and then she will take it to Amu.

The holographic Warden looks at her from his glass-walled cage. His expression remains dubious, fearful, with a layer of contempt. Theowane says nothing as she casually walks over to the panorama window. She gazes across the blasted ground. Though the diggers continue to reform the landscape, she never sees any actual improvement.

Theowane stares for a few moments longer, then turns to meet the Warden's eyes. "You pride yourself so much in having human emotions and human reactions, Warden, but you're naive. You don't know how to hide things from other people. I can read your reactions as clearly as if they were spelled out on a screen."

The Warden blinks at her. "I do not understand."

"I caught you yesterday."

He extends his hands forward until the image fuzzes near the edge of the forcewalls. "What do you mean?"

"The boy," Theowane says. "You recognized him. It was painfully obvious. You know who he is. You know why he's here —and it isn't because of that crazy story he told us. Explain it to me now."

The Warden hesitates a moment, then hardens his face into a stoic mask. "I don't know what you are talking about."

Theowane raises her eyebrows. She reaches out and caresses the control panel. "I can turn the worm loose and delete you." That doesn't seem to frighten the Warden; she has used the same threat too many times before.

"Then you will lose whatever information you imagine I have."

"Perhaps I can find some way to make you feel pain," she says.

The Warden shrugs. "I am not afraid anymore."

In all her taunting, Theowane has taught the Warden as much about herself as she has learned from him. He knows exactly how to infuriate her.

"I'll inform Amu," she says, trying to regain her composure. "That will stifle whatever plans you are hatching."

Theowane straightens away from the window and sees the Warden turn his head, flicking his glance to look outside. Sensing something, hearing a muffled sound too close, she whirls around—

The giant automatic digger rears up and plunges through the glass. With its great scooping and digging gears churning, it claws out the poured-stone and insulation, ripping girders and breaching the wall.

Theowane stumbles back, sucking in a breath to scream as the deadly, acid-drenched air of Bastille rushes inside.

• • •

"You're quiet today," Amu says as he leads the boy down into one of the lower levels. Smells of oil, dirt, and stale air fill the tunnels.

"Introspective," Dybathia corrects. He thinks that word will better disarm Amu. He has not thought his silence and uneasiness would be so noticeable, but then he remembers that Amu is a master at studying other people.

"Ah, introspective is it?" Amu's lips curl in amusement.

"I have been through a lot in the last few days."

Amu accepts this and continues leading him down to where the corridors widen into larger chambers hewn from the rock. Amu spends hours showing him distillation ponds that remove the alkaloid poisons from the seawater. Like a proud father, Amu demonstrates the rows of plants growing under garish artificial sunlight, piped in and intensified through optical-fiber arrays stretching through the rock to surface collectors.

Other prisoners work at their tasks and seem to move more quickly when Amu watches them. Dybathia wonders how they can consider this to be so different from working under another kind of master.

Amu continues to talk about his grand vision, how they have made their colony self-sufficient. It has been difficult at first without supply ships from the Federation, but they have overcome those obstacles and now have everything they did before—except their prison.

Then Amu speaks in a dreamier voice, explaining about the terraforming activities, how he has switched the diggers to mining materials useful for their own survival, rather than supplying *ubermindist* offplanet. The floater harvesters are spreading algae and Earth plankton that have been tailored to Bastille's environment. They are resculpting the atmosphere of the planet, making it a place where humans will one day be able to walk outside and in peace. Amu's long-term goals and his naive sense of wonder disgust Dybathia, but he keeps his feelings hidden. The boy will know when the time has come.

Amu says something he thinks is funny. Dybathia isn't paying attention, but automatically snorts in response. Amu nods, approvingly.

When alarm klaxons belch out and echo in the tunnel, the noise startles Dybathia, even though he has been expecting it.

• • •

My life-preservation overrides force me to close the airlock on the other end of the corridor to keep Bastille air from penetrating farther into the complex. I do not resist the impulse. I know it will trap Theowane inside.

She sprawls on the floor, trying to crawl forward. The floor is smooth and slippery, and she cannot get enough purchase to move herself. Her eyes are wide with horror. Her lips turn brown, then purplish as she gasps, and the sulfuric acid eats out her lungs. I force myself to watch, for all the times she has watched me.

The digging machine, sensing that it has been led astray, stops clawing and churning, then uses its scanners to reorient itself. The big vehicle clanks and drops clods of dirt and shattered rock as it backs outside.

Theowane croaks words. "Open—open door!"

"Sorry, Theowane. That would endanger the colony."

Before, I was afraid of the worm, which forbade me to do anything against Theowane and the other prisoners. But the worm, though deadly, is not intuitive and is unable to extrapolate the consequences of my actions. I will take the risk, for my son. I can do much damage, while doing nothing overt.

I have used an old sensor-loop taken from the archives of the digging machines' daily logs. Broadcasting this sensor-loop along with an override signal to one nearby digger, I made the machine think it saw a different landscape, where the route of choice led it directly through the viewing window.

The chamber has filled with Bastille's air, and I begin to see static discharges as the corrosive atmosphere eats into the microchips, the layers that form the computer's brain, my Simulated Personality—and the worm.

But the auxiliary computer core lies deep and unreachable below the lower levels. Bastille's acid atmosphere will destroy the main system here, where the worm has been added, but within a fraction of a second my own backup in the auxiliary computer will kick in. I should lose consciousness for only an instant before I am recreated.

My only wonder is whether the other Me will be me after all, or only a Simulated Personality that thinks it is.

Theowane lies dead but twitching on the floor, sprawled out in front of me. Blotches cover her skin. It is difficult for me to see anything now, with the images growing distorted and fuzzy, breaking up. I feel no pain, only a sense of displacement.

In the last moment, even the forcewalls seem to be gone. I have conquered the worm.

• • •

Dybathia watches Amu closely as the alarms sound. The leader stiffens and looks around. The other prisoners run to stations. Amu claps his hands and bellows orders at them. His face looks concerned: he doesn't understand what is happening.

Dybathia gives him no time to understand.

Amu bends down to him. "We've got to get you to a safe place. I don't know what's going on—"

In that moment, Dybathia brings up the prison knife taken from Amu's table, pushing all the wiry strength of his body behind it. He drives the dull point under Amu's chin, tilting it sideways, and slashes across his throat. He has only one chance. He has no special training. Only his heritage.

Blood sprays out. Amu grunts, falling to his knees and backward. Scarlet spatters the silver of his beard, and the whites of his eyes grow red from burst capillaries. He reaches out with a hand, but Dybathia dances back, holding the dripping knife in his hand.

Amu's expression is complete shock shadowed with pain and confusion. He tries to talk, but only gurgles come out.

Dybathia kneels and hisses. "How? Is that what you're trying to say? *How?* Are you amazed because your psyche assessor detected no brainwashing? You forgot to consider that maybe I wasn't brainwashed, that maybe I *wanted* to do this because I hate you so much. I am free to act. I have no special training."

The light fades behind Amu's eyes, but the confusion seems as great. Dybathia continues. "My father was a great man, an important man—a fleet commander. He became an *ubermindist* addict, and that was a great secret. Does that mean I am not supposed to love him? That I wasn't supposed to try to help him? Do you know what happens when an *ubermindist* addict is cut off from his supply?"

Dybathia kneels beside the dying man to make sure his words come clear. "The withdrawal fried my father's nerves. He lost all muscle control. He went into a constant seizure for eight days—his mind took that long to burn out. He went blind from the hemorrhages. His body was snapped and broken by his own convulsions. You caused that, Amu. You did that to him, and now I did this to you. My choice. My revenge."

But Amu is already dead. Dybathia does not know how much he understood at the last. The only sound Dybathia hears is his own breathing, a monotonous wheeze that fills his ears. The boy stands without moving as several other prisoners shout and come running toward him.

• • •

Inside her office, the Praesidentrix has chosen a honey-colored sky with a brilliant white sun overhead. She finds it soothing. For the first time in ages, she feels like smiling.

The First Secretary stands at the doorway, interrupting her reverie. "You asked to see me, Madame?"

She turns to him. For a moment he wears a fearful expression, as if he thinks she has caught him at something. She nods to make him feel at ease. "I've just received word from the Warden on Bastille. We have two gunships in orbit and all prisoners are now subdued. Amu and Theowane are both dead."

The First Secretary takes a step backward in astonishment. He looks for someplace to sit down, but the Praesidentrix has no other chairs in her office. "But how?" He raises his voice. "How!"

"I placed an operative on Bastille. A . . . young man."

"An operative? But I thought Amu had equipment to detect any training alterations."

The Praesidentrix pulls her lips tight. "The young man's father died from *ubermindist* withdrawal after the prison takeover. I believed he had sufficient motivation to kill Amu. He was free to act."

The First Secretary sputters and keeps looking for a place to sit. "But how did you know? What did you do?"

"He acted as a catalyst to spur the Warden into taking a more drastic action than he was likely to take on his own, with nothing else at stake. Remember, we built the Warden's Artificial Personality. I knew exactly how he would react to certain pressures." She waves a hand, anxious to get rid of the First Secretary so she can use the subspace radio again. "I just thought you'd like to know. You're dismissed."

He stumbles backward, unable to find words. He stops and turns back to the Praesidentrix, but she closes the door on him. The subspace projection chimes, announcing an incoming transmission. She sighs with a pride and contentedness she has not felt in quite some time. He has called her even before she could contact him.

The Warden's image appears in front of her like a painful memory. It is as she remembers her consort when he was a dashing and brave commander, streaking through hyperspace nodes and knitting the Federation together with his strength.

The Warden is only a simulation, though, intangible and far away. But that would not be much different from their original romance, with her consort flitting off through the Galaxy for three-quarters of the year while she held the reins of government at home. She had rarely held him anyway; but they had spoken often through the private subspace link.

They greet each other in the same breath and then the widowed Praesidentrix begins catching up on all the things she has wanted to say to him, repeating all the things she did tell him while he writhed in delirium from his withdrawal, while she had concocted a false story about his fatal "accident" in order to avert a scandal.

But first she must say how proud she is of their son.

DIFFERENT DAY

K. TEMPEST BRADFORD

K. Tempest Bradford's fiction has appeared in or is forthcoming from *Electric Velocipede, Podcastle,* and *Strange Horizons.* In addition to writing, she's worked in the editorial trenches of several magazines, and is currently the managing editor for *Fantasy Magazine.*

Bradford says that she's an "un-fan" of how SF on television and film often depicts each alien race as a monoculture. "When characters go to alien planets, they generally deal with one government, one group of people, one culture, as if that planet is made up of one huge, happy group who work together and have no internal differences," she said.

So she started thinking about what it would be like if the aliens that came here had the same problems we have—fighting between groups and cultures and such. "I also thought it would be nice to show that they wouldn't necessarily come to America first," she said. "Or, if they did, it wouldn't be because they think we're superior."

DIFFERENT DAY

I didn't pay much attention to the aliens at first. Oh, if you mean like that first week, then yeah, we were scared and hiding and shit like everyone else. But once the whole thing calmed down and everything went back to normal I didn't spend that much time thinking about them.

It's all well and good to come down from space and promise you can fix the ozone or whatever, but any group of people—aliens, sorry—that come to this planet and start out by talking to *our* government have to be seriously doubted. All the countries on all the continents and they think we're the most likely to care about cleaning up the environment? Ha ha, yeah right.

Anyway, like I said, after that first scare I didn't pay a lot of attention to them. Not like my daughter with her t-shirts and webpages and all that. My little corner of the world wasn't going to change.

Don't get me wrong. I'm not a head-in-the-sand kind of guy. I read newspapers from all over on my Google News. I knew about how other countries were mad that those—whatchacall'em? . . . By-er-nam-yan? Yeah—them Byernamian aliens were making deals with us like America has some kind of power to decide stuff for the whole planet. Thing is, no matter how many threats they make, I live in Mason fucking Ohio. Nothing ever happens here until it's happened somewhere else at least five times. Aliens or not, I still have to be at work on Monday and take my son to karate on Tuesdays and Thursdays.

It got really messed up when the other aliens came, though. The other ones. You know, the ah . . . Deb . . . Debachhhk—whatever. I can't make that sound—neither can anyone on CNN. My wife and I call them the African Aliens because they have that weird head shape.

I was pulling an all-nighter here at the store—correcting the bedroom set inventory my stupid nephew screwed up—when I heard Nelson

Mandela on the radio announcing that he'd been negotiating with aliens too, and that they were from the same planet as the Byerwhosits but a different tribe or somethin'. And you know that it was no mistake that shit was broadcast when it was 4 A.M. here.

Now see, *that* was when I started paying attention. Cuz those first aliens had promised to do something about global warming, but here the African Aliens come to tell us that they were lying. Flat out. Those Byernams don't even have access to the technology. And here we'd given them, what, half of the global soy crop already? For nothing?

I tell you though, even though they freak me out a little, I gotta respect those African Aliens. They deal with Mandela and the Dalai Lama and only them two. They did their homework before showing up here. Mandela and the Lama are the only two guys on the planet I would trust not to screw everybody else over. Of course, my wife is pissed that they don't have a woman in there, too. Knowing her, she'd probably want it to be Oprah.

Hey look, all I'm sayin' is that if the African Aliens are as powerful as they say they are, then I want someone with a little global perspective negotiating with them. This new President, he's got his head on straight, yeah. But he has enough to deal with, cleaning up after the last administration. A messed up economy, the Constitution used for toilet paper, all that crap about torture—you know, almost every other country hated us *before* President Dipshit made that bad deal, now they *all* do. Maybe Mandela and the Lama can fix the mess he made without starting another damn war.

Then again, if the Byernamers hadn't made such a big show of making first contact in the middle of the Super Bowl halftime show, the government probably wouldn't have ever told us about them *or* the soy deal. We'd be just as clueless as the Chinese were—and don't tell me you weren't floored when that bit came out about Mao being in contact with that other *other* tribe of aliens. 50 years ago and no one knew for all this time! I can't believe that dude is still alive somewhere out in space.

And you notice how quick the Chinese got their asses out of Tibet after the Dalai Lama talked about it on Al Jazeera? Makes me wonder what else they don't want us to know.

No, you know what, it makes me worry. All these different aliens showing up and putting us in the middle of their fights that've been going on for centuries? Something tells me we won't come out ahead no matter what we do. We had enough problems of our own before any of *them* showed up. Now we have to deal with international and inter . . . space relations. Who has the right to talk to who and negotiate what and all else. And we *still* have global warming!

The aliens don't care, though. They're too busy fighting. It's like what they came here to get out of us is secondary—they still have to learn how to get on with each other.

You know, I used to think that the best part of space travel would be getting away from folk you can't stand. Just put all your people on a spaceship and go. What's the use if you all just end up in the same places arguing over the same ol' shit?

So no, I'm not letting my daughter sign up for that colony thing the African Aliens are setting up. She just turned sixteen, and thank God for that parental consent requirement. This whole "cultural exchange" thing to fix global warming, it just doesn't sit right. What do they need with a million people? To go off to some planet and do what? For who? We won't even be able to communicate with them for five years. I don't think so. Not *my* daughter.

We should have been solving our own problems instead of counting on some damn handout from the sky. So you know what? I told her no. Don't make the same mistakes they did, I said. It'll just be the same shit, different planet. And if you have to deal with the same old shit no matter where you go, so you might as well stay right here and do it at home.

Yeah, she's mad at me now, but she'll have other chances. Won't be long before all the other aliens out there show up. A billion stars in the sky? There's got to be more than just three kinds.

TWILIGHT OF THE GODS

JOHN C. WRIGHT

John C. Wright is the author of nine novels including the recent *Null-A Continuum*, an authorized sequel to A.E. van Vogt's *World of Null-A*. The first book in Wright's Chaos Chronicles series—*The Orphans of Chaos*—was a finalist for the Nebula Award. His first novel, *The Golden Age*, was a finalist for the John W. Campbell Memorial Award for best SF novel of the year. He is also a retired attorney, newspaperman, and newspaper editor, who lives in the commonwealth of Virginia with his wife, author L. Jagi Lamplighter, and his three children Orville, Wilbur, and Just Wright.

"Twilight of the Gods" is a sequel to Wright's short stories "Not Born a Man" and "Farthest Man From Earth," and is his attempt to tell the story of Wagner's The Ring of the Nibelung in space. "All three tales take place in a common background or future history, where the human race has discovered the secret of immortality on 36 Ophiuchi," Wright said. "Only an incentive such as eternal youth, in my opinion, could motivate the human race to overcome the near-infinite expense and hardship of interstellar travel."

TWILIGHT OF THE GODS

Tall golden doors loomed up behind the dais of the throne. Behind those doors, it was said, the Main Bridge of the *Twilight of the Gods* reposed, a chamber dim and vast, with many altars studded all with jeweled controls set before the dark mirrors of the Computer. But Acting Captain Weston II found the chamber oppressive, and did not like the mysterious dark mirrors of the Computer watching him, and so, since his father's death many years ago, this white high chamber before the golden doors was used as his hall of audience.

The chamber was paved in squares of gold and white, with pillars of gold spaced along white walls. Hanging between the pillars were portraits of scenes from somewhere in the ship the Captain had never seen; fields of green plants, some taller than a man, growing, for some reason, along the deck rather than in shelves along the walls. In the pictures, the deck was buckled and broken, rising and falling in round slopes (perhaps due to damage from a Weapon of the Enemy) with major leaks running across it. The scenes took place in some hold or bay larger than any Acting Captain Weston II had seen or could imagine; the overhead bulkhead was painted light blue, some sort of white disruption like steam-clouds floating against it. In many pictures, the blue overhead was ruptured by a large yellow many-rayed circular explosion, perhaps, again, of a Weapon.

In most pictures were sheep or other animals, and young crewmen and women, out of uniform, blissfully ignoring the explosion overhead, and doing nothing to stop the huge leaks, one of which had ducks swimming in it.

Acting Captain Weston II found the pictures soothing, but disturbing. He often wondered if the artist had been trying to show how frail and foolish men are, that they will trip lightly through their little lives without a thought to the explosions and disasters all about them. Perhaps he preferred this chamber for that reason.

What the original use and name of this chamber had been in days gone past, no man of the Captain's Court could tell, not even his withered and aged Computerman.

The chamber now was bare, except that the Computerman approached the throne and knelt to Weston. "My lord," he said. His face was worn and haggard, his garb simple, rough, and belted with a hank of rope. The Computerman's eyes showed red and staring, a certain sign of the many long nightwatches he had spent writhing in the grip of the holy drug, which allowed his brethren to commune with the Computer.

"Why do you come unbidden unto me?" Weston asked sternly. "I know you await another,"

The Computerman replied. "It is to warn you against that other, that I am come."

The Acting Captain raised his hand, but the Computerman said swiftly, "Bid me not to go! Unless you would not heed the will of the Computer in this thing, the Computer which knows all, indeed, even things most secret and shameful."

The Captain had a troubled look upon his face, and sat back with one hand clutching the front of his jeweled coat, as if to hide something behind his hand, something, perhaps, on a necklace hidden beneath his tunic. "What shame?" he said.

"Every child knows the story of the Ring of Last Command," the Computerman said. "Of how, when the Sixth Barrage destroyed the lights and power of the second hundred decks, and Weapon of the Enemy opened the Great Chasm in the hull, reaching from the stars below almost to the thousandth deck, the first Captain, Valdemar, capitulated to the Enemy, and allowed a Boarding Party to come in from the Void Below the Hull. Decks Three Hundred through Seven Hundred Seventy rebelled, and followed bright Alverin into battle against the traitor Captain. But the Captain was not found, and his Ring of Final Command was lost. The ring, they say, can waken the Computers all again, and send the Weapons of the Twilight down into the Void."

"Children's fairy-tales," the Captain said.

"Yet, I deem, they tempt you," the Computerman said.

The Captain was silent.

"This prisoner which the giant brings; he had a ring inscribed with circuits, did he not? A ring which matches the descriptions of the Command Ring? You dream of learning the Secret Word which controls that Ring, and of conquering the world, of driving back the tall elves from decks above, where they fly and know no weight, and compelling the twisted dwarves from Engineering to obedience to your reign, and, one day, who knows? you think you will drive forth the Destroyers, and the servants of the enemy who infest the many antispinward decks, and hurl them down into the Void from whence they came. You dream a dream of vile pride; you are corrupted with temptation."

The Captain rose angrily from his throne. "Stop! Do you think your holy office will protect you from my wrath? Were there such a ring as legends say, for certain I would seize it to my own. And who would dare deny me? You? You?"

But the Computerman bowed in all humility, and said, "My lord knows there can be no such ring. A ring to waken the computers, indeed! Our faith informs us that the Computers do not sleep, that their screens are not dark, not to eyes that keep the faith. I and my brethren commune with the computers each nightwatch, and it gives us secret knowledge."

"My father told me the Computer screens once were bright to every eye, and a voice like a man's voice spoke from them, every man, even the humblest, could hear that voice. Before the Fifth Barrage, in his youth, he had seen them shining, and heard the voice."

"Men knew less sin in those days, my lord."

At that moment came a noise at the doors before them, not the golden doors of the Bridge, but the silver doors leading to the outer part of the palace and to the corridors and warrens of the great city of Forecomcon. The silver doors swept wide; here were twenty pikemen of the Gatewatch, dressed in blue and silver, and here, garbed hugely in the gray-green of the ancient order of Marines, strode in the giant.

The giant's shoulder was taller than a tall man's head, but his hair and beard were white with age. For he was the last of his kind, born to serve as a Marine, created by the lost arts of the Medical House, back when the Twilight was young. His name was Carradock.

In one hand Carradock held a mighty weapon like a spear, made by ancient and forgotten arts. The weapon could shoot bullets like a musket, except that it could fire many at a time, yet the bullets were slow, and would not pierce the bulkheads, or damage the equipment, and so the weapon was lawful according to the Weapons Law.

In Carradock's other hand was a chain. Bound by that chain, manacled and fettered, was a strange, dark man, wearing a uniform of silver-white, unlike any uniform known to Weston's lore. The man had pale hair like an upper-deck elf, and, like them, he was tall. But he was darkened and scarred by radiation, like the dwarves of engineering, or like those who lived near the Great Chasm, the Lesser Chasm, or the Hole, or near any other place the Weapons of the Enemy had blown up through the world. He was muscled like a down-deck dwarf, with thicker muscles than Weston had ever seen, except, perhaps for those on Carradock.

The Gatewatch lieutenant spoke up out of turn, coming forward and saying, "My lord! I pray you, let not this man alone in audience with you! He has the strength of three men."

"Then let him be bound with three men's chains, but I will speak alone to him."

The prisoner in silver-white stood, face calm, staring at the Captain. His face was still, his demeanor quiet. He seemed neither proud nor humble, but he stood like a man surrounded by a great silent open space, wherein nothing could be hidden from him, nor anything approach to harm him.

When he did not kneel, the Gatewatch pikemen struck him in the back of his knees with the butts of their spears. But the muscles of the prisoner's legs were strong, and did not bend when struck. Three of the Gatewatch put their hands on his shoulders to force him down. The prisoner watched them calmly, but would not budge.

"Leave him stand," the Captain ordered. The men stepped back. Then the Captain said, "Where are his wounds? He has no new scars. I ordered him put to torment. Bring forth the Apprentice Torturer."

But the lieutenant said, "Sire, the Apprentice Torturer fled after you ordered the Master Torturer tortured to death. After, none of the lesser torturers would approach this prisoner. They refused to obey your order."

The Computerman was still standing near the throne. He leaned forward and whispered, "Sire, why did you order the Master Torturer put to the question? I guess this: this prisoner told you that he had told the Master Torturer the Words which command the ring. The Master Torturer denied it. You conceived a jealous suspicion, and feared the Master Torturer craved the ring, and knew the Word. Do I guess aright?"

The Captain stood. "Leave me! All of you, except my giant, leave me! You, as well, Computerman!"

The lieutenant said, "Sire, shall we bring the other prisoner in now as well? The blind man we found wondering the Inner Corridor?"

"What care I for wandering beggars? Leave me, all!"

But the Computerman would not leave until the Gatewatch came to drag him away. The Computerman was shouting, "Beware the thing you covet! Beware! It is a thing accursed! All who do not possess it will crave it! It will drive you to madness; it will drive you to destroy your trusted servants, as you have destroyed your Torturer! Eschew this thing! Cast it away! The Computer cannot be controlled by it!" But by then the Gatewatch had gently pulled the old man out of the chamber and closed the door behind them.

Acting Captain Weston II sat upon his throne again, and bent his gaze upon the dark, scarred man before him. The man did not fidget or stir, but stood, calm and silent; and the giant stood waiting behind him.

"Speak!" ordered Weston.

The man said, "I have nothing more to say." His voice was soft and pleasant to the ear.

"The Old Code requires you to speak to a superior officer. What is your name and station, rank and duty?"

"I am Henwas, son of Himdall. I come from Starwell. My rank is Watchman. I am come to report to the true Captain."

"There are no Watchmen; the order is defunct. After the Boarding by the Enemy, all the outer Hull was laid to waste. No; you are no Watchman. You have the look of an aftman farmer about you."

"I was not born a Watchman; indeed, I was born a farmer. My village is called Aftshear, in the secondary engine core, near the Axis, where the world has no weight. My youth was spent tending the many plants and green growing things from whence come our air, and life. But I was captured by the Enemy, and, for a time, was a slave. I escaped, and fled below decks, where every step is a crushing weight, and the air is poisoned by the radiations of the Seventh Barrage. The servants of the Enemy feared the radiation, and could not tolerate the weight, and did not pursue me. Crawling, I went still lower, till I was nearly crushed. Then I came upon a place where nothing was below me, except for the stars.

"There I was found by Himdall, last of all Watchmen, in the midst of a deserted place and empty corridors, a chamber lit, and filled with sweet air, although surrounded by darkness and poison on every side.

"Himdall nursed me back to health, and taught to me his art, and showed to me the Starwell, at whose deep bottom the stars underfoot turn and turn again. And I became a Watchman in truth, and was adopted as his son. And for long years I kept watch on the Enemy stars, and saw the slow, grave motions."

Weston asked: "And do you believe the heresy which says the stars which move are not mere colored lights, but the Ships from which the Enemy, in ancient times, came forth?"

"I do. And yet among those lights, are four Ships friendly to our own, sent out, as we were, in ages past, from Earth. Their names I think you know: the *Götterdämmerung*, the *Apocalypse*, the *Armageddon*, and the *Ragnarök*."

Weston stirred uneasily upon his throne. "I tell you the original Captain betrayed the crew, and fled. This happened when my father was a boy. He was Acting Captain; now I am the Acting Captain."

"By what right do you call yourself so?"

Weston shouted angrily, "By right of blood succession!" Then he was quiet, and he said quietly, "You may give any report you must give to me."

"Very well," said Henwas Watchman, and he recited all he had said when first he had been brought before Weston: "The Eighth Barrage, which has been approaching for so many years, has turned aside, and seeks now to strike the *Armageddon*. The missiles and small ships of that Barrage shall smite their target starting twelve years hence, with a bombardment lasting a year or two, peaking fourteen years hence and diminishing thereafter. We shall not be struck by it; presumably the masters of Enemy now know we were boarded by the sixty armies from the landing party from the Dreadnought *Kzalcurrang-Achai*, which, in our speech, is named the *Hungry Indeed For Battle*.

"I further report that our escort ships, the *Revenge* and the *Vendetta*, were destroyed between thirteen and seven years ago by picket ships launched from the *Tzazalkiurung*, which, in our speech, is named *Ready To Do Grave Harm*. This ship is presently four light-minutes off our port bow, where it has remained for seventy years, no doubt waiting to see if it must render aid to the *Kzalcurrang-Achai*.

"Yet the main sweep of the Destroyer fleet has passed beyond us and done us no hurt. We are in the midst of some eighty Dreadnoughts and four motile planets. Their Crown ships are within eight light-minutes of us now, and have not maneuvered to avoid us by a further distance. Asteroids from the shattered planet called War Storm are all about us in each direction, and perhaps hide us from the main body of the Enemy, and from the Crown Ships, which take no heed of us, but proceed against the *Armageddon* and the *Götterdämmerung*. Of the *Apocalypse* there has been no sign for thirty years. The *Ragnarök* is hidden by a great light; either she maneuvers, or she is in full retreat."

The Captain was sarcastic. "And you believe all this? That the fate of our world depends on the motions of these little colored lights?"

"I have one thing further to report. The escort ship *Hermes Trismegistus* out from the *Götterdämmerung* has entered an orbit of the Enemy planet called Promise of Destruction. She maneuvers without any flare, and will not be seen by the Enemy. The orbit will carry the *Hermes Trismegistus* to us before the decade ends. It is a rescue ship. When the officers from the *Hermes* come aboard, power and light will be restored to all sections, the wounded and the poisoned will be healed by their knowledge; and those who have not kept faith will be punished. If you have been disobedient, you will be taken before the Court Martial."

The Captain sneered. "My nurse, when I was but a babe, would terrify me with tales of the Court Martial and the Day of Judgment that would come when the Earthmen would come up from Heaven underfoot. But you shall not live long enough to find the truth of these things, unless the medicine of the Earthmen knows how to resurrect the dead."

The Watchman said simply, "I have lived near the radiations of the outer hull. I have the disease. I know the hour of my death is not far off. Why else would I be willing to bear the cursed ring?"

Weston drew on a chain around his neck. Up from inside his jeweled coat he drew out the ring. It was gold, inscribed with delicate circuitry, and set with gray stone. In the middle of the stone gleamed a strange light, which showed that the power of the ring still lived.

"Tell me the word which commands this ring."

"I may only tell the Captain."

"I am Captain! I am he! There is no Captain Valdemar! He is myth! Even were there such a man, he would be long dead, a hundred years or more gone by! I am the true Captain!"

"A true Captain would use the power, not for himself, but to complete the mission, and discharge the great Weapons the stories say our world carries at its Axis," the Watchman said softly.

"And if that were my intention . . . ?"

"Then you would not have chained me," said the Watchman, rattling his manacles.

The Captain sat until he felt his anger cool within him. Then he spoke in a voice most reasonable and even, "Watchman, if I could persuade you that there are no worlds hanging in the Void beneath our world, no Dreadnoughts of the Enemy, no war, except for the wars fought with the Enemy aboard our Ship, between here and Midline Darkhall, and spinward toward the Lesser Chasm, what then? If there is no world outside our world, no Weapons to fire, what reason have you them to withhold from me the Ring of Final Command?"

"No reason," said the Watchman. "If there were no worlds below our feet, I would give the ring's commands to you."

"Then reckon this: If you are right, and there is a war in space below us, then this ship, and all aboard, were sent into that war, to fight, perhaps, to die, all in order to defend the ship called Earth from our Great Enemy."

"Earth is not a ship. It is a planet. Earth is inside out, for the crew there live on the outer hull, and their air is outward from them. On Earth, gravity is backwards, and draws them toward their axis, so that they stand with their feet on the hull, with their heads looking down toward the stars."

"Be that as it may; the Earthmen sent these great ships far out into space to fight their wars, not so? This they did with all wisdom and intention, knowing that even the swiftest flight across the Void would take generations, not so?"

"It is so."

"I ask you then, in all candor, how could this be? Who but a madman would dispatch his armies to fight across the Void, sending them to battlefields so far that the grandchildren of those sent out would be the only soldiers on the field?"

"I know not: yet it was done."

"Leaving us ignorant of all? No one has even seen the Enemy stars, nor do we know them. How have we become so ignorant so soon?"

"My master said once that the Computer spoke to all the children, and instructed them. When the Computer fell silent, there were no written things aboard with which to teach the children. Much was lost; more was lost in the confusion of the wars and darkenings. What we know, we know by spoken lore; but in the past, all men knew the priestly arts, and could read the signs."

Weston waved his hand impatiently, as if this were nothing to the point. "Heed me. I tell you, I have led men into battle, not once, but many times, both against the rebel elves of Alverin, and against the Enemy. Will you take me at my word, that no battle could be fought, nor any force commanded, unless the soldiers are willing to die for one another, or for their home corridors?"

"I believe it."

"Now then: who aboard this ship is willing to die for Earth, which no one has ever seen; or is willing to die for those aboard the other ships of which myths speak; the *Götterdämmerung* or the *Apocalypse*? Are the crews and peoples of those mythic worlds willing to die for us? If so, why? Perhaps their great-grandfathers knew our great-grandfathers back when Earth first made us, but who knows them now? Do you see? Wars over such length of time cannot be possible."

But the Watchman said, "The medicine of those times past was much greater than our own, and men expected lives many hundreds of years in length, due to things they had put inside their bodies; things we do not have, and cannot make with our scant arts. To the immortals, wars, no matter how long, are done with swiftly."

The Captain knew a moment of doubt. His gaze rested on his giant; a man made huge and strong by arts the Captain knew had been lost. He also knew the old tales, which said that, before the Medical House was destroyed during the Second Barrage, all officers were young and ageless, able to see in the dark like cats, strong as dwarves, and instantly cured of any wound, poison, or hurt.

"Even were there such a war," the Captain slowly said, "If we are, as you say, deep in the ranks of the Enemy, overlooked and ignored, to fire our Weapons now would mean the destruction of this world, if not now, then in the time of our children."

At that moment came a great commotion at the silver doors, a sound of trumpets and alarms. There came a banging at the doors, and the lieutenant rushed in, his sword drawn.

"Sire," called the lieutenant, "The rebels from abovedecks attack in great force! Alverin himself leads them! Already he has been struck by a dozen arrows; each time he plucks them forth and laughs. The men . . . the men are saying he is an Earthman!"

"Rally the men. Draw down the great doors at Spinhall Common Fork and at the Underroad. Flood the stairwells leading to deck Eight Thirty Six with oil. Then, withdraw the men behind the Great Barrier Wall and close the High Gate. Use hand pumps to withdraw some part of the air from the circular approach corridor; this will seal all doors beyond the power of any battering-ram to breach."

"But if he brings unlawful weapons? Explosives?"

"Fool. Alverin has never broken the Weapon Law; never cheated a treaty; never lied. Why do you think his rebellion does so poorly? They must be mad things to attack us now."

"Will you come to lead us?"

"Presently; first I must do otherwise. Go!"

And when the man had left, Weston said to the Watchman Henwas, "With this Ring, I could call upon the Computer to close and open doors at will, extinguish lights, drain corridors of air. Tell me the Words!"

But Henwas said, "You did not think to hide the ring when your lieutenant entered here. He saw it. If he craves its power as much as you, he will be gathering men to lead against you here to seize the ring."

"There is no more time for talk. Say the words, or I will order my giant to snap you like a wire!"

"You cannot escape the curse of the ring. Whoever does not have the ring craves to have it. So my master Himdall was told by the strange blind man who gave it first to him."

"Strange blind man?"

"Perhaps he thought the curse would be alleviated if the ring were given to so remote a hermit as my master."

"And did your master say what this man's appearance was?"

"Many times, for he was most peculiar. The wanderer, he wore his hair long, like those of the lower decks, but walked with a staff, like an upper-deck man not used to our weight. He wore a wide-brimmed hat, like the men of the Greenhouses, where the light controls never dim their fierce glare; but he wore cusps of black glass before his eyes, like a darklander out here where lights still glow. On each shoulder he carried a bird, like men who walk in fear of poisoned corridors, who, when they see their pets keel over, flee."

"Carradock! Go tell the Gatewatch to bring the other prisoner in! The description matches; it is he."

When the giant was at the door, speaking to the guard, the Watchmen flexed his muscles hugely, and the chains about his wrists snapped free. He bent down and tugged the chains about his ankles; the links bent and broke; but, by then, the giant had seen, and flung himself back across the room to fall upon the Watchman with his full strength.

For a moment they strove against each other, limbs intertwined, muscles knotted. Their strength was equal, yet the aged giant was more cunning in the art of wrestling; the giant twisted and flung the Watchman to the ground and fell atop him. By this time the guards from the door had run forward, and stood with pikes ready, but could find no opening, and dared not strike for fear of hitting the giant.

When he rose, the giant had the Watchman's arms pinned painfully behind his back, his hands twisted up. The giant was grinning. "You are a worthy opponent," he whispered, panting.

"You also," said the Watchman, as blood trickled down his face.

A moment later a second group of knights and pikemen came in the chamber, escorting an old man in a broad black hat. The old man walked leaning on a staff; two black birds clung to the shoulders of his long cape. The cape was fastened with a steel ornament shaped like a spiked wheel.

"Lieutenant! Why does he come before me unchained, garbed in no uniform, holding his stick? Were these things not taken from him at the door of his cell?"

"Sire!" stammered the lieutenant, "We found him now, not in his cell, but walking the corridors leading to the palace, singing a carol."

"A carol?"

The stranger lifted his head. As the hat brim tilted up, Weston saw the man wore round disks of black glass before his eyes. The stranger sang,

"Woe my child! Woe is me! My son was born while falling free! Cannot endure Earth gravity, he never shall come home, not he, but evermore, forevermore, shall fly the airless deep, fly free!"

"That is an old song," said Weston.

"I am an old man," the stranger replied.

"I think you are Valdemar," said Weston.

"Then why do you not salute me?"

"Valdemar was a traitor!"

"Then why do you not embrace me as a brother, my fellow traitor?"

"What treason do you say I do?" asked Weston.

"The same as mine; you covet the ring. But I cannot use it; when the Chief Engineer Alberac learned I had let the Enemy aboard, he bound all the main circuits of the Computer to a single overall command; and wrought that command into the ring you hold, leaving all other systems on automatic. Lauren, the Ship's Psychiatrist, and I, we traveled to the Engine Room, and we deceived poor Alberac and seized the ring. But Alberac had wrought more cunningly than I had guessed, and had programmed the ring, such that whenever it was used, any other member in the computer then would know from where and from whom the ring's commands had come. The Enemy would bend all their forces toward its capture, were there any Enemy aboard. You see? The ultimate power of command, yet it can be used only by someone not afraid to die. Where to find such absolute devotion to one's duty? Many years I searched the halls of this great ship, from the Ventilation Shafts where pirates aboard their giant kites fly the hurricanes from level to level, down to the swamps and stench of the Sewermen, who silently take the dead away, and, in the darkness, use secret arts to recycle all foul things to air and light again. Only one man I found had not deserted his post; Himdall, last of the Watch, and most faithful. Surrounded by the enemy, abandoned, alone, yet true to his duty. And look! Here is his son, equally as faithful as is he. Equally as doomed."

Henwas called out, "Captain, I wish to report the Enemy Crown Ships are nigh to us, believing our world conquered and desolate, and are presently vulnerable to the discharge of our weapons!"

Several of the knights stared at the black-cloaked stranger in awe. "It is Valdemar!" said one. "Captain!" another whispered, and a third said, "Can it be he?"

One of the pikemen in the room was looking, not at Valdemar, but at Weston. This pikeman spoke out, saying, "My lord? You have the Command Ring?" But there was envy in his eyes, and he stepped toward the throne. But a knight, dressed all in ribbons and fine clothes, drew his rapier and touched that pikeman on the shoulder with the naked blade, so that the man was frightened, and stopped. The knight spoke to Weston, saying, "The rumor of the ring draws Alverin and all his tall, frail men. This old dribbler, if he is Valdemar, came also for its lure. I think the squat and surly dwarves who serve the fat Lord of Engineering cannot be far behind. The ring is surely cursed, my lord. It were better cast into a pit."

A second knight, this a tall man from Cargobay, said, "My lord! The stranger rambles at length. He hopes for delay. Perhaps he is in league with Alverin's people."

The giant said to the Stranger, "Captain Valdemar. I am Carradock son of Cormac. My father died in the battle of Foresection Seven Hold, killing the great champion of the Enemy. My father was an Earthman, born beneath blue skies, and he did not desert his post, even at his death. By his name, and in return for the vengeance I owe you for his death at the hands of the Enemy whom you allowed aboard, I ask this question: Why?"

"Broad question. Why what?"

"Why did you surrender to the Enemy, and allow them to land sixty armies into our halls?"

"Is that your full question? Are you not also going to ask why, on the day of the Last Burn, did our drive core suddenly accidentally ignite? Why the Enemy vessel was struck amidships with a line of flame a hundred miles long, sterilizing half their outer decks? Why, to this day, they have not landed a thousand armies more, and why can they barely keep the empire to our antispinward supplied with arms and food, and that with picket ships which, till recently, were kept at bay by our escort ship *Revenge*? Why they dare not bombard the Twilight into flaming ruin, for fear of striking dead their own armies? And, best of all, why does the Sirdar-Emperor aboard this ship, the son of the Leader of the Boarding Party, why has he reported to his masters that the ship is taken? This last question I can answer: the Destroyers would certainly annihilate this vessel with their great weapons were they to learn that we still lived, and fought, and still ruled the inner decks as far spinward as Waterstore and forward as Airbay and Greenlitfield."

"Watchman," said the giant, "If you will promise not to escape, I will release one arm of yours. And I will trust your promise, knowing that, of all orders and ranks of men, Watchmen are the most true and trustworthy; for the good of the ship relies on the honesty of their reports."

"Why do you wish to let go my hand?" the Watchman asked.

"So that my own hand shall be free to salute my Captain, as he has asked."

"I agree," said the Watchman. And the Carradock raised his huge hand and saluted Valdemar. There were tears in Carradock's eyes.

Weston was livid. "Tell me the Word to unleash the power of the ring! Tell! Or I swear you die this moment, traitor!"

Valdemar said, "I know many secret words of high Command; words to open doors or trigger circuits which only open to my voice, doors leading down into secret corridors, accessways, and crawlspaces where no designers ever meant a human being to go. Every inch of all thousand decks of this vast ship I know, for it is mine, and I have never renounced my claim to it. I know words to darken lights, and still the airs to silence, or to send them rushing up again. But one word I do not know: the word which Himdall whispered to ring when he took it for his own."

Now a group of twelve Computermen came into the chamber, carrying staves and bludgeons. The pikemen in silver and blue lowered their lances, but confusedly, some pointing at the Computermen, some at the black stranger, and one or two at the Watchman whom the giant still gripped. Three pikemen began walking toward the throne in a menacing fashion, but when the lieutenant called sharply out to them, these three hesitated, and stood uncertainly.

The Chief Computerman was near the silver doors. He waved his truncheon, and called out, "Weston! Give up the ring! It is false and has no power! Do not dream you can control the doors and lights and weapons of the world! Only the Computer can control these things, and it heeds only our holy order!"

"It that so indeed?" spoke the dark stranger. He pointed his staff at the silver doors and spoke a single harsh syllable. Immediately the silver doors swung shut, and there was a sound of great bolts slamming home. The Computerman jumped forward to avoid the doors. "No doubt," hissed

Valdemar, "These doors reacted of their own accord, from a wish to keep mere riff-raff and sweepings of the corridors from blowing in to botch the brew."

"Edgal! Sindal! Garvoris!" called out Weston to three of his knights, "Kill Valdemar upon this instant! If he knows not the word to command the ring, then he is not any use to me."

"Other words I know," Valdemar mildly replied. And he shouted; the chamber dimmed into utter darkness. During the moment as the lights failed, Henwas saw Valdemar leap and spin lightly into the air, surrounded by a great gray circle of cloak, and by the flutter of his two dark, shrieking birds. With one hand, as he leaped, Valdemar drew out a breathing tube from his collar and put it to his mouth and nose; his other hand drew a hidden sword-blade from his staff. The staff-end, which had been the scabbard, fell away, smoking. Valdemar spun, disemboweling one oncoming knight with a kick, hidden knives unfolding from his boot spurs. In one smooth motion it was done; and the two other knights rushing forward missed him with their pikes as he leaped, swirling his cloak about the head of one of them. While the man was tangled in the weighted net hidden below the cloak, Valdemar slashed him to death with a stroke of his shining sword, which he held under his palm, against his fore-arm, after the fashion of blind-fighters.

Then it was dark. There came a noise and shattering explosion of light. In the flare of the explosion, the corpse of the one knight standing near where the smoking cane-end had been abandoned could be briefly seen, headless, bloody, arms flailing as it fell. The hollow tube had contained some shrapnel which had been scattered among the pikemen and guards. Their chests and faces were bloody. Screams were starting. One man was blubbering like a baby. Henwas heard a hiss, smelled the fetid, dizzying smell of poisonous gas radiating from the corner of the chamber where Valdemar had been.

All was noise, screams, horn-calls, darkness, confusion, the stench of blood, the smell of poison.

Henwas was awed by the destruction. Was the Captain truly blind?

There was another flare of light; the lieutenant stood with an illegal hand-weapon blazing in his fist, his face blood-red, contorted with murderous wrath; he was shouting, "Suffer not to live who breaks the weapon code! Who kills the Ship kills all . . . " The lieutenant had been driven beyond all reason by the traitor-captain's use of poisons and explosives, which could damage air filters and bulkhead seals; he reckoned nothing for the illegality of his own weapon.

The ornament which Valdemar had used as a cloak-pin spun shining out of the darkness and struck the lieutenant's hand. The disk was razor-sharp; it severed the lieutenant's fingers. The hand-weapon fell. Again it was dark.

Weston shouted, "Carradock! Save the Watchman . . . " and then he cried out in great pain, having betrayed his location by his shout.

Someone struck at Henwas with a bludgeon; with his free hand (for the other was still gripped by the giant) Henwas reached out and seized the arm wielding the bludgeon, and the bones broke under the strength of his fingers. At first, he was amazed and angered, for he did not think that any in that chamber would risk his harm; but under hand he felt the rough-spun cloth of a Computerman.

Then the giant was dragging him to one side. Henwas heard a clash of blades, a hoarse cry, where he had just been standing. Now the giant held him still.

By some odor or noise or pressure close at hand, Henwas felt an intuition that Valdemar was nearby, silent in the darkness.

The giant still had him by one arm; but, even so, Henwas did not move or speak, for fear of someone hearing. There was a ruckus in the blackness all around them, the clash of arms. Henwas suspected that the Computermen or the pikemen were in rebellion, and thought, under cover of darkness and confusion, to steal the ring.

Valdemar's voice slithered out of the blackness: "Carradock, I ask you, by your ancient oaths, now to be obedient to me, and bring the Watchman to the throne where Weston is. We will seize the ring. When you call to him, he will answer, thinking you loyal."

Henwas was amazed that any man who used explosives aboard the Ship could say words like 'oath' and 'loyalty' and not be choked. But he feared a coming tragedy; Carradock and Valdemar both were resolute, brave men. He knew the giant would not break fealty with Weston, who, however unworthy, was his lord. He knew as well that Valdemar, who might admire the giant, would not hesitate an instant to cheat, deceive or murder him, the moment that such crimes became useful to his grand design.

The giant made no noise. Henwas was not surprised.

Valdemar spoke again: "Unfortunate that you must betray Weston, who is your lord, but the mission goals require it. Fret not; treason is only bitter at first. The soul grows easily accustomed . . . "

Carradock lashed the bayonet of his weapon through the air toward the voice. He struck nothing. By some trick or sleight, Valdemar had made his voice seem to come from where it was not.

"Henwas!" Valdemar whispered, sounding very near. "Call out, that I may hear where the giant stands, and slay him."

But Henwas did not want the giant to die, and did not answer. "Henwas, Carradock! Both of you have disobeyed my direct command in time of war; for this I instantly condemn you. I now release the deadly vapor. Breathe, and perish . . . "

Henwas knew this was some feint to compel them to move or act, so he doubted, and stayed still; and perhaps the giant suspected this a ruse as well, but staked no chance on it.

Carradock discharged his weapon straight up into the air. In the momentary muzzle-flare, Valdemar could be seen, crouching like a great black bat near the floor, white blade in his hand, point poised across his back like the sting of a scorpion.

The giant dropped the barrel of his weapon and fired again. Valdemar flopped and fell limply. The giant fired many times.

At that moment, the great gold doors behind the throne opened a crack. There was a weak light from the Main Bridge beyond, dusky blue service-lights said to burn forever. Silhouetting against that light, Henwas could see the staggering figure of Acting Captain Weston, who was pierced and bleeding.

By the slim crack of light from the door, the huddled figure of Valdemar could be seen, bleeding terribly. "Accept my surrender," whispered Valdemar, "for I am wounded unto death."

The giant stepped forward. "I repent, that when finally I had found a man worth serving, the true Captain from the young days of the world, he sullied his hands with unlawful weapons. Your surrender I accept, for memory of the nobility once you had." A pause, then: "Can you hear me?"

And when he bent over the huddled figure, Valdemar, hearing the sound of his voice, flung up his hand and threw a poisoned dagger into the open mouth of the giant, piercing the roof of his mouth.

"Nothing is unlawful, nothing noble in war!" Valdemar screamed in anger.

The white-haired and ancient giant staggered forward and fell onto the supine body of Captain Valdemar, crushing him down. And perhaps the giant, falling, had struck down with his knife or hands, for the body of Valdemar was crushed and was not seen to move again.

As the giant fell, Valdemar cried a single word of command and then was silent.

The moment the giant had unhanded him, Henwas bounded across the chamber toward Weston. A knight rose up before him, like a ghost in the gloom, brandishing a rapier; but Henwas, scarred by radiation, knew no fear, came forward, was stabbed in the shoulder painfully, but struck in the knight's skull with his fist.

He nearly had his hands on the wounded Weston, who, sobbing, was crawling through the golden doors into the vast dark chamber beyond, when a pike-stroke from behind Henwas cut into the muscles of his leg and toppled him. In a moment, the pikeman had him by the hair, and was pressing a dirk against his throat, even as Henwas' hands closed around the bracelet-ringed ankle of Weston's jeweled boot.

Weston drew a bloody hand out from underneath his gem-studded coat. "This is my death-wound," he panted, staring in horror at the heart's blood in his palm, "I am slain . . . "

Meanwhile, Valdemar's last spoken word had its effect. There was a noise like that of bolts being drawn back and of doors opening; and the pictures which lined the walls swung free in their frames, and from half a dozen secret doors, lights and trumpet-noise issued forth.

Into the chamber from these secret doors came suddenly the tall pale men of Overdeck, garbed all in green, some with breastplates and helms of polished steel, carrying bows and tall spears and slim straight swords.

The knights of the above-world were tall and fair and terrible to look upon, and they were singing their war-song. Not one of them was pock-marked, or scarred, or showed any sign of the radiation diseases which those who live on lower decks, to their sorrow, know only too well. Before them, came the white starbanner of Alverin.

Many carried bows and cross-bows, for, although the Over-men are weaker in their legs and bodies than are other men, their arms are sinewy and their eyes are keen.

Alverin himself came forth, his uniform as green as leaves, and from his wide shoulders hung one of the fair white winged cloaks those who live at the Axis of the world use to steer themselves in flight. His hair was as yellow as the corn his people grow in Greenhold; his eyes were blue and bright, and shone with a light of stern command.

Now Alverin raised his straight slim sword and called upon those within the chamber to surrender, saying, "Whoso lays down his arms, shall be spared, and set free, I vow, suffering no hurt nor any dishonor!"

Because the rumor of Alverin's honesty and clemency was so well known, the knights and pikemen in that chamber instantly threw down their swords and pole-arms. None had heart to fight, seeing their leader, Weston, lay swooning with his life blood bubbling out of him. The weapons fell ringing to the chamber floor.

But one of the Computermen seized up a pike and, with a terrible cry, cast it straight into Alverin's breast. Alverin staggered backward, pierced through the heart and lungs. In that same instant of time, the man who had cast the pike was stricken through his arm by three arrows. Yet these shots were not ill-aimed; for Alverin's men, by custom, spoke before they struck, wounded rather than slew.

Alverin drew the pike-head out from his bloody chest and wiped the blood away. The wound closed up into a scar and then Alverin's chest grew fair and smooth again. He cast the bloody pike aside. "I am an Earthman; I was born beneath blue sky!" he called out. To the wounded man, he said, "The knowledge of the men who made this entire world have made me as I am, and I am not to be slain by your small weapons." And he ordered his physician to tend to the wounded among the enemy, even the man who had smitten him.

Alverin turned. He saw Valdemar laying motionless, his body crushed beneath the fallen giant. "So," Alverin whispered, "These secret paths you showed to us were not a trap. Did you play us true, this once, old liar? If so, where is the ring?"

Now he turned again. In the threshold of the golden doors leading to the Main Bridge, a pikeman still crouched above Henwas the Watchman, a steady knife still touching the prone man's throat. Henwas was bleeding at the shoulder and the leg, and yet his face was remote and calm, as if no wound nor pain could trouble him.

Alverin stepped forward till he could see, lying in the shadow of the door, dying, Acting Captain Weston II, and, in his bloodstained hand, the ring.

Beyond was the Bridge, a large dimly lit cathedral of a space, surrounded on all sides by the darkened screens of the Computer.

Weston croaked, "Pikeman. Slit the Watchman's throat if the rebel-king steps forward one step more."

"Weston," said Alverin in a soft, stern voice, "Yield up to me the ring. I will restore to all the world, the light, the power, and the justice, which, by right, should have been ours. You have my solemn promise that all your men shall be dealt with justly."

"Should I believe a mutineer? You betrayed Valdemar," hissed Weston wearily.

"After he surrendered to the Enemy. Free men follow leaders into battle, and render him the power of Command, only while he does their will, in pursuit of a just war, or in defense against hostility. That power of Command, incapable of destruction, returned to the free men of this ship, upon Valdemar's abdication of it. By their fair and uncoerced election, I was tendered the Command, and so am Captain. That trust I hold sacred; render me the ring, and I shall see this world prosper."

"Prosper? Are we not surrounded by enemy worlds?" Weston asked softly.

"We are too humble for their attention," Alverin said, "If we do not offend them, they will pay us no more heed."

"And if the ring is used to launch the fabled Weaponry at World's Core?" Weston now raised himself on one elbow. His face was pasty-white, his eyes wild and sick.

"Then the world dies, if not in this generation, then in the next."

The lieutenant, his hand being bandaged by a tall pale doctor, spoke up, "Sire! Yield the ring to Alverin! Even we, so many years his foe, acknowledge his justice, wisdom, and trueheartedness. If any man is deserving of empire, it is such a man as this!"

But Henwas, who still had him by the ankle, said a voice of calm command, "In your last moment, sir, I pray you be a Captain truly. Use the ring, or give it me, to complete the mission of the *Twilight of the Gods*. We both are dying, you of wounds, me of radiation poison and disease. Should we, in such a time as this, abandon our posts and sue for peace? This whole world was made for war."

"Pikeman, stand away. Here, Watchman; take the accursed thing. Do your duty; kill all my enemies, you, them, everyone. And be damned to you all." With a curse on his lips, Weston slid into death, and his cold hand gave the ring to Henwas.

Henwas came up to his knees and thrust the pikeman down across the dais' stairs. Such was the strength of his arm that the man was flung many yards away. Alverin and the elves started forward suddenly, but Henwas, leaning inward from the golden door, reached and touched the shining ring against the dark, cold mirrored corner of the nearest of the many computer screens which filled the huge, black bridge.

He spoke the words: "Eternal Fidelity. I am forever loyal." And all the mirrors flamed to life and shone with purest light. On each screen images appeared, words, symbols, strange letters and equations, and everywhere, the thousand shining lights of all the Enemy stars.

A pure and perfect voice, like no voice ever to be made by lips or tongue of man, rang out: "READY."

Several of the Computermen screamed in fear or shouted with joy. One sank down to his knees and cried out, "Oh, that I have seen this day!" Even the knights and guards of Weston's, and Alverin's tall men, stood speechless, eyes wide.

But the Chief Computerman called out for the men to avert their eyes, "This is a deception of the Enemy! The Computer cannot speak to men, except through us!" But one of the knights smote him across the face with his fist. The Chief Computerman fell to the deck, and lay sullen, wiping his mouth, weeping and afraid to speak again.

One of the overman knights raised his bow, and spoke in a soft, clear voice, "Noble lord Alverin! We have heard the word which can command the ring. One shot, and all the world shall be yours!"

"Nay, Elromir," spoke Alverin, "Not even to win empires will I have such a blow be struck, against a man wounded and unarmed."

The Watchman, kneeling, said, "Computer! Are there weapons at this world's core, ready to strike out against our enemies?"

"ALL WEAPON SYSTEMS AT READY. TARGETS ACQUIRED. FIRING SEQUENCES READY TO INITIATE. STANDING BY."

Alverin said, "Watchman, I pray you, wait! You will unleash a storm of fire! None save me aboard this ship even recall the origins of this war, its purpose, or its cause. Why do you condemn all the nations, lands, and peoples, here aboard the *Twilight,* to be obliterated? Think of those born innocent, years after this dreadful ship of war was launched. Our Captain betrayed us; we have surrendered; let it rest at that."

Henwas said, "When the stranger, whom I now know to have been Valdemar, gave my master Himdall this dread ring, he did so with these words: 'You alone shall know when the waiting is completed, when the enemy grows lax, and deems us dead.' Only now do I understand the Captain's purpose after all these years, even from before my birth. The other ships we know only as names of glory, these ships are hard beset by that great foe which ruined and overthrew our world so long ago; and our true world Earth, though we have forgotten it, still calls to us to fight in her defense. The Captain expected us to fight and die for the glory of the fleet, to die, if need be, to have all the *Twilight* die, if it would forward the mission goals, and accomplish our duty."

Alverin said, "But, those aboard the other ships, why do you give such love and loyalty to them, that you are willing to call destruction down on all our world, for the sake of those whom you have never seen, and do not know?"

"I will not live to see salvation, yet I know it comes," said Henwas, "I never knew the other men who serve aboard those other ships; yet I know that there are those aboard them who would gladly do for me what I now do for them. That knowledge is enough for me."

One of the knights, evidently realizing the Henwas meant to do an act which would provoke the Enemy to destroy the world, stooped, picked up a fallen dagger, and, before any of Alverin's men could think to stop him, threw it. The dagger spun and landed fair on the middle of Henwas' back. Henwas, back arched, eyes blind with pain, now shouted, "Computer! Shut these doors!"

"ACKNOWLEDGED. ALL STATIONS NOTIFIED OF OVERRIDE COMMAND LOCATION."

The men in the room swept forward like a tide, but too late; the golden doors fell to, and shut in their faces.

Alverin raised his hand, and cried out with a great voice to rally his men. "Alberac's curse has told all the computer screens now where the ring hides! The Enemy will sweep this area with fire, exploding all the decks below us if they need be! Come! We must be gone! It may be already too late . . . " And he set his men passing swiftly out of the chamber. He and his paladins stood on the dais before the golden doors, unwilling to depart till all the men had gone before them.

And as they stood so, through the doors, they heard the great, chiming and inhuman voice call out, "WEAPONS FREE. INITIATING LAUNCH. WARHEADS AWAY."

There came a noise like thunder. And a great voice echoing from every wall rang out; and it was the Watchman's voice, tremendously amplified, and echoing throughout every corridor of every nation of the great ship. They heard the Watchman call out, saying, "I have seen it! I have seen it! And the heavens are consumed with light!"

Then, more softly, they heard the great voice say, "Father! If you see this, you shall know; I did not leave my post . . . "

And then, even more softly: "Computer, now destroy this ring, and let its curse be ended, and return all functions to their proper stations and commands . . . "

Light returned to the chamber where they where, and they heard, as from far off, a great noise of wonder, as of many voices of people near and far, all crying out at once. And they knew that light returned to darkened places which had known no light for years beyond count.

One of the knights took hold of Alverin's cape. "Sire, look!" and he pointed to where the giant Carradock lay.

Of Valdemar's body there was no sign. He was gone.

"Look there." One of the knights, in wonder, pointed upward to where the two black birds were huddled among the pillar-tops, bundles of black feathers, croaking.

"They are his magpies," said Alverin softly. "Even in ancient times, from before he was blind, he always kept such birds near him, to remind him of what he dared not forget." And, to himself, he murmured, "Or perhaps, since all this was arranged by his cunning, perhaps it is I who am blind, or who have forgotten . . . "

One of the black birds croaked, and spoke in a voice like a man's voice: "No matter what the cost. The Mission goals must be accomplished. No matter what the cost."

The other black bird croaked and said, "All's fair in war. All's fair. All's fair."

Alverin and his men departed from that place, and did not look back.

WARSHIP

GEORGE R. R. MARTIN
and GEORGE GUTHRIDGE

George R. R. Martin is the best-selling author of the Song of Ice and Fire epic fantasy series and a range of other novels such as *Fevre Dream, The Armageddon Rag,* and *Dying of the Light.* He is a prolific author of short stories, which have garnered numerous nominations and wins for the field's major awards, including the Hugo, Nebula, Stoker, and World Fantasy Awards.

George Guthridge is the author of several novels, including *The Madagascar Manifesto* (with Janet Berliner). He's also written dozens of short stories, which have appeared in *Amazing Stories, The Magazine of Fantasy & Science Fiction,* and in numerous anthologies. He has won the Bram Stoker Award for best novel, and has been a finalist for both the Hugo and Nebula Awards.

"Warship" is the very first SF story Martin ever tried to sell professionally. "Tried" being the operative word. It wasn't until some years later when he showed the story to his friend George Guthridge—who saw something in it, and offered to rewrite it—that the story found a home in the pages of *The Magazine of Fantasy & Science Fiction.*

WARSHIP

Invulnerable, she is. Earth's answer to Sarissa's defiance of Earth authority, she carries fourteen lasercannon, dual solar guns, a belly filled with conventionally armed missiles. Self-repairing, computerized to a point approaching sentience, she has backup systems should any instruments prove defective—supervisory capacities should any of her crew of fifty-one prove derelict. She is powered by two Severs-stardrive engines.

She is *Alecto*.

Graciously, gloriously she began her cruise homeward at five times lightspeed, her duralloy awash with starlight. Now she had stopped. Behind her, once reddened by Doppler shift, Sarissa's sun is again gold.

• • •

He was the last of the crew, and his strength was waning. First Dutyman Lewis Akklar found solace in those facts, an emotion he felt but could not explain, something similar to what he once had felt toward the paintings of Degas and Renoir. He was sitting in the command chair, his eyes dull; now a smile creased his lips, turned the left corner of his mouth slightly upward. Back and forth, slowly back and forth he continued to swivel the chair. The smile broadened.

His legs were outstretched, and his pants, plastic and sweat-soaked, clung wetly to his legs. His face throbbed with heat; his temperature, he knew, was about 104 degrees. His hair—straight, black—was unkempt, and it occurred to him he needed a shave and shower, some sleep. That, too, he found ironic.

Except for the low humming of the instrument panel and an occasional click as a switch cut in, the bridge around him was empty.

On three sides the silent impersonal instruments winked their multicolored lights off and on in ever-changing patterns. Above him the viewscreen revealed its endless stars: an expanse of coldness and loneliness. He knew Sol was the bright yellow star in the lower right-hand corner of the screen. Somehow he did not give a damn anymore.

So this was how it was to end. Belford, Petrovovich, Captain Doria, Lieutenant Judanya Kahr: all his friends and shipmates—killed by disease. Though capable of firing some of the most sophisticated weaponry ever installed in a spacecraft, the crew had not realized until too late for retaliation that the Sarissi emissaries had smuggled aboard a biological agent. Now only Ak-klaf, a clerk-holographer, remained.

Again he was conscious of the viewscreen. The galaxy seemed adazzle with pinpricks of light. Stars, knots in a salmon net, faces in a classroom: his mind had insisted upon those comparisons ever since he had volunteered for the international draft back home in the Republic of the Aleutians. Yet the loneliness he felt toward those images had preceded that induction by several years. It had been loneliness, he now knew—not wanderlust—which in mid-semester had taken him from those schoolchildren and set him upon the grease-blackened deck of the *Ulak* out of Cold Bay, the nets piled at his feet overlay upon neat overlay, the sea slapping the hull and the gulls cawing overhead as they waited to alight, wings lifting, should the cook dump the garbage. He had loved the ship, the chilling, constant fog; the fishing voyage had neither erased nor intensified his loneliness, but at least had given him reason for it.

He pressed a button in a console next to the chair. The door nearest the central control-panel hummed open. He rose, hands clutching the armrests to steady himself, and stumbled across the room, paused at the door—hands against the jamb. Then wild-eyed and smiling, he staggered down the dimly lit corridor.

"Judanya," he said.

He pressed a wall button, a second door opened. Twenty sheeted figures, most on mattresses on the floor, lay within the small sickbay. Lieutenant Kahr was near the rear wall, an oxygen tent enclosing her, a sheet tucked neatly under her arms; she was the only one of the dead whose face was uncovered.

The oxygen tent crinkled when he folded back the side. He had been unable to force himself to close her eyelids; she gazed toward him unseeing, his form blackly mirrored within the pupils. With the back of his hand he touched her cold, cold cheek. Her lips were thin; her nose, sharply angular, made her face appear narrow. Except for a Mohawk-like mane of black hair, she was bald. The sight of her head slightly startled him; somehow he had thought death would overtake style, and her hair would grow back as long as it was when she had first boarded the ship two years earlier.

He combed the hair with his fingers. "Judanya," he whispered. Light shone upon her forehead. He drew the sheet down over her breasts, her abdomen, down over her legs. He looked upon her as he had many times before: wanting her, not wanting her. Though she had sometimes slept with him, she had never loved him. Lengthy cohabitations between officers and enlisted had been discouraged, and she had refused to jeopardize her career for what she considered the insipid emotions he associated with sexuality; she needed orgasms, she had told him once, merely to relax. On his knees as though before an idol, he folded the sheet, overlay upon neat overlay, at her feet. Her pubic triangle looked at him. He bent forward and pressed his lips to her kneecap, his fingertips squeezing the back of her leg. "Judanya." Tears welled. Back home, he knew, people were dying, laughing, loving. Such was the terror of it all, the terror and the loneliness he had felt within that crowded classroom back in Dutch Harbor: the knowledge that, whatever joy or sorrow he experienced, there existed emotions and happenings beyond his comprehension—people he could neither know nor touch nor even really imagine. Life would go on whether he was alive or not.

Unless, of course, the ship fell into Sarissi hands. Or if the members of an Earth ship contracted the disease and brought it home with them. Then all Earth would know of him, if only to hate. All would die. In a way—perhaps, he told himself, it was the fever—the notion appealed to him. Loneliness had brought him here; here, in death, his loneliness could end.

It was for Judanya—not for himself or humanity—that he would place the charges. For Judanya, who had been all duty and dispassion.

Judanya, who to him was the ship.

He left her, went to the armory for plastic explosives and an armload of looped fusewire, then returned to the control room. He flopped down in the command chair, so exhausted and feverish he could hardly breathe, and sat with his head in his hands. Finally, straightening, he sighed and lifted the vocoder from its cradle in the console. Except for his perfunctory remarks earlier in the day, the log had not been kept for weeks.

"Transcription of First Duty-man Lewis Akklar continuing at . . . " He glanced at his watch. "Sixteen thirty-one hours. I have just come back from sickbay, having said good-by to my shipmates."

He paused and for a few moments just sat staring at the blankness of the forward wall. At last he shook himself from his daydreams and resumed speaking.

"The computers analyzed the disease as some sort of virus. How the Sarissi smuggled the agent on board remains a mystery. We took all normal precautions against such a danger, including standard sterilization and quarantine procedures.

"The plague had an extremely long incubation period. The first outbreak was five weeks ago, nearly two months after we began the return trip to Earth. But once it struck, it spread rapidly, killing within a period of forty-eight hours after the first symptoms—fever and a rawness about the eyes—appeared. The reception delegation, including Captain Doria, died first.

"The med scanners failed to isolate the cause of the disease, or to devise a workable cure or preventative. Both of the ship's doctors died early. Gradually all efforts to combat the disease ceased."

He stopped suddenly and rubbed his left eye. The pain was growing worse. His hand went to the control panel, and the soft blue lighting dimmed to darkness.

"The damned plague is—seems—unbeatable. After half the crew was dead, Acting Captain Kahr took extreme steps to save the rest of us. She cut the stardrive engines and, retro-firing, slowed us to a stop; then she had the bodies jettisoned. We moved the remaining crew from room to room and opened outside hatches and interior doors, hoping the vacuum would kill the disease. Finally Lieutenant Kahr even jettisoned some of those who had shown symptoms. There was—a mutiny. We killed those who fought. But it was no use. It was all for nothing. All that blood. For nothing."

He frowned in the darkness as the memories came flooding back. "People just kept dying," he said. "Maybe the contagion had already spread to everyone during the incubation period. Nearly everyone had had contact with everyone else, at least indirectly, during our return flight. Or maybe it spread through the air ducts, even after we switched to the back-up system. I don't know. I just don't know. All the med facilities this ship has—yet nothing worked."

There was a long silence; Akklar watched the lights blink on and off, listened to the hum of the instruments, smelled the clean, heavy smell of machine. He set the vocoder down carefully on the armrest and looked a final time at the viewscreen filled with stars. "I should close with some . . . some memorable last words," he said, not lifting the vocoder but pushing the on-button with his thumb. His voice sounded hollow. "But I seem to have run out of words." A moment passed, and he looked out into the stars, saw children's faces, a salmon net, saw the ship within that net, not struggling but hanging by its gills like the time the net had torn and the fishing crew had spent all afternoon taking but one six-pound King. "No," he said. "I don't have any final words at all."

Slowly standing, he walked quietly from the room—passing this time through a door to his left. The door closed behind him with the softest of whispers.

He moved along the corridors toward the ship's belly, planting plastic explosives in various niches and linking up the fuse wire. He thought he heard fire doors close behind; he told himself it was only his imagination. The fire-control panel along the baseboard began to hiss. By the time he reached the warhead vault, the steam from the panel had turned to foam and lay like giant puffy snakes around his legs.

The vault door opened—halfway, immediately closed again. The hissing grew louder. The foam was now up to his thighs and climbing rapidly. He tried the door button again. Still no response. He found it ironic that the ship was malfunctioning just at the time the last of the crew was about to die. But the fact that the door would not open did not matter anyway. The chain reaction from the plastic explosives would trigger the warheads whether or not the door was open. He mashed a handful of explosive into the corner of the door, jabbed in both the relay and detonator fuses, and stepped back, sloshing through the foam. He paused, trying unsuccessfully to remember Judanya's face.

The foam was to his chest.

He squeezed the detonator.

A dull, faraway boom echoed through the ship, and back on the bridge all the multi-colored lights on the instrument panels went black. On the main viewscreen, the stars quite suddenly winked out.

• • •

Finally she has rid herself of the last of them—the humans, the diseased vermin. And she has saved herself from becoming a crippled hulk. The fire doors buffered the explosion; the flooding of herself short-circuited all but one of the wads of explosive.

Now her intelligence moves through herself—checking, re-checking. Relays click. Circuits buzz. Signals indicate a jagged hole in hull Subsection 37c. Instantly she activates her self-repair units. Liquid sealant oozes and hardens to plug minor holes. Duralloy plates are rigged and methodically secured to close the major one. Her secondary monitor system then surveys damage to all systems and files extensive reports with her central computer banks. Again she sets the self-repair units to humming, and one by one the damaged areas are repaired or replaced. Damage to the Severs-stardrive engines has been extensive; this too is corrected.

Now she checks her position. Alarms sound. She is off course and hanging dead in space.

Reports and corrections flow through herself in a steady stream. Time passes. Scanners and medi-probes scrutinize those bodies still aboard ship. All are lifeless. The plan has been successful. All crew members having been exposed to the virus, all were expendable; she could not allow possible contagion to occur by bringing them home. To insure that, she sucked the virus spores into her air ducts, transferred them each time Kahr ordered an airlock opened, infected the food and water supply whenever possible.

A low rumbling begins, climbs to a piercing shriek as she starts her great Severs-stardrive engines. On the bridge the lights dance dizzily as she calculates the course to Earth and feeds corrections to Navigation. Rockets fire.

She moves—invulnerable, disease-free. Mother and mistress to the shuttlecraft which service her, *Alecto* returns to her old orbit.

SWANWATCH

YOON HA LEE

Yoon Ha Lee's work has appeared in *The Magazine of Fantasy & Science Fiction, Clarkesworld, Fantasy Magazine, Ideomancer, Lady Churchill's Rosebud Wristlet, Farrago's Wainscot,* and *Sybil's Garage.* She's also appeared in the anthologies T*wenty Epics, Year's Best Fantasy #6,* and *Science Fiction: The Best of 2002.* A new story is forthcoming in *Electric Velocipede.*

Lee says that she plays several instruments and composes as a hobby. Learning to use a piece of music software called Logic Studio gave her some ideas about how musicians in the future might compose, which helped in the development of this story. "Swanwatch" is about the intersection of life and music and black holes. In the story, Lee explores the notion of an interstellar society that holds suicide art in high esteem. And what could be more perfect for that purpose than a black hole?

SWANWATCH

Officially, the five exiles on the station were the Initiates of the Fermata. Unofficially, the Concert of Worlds called them the swanwatch.

The older exiles called themselves Dragon and Phoenix, Tiger and Tortoise, according to tradition based in an ancient civilization's legends. The newest and youngest exile went by Swan. She was not a swan in the way of fairy tales. If so, she would have had a history sung across the galaxy's billions of stars, of rapturous beauty or resolute virtue. She would have woven the hearts of dead stars into armor for the Concert's soldiers and hushed novae to sleep so ships could safely pass. However, she was, as befitted the name they gave her, a musician.

Swan had been exiled to the station because she had offended the captain of a guestship from the scintillant core. In a moment of confusion, she had addressed him in the wrong language for the occasion. Through the convolutions of Concert politics, she wound up in the swanwatch.

The captain sent her a single expensive message across the vast space now separating them. It was because of the message that Swan first went to Dragon. Dragon was not the oldest and wisest of the swanwatch; that honor belonged to Tortoise. But Dragon loved oddments of knowledge, and he could read the calligraphy in which the captain had written his message.

"You have good taste in enemies," Dragon commented, as though Swan had singled out the captain. Dragon was a lanky man with skin lighter than Swan's, and he was always pacing, or whittling appallingly rare scraps of wood, or tapping earworm-rhythms upon his knee.

Swan bowed her head. *I'd rather not be here, and be back with my family.* She didn't say so out loud, though. That would have implied a disregard for Dragon's company, and she was already fond of Dragon. "Can you read it?" she asked.

"Of course I can read it, although it would help if you held the message right side up."

Swan wasn't illiterate, but there were many languages in the Concert of Worlds. "This way?" Swan asked, rotating the sheet.

Dragon nodded.

"What does it say?"

Dragon's foot tapped. "It says: 'I look forward to hearing your masterpiece honoring the swanships.' Should I read all his titles, too?" Dragon's ironic tone made his opinion of the captain's pretensions quite clear. "They take up the rest of the page."

Swan had paled. "No, thank you," she said. The swanwatch's official purpose was as a retreat for artists. Its inhabitants could only leave upon presenting an acceptable masterwork to the judges who visited every decade. In practice, those exiled here lacked the requisite skill. The captain's message clearly mocked her.

Like many privileged children, Swan had had lessons in the high arts: music and calligraphy, fencing and poetry. She could set a fragment of text to a melody, if given the proper mode, and play the essential three instruments: the zither, the flute, and the keyboard. But she had never pursued composing any further than that, expecting a life as a patron of the arts rather than an artist herself.

Dragon said, kindly, "It's another way of telling you your task is impossible."

Swan wondered if Dragon was a composer, but would not be so uncouth as to ask. "Thank you for reading me the letter," she said.

"It was my pleasure," Dragon said. It was obvious to him that Swan was determined to leave the Initiates and return home, however difficult the task and however much home might have changed in the interim. Kind for a second time, he did not disillusion her about her chances.

• • •

Tiger was a tall woman with deceptively sweet eyes and a rapacious smile. When Swan first met her, she was afraid that Tiger would gobble her up in some manner peculiar to the Initiates. But Tiger said only, "How are you settling in?"

Swan had a few reminders of her home, things she had been allowed to bring in physical form: a jewelry box inlaid with abalone, inherited from her deceased mother; a silver flute her best friend had given her. The official who had processed Swan's transfer to the station had reminded her to choose carefully, and had said she could bring a lot more in scanned form, to be replicated at the station. But where homesickness was concerned, she wanted the real item, not a copy.

Swan thought about it, then said, "I'll adjust."

Tiger said, "We all do." She stretched, joints creaking. "You've seen the duty roster, I trust. There's a swanship coming in very soon. Shall I show you what to do?"

Although Swan could have trusted the manuals, she knew she would be sharing swanwatch with Tiger and the others for a long time. If Tiger was feeling generous enough to explain the procedures to her, best not to offend Tiger by declining.

Together, Tiger and Swan walked the long halls of their prison to the monitoring room. "You can do this from anywhere on the station," Tiger said. "The computers log everything, and it only requires a moment's attention for you to pray in honor of the swanship's valor, if you believe in that at all. Once you've been here a while, you'll welcome the ritual and the illusion that you matter. They do value ritual where you come from, don't they?"

"Yes," Swan said.

"How much of the fermata did you see on your way here?"

"They wouldn't let me look." In fact, Swan had been sedated for her arrival. New Initiates sometimes attempted escape. "They said I'd have plenty of time to stare at the grave-of-ships as an Initiate."

"Quite right," Tiger said, a little bitterly.

Doors upon doors irised before them until at last they reached the monitoring room. To Swan's surprise, it was a vast hall, lined with subtly glowing banks of controls and projective screens. Tiger grasped Swan's shoulder firmly and steered her to the center of the hall. "The grave-of-ships," Tiger said, adding an honorific to the phrase. "Look!"

Swan looked. All around them were the projected images of swanships in the first blush of redshift, those who had cast themselves into the fermata and left their inexorably dimming shadows: the Concert of Worlds' highest form of suicide art. In any number of religions, the swanships formed a great fleet to battle the silence at the end of time. Some societies in the

Concert sent their condemned in swanships to redeem themselves, while others sent their most honored generals.

"The ship doesn't need our assistance, does it?" Swan said.

"What, in plunging into a black hole?" Tiger said dryly. "Not usually, no."

Tiger muttered a command, and all the images flickered away save that of the incoming swanship and its escort of three. The escort peeled away; the swanship flew straight toward the fermata's hidden heart, indicated in the displays by a pulsing point.

Swan did not know how long she watched that fatal trajectory.

Tiger tapped Swan on the shoulder. "Breathe, cygnet. It's not coming back. You'll just see the ship go more and more slowly as it approaches the event horizon forever, and you don't want to pass out."

"How many people were on the ship?" Swan said.

"You want statistics?" Tiger said approvingly. Tiger, Swan would learn, was a great believer in morbid details. She showed Swan how to look up the basic things one might wish to know about a swanship: its crew and shipyard of origin, its registry, the weapons it brought to the fight at the end of time.

"I had thought it would be more spectacular," Swan said, gazing back at the swanship's frozen image. "Even if I knew about the—the physics involved."

"What were you expecting, cygnet? False-color explosions and a crescendo in the music of your mind?" Tiger saw Swan bite her lip. "It wasn't hard to guess how you'd try to escape, little musician. It's too bad you can't ask Tortoise to write music for your freedom, but all Tortoise does anymore is sleep."

"I wouldn't ask that of Tortoise," Swan said. "But I have to understand the swanships if I am to compose for them."

"Poor cygnet," Tiger said. "You'll learn to set hope aside soon enough."

Tiger kissed Swan on the side of the mouth, not at all benevolently, then walked away.

In the silence, Swan listened to the ringing in her ears, and shivered.

• • •

After her nineteenth swanship, Swan hunted through the station's libraries—updated each time a swanship and its entourage came through—for material on composition. She read interactive treatises on music theory for six hours, skipping lunch and dinner: modes and keys, time signatures and rhythms, tones and textures, hierarchies of structure. The result was a vile headache. The Concert of Worlds was as rich in musical forms as it was in languages, and despite Swan's efforts to be discriminating, she ran into contradictory traditions.

Swan returned to the three instruments she knew, zither, flute, and keyboard. The station replicated the first and third for her according to her specifications. Drawing upon the classics she had memorized in childhood and the libraries' collection of poetry, she practiced setting texts to music. Sometimes she did this in the station's rock garden. The impracticality of the place delighted her absurdly.

Dragon often came to listen, offering neither encouragement nor criticism. Rather than applauding, he left her the figurines he whittled. Swan decorated her room with them.

"Are you an artist?" she asked Dragon once after botching her warm-up scales on the flute.

"No," Dragon said. "I could play a chord or two on your keyboard, but that's all."

Swan turned her hand palm-up and stepped away from the keyboard, offering. Smiling, he declined, and she did not press him.

After fifty-seven swanships—months as the station reckoned time—Swan asked the others if she could move her keyboard into the observation room. Dragon not only agreed, but offered to help her move it, knowing that Swan felt uneasy around the station's mechanical servitors. Phoenix said she supposed there was no harm in it. Tiger laughed and said, "Anything for you, cygnet." Swan was horribly afraid that Tiger meant it. Tortoise didn't respond, which the others assured her was a yes.

Swan wrote fragments of poetry for each ship thereafter, and set them to music. The poetry itself was frequently wretched—Swan was honest enough with herself to admit this—but she had some hope for the music. She was briefly encouraged by her attempts at orchestration: bright, brassy fanfares for ships that had served in battles; shimmering chords for ships built with beauty rather than speed in mind; the menacing clatter of drums for those rare ships that defied their fate and swung around to attack the station.

Tiger deigned to listen to one of Swan's fragments, despite her ordinary impatience for musical endeavors. "Orchestrate a battle; orchestrate a piece of music. This isn't the only language that uses the same verb for both. Your battle, cygnet, is a hundred skirmishes and no master plan. If you plan to do this for every swanship that is and has ever been, you'll die of old age before you're finished."

"I'm no general," Swan said, "but I have a battle to fight and music to write."

"I can't decide whether your persistence is tiresome or admirable," Tiger said. But she was smiling, and although she didn't seem to realize it, her foot was still tapping to the beat.

Swan had already returned to the keyboard, sketching a theme around the caesuras of an ancient hymn. Lost in visions of ships stretched beyond recognition, she did not hear Tiger leave.

• • •

Phoenix had held herself aloof from Swan after their initial introduction. This was not a matter of personal ill-will, as Dragon told Swan. Phoenix didn't hold anyone but herself in high regard, and she locked herself away in pursuit of her own art, painting.

Perhaps Swan's diligence impressed Phoenix at last. It was hard to say. Tiger paid as little attention to Phoenix as possible, and urged Swan to do likewise. "She's forever painting nebulae and alien landscapes, then burning the results," Tiger said contemptuously. "What's the point, then?"

Dragon said that everyone was entitled to a few quirks. Tiger remarked that anyone would say that of a former lover. At that point, Swan excused herself from the conversation.

"I have heard that you started the first movement of your symphony. I should like to hear it," Phoenix said to Swan through the station's most impersonal messaging system.

So Swan invited her to the observation room at an hour when no swanships were scheduled to arrive. She played the flute—her best instrument—to the station's recordings of the other parts; the libraries had included numerous sequencers.

Phoenix applauded when Swan had finished. Her expression was reluctantly respectful. Gravely, she said, "This captain of yours—"

He's not mine, Swan thought, *although perhaps I am his.*

"—do you know anything of his musical preferences?"

Swan shook her head. "I tried to find out," she said. After all, if the captain had possessed enough influence to send her to the swanwatch, he might also be able to influence the selection of judges. "He commissioned a synesthetic opera once, which I have no recording of. Beyond that, who knows how he interprets the grave-of-ships? And if I am to do each swanship justice, shouldn't I draw upon the musical traditions of their cultures? Some of them contradict each other. How am I to deal with this in a single finite symphony?"

Phoenix lifted an eyebrow, and Swan felt ashamed of her outburst. "Do you know why we're here, Swan?" she asked. She was not referring to their official mission of contemplating the fermata to further their art.

"It seemed impolite to ask," Swan said.

"Tiger is a war criminal," Phoenix said. "Tortoise is a scholar who resigned and came here to protest the policies of some government that has since been wiped out of time. It might even have done some good, in the strand of society where he was famous. I, of course, am here as unjustly as you are." She did not elaborate.

"And Dragon?"

Phoenix smiled thinly. "You should ask Dragon yourself. It might make you think twice about your symphony."

• • •

Swan wouldn't have realized anything was wrong if Tiger hadn't sent her a message while she was in the middle of working on her second movement. The idea had come to her in the middle of her sleep shift, and she was kneeling at the zither, adjusting the bridges.

"Urgent message from Tiger," the station informed her.

"Go ahead," Swan said absently, trying to decide what mode to tune to.

Tiger's voice said, "Hello, cygnet. It's Tortoise's watch, but he seems to be asleep as usual, and you might be interested in going to the observation room."

Tiger's tone was lazy, but she had flagged the message as urgent. What was going on?

"Station," Swan said, "who's in the observation room now?"

"No one," it said.

"Is there a swanship scheduled to arrive soon?"

"There is an unscheduled swanship right now."

Swan rose and ran to the observation room.

Tiger had been correct about the importance of ritual. No matter how smoothly a ship descended into the fermata, Swan always checked the ship's status. Swanships did occasionally arrive off-schedule, but she wondered why Tiger had sounded concerned.

So she looked at the ship, which was tiny, with an underpowered sublight drive, and its crew, a single person: Gazhien of the *Circle of Swords.*

She knew that name, although ages had passed since she had used it. It was Dragon.

She asked the station what the *Circle of Swords* was. It had been a swanship nearly a century ago, and all but one member of the crew had passed into the fermata on it.

"Swan to Dragon," she said to the tiny ship, which was one of the station's shuttles. "Swan to Dragon. Please come back!"

After a heartstopping moment, Dragon replied, "Ah, Swan."

Swan could have said, *What do you think you're doing?*, but they both knew that. Instead, she asked, "Why now, and not tomorrow, or the day before? Why this day of all days, after a century of waiting?"

"You are as tactful as ever," Dragon said, "even about the matter of my cowardice."

"*Please*, Dragon."

Dragon's voice was peculiarly meditative. "Your symphony reminds me of my duty, Swan. I came here a long time ago on the *Circle of Swords.* It was one of the proudest warships of—well, the nation has since passed into anarchy. I was the only soldier too afraid of my fate to swear the sacred oath to *sing always against the coming silence.* As punishment, they left me here to contemplate my failure, forever separated from my comrades."

"Dragon," Swan said, "they're long gone now. What good will it do them, at this end of time, for you to die?"

"The Concert teaches that the fermata is our greatest form of immortality—"

"Dead is dead," Swan said. "At this end of time, what is the hurry?"

The door whisked open. Swan looked away from the ship's image and met Tiger's curious eyes.

"Damn, 'Zhien," Tiger said respectfully. "So you found the courage after all."

"That's not it," Swan said. "The symphony wasn't supposed to be about the glory of death."

Loftily, Tiger said, "Oh, *I'd* never perform suicide art. There's nothing pretty about death. You learn that in battle."

After a silence, Dragon said, "What did you intend, then, Swan?"

The question brought her up short. She had been so absorbed in attempting to convey the swanships' grandeur that she had forgotten that real people passed into the fermata to send their souls to the end of time. "I'll change my music," she said. "I'll delete it all if I have to."

"Please don't," Dragon said. "I would miss it greatly." A faint swelling of melody: his ship was playing back one of her first, stumbling efforts.

"You'll miss it forever if you keep going."

"A bargain, then," Dragon said. "I was never an artist, only a soldier, but a hundred years here have taught me the value of art. Don't destroy your music, and I'll come back."

Swan's eyes prickled. "All right."

Tiger and Swan watched as Dragon's ship decelerated, then reversed its course, returning to the station.

"You've sacrificed your freedom to bring him back, you know," Tiger said. "If you finish your symphony now, it will lack conviction. Anyone with half an ear will be able to tell."

"I would rather have Dragon's life than write a masterpiece," Swan said.

"You're a fool, cygnet."

Only then did Swan realize that, in her alarm over the situation, she had completely forgotten the theme she had meant to record.

• • •

Dragon helped Swan move the keyboard out of the observation room and into the rock garden. "I'm glad you're not giving up your music," he remarked.

She looked at him, really looked at him, thinking of how she had almost lost a friend. “I’m not writing the symphony,” she said.

He blinked.

“I’m still writing music,” Swan assured him. “Just not the captain’s symphony. Because you were right: it’s impossible. At least, what I envisioned is impossible. If I dwell upon the impossible, I achieve nothing. But if I do what I can, where I can—I might get somewhere.”

She wasn’t referring to freedom from the swanwatch.

Dragon nodded. “I think I see. And Swan—” He hesitated. “Thank you.”

“It’s been a long day,” she said. “You should rest.”

“Like Tortoise?” He chuckled. “Perhaps I will.” He ran one hand along the keyboard in a flurry of notes. Then he sat on one of the garden’s benches and closed his eyes, humming idly.

Swan studied Dragon’s calm face. Then she stood at the keyboard and played several tentative notes, a song for Dragon and Phoenix and Tiger. A song for the living.

SPIREY AND THE QUEEN

ALASTAIR REYNOLDS

Alastair Reynolds is the author of eight novels and about thirty short stories. His fiction frequently shares the setting of his novel *Revelation Space.* His stories have appeared mostly in the British magazine *Interzone,* but also in several anthologies, such as *The New Space Opera, Eclipse Two, One Million A. D.,* and *Constellations.* He is a winner of the British Science Fiction Award, and his work has often been reprinted in the various best-of-the-year annuals.

In his collection, *Zima Blue and Other Stories,* Reynolds says that "Spirey and the Queen" was a "pig" to write, and that it was a relief to get it out of his system. "The motor of plot only kicked in when I started looking at the story in thriller terms: spies, defectors, that kind of thing," he said, and added that he always had the vague intention of returning to the milieu someday, if only to find out what happens after the last line of the story.

SPIREY AND THE QUEEN

Space war is godawful *slow.*

Mouser's long-range sensors had sniffed the bogey two days ago, but it had taken all that time just to creep within kill-range. I figured it had to be another dud. With ordnance, fuel, and morale all low, we were ready to slink back to Tiger's Eye anyway; let one of the other thickships pick up the sweep in this sector.

So—still groggy after frogsleep—I wasn't exactly wetting myself with excitement, not even when *Mouser* started spiking the thick with combat-readiness psychogens. Even when we went to Attack-Con-One, all I did was pause the neurodisney I was tripping (*Hellcats of Solar War Three,* since you asked), slough my hammock, and swim languidly up to the bridge.

"Junk," I said, looking over Yarrow's shoulder at the readout. "War debris or another of those piss-poor chondrites. Betcha."

"Sorry, kid. Everything checks out."

"Hostiles?"

"Nope. Positive on the exhaust; dead ringer for the stolen ship." She traced a webbed hand across the swathe of decorations that already curled around her neck. "Want your stripes now or when we get back?"

"You actually think this'll net us a pair of tigers?"

"Damn right it will."

I nodded, and thought: *She isn't necessarily wrong.* No defector, no stolen military secrets reaching the Royalists. Ought to be worth a medal, maybe even a promotion.

So why did I feel something wasn't right?

"All right," I said, hoping to drown qualms in routine. "How soon?"

"Missiles are already away, but she's five light-minutes from us, so the quacks won't reach her for six hours. Longer if she makes a run for cover."

"Run for cover? That's a joke."

"Yeah, hilarious." Yarrow swelled one of the holographic displays until it hovered between us.

It was a map of the Swirl, tinted to show zones controlled by us or the Royalists. An enormous, slowly rotating disk of primordial material, 800 AU edge to edge; wide enough that light took more than four days to traverse it.

Most of the action was near the middle, in the light-hour of space around the central star Fomalhaut. Immediately around the sun was a material-free void that we called the Inner Clearing Zone, but beyond that began the Swirl proper: metal-rich lanes of dust condensing slowly into rocky planets. Both sides wanted absolute control of those planet-forming Feeding Zones—prime real estate for the day when one side beat the other and could recommence mining operations—so that was where our vast armies of wasps mainly slugged things out. We humans—Royalist and Standardist both—kept much further out, where the Swirl thinned to metal-depleted icy rubble. Even hunting the defector hadn't taken us within ten light-hours of the Feeding Zones, and we'd become used to having a lot of empty space to ourselves. Apart from the defector, there shouldn't have been anything else out here to offer cover.

But there was. Big, too, not much more than a half light-minute from the rat.

"Practically pissing distance," Yarrow observed.

"Too close for coincidence. What is it?"

"Splinter. Icy planetesimal, you want to get technical."

"Not this early in the day." But I remembered how one of our tutors back at the academy put it: *Splinters are icy slag, spat out of the Swirl. In a few hundred thousand years there'll be a baby solar system around Fomalhaut, but there'll also be shitloads of junk surrounding it, leftovers on million-year orbits.*

"Worthless to us," Yarrow said, scratching at the ribbon of black hair that ran all the way from her brow to fluke. "But evidently not too ratty."

"What if the Royalists left supplies on the splinter? She could be aiming to refuel before the final hop to their side of the Swirl."

Yarrow gave me her best withering look.

"Yeah, okay," I said. "Not my smartest ever suggestion."

Yarrow nodded sagely. "Ours is not to question, Spirey. Ours is to fire and forget."

• • •

Six hours after the quackheads had been launched from *Mouser,* Yarrow floated in the bridge, fluked tail coiled beneath her. She resembled an inverted question mark, and if I'd been superstitious I'd have said that wasn't necessarily the best of omens.

"You kill me," she said.

An older pilot called Quillin had been the first to go *siren*—first to swap legs for tail. Yarrow followed a year later. Admittedly it made sense, an adaptation to the fluid-filled environment of a high-gee thickship. And I accepted the cardiovascular modifications that enabled us to breathe thick, as well as the biomodified skin, which let us tolerate cold and vacuum far longer than any unmodified human. Not to mention the billions of molecule-sized demons that coursed through our bodies, or the combat-specific psycho-modifications. But swapping your legs for a tail touched off too many queasy resonances in me. Had to admire her nerve, though.

"What?" I said.

"That neurodisney shit. Isn't a real space war good enough for you?"

"Yeah, except I don't think this is it. When was the last time one of us actually looked a Royalist in the eye?"

She shrugged. "Something like four hundred years."

"Point made. At least in *Solar War Three* you get some blood. See, it's all set on planetary surfaces—Titan, Europa, all those moons they've got back in Sol system. Trench warfare, hand-to-hand stuff. You know what adrenalin is, Yarrow?"

"Managed without it until now. And there's another thing: don't know much about Greater Earth history, but there was never a Solar War Three."

"It's conjectural," I said. "And in any case it almost happened; they almost went to the brink."

"Almost?"

"It's set in a different timeline."

She grinned, shaking her head. "I'm telling you, you kill me."

"She made a move yet?" I asked.

"What?"

"The defector."

"Oh, we're back in reality now?" Yarrow laughed. "Sorry, this is going to be slightly less exciting than *Solar War Three*."

"Inconsiderate," I said. "Think the bitch would give us a run for our money." And as I spoke the weapons readout began to pulse faster and faster, like the cardiogram of a fluttering heart. "How long now?"

"One minute, give or take a few seconds."

"Want a little bet?"

Yarrow grinned, sallow in the red alert lighting. "As if I'd say no, Spirey."

So we hammered out a wager; Yarrow betting fifty tiger-tokens the rat would attempt some last-minute evasion. "Won't do her a blind bit of good," she said. "But that won't stop her. It's human nature."

Me, I suspected our target was either dead or asleep.

"Bit of an empty ritual, isn't it."

"What?"

"I mean, the attack happened the best part of five minutes ago, realtime. The rat's already dead, and nothing we can do can influence that outcome."

Yarrow bit on a nicotine stick. "Don't get all philosophical on me, Spirey."

"Wouldn't dream of it. How long?"

"Five seconds. Four . . . "

She was somewhere between three and four when it happened. I remember thinking that there was something disdainful about the rat's actions: she had deliberately waited until the last possible moment, and had dispensed with our threat with the least effort possible.

That was how it felt, anyway.

Nine of the quackheads detonated prematurely, far short of kill-range. For a moment the tenth remained, zeroing in on the defector—but instead it failed to detonate, until it was just beyond range.

For long moments there was silence while we absorbed what had happened. Yarrow broke it, eventually.

"Guess I just made myself some money," she said.

• • •

Colonel Wendigo's hologram delegate appeared, momentarily frozen before shivering to life. With her too-clear, too-young eyes she fixed first Yarrow and then me.

"Intelligence was mistaken," she said. "Seems the defector doctored records to conceal the theft of those countermeasures. But you harmed her anyway?"

"Just," said Yarrow. "Her quackdrive's spewing out exotics like Spirey after a bad binge. No hull damage, but . . . "

"Assessment?"

"Making a run for the splinter."

Wendigo nodded. "And then?"

"She'll set down and make repairs." Yarrow paused, added: "Radar says there's metal on the surface. Must've been a wasp battle there, before the splinter got lobbed out of the Swirl."

The delegate nodded in my direction. "Concur, Spirey?"

"Yes sir," I said, trying to suppress the nervousness I always felt around Wendigo, even though almost all my dealings with her had been via simulations like this. Yarrow was happy to edit the conversation afterward, inserting the correct honorifics before transmitting the result back to Tiger's Eye—but I could never free myself of the suspicion that Wendigo would somehow unravel the unedited version, with all its implicit insubordination. Not that any of us didn't inwardly accord Wendigo all the respect she was due. She'd nearly died in the Royalist strike against Tiger's Eye fifteen years ago—the one in which my mother was killed. Actual attacks against our two mutually opposed comet bases were rare, not happening much more than every other generation—more gestures of spite than anything else. But this had been an especially bloody one, killing an eighth of our number and opening city-sized portions of our base to vacuum. Wendigo was caught in the thick of the kinetic attack.

Now she was chimeric, lashed together by cybernetics. Not much of this showed externally—except that the healed parts of her were too flawless, more porcelain than flesh. Wendigo had not allowed the surgeons to regrow her arms. Story was she lost them trying to pull one of the injured through an open airlock, back into the pressurized zone. She'd almost made it, fighting against the gale of escaping air. Then some no-brainer hit the emergency door control, and when the lock shut it took Wendigo's arms off at the shoulder, along with the head of the person she was saving. She wore prosthetics now, gauntleted in chrome.

"She'll get there a day ahead of us," I said. "Even if we pull twenty gees."

"And probably gone to ground by the time you get there, too."

"Should we try a live capture?"

Yarrow backed me up with a nod. "It's not exactly been possible before."

The delegate bided her time before answering. "Admire your dedication," she said, after a suitably convincing pause. "But you'd only be postponing a death sentence. Kinder to kill her now, don't you think?"

• • •

Mouser entered kill-range nineteen hours later, a wide pseudo-orbit three thousand klicks out. The splinter—seventeen by twelve klicks across—was far too small to be seen as anything other than a twinkling speck, like a grain of sugar at arm's length. But everything we wanted to know was clear: topology, gravimetrics, and the site of the downed ship. That wasn't hard. Quite apart from the fact that it hadn't buried itself completely, it was hot as hell.

"Doesn't look like the kind of touchdown you walk away from," Yarrow said.

"Think they ejected?"

"No way." Yarrow sketched a finger through a holographic enlargement of the ship, roughly cone-shaped, vaguely streamlined just like our own thickship, to punch through the Swirl's thickest gas belts. "Clock those dorsal hatches. Evac pods still in place."

She was right. The pods could have flung them clear before the crash, but evidently they hadn't had time to bail out. The ensuing impact—even cushioned by the ship's manifold of thick—probably hadn't been survivable.

But there was no point taking chances.

Quackheads would have finished the job, but we'd used up our stock. *Mouser* carried a particle beam battery, but we'd have to move uncomfortably close to the splinter before using it. What remained were the molemines, and they should have been perfectly adequate. We dropped fifteen of them, embedded in a cloud of two hundred identical decoys. Three of the fifteen were designated to dust the wreck, while the remaining twelve would bury deeper into the splinter and attempt to shatter it completely.

That at least was the idea.

It all happened very quickly, not in the dreamy slow-motion of a neurodisney. One instant the molemines were descending toward the splinter, and then the next instant they weren't there. Spacing the two instants had been an almost subliminally brief flash.

"Starting to get sick of this," Yarrow said.

Mouser digested what had happened. Nothing had emanated from the wreck. Instead, there'd been a single pulse of energy seemingly from the entire volume of space around the splinter. Particle weapons, *Mouser* diagnosed. Probably single-use drones, each tinier than a pebble but numbering hundreds or even thousands. The defector must have sown them on her approach.

But she hadn't touched us.

"It was a warning," I said. "Telling us to back off."

"I don't think so."

"What?"

"I think the warning's on its way."

I stared at her blankly for a moment, before registering what she had already seen: arcing from the splinter was something too fast to stop, something against which our minimally armored thickship had no defense, not even the option of flight.

Yarrow started to mouth some exotic profanity she'd reserved for precisely this moment. There was an eardrum-punishing bang and *Mouser* shuddered—but we weren't suddenly chewing vacuum.

And that was very bad news indeed.

Antiship missiles come in two main flavors: quackheads and sporeheads. You know which immediately after the weapon has hit. If you're still thinking—if you still exist—chances are it's a sporehead. And at that point your problems are just beginning.

Invasive demon attack, *Mouser* shrieked. Breather manifold compromised . . . which meant something uninvited was in the thick. That was the point of a sporehead: to deliver hostile demons into an enemy ship.

"Mm," Yarrow said. "I think it might be time to suit up."

Except our suits were a good minute's swim away, into the bowels of *Mouser,* through twisty ducts that might skirt the infection site. Having no choice, we swam anyway, Yarrow insisting I take the lead even though she was a quicker swimmer. And somewhere—it's impossible to know exactly where—demons reached us, seeping invisibly into our bodies via the thick. I couldn't pinpoint the moment; it wasn't as if there was a jagged transition between lucidity and demon-manipulated irrationality. Yarrow and I were terrified enough as it was. All I know is it began with a mild agoraphilia: an urge to escape *Mouser*'s flooded confines. Gradually it phased into claustrophobia, and then became fully fledged panic, making *Mouser* seem as malevolent as a haunted house.

Yarrow ignored her suit, clawing the hull until her fingers spooled blood.

"Fight it," I said. "It's just demons triggering our fear centers, trying to drive us out!"

Of course, knowing so didn't help.

Somehow I stayed still long enough for my suit to slither on. Once sealed, I purged the tainted thick with the suit's own supply—but I knew it wasn't going to help much. The phobia already showed that hostile demons had reached my brain, and now it was even draping itself in a flimsy logic. Beyond the ship we'd be able to think rationally. It would only take a few minutes for the thick's own demons to neutralize the invader—and then we'd be able to reboard. Complete delusion, of course.

But that was the point.

• • •

When something like coherent thought returned I was outside.

Nothing but me and the splinter.

The urge to escape was only a background anxiety, a flock of stomach butterflies urging me against returning. Was that demon-manipulated fear or pure common sense? I couldn't tell—but what I knew was that the splinter seemed to be beckoning me forward, and I didn't feel like resisting. Sensible, surely; we'd exhausted all conventional channels of attack against the defector, and now all that remained was to confront her on the territory she'd staked as her own.

But where was Yarrow?

Suit's alarm chimed. Maybe demons were still subjugating my emotions, because I didn't react with my normal speed. I just blinked, licked my lips, and stifled a yawn.

"Yeah, what?"

Suit informed me: something massing slightly less than me, two klicks closer to the splinter, on a slightly different orbit. I knew it was Yarrow; also that something was wrong. She was drifting. In my blackout I'd undoubtedly programmed suit to take me down, but Yarrow appeared not to have done anything except bail out.

I jetted closer. And then saw why she hadn't programmed her suit. Would have been tricky. She wasn't wearing one.

• • •

I hit ice an hour later.

Cradling Yarrow—she wasn't much of a burden in the splinter's weak gravity—I took stock. I wasn't ready to mourn her, not just yet. If I could quickly get her to the medical suite aboard the defector's ship there was a good chance of revival. But where the hell was the wreck?

Squandering its last reserves of fuel, suit had deposited us in a clearing among the graveyard of ruined wasps. Half-submerged in ice, they looked like scorched scrap-iron sculptures, phantoms from an entomologist's worst nightmare. So there'd been a battle here, back when the splinter was just another drifting lump of ice. Even if the thing was seamed with silicates or organics, it would not have had any commercial potential to either side. But it might still have had strategic value, and that was why the wasps had gone to war on its surface. Trouble was—as we'd known before the attack—the corpses covered the entire surface, so there was no guessing where we'd come down. The wrecked ship might be just over the nearest hillock—or another ten kilometers in any direction.

I felt the ground rumble under me. Hunting for the source of the vibration, I saw a quill of vapor reach into the sky, no more than a klick away. It was a geyser of superheated ice.

I dropped Yarrow and hit dirt, suit limiting motion so that I didn't bounce. Looking back, I expected to see a dimple in the permafrost, where some rogue had impacted.

Instead, the geyser was still present. Worse, it was coming steadily closer, etching a neat trench. A beam weapon was making that plume, I realized—like one of the party batteries aboard ship. Then I wised up.

That was *Mouser.* The demons had worked their way into its command infrastructure, reprogramming it to turn against us. Now *Mouser* worked for the defector.

I slung Yarrow over one shoulder and loped away from the boiling impact point. Fast as the geyser moved, its path was predictable. If I made enough lateral distance the death-line would sear past—

Except the damn thing turned to follow me.

Now a second flanked it, shepherding me through the thickest zone of wasp corpses. Did they have some significance for the defector? Maybe so, but I couldn't see it. The corpses were a rough mix of machines from both sides: Royalist wasps marked with yellow shell symbols, ours with grinning tiger-heads. Generation thirty-five units, if I remembered Mil-Hist, when both sides toyed with pulse-hardened optical thinkware. In the seventy-odd subsequent generations there'd been numerous further jumps: ur-quantum logics, full-spectrum reflective wasp armor, chameleoflage, quackdrive powerplants, and every weapon system the human mind could devise. We'd tried to encourage the wasps to make these innovations for themselves, but they never managed to evolve beyond strictly linear extrapolation. Which was good, or else we human observers would have been out of a job.

Not that it really mattered now.

A third geyser had erupted behind me, and a fourth ahead, boxing me in. Slowly, the four points of fire began to converge. I stopped, but kept holding Yarrow. I listened to my own breathing, harsh above the basso tremor of the drumming ground.

Then steel gripped my shoulder.

• • •

She said we'd be safer underground. Also that she had friends below who might be able to do something for Yarrow.

"If you weren't defecting," I began, as we entered a roughly hewn tunnel into the splinter's crust, "what the hell was it?"

"Trying to get home. Least that was the idea, until we realized Tiger's Eye didn't want us back." Wendigo knuckled the ice with one of her steel fists, her suit cut away to expose her prosthetics. "Which is when we decided to head here."

"You almost made it," I said. Then added: "Where were you trying to get home from?"

"Isn't it obvious?"

"Then you did defect."

"We were trying to make contact with the Royalists. Trying to make peace." In the increasingly dim light I saw her shrug. "It was a long shot, conducted in secrecy. When the mission went wrong, it was easy for Tiger's Eye to say we'd been defecting."

"Bullshit."

"I wish."

"But you sent us."

"Not in person."

"But your delegate—"

"Is just software. It could be made to say anything my enemies chose. Even to order my own execution as a traitor."

We paused to switch on our suit lamps. "Maybe you'd better tell me everything."

"Gladly," Wendigo said. "But if this hasn't been a good day so far, I'm afraid it's about to go downhill."

• • •

There had been a clique of high-ranking officers who believed that the Swirl war was intrinsically unwinnable. Privy to information not released to the populace, and able to see through Tiger's Eye's own carefully filtered internal propaganda, they realized that negotiation—contact—was the only way out.

"Of course, not everyone agreed. Some of my adversaries wanted us dead before we even reached the enemy." Wendigo sighed. "Too much in love with the war's stability—and who can blame them? Life for the average citizen in Tiger's Eye isn't that bad. We're given a clear goal to fight for, and the likelihood of any one of us dying in a Royalist attack is small enough to ignore. The idea that all of that might be about to end after four hundred years, that we all might have to rethink our roles . . . well, it didn't go down too well."

"About as welcome as a fart in a vac-suit, right?"

Wendigo nodded. "I think you understand."

"Go on."

Her expedition—Wendigo and two pilots—had crossed the Swirl unchallenged. Approaching the Royalist cometary base, they had expected to be questioned—perhaps even fired upon—but nothing had happened. When they entered the stronghold, they understood why.

"Deserted," Wendigo said. "Or we thought so, until we found the *Royalists.*" She expectorated the word. "Feral, practically. Naked, grubby subhumans. Their wasps feed them and treat their illnesses, but that's as far as it goes. They grunt, and they've been toilet-trained, but they're not quite the military geniuses we've been led to believe."

"Then . . . "

"The war is . . . nothing we thought." Wendigo laughed, but the confines of her helmet rendered it more like the squawking of a jack-in-the-box. "And now you wonder why home didn't want us coming back?"

• • •

Before Wendigo could explain further, we reached a wider bisecting tunnel, glowing with its own insipid chlorine-colored light. Rather than the meandering bore of the tunnel in which we walked, it was as cleanly cut as a rifle barrel. In one direction the tunnel was blocked by a bullet-nosed cylinder, closely modeled on the trains in Tiger's Eye. Seemingly of its own volition, the train lit up and edged forward, a door puckering open.

"Get in," Wendigo said. "And lose the helmet. You won't need it where we're going."

Inside I coughed phlegmy ropes of thick from my lungs. Transitioning between breathing modes isn't pleasant—more so since I'd breathed nothing but thick for six weeks. But after a few lungfuls of the train's antiseptic air, the dark blotches around my vision began to recede.

Wendigo did likewise, only with more dignity.

Yarrow lay on one of the couches, stiff as a statue carved in soap. Her skin was cyanotic, a single, all-enveloping bruise. Pilot skin is a better vacuum barrier than the usual stuff, and vacuum itself is a far better insulator against heat loss than air. But where I'd lifted her my gloves had embossed fingerprints into her flesh. Worse was the broad stripe of ruined skin down her back and the left side of her tail, where she had lain against the splinter's surface.

But her head looked better. When she hit vac, biomodified seals would have shut within her skull, barricading every possible avenue for pressure, moisture, or blood loss. Even her eyelids would have fused tight. Implanted glands in her carotid artery would have released droves of friendly demons, quickly replicating via nonessential tissue in order to weave a protective scaffold through her brain.

Good for an hour or so—maybe longer. But only if the hostile demons hadn't screwed with Yarrow's native ones.

"You were about to tell me about the wasps," I said, as curious to hear the rest of Wendigo's story as I was to blank my doubts about Yarrow.

"Well, it's rather simple. They got smart."

"The wasps?"

She clicked the steel fingers of her hand. "Overnight. Just over a hundred years ago."

I tried not to look too overwhelmed. Intriguing as all this was, I wasn't treating it as anything other than an outlandish attempt to distract me from the main reason for my being here, which remained killing the defector. Wendigo's story explained some of the anomalies we'd so far encountered—but that didn't rule out a dozen more plausible explanations. Meanwhile, it was amusing to try and catch her out. "So they got smart," I said. "You mean our wasps, or theirs?"

"Doesn't mean a damn anymore. Maybe it just happened to one machine in the Swirl, and then spread like wildfire to all the trillions of other wasps. Or maybe it happened simultaneously, in response to some stimulus we can't even guess at."

"Want to hazard a guess?"

"I don't think it's important, Spirey." She sounded as though she wanted to put a lot of distance between herself and this topic. "Point is, it happened. Afterward, distinctions between us and the enemy—at least from the point of view of the wasps—completely vanished."

"Workers of the Swirl unite."

"Something like that. And you understand why they kept it to themselves, don't you?"

I nodded, more to keep her talking.

"They needed us, of course. They still lacked something. Creativity, I guess you'd call it. They could evolve themselves incrementally, but they couldn't make the kind of sweeping evolutionary jumps we'd been feeding them."

"So we had to keep thinking there was a war on."

Wendigo looked pleased. "Right. We'd keep supplying them with innovations, and they'd keep pretending to do each other in." She halted, scratching at the unwrinkled skin around one eye with the alloy finger of one hand. "Clever little bastards."

• • •

We'd arrived somewhere.

It was a chamber, large as any enclosed space I'd ever seen. I felt gravity; too much of the stuff. The whole chamber must have been gimbaled and spun within the splinter, like one of the gee-load simulators back in Tiger's Eye. The vaulted ceiling, hundreds of meters "above," now seemed vertiginously higher.

Apart from its apex, it was covered in intricate frescos—dozens of pictorial facets, each a cycling hologram. They told the history of the Swirl, beginning with its condensation from interstellar gas, the ignition of its star, the onset of planetary formation. Then the action cut to the arrival of the first Standardist wasp, programmed to dive into the Swirl and breed like a rabbit, so that one day there'd be a sufficiently huge population to begin mining the thing; winnowing out metals, silicates, and precious organics for the folks back home. Of course, it never happened like that. The Royalists wanted in on the action, so they sent their own wasps, programmed to attack ours. The rest is history. The frescos showed the war's beginning, and then a little while later the arrival of the first human observers, beamed across space as pure genetic data, destined to be born in artificial wombs in hollowed out comet-cores, raised and educated by wasps, imprinted with the best tactical and strategic knowledge available. Thereafter they taught the wasps. From then on things heated up, because the observers weren't limited by years of timelag. They were able to intervene in wasp evolution in realtime.

That ought to have been it, because by then we were pretty up-to-date, give or take four hundred years of the same.

But the frescos carried on.

There was one representing some future state of the Swirl, neatly ordered into a ticking orrery of variously sized and patterned worlds, some with beautiful rings or moon systems. And finally—like medieval conceptions of Eden—there was a triptych of lush planetary landscapes, with weird animals in the foreground, mountains and soaring cloudbanks behind.

"Seen enough to convince you?" Wendigo asked.

"No," I said, not entirely sure whether I believed myself. Craning my neck, I looked up toward the apex.

Something hung from it.

It was a pair of wasps, fused together. One was complete, the other was only fully formed, seemingly in the process of splitting from the complete wasp. The fused pair looked to have been smothered in molten bronze, left to dry in waxy nodules.

"You know what this is?" Wendigo asked.

"I'm waiting."

"Wasp art."

I looked at her.

"This wasp was destroyed mid-replication," Wendigo continued. "While it was giving birth. Evidently the image has some poignancy for them. How I'd put it in human terms I don't know . . . "

"Don't even think about it."

I followed her across the marbled terrazzo that floored the chamber. Arched porticos surrounded it, each of which held a single dead wasp, their body designs covering a hundred generations of evolution. If Wendigo was right, I supposed these dead wasps were the equivalent of venerated old ancestors peering from oil paintings. But I wasn't convinced just yet.

"You knew this place existed?"

She nodded. "Or else we'd be dead. The wasps back in the Royalist stronghold told us we could seek sanctuary here, if home turned against us."

"And the wasps—what? Own this place?"

"And hundreds like it, although the others are already far beyond the Swirl, on their way out to the halo. Since the wasps came to consciousness, most of the splinters flung out of the Swirl have been infiltrated. Shrewd of them—all along, we've never suspected that the splinters are anything other than cosmic trash."

"Nice décor, anyway."

"Florentine," Wendigo said, nodding. "The frescos are in the style of a painter called Masaccio; one of Brunelleschi's disciples. Remember, the wasps had access to all the cultural data we brought with us from GE—every byte of it. That's how they work, I think—by constructing things according to arbitrary existing templates."

"And there's a point to all this?"

"I've been here precisely one day longer than you, Spirey."

"But you said you had friends here, people who could help Yarrow."

"They're here all right," Wendigo said, shaking her head. "Just hope you're ready for them."

On some unspoken cue they emerged, spilling from a door which until then I'd mistaken for one of the surrounding porticos. I flinched, acting on years of training. Although wasps have never intentionally harmed a human being—even the enemy's wasps—they're nonetheless powerful, dangerous machines. There were twelve of them, divided equally between Standardist and Royalist units. Six-legged, their two-meter-long, segmented alloy bodies sprouted weapons, sensors, and specialized manipulators. So far so familiar, except that the way the wasps moved was subtly wrong. It was as if the machines choreographed themselves, their bodies defining the extremities of a much larger form, which I sensed more than saw.

The twelve whisked across the floor.

"They are—or rather *it* is—a queen," Wendigo said. "From what I've gathered, there's one queen for every splinter. Splinterqueens, I call them."

The swarm partially surrounded us now—but retained the brooding sense of oneness.

"She told you all this?"

"Her demons did, yes." Wendigo tapped the side of her head. "I got a dose after our ship crashed. You got one after we hit your ship. It was a standard sporehead from our arsenal, but the Splinterqueen loaded it with her own demons. For the moment that's how she speaks to us—via symbols woven by demons."

"Take your word for it."

Wendigo shrugged. "No need to."

And suddenly I knew. It was like eavesdropping a topologist's fever dream—only much stranger. The burst of Queen's speech couldn't have lasted more than a tenth of a second, but its afterimages seemed to persist much longer, and I had the start of a migraine before it had ended. But like Wendigo had implied before, I sensed planning—that every thought was merely a step toward some distant goal, the way each statement in a mathematical proof implies some final *QED*.

Something big indeed.

"You deal with that shit?"

"My chimeric parts must filter a lot."

"And she understands you?"

"We get by."

"Good," I said. "Then ask her about Yarrow."

Wendigo nodded and closed both eyes, entering intense rapport with the Queen. What followed happened quickly: six of her components detached from the extended form and swarmed into the train we had just exited. A moment later they emerged with Yarrow, elevated on a loom formed from dozens of wasp manipulators.

"What happens now?"

"They'll establish a physical connection to her neural demons," Wendigo said. "So that they can map the damage."

One of the six reared up and gently positioned its blunt, anvil-shaped "head" directly above Yarrow's frost-mottled scalp. Then the wasp made eight nodding movements, so quickly that the motion was only a series of punctuated blurs. Looking down, I saw eight bloodless puncture marks on Yarrow's head. Another wasp replaced the driller and repeated the procedure, executing its own blurlike nods. This time, glistening fibers trailed from Yarrow's eight puncture points into the wasp, which looked as if it was sucking spaghetti from my compatriot's skull.

Long minutes of silence followed, while I waited for some kind of report.

"It isn't good," Wendigo said eventually.

"Show me."

And I got a jolt of Queen's speech, feeling myself *inside* Yarrow's hermetically sealed head, feeling the chill that had embraced her brain core, despite her pilot augs. I sensed the two intermingled looms of native and foreign demons, webbing the shattered matrix of her consciousness.

I also sensed—what? Doubt?

"She's pretty far gone, Spirey."

"Tell the Queen to do what she can."

"Oh, she will. Now that she's glimpsed Yarrow's mind, she'll do all she can not to lose it. Minds mean a lot to her—particularly in view of what the Splinterqueens have in mind for the future. But don't expect miracles."

"Why not? We seem to be standing in one."

"Then you're prepared to believe some of what I've said?"

"What it means," I started to say—

But I didn't finish the sentence. As I was speaking the whole chamber shook violently, almost dashing us off our feet.

"What was that?"

Wendigo's eyes glazed again, briefly.

"Your ship," she said. "It just self-destructed."

"What?"

A picture of what remained of *Mouser* formed in my head: a dulling nebula, embedding the splinter. "The order to self-destruct came from Tiger's Eye," Wendigo said. "It cut straight to the ship's quackdrive subsystems, at a level the demons couldn't rescind. I imagine they were rather hoping you'd have landed by the time the order arrived. The blast would have destroyed the splinter."

"You're saying *home* just tried to kill us?"

"Put it like this," Wendigo said. "Now might not be a bad time to rethink your loyalties."

• • •

Tiger's Eye had failed this time—but they wouldn't stop there. In three hours they'd learn of their mistake, and three or more hours after that we would learn of their countermove, whatever it happened to be.

"She'll do something, won't she? I mean, the wasps wouldn't go to the trouble of building this place only to have Tiger's Eye wipe it out."

"Not much she can do," Wendigo said, after communing with the Queen. "If home chooses to use kinetics against us—and they're the only weapon which could hit us from so far—then there really is no possible defense. And remember there are a hundred other worlds like this, in or on their way to the halo. Losing one would make very little difference."

Something in me snapped. "Do you have to sound so damned indifferent to it all? Here we are talking about how we're likely to be dead in a few hours and you're acting like it's only a minor inconvenience." I fought to keep the edge of hysteria out of my voice. "How do you know so much anyway? You're mighty well informed for someone who's only been here a day, Wendigo."

She regarded me for a moment, almost blanching under the slap of insubordination. Then Wendigo nodded, without anger. "Yes, you're right to ask how I know so much. You can't have failed to notice how hard we crashed. My pilots took the worst."

"They died?"

Hesitation. "One at least—Sorrel. But the other, Quillin, wasn't in the ship when the wasps pulled me out of the wreckage. At the time I assumed they'd already retrieved her."

"Doesn't look that way."

"No, it doesn't, and . . . " She paused, then shook her head. "Quillin was why we crashed. She tried to gain control, to stop us landing . . . " Again Wendigo trailed off, as if unsure how far to commit herself. "I think Quillin was a plant, put aboard by those who disagreed with the peace initiative. She'd been primed—altered psychologically to reject any Royalist peace overtures."

"She was born like that—with a stick up her ass."

"She's dead, I'm sure of it."

Wendigo almost sounded glad.

"Still, you made it."

"Just, Spirey. I'm the humpty who fell off the wall twice. This time they couldn't find all the pieces. The Splinterqueen pumped me full of demons—gallons of them. They're all that's holding me together, but I don't think they can keep it up forever. When I speak to you, at least some of what you hear is the Splinterqueen herself. I'm not really sure where you draw the line."

I let that sink in, then said: "About your ship. Repair systems would have booted when you hit. Any idea when she'll fly again?"

"Another day, day and a half."

"Too damn long."

"Just being realistic. If there's a way to get off the splinter within the next six hours, ship isn't it."

I wasn't giving up so easily. "What if wasps help? They could supply materials. Should speed things."

Again that glazed look. "All right," she said. "It's done. But I'm afraid wasp assistance won't make enough difference. We're still looking at twelve hours."

"So I won't start any long disneys." I shrugged. "And maybe we can hold out until then." She looked unconvinced, so I said: "Tell me the rest. Everything you know about this place. *Why*, for starters."

"Why?"

"Wendigo, I don't have the faintest damn idea what any of us are doing here. All I do know is that in six hours I could be suffering from acute existence failure. When that happens, I'd be happier knowing what was so important I had to die for it."

Wendigo looked toward Yarrow, still nursed by the detached elements of the Queen. "I don't think our being here will help her," she said. "In which case, maybe I should show you something." A near-grin appeared on Wendigo's face. "After all, it isn't as if we don't have time to kill."

• • •

So we rode the train again, this time burrowing deeper into the splinter.

"This place," Wendigo said, "and the hundred others already beyond the Swirl—and the hundreds, thousands more that will follow—are *arks*. They're carrying life into the halo, the cloud of leftover material around the Swirl."

"Colonization, right?"

"Not quite. When the time's right the splinters will return to the Swirl. Only there won't be one anymore. There'll be a solar system, fully formed. When the colonization does begin, it will be of new worlds around Fomalhaut, seeded from the life-templates held in the splinters."

I raised a hand. "I was following you there . . . until you mentioned life-templates."

"Patience, Spirey."

Wendigo's timing couldn't have been better, because at that moment light flooded the train's brushed-steel interior.

The tunnel had become a glass tube, anchored to one wall of a vast cavern suffused in emerald light. The far wall was tiered, draping rafts of foliage. Our wall was steep and forested, oddly curved waterfalls draining into stepped pools. The waterfalls were bent away from true "vertical" by

Coriolis force, evidence that—just like the first chamber—this entire space was independently spinning within the splinter. The stepped pools were surrounded by patches of grass, peppered with moving forms that might have been naked people. There were wasps as well—tending the people.

As the people grew clearer I had that flinch you get when your gaze strays onto someone with a shocking disfigurement. Roughly half of them were *males.*

"Imported Royalists," Wendigo said. "Remember I said they'd turned feral? Seems there was an accident, not long after the wasps made the jump to sentience. A rogue demon, or something. Decimated them."

"They have both sexes."

"You'll get used to it, Spirey—conceptually anyway. Tiger's Eye wasn't always exclusively female, you know that? It was just something we evolved into. Began with you pilots, matter of fact. Fem physiology made sense for pilots—women were smaller, had better gee-load tolerance, better stress psychodynamics, and required fewer consumables than males. We were products of bioengineering from the outset, so it wasn't hard to make the jump to an all-fem culture."

"Makes me want to . . . I don't know." I forced my gaze away from the Royalists. "Puke or something. It's like going back to having hair all over your body."

"That's because you grew up with something different."

"Did they always have two sexes?"

"Probably not. What I do know is that the wasps bred from the survivors, but something wasn't right. Apart from the reversion to dimorphism, the children didn't grow up normally. Some part of their brains hadn't developed right."

"Meaning what?"

"They're morons. The wasps keep trying to fix things of course. That's why the Splinterqueen will do everything to help Yarrow—and us, of course. If she can study or even capture our thought patterns—and the demons make that possible—maybe she can use them to imprint consciousness back onto the Royalists. Like the Florentine architecture I said they copied, right? That was one template, and Yarrow's mind will be another."

"That's supposed to cheer me up?"

"Look on the bright side. A while from now, there might be a whole generation of people who think along lines laid down by Yarrow."

"Scary thought." Then wondered why I was able to crack a joke, with destruction looming so close in the future. "Listen, I still don't get it. What makes them want to bring life to the Swirl?"

"It seems to boil down to two . . . *imperatives*, I suppose you'd call them. The first's simple enough. When wasps were first opening up Greater Earth's solar system, back in the mid-twenty-first century, we sought the best way for them to function in large numbers without supervision. We studied insect colonies and imprinted the most useful rules straight into the wasps' programming. More than six hundred years later, those rules have percolated to the top. Now the wasps aren't content merely to organize themselves along patterns derived from living prototypes. Now they want to become—or at least give rise to—living forms of their own."

"Life envy."

"Or something very like it."

I thought about what Wendigo had told me, then said: "What about the second imperative?"

"Trickier. Much trickier." She looked at me hard, as if debating whether to broach whatever subject was on her mind. "Spirey, what do you know about Solar War Three?"

• • •

The wasps had given up on Yarrow while we traveled. They had left her on a corniced plinth in the middle of the terrazzo, poised on her back, arms folded across her chest, tail and fluke draping asymmetrically over one side.

"She didn't necessarily fail, Spirey," Wendigo said, taking my arm in her own unyielding grip. "That's only Yarrow's body, after all."

"The Queen managed to read her mind?"

There was no opportunity to answer. The chamber shook, more harshly than when *Mouser* had exploded. The vibration keeled us to the floor, Wendigo's metal arms cracking against the tessellated marble. As if turning in her sleep, Yarrow slipped from the plinth.

"Home," Wendigo said, raising herself from the floor.

"Impossible. Can't have been more than two hours since *Mouser* was hit. There shouldn't be any response for another four!"

"They probably decided to attack us regardless of the outcome of their last attempt. Kinetics."

"You sure there's no defense?"

"Only good luck." The ground lashed at us again, but Wendigo stayed standing. The roar that followed the first impact was subsiding, fading into a constant but bearable complaint of tortured ice. "The first probably only chipped us—maybe gouged a big crater, but I doubt that it ruptured any of the pressurized areas. Next time could be worse."

And there *would* be a next time, no doubt about it. Kinetics were the only weapon capable of hitting us at such long range, and they did so by sheer force of numbers. Each kinetic was a speck of iron, accelerated to a hair's breadth below the speed of light. Relativity bequeathed the speck a disproportionate amount of kinetic energy—enough that only a few impacts would rip the splinter to shreds. Of course, only one in a thousand of the kinetics they fired at us would hit—but that didn't matter. They'd just fire ten thousand.

"Wendigo," I said. "Can we get to your ship?"

"No," she said, after a moment's hesitation. "We can reach it, but it isn't fixed yet."

"Doesn't matter. We'll lift on auxiliaries. Once we're clear of the splinter we'll be safe."

"No good, either. Hull's breached—it'll be at least an hour before even part of it can be pressurized."

"And it'll take us an hour or so just to get there, won't it? So why are we waiting?"

"Sorry, Spirey, but—"

Her words were drowned by the arrival of the second kinetic. This one seemed to hit harder, the impact trailing away into aftergroans. The holographic frescos were all dark now. Then—ever so slowly—the ceiling ruptured, a huge mandible of ice probing into the chamber. We'd lost the false gravity; now all that remained was the splinter's feeble pull, dragging us obliquely toward one wall.

"But what?" I shouted in Wendigo's direction.

For a moment she had that absent look, which said she was more Queen than Wendigo. Then she nodded in reluctant acceptance. "All right, Spirey. We play it your way. Not because I think our chances are great. Just that I'd rather be doing something."

"Amen to that."

It was uncomfortably dim now, much of the illumination having come from the endlessly cycling frescos. But it wasn't silent. Though the groan of the chamber's off-kilter spin was gone now, what remained was almost as bad: the agonized shearing of the ice that lay beyond us. Helped by wasps, we made it to the train. I carried Yarrow's corpse, but at the door Wendigo said: "Leave her."

"No way."

"She's dead, Spirey. Everything of her that mattered, the Splinterqueen already saved. You have to accept that. It was enough that you brought her here, don't you understand? Carrying her now would only lessen your chances—and that would really have pissed her off."

Some alien part of me allowed the wasps to take the corpse. Then we were inside, helmeted up and breathing thick.

As the train picked up speed, I glanced out the window, intent on seeing the Queen one last time. It should have been too dark, but the chamber looked bright. For a moment I presumed the frescos had come to life again, but then something about the scene's unreal intensity told me the Queen was weaving this image in my head. She hovered above the debris-strewn terrazzo—except that this was more than the Queen I had seen before. This was—what?

How she saw herself?

Ten of her twelve wasp composites were now back together, arranged in constantly shifting formation. They now seemed more living than machine, with diaphanous sunwings, chitin-black bodies, fur-sheened limbs and sensors, and eyes that were faceted crystalline globes, sparkling in the chamber's false light. That wasn't all. Before, I'd sensed the Queen as something implied by her composites. Now I didn't need to imagine her. Like a ghost in which the composites hung, she loomed vast in the chamber, multiwinged and brooding—

And then we were gone.

We sped toward the surface for the next few minutes, waiting for the impact of the next kinetic. When it hit, the train's cushioned ride smothered the concussion. For a moment I thought we'd made it, then the machine began to decelerate slowly to a dead halt. Wendigo convened with the Queen, and told me the line was blocked. We disembarked into vacuum.

Ahead, the tunnel ended in a wall of jumbled ice.

After a few minutes we found a way through the obstruction, Wendigo wrenching aside boulders larger than either of us. "We're only half a klick from the surface," she said, as we emerged into the unblocked tunnel beyond. She pointed ahead, to what might have been a scotoma of absolute blackness against the milky darkness of the tunnel. "After that, a klick overland to the wreck." She paused. "Realize we can't go home, Spirey. Now more than ever."

"Not exactly spoiled for choice, are we."

"No. It has to be the halo, of course. It's where the splinter's headed anyway; just means we'll get there ahead of schedule. There are other Splinterqueens out there, and at the very least they'll want to keep us alive. Possibly other humans as well—others who made the same discovery as us, and knew there was no going home."

"Not to mention Royalists."

"That troubles you, doesn't it?"

"I'll deal with it," I said, pushing forward.

The tunnel was nearly horizontal, and with the splinter's weak gravity it was easy to make the distance to the surface. Emerging, Fomalhaut glared down at us, a white-cored, bloodshot eye surrounded by the wrinkle-like dust lanes of the inner Swirl. Limned in red, wasp corpses marred the landscape.

"I don't see the ship."

Wendigo pointed to a piece of blank caramel-colored horizon. "Curvature's too great. We won't see it until we're almost on top of it."

"Hope you're right."

"Trust me. I know this place like, well . . . " Wendigo regarded one of her limbs. "Like the back of my hand."

"Encourage me, why don't you."

Three or four hundred meters later we crested a scallop-shaped rise of ice, and halted. We could see the ship now. It didn't look in much better shape than when Yarrow and I had scoped it from *Mouser.*

"I don't see any wasps."

"Too dangerous for them to stay on the surface," Wendigo said.

"That's cheering. I hope the remaining damage is cosmetic," I said. "Because if it isn't—"

Suddenly I wasn't talking to anyone.

Wendigo was gone. After a moment I saw her, lying in a crumpled heap at the foot of the hillock. Her guts stretched away like a rusty comet-tail, halfway to the next promontory.

Quillin was fifty meters ahead, having risen from the concealment of a chondrite boulder.

When Wendigo had mentioned her, I'd put her out of my mind as any kind of threat. How could she pose any danger beyond the inside of a thickship, when she'd traded her legs for a tail and fluke, just like Yarrow? On dry land, she'd be no more mobile than a seal pup. Well, that was how I'd figured things.

But I'd reckoned without Quillin's suit.

Unlike Yarrow's—unlike any siren suit I'd ever seen—it sprouted legs. Mechanized, they emerged from the hip, making no concessions to human anatomy. The legs were long enough to lift Quillin's tail completely free of the ice. My gaze tracked up her body, registering the crossbow which she held in a double-handed grip.

"I'm sorry," Quillin's deep voice boomed in my skull. "Check-in's closed."

"Wendigo said you might be a problem."

"Wise up. It was staged from the moment we reached the Royalist stronghold." Still keeping the bow on me, she began to lurch across the ice. "The ferals were actors, playing dumb. The wasps were programmed to feed us bullshit."

"It isn't a Royalist trick, Quillin."

"Shit. See I'm gonna have to kill *you* as well."

The ground jarred, more violently than before. A nimbus of white light puffed above the horizon, evidence of an impact on the splinter's far side. Quillin stumbled, but her legs corrected the misstep before it tripped her forward.

"I don't know if you're keeping up with current events," I said. "But that's our own side."

"Maybe you didn't think hard enough. Why did wasps in the Swirl get smart before the trillions of wasps back in Sol system? Should have been the other way round."

"Yeah?"

"Of course, Spirey. GE's wasps had a massive head start." She shrugged, but the bow stayed rigidly pointed. "Okay, war sped up wasp evolution here. But that shouldn't have made so much difference. That's where the story breaks down."

"Not quite."

"What?"

"Something Wendigo told me. About what she called the second imperative. I guess it wasn't something she found out until she went underground."

"Yeah? Astonish me."

Well, something astonished Quillin at that point—but I was only marginally less surprised by it myself. An explosion of ice, and a mass of swiftly moving metal erupting from the ground around her. The wasp corpses were partially dismembered, blasted, and half-melted—but they still managed to drag Quillin to the ground. For a moment she thrashed, kicking up plumes of frost. Then the whole mass lay deathly still, and it was just me, the ice, and a lot of metal and blood.

The Queen must have coaxed activity out of a few of the wasp corpses, ordering them to use their last reserves of power to take out Quillin.

Thanks, Queen.

But no cigar. Quillin hadn't necessarily meant to shoot me at that point, but—bless her—she had anyway. The bolt had transected me with the precision of one of the Queen's theorems, somewhere below my sternum. Gut-shot. The blood on the ice was my own.

• • •

I tried moving.

A couple of light-years away I saw my body undergo a frail little shiver. It didn't hurt, but there was nothing in the way of proprioceptive feedback to indicate I'd actually managed to twitch any part of my body.

Quillin was moving, too. Wriggling, that is, since her suit's legs had been cleanly ripped away by the wasps. Other than that she didn't look seriously injured. Ten or so meters from me, she flopped around like a maggot and groped for her bow. What remained of it anyway.

Chalk one to the good guys.

By which time I was moving, executing a marginally quicker version of Quillin's slug crawl. I couldn't stand up—there are limits to what pilot physiology can cope with—but my legs gave me leverage she lacked.

"Give up, Spirey. You have a head start on me, and right now you're a little faster—but that ship's still a long way off." Quillin took a moment to catch her breath. "Think you can sustain that pace? Gonna need to, if you don't want me catching up."

"Plan on rolling over me until I suffocate?"

"That's an option. If this doesn't kill you first."

Enough of her remained in my field-of-view to see what she meant. Something sharp and bladelike had sprung from her wrist, a bayonet projecting half a meter ahead of her hand. It looked like a nasty little toy—but I did my best to push it out of mind and get on with the job of crawling toward the ship. It was no more than two hundred meters away now—what little of it protruded above the ice. The external airlock was already open, ready to clamp shut as soon as I wriggled inside—

"You never finished telling me, Spirey."

"Telling you what?"

"About this—what did you call it? The second imperative?"

"Oh, that." I halted and snatched breath. "Before I go on, I want you to know I'm only telling you this to piss you off."

"Whatever bakes your cake."

"All right," I said. "Then I'll begin by saying you were right. Greater Earth's wasps should have made the jump to sentience long before those in the Swirl, simply because they'd had longer to evolve. *And that's what happened.*"

Quillin coughed, like gravel in a bucket. "Pardon?"

"They beat us to it. About a century and a half ago. Across Sol system, within just a few hours, every single wasp woke up and announced its intelligence to the nearest human being it could find. Like babies reaching for the first thing they see." I stopped, sucking in deep lungfuls. The wreck had to be closer now—but it hardly looked it.

Quillin, by contrast, looked awfully close now—and that blade awfully sharp.

"So the wasps woke," I said, damned if she wasn't going to hear the whole story. "And that got some people scared. So much, some of them got to attacking the wasps. Some of their shots went wide, because within a day the whole system was one big shooting match. Not just humans against wasps—but humans against humans." Less than fifty meters now, across much smoother ground than we'd so far traversed. "Things just escalated.

Ten days after Solar War Three began, only a few ships and habitats were still transmitting. They didn't last long."

"Crap," Quillin said—but she sounded less cocksure than she had a few moments before. "There was a war back then, but it never escalated into a full-blown Solar War."

"No. It went the whole hog. From then on every signal we ever got from GE was concocted by wasps. They dared not break the news to us—at least not immediately. We've only been allowed to find out because we're never going home. Guilt, Wendigo called it. They couldn't let it happen again."

"What about our wasps?"

"Isn't it obvious? A while later the wasps here made the same jump to sentience—presumably because they'd been shown the right moves by the others. Difference was, ours kept it quiet. Can't exactly blame them, can you?"

There was nothing from Quillin for a while, both of us concentrating on the last patch of ice before Wendigo's ship.

"I suppose you have an explanation for this, too," she said eventually, swiping her tail against the ground. "C'mon, blow my mind."

So I told her what I knew. "They're bringing life to the Swirl. Sooner than you think, too. Once this charade of a war is done, the wasps breed in earnest. Trillions out there now, but in a few decades it'll be *billions* of trillions. They'll outweigh a good-sized planet. In a way the Swirl will have become sentient. It'll be directing its own evolution."

I spared Quillin the details—how the wasps would arrest the existing processes of planetary formation so that they could begin anew, only this time according to a plan. Left to its own devices, the Swirl would contract down to a solar system comprised solely of small, rocky planets—but such a system could never support life over billions of years. Instead, the wasps would exploit the system's innate chaos to tip it toward a state where it would give rise to at least two much larger worlds—planets as massive as Jupiter or Saturn, capable of shepherding leftover rubble into tidy, world-avoiding orbits. Mass extinctions had no place in the Splinterqueens' vision of future life.

But I guessed Quillin probably didn't care.

"Why are you hurrying, Spirey?" she asked between harsh grunts as she propelled herself forward. "The ship isn't going anywhere."

The edge of the open airlock was a meter above the ice. My fingers probed over the rim, followed by the crest of my battered helmet. Just lifting myself into the lock's lit interior seemed to require all the energy I'd already expended in the crawl. Somehow I managed to get half my body length into the lock.

Which is when Quillin reached me.

There wasn't much pain when she dug the bayonet into my ankle, just a form of cold I hadn't imagined before, even lying on the ice. Quillin jerked the embedded blade to and fro, and the knot of cold seemed to reach out little feelers into my foot and lower leg. I sensed she wanted to retract the blade for another stab, but my suit armor was gripping it tight.

The bayonet taking her weight, Quillin pulled herself up to the rim of the lock. I tried kicking her away, but the skewered leg no longer felt a part of me.

"You're dead," she whispered.

"News to me."

Her eyes rolled wide, then locked on me with renewed venom. She gave the bayonet a violent twist. "So tell me one thing. That story—bullshit, or what?"

"I'll tell you," I said. "But first consider this." Before she could react I reached out and palmed a glowing panel set in the lock wall. The panel whisked aside, revealing a mushroom-shaped red button. "You know that story they told about Wendigo, how she lost her arms?"

"You weren't meant to swallow that hero guff, Spirey."

"No? Well, get a load of this, Quillin. My hand's on the emergency pressurization control. When I hit it, the outer door's going to slide down quicker than you can blink."

She looked at my hand, then down at her wrist, still attached to my ankle via the jammed bayonet. Slowly the situation sank in. "Close the door, Spirey, and you'll be a leg short."

"And you an arm, Quillin."

"Stalemate, then."

"Not quite. See, which of us is more likely to survive? Me inside, with all the medical systems aboard this ship, or you all on your lonesome outside? Frankly, I don't think it's any contest."

Her eyes opened wider. Quillin gave a shriek of anger and entered one final, furious wrestling match with the bayonet.

I managed to laugh. "As for your question, it's true, every word of it." Then, with all the calm I could muster, I thumbed the control. "Pisser, isn't it."

• • •

I made it, of course.

Several minutes after the closing of the door, demons had lathered a protective cocoon around the stump and stomach wound. They allowed me no pain—only a fuzzy sense of detachment. Enough of my mind remained sharp to think about my escape—problematic given that the ship still wasn't fixed.

Eventually I remembered the evac pods.

They were made to kick away from the ship fast, if some quackdrive system went on the fritz. They had thrusters for that—nothing fancy, but here they'd serve another purpose. They'd boost me from the splinter, punch me out of its grav well.

So I did it.

Snuggled into a pod and blew out of the wreck, feeling the gee-load even within the thick. It didn't last long. On the evac pod's cam I watched the splinter drop away until it was pebble-sized. The main body of the kinetic attack was hitting it by then, impacts every ten or so seconds. After a minute of that the splinter just came apart. Afterward, there was only a sooty veil where it had been, and then only the Swirl.

I hoped the Queen had made it. I guess it was within her power to transmit what counted of herself out to sisters in the halo. If so, there was a chance for Yarrow as well. I'd find out eventually. Then I used the pod's remaining fuel to inject me into a slow, elliptical orbit, one that would graze the halo in a mere fifty or sixty years.

That didn't bother me. I wanted to close my eyes and let the thick nurse me whole again—and sleep an awfully long time.

PARDON OUR CONQUEST

ALAN DEAN FOSTER

Alan Dean Foster is the bestselling author of several dozen novels, and is perhaps most famous for his Commonwealth series, which began in 1975 with the novel *Midworld*. The most recent in that series, *Quofum*, was published in 2008, and a new Commonwealth book featuring the popular characters Pip and Flinx—*Flinx Transcendent*—should be out around the same time as this anthology. Also forthcoming is *The Human Blend*, the first book of a new SF trilogy for Del Rey. Foster's short fiction has appeared in numerous anthologies and in magazines such as *The Magazine of Fantasy & Science Fiction, Analog*, and *Jim Baen's Universe*. A new collection, *Exceptions to Reality*, came out in 2008.

Like the forthcoming *Flinx Transcendent,* this story takes place in Foster's Commonwealth milieu. Foster said it was inspired by the idea that there are various ways to conquer. "Sometimes simply persuading an opponent that your way is better can achieve the desired end," he said. "I always thought killing an opponent was a poor way of convincing him of the rightness of your argument."

PARDON OUR CONQUEST

Admiral Gorelkii shifted his seat on the meter-thick, jewel-encrusted, ceremonial golden cushion that rose behind the sweeping transparent arc of the solid crystal crescent moon, and fumed. His substantial pale gray bulk was draped in a bloom of multihued embroidered standards, each one representing one of the ancient Great Hordes that together comprised the Empire of the Three Suns. They weighed on him physically as well as historically. The wearing of the standards was a great honor accorded to a select few only on the most extraordinary occasions.

Unfortunately for him, today's extraordinary occasion was one of surrender.

His courage and willingness in accepting the responsibility for heading the disagreeable negotiations was recognized on all five inhabited worlds of the three systems that comprised the Empire. That did not mean he looked forward to the impending ceremony. What the exact details would consist of he did not know. What specific protocol was to be followed he did not know.

No doubt the conquerors of the Empire would be enlightening him in due course.

The Falan had never been a species to hesitate. Imbued with the heady wine of discovery and an assurance of their own superiority, they had looked forward to the steady expansion of their Empire in the direction of the arm of the galaxy that held a greater density of star systems than their own immediate vicinity. Following initial exploration they had discovered, explored, charted, and engaged in the successful colonization of two new habitable systems.

Then they had found Drax IV.

So it was called by the short, multi-legged, hard-carapaced creatures who inhabited the cities and towns they had excavated beneath its jungles and forests. Mild in temperament, absurd in appearance, they claimed to be part of a vast interstellar dominion called the Commonwealth. Vast, small, or imaginary, their polite insistence did nothing to deter the aggressive Falan. It was announced that the system of Drax would be incorporated into the Empire forthwith, and any foolish resistance met with fire and destruction on a planetary scale. Declaring war, the Falan proceeded to open hostilities by unleashing a small example of their firepower on a little-populated corner of the planet.

Subsequent to this ferocious demonstration, the inhabitants requested some time to contemplate their limited alternatives. While any military prowess on their part remained undetermined, they proved expert in the arts of obfuscation and delay. Eventually the patience of the Falan, never extensive to begin with, ran out.

This happened to coincide with the arrival of a fleet of fifty warships, which was considerably more than the two dozen or so the Empire could muster. When informed that this was a scouting force sent to determine the precise nature of the threat that had been levied against Drax, and that the main armada of the so-called Commonwealth had not even been assembled, consternation and despair among the Falan was followed by reluctant but unavoidable capitulation.

Gorelkii and his frustrated fellow career officers would have preferred to test the strength of the enemy warships in battle. As for the claim that they represented only a scouting force, such alien assertions could not be verified. They might be composed of nothing more than bluster on the part of the inhabitants of Drax. But Gorelkii and his comrades had been overridden by the Polity of the Three Suns, whose fear of utter annihilation if hostilities commenced was a realistic extrapolation based on their own fractious racial history.

"The Falan must be preserved," he had been informed solemnly. "We will build our strength in secret, improve our weapons, advance our science. In time we will throw off the yoke of the enemy and carry the battle to its homeworlds."

Fifty warships, he thought as he sat behind the glittering crescent moon. Scouting force. It was scarce to be believed. When queried, the inhabitants of Drax IV had declined to elaborate on the actual size and extent of their mysterious "Commonwealth." Though not looking forward to negotiating the formal terms of surrender, Gorelkii knew that it would buy the Falan time to learn exactly what they were up against. Learning that, they would be able to prepare their inevitable unstoppable response.

Adjutant Bardanat entered through the wide, arched entrance of rippling metal. The muscles of his heavy bipedal form bulged beneath his gleaming uniform and his small black eyes glittered beneath a single thrust of projecting bone. One tri-fingered hand snapped ceilingward in salute. His tone was its usual clipped, wholly professional self, save for what Gorelkii took to be a touch of bemusement.

"The diplomatic representatives of the Commonwealth are here, Grand Admiral." Bardanat hesitated and his voice lost some of its formal stress. "They are . . . they are . . . "

"Well, pour it out, Adjutant! *What* are they?"

Bardanat's fleshy eyefolds contracted in his species' equivalent of a blink. "Not what I expected, Admiral."

Gorelkii snorted through the single large respiratory opening set high in the center of his chest and below his thick neck. The nostril was framed by ribbons of valor that had been permanently encased in gleaming protective transparencies. The color tint of each transparency indicated the level of accomplishment that accented each ribbon.

"It doesn't matter what you expected, or I. We must deal with them." He gestured with a powerful, double-jointed arm. "Admit them."

He readied himself. Though his people had been defeated without a shot having been fired, a missile being unleashed, or an energy beam deployed, he would attempt to bargain as an equal. The Admiral could rant and rave with the most voluble politician. He could be out-argued, but he could not be intimidated. It was one of the reasons he had been chosen to head the negotiations. It was universally conceded among the Polity that no one in the Empire was likely to obtain better terms than Grand Admiral Gorelkii.

Steeping to the left, Adjutant Bardanat assumed a position of ready respect. Legs contracted, upper body straight and stiff, eyes forward, he would hold that position until his muscles screamed for relief or Gorelkii directed him to stand down.

Two shapes were approaching from the far end of the formal antechamber, walking toward him from the towering main entry arch. Gorelkii could not keep from tensing. What would they demand? How would they treat him personally? What kind of confrontational species had the resources to send forth a force of fifty warships merely to scout a confrontation?

When at last the pair finally halted before the curve of the crescent moon, he was shocked by their size. The spindly, big-eyed one he knew from images sent back from Drax. Presently standing on four limbs with another four upraised, it inclined feathery antennae in his direction. A bright blue-green in color, it looked fragile and harmless.

Though bipedal like the Falan, the creature standing beside the thranx appeared even less threatening. So soft was it that one could actually see bits of its exposed flesh moving after it had come to a stop. A strange white growth emerged from the top of its skull and also covered much of the lower half of its face. It would take little effort, Gorelkii thought, to crush them both, splintering the thranx-thing and smashing its taller companion to a pulp.

Should he give in to the natural impulse, however, he knew it would put something of a damper on the forthcoming negotiations. He forced down his instinctive feelings and kept his massive three-fingered hands locked together in front of him.

Lumbering forward, Bardanat checked to make sure the translator positioned in front of his cutting teeth was operational before he began to declaim forcefully without looking to left or right. "I present to you Grand Admiral Gorelkii-vant, Destroyer of Worlds, Sovereign of the Nation-Clan Hasekar, Supreme Commander of the First Fleet Majestic, Defender of Empire, Scion of the Second Sun!"

His soft mouth parting to reveal tiny white teeth behind his own hair-thin translation device, the white-haired biped stepped forward and thrust a limb across the crystal arc in Gorelkii's direction. "Hi, I'm Bill. William Chen-Khamsa, but my friends all call me Bill." Gesturing at his hard-shelled companion, he added, "That's the Eint Colvinyarev. He's from Hivehom and I'm from Earth."

Scuttling sideways, Adjutant Bardanat leaned slightly toward his commander and whispered. "The extended limb of the human creature, Grand Admiral. I believe you are supposed to make contact with the end."

Baffled but adaptive, Gorelkii reached out with a massive hand. Unable with his more numerous but much smaller fingers to envelop it all, the human creature took two of the three thick proffered fingers and shook them up and down several times. Releasing its lightweight but assured grasp, it then stepped back.

"Pleased to meet you, Admiral." Gesturing with its head, the being indicated Gorelkii's expansive torso. "Are those awards on your chest? I don't know their individual significance, of course, but even a visitor like myself can see that they're very impressive!"

Flattery as an opening ploy, Gorelkii told himself. Somewhat unexpected, given that he was the supine party. He would not succumb to it of course. Still, there was no harm in utilizing his personal history to make an impact on this unimposing pair. He proceeded to do so.

When he had finished, the thranx dipped its head and antennae low in his direction. "Most impressive! I can see that the Polity of the Three Suns chose from among the best of your kind to represent them."

"The Polity makes no mistakes!" Gorelkii's voice reverberated through the vaulted, effusively decorated audience chamber. "Though we have surrendered to your forces, we have not been defeated, as no actual combat has taken place."

"We agree absolutely." Though massing far less than the average Falan, the human's eyes were the same size. The Bill's were blue, a color that fascinated Gorelkii. All Falan eyes were black or shades of very dark gray. "We consider ourselves fortunate to have escaped your wrath."

Intriguing though the diversion was, Gorelkii ceased musing on the startlingly bright color of alien eyes. "Excuse me?"

"Clearly after learning more about you and your kind, any conflict between our three species would have resulted in terrible losses on our side. We would have been devastated! We are so very grateful that you have deigned to refrain from destroying us."

"Yes, *ccr!lk*." Folding its forelegs beneath its abdomen, the thranx executed a deep bow. "Gratitude compels us to abase ourselves before you."

What was going on here? Gorelkii thought confusedly. What kind of game were these representatives playing at? He bemoaned his ignorance of the culture of the triumphant species. He did not know enough to recognize if he was being mocked. In the absence of such data he could only improvise his responses.

"Yes—well, the casualties the combined fleets would have wreaked on your forces would have been terrible!"

"Truly, we are aware." The thranx rose out of its forward-inclining stance to regard the Admiral with golden compound eyes. "It is out of this awe and respect that we most cordially invite you to bring the Empire of the Three Suns into the Commonwealth."

Ah, there it was, at last! Gorelkii told himself with satisfaction. Couched in respectful, almost deferential terms, but unmistakable none the less. On familiar rhetorical ground once again, he immediately challenged.

"You propose to absorb us into your own federation! Well I can tell you, both as an Admiral of the Falan and as . . . !"

"No, no, you've got it all wrong!" So absurd a picture did the human present, with its waving little arms and wide eyes, that Gorelkii did not take exception to the clumsy interruption. "Colvinyarev speaks honestly when he says it's an invitation. If it so wishes, the Empire can go on its happy way with as little or as much contact with the Commonwealth as it desires. There is no compulsion to participate of any kind."

The thranx gestured first-degree concurrence, though the elaborate gesticulations of foothands and truhands meant nothing to the Admiral. "Many intelligent species besides our own are members of the Commonwealth. Some in full, some only in part. The only thing we have in absolute common is sentience. Several participate actively in decisions of Commonwealth policy, others tend to their own world or worlds and leave policy making to the rest." A small truhand gestured. "The Falan would surely rank among the most impressive species ever to join."

Despite the resolve with which he had determined to enter into the negotiations, Gorelkii found himself slightly dazed. Nothing was proceeding as expected. He resolved to force matters back onto a familiar keel.

"It is for the Polity and not me to consider such topics. I sit before you only to settle formal matters of surrender." He leaned forward, his massive bulk greater than that of human and thranx combined, his jet black eyes glittering challengingly. "First we will dispose of the matter of reparations . . . "

Human and thranx looked at one another. "What reparations?" The human turned back to face the Admiral. "A couple of your ships inflicted some minor damage on Drax IV. Nothing that can't be fixed. Forget about it. What's a little petty devastation between friends?"

Once again Gorelkii's eyepads performed the Falan blink. "No reparations?"

The human showed its teeth again. "No reparations."

"Very well then." The Admiral drew himself up. "We will proceed to the highly sensitive matter of disarmament, which I assure you the Polity will regard with the most . . . "

This time it was the thranx who broke in. "You can keep and maintain all of your ships."

"*All* of them?" the Adjutant blurted. "All three fleets?" It was an outrageous breach of protocol, but Gorelkii could hardly chastise Bardanat for speaking out. The Admiral was equally shocked

"Well, of course," the human replied cheerfully. "They're *your* ships, after all."

"Restriction of movement, then." Recovering, Gorelkii cast a warning look in Bardanat's direction to remind the Adjutant who and where he was.

"No restrictions." Instead of meeting the Admiral's eyes, the human was leaning forward to examine the arc of the crescent moon. "This is really beautiful workmanship. I can't find a single flaw or inclusion. I know that the crafts folk who fashioned it would find ready acceptance on many worlds of the Commonwealth. As I said, they're your ships."

Gorelkii's thoughts were awhirl. "Commonwealth military garrisons on the five worlds. How extensive?"

The human looked again at his thranx companion. "Why would we want to establish a military presence on any of your worlds? You're not part of the Commonwealth. Yet, anyway."

"But," the thranx added, "we would be flattered if you would situate some of your forces—completely independent, of course—on several of our worlds. Given the impression the Falan have made on the peoples of the Commonwealth, I'm certain their presence would be both welcome and admired."

"Wait . . . " Gorelkii struggled to gather himself. "You want *us* to establish a military presence on some of *your* worlds?"

The human's head bobbed lightly up and down. "Would you do us that honor?"

Honor. No reparations. No disarmament. Everything the two representatives had said so far was suggestive of craven cowardice. Or . . . ?

Gorelkii was a soldier. He knew how to fight. He even knew how to surrender. His long and distinguished career had prepared him for both eventualities. But nothing he had experienced or studied had prepared him for negotiations like this.

"I am sure," he said quickly, "that the Polity would be most pleased to place representatives of the Empire's military on as many of your worlds as would be allowed."

"Excellent!" As far as Gorelkii could ascertain, the human's expression of delight was sincere. "We would be pleased to engage in cultural and commercial exchanges as well. According to whatever procedures and restrictions your government decides to impose."

"Yes, well, as I have already mentioned, I am not empowered to negotiate such matters."

The human's head moved again, the white growth covering part of his face bobbing with the movement. "I'm positive others can work out the details." He looked to his colleague. "I think that's about it, Col."

"Yes," the thranx agreed. He eyed the Admiral. "Is there anything else you would like to discuss, your excellency? If you have the time, we would be flattered to invite you to a reception to be given aboard our ship, currently in stationary orbit above this city. You may of course bring with you any relations or friends that you would like. As our food synthesizers are programmed to satisfy the nutritional requirements of many species, I am sure they can create victuals that you would find of culinary interest, *srral!k*."

Gorelkii hesitated. The negotiations had gone well. No, amazingly well. Far, far better than even the most pessimistic member of the Polity could have imagined. He considered the thranx's offer. Refusing an invitation might be construed as an affront. It would be foolish to risk all that had been attained over such a slight request. Besides which he could not deny holding a personal interest in learning as much as he could about these obscenely deferential creatures.

"I accept your invitation." He indicated the stiff-legged Bardanat. "My Adjutant will handle the details. But I warn you," he added, "the details of these proceedings have been exhaustively recorded by multiple concealed sources. Any attempt at a future date to alter the terms of surrender will be met with—"

The visitors' penchant for interruption struck yet again. "Oh, let's not call it that," the human insisted. " 'Surrender' is such an unsociable term. I believe the official documents to be agreed upon are titled 'Instruments of Eternal and Lasting Friendship between the Commonwealth of the Humanx and the Grand and Indivisible Empire of the Three Suns.' They are already being communicated to your Polity for formal final review and execution."

Gorelkii tapped his translator. In the course of negotiations he had fully expected to hear the term "execution" employed, but before now, and not in relation to bureaucratic formalities.

"We do have one last request." The human was eyeing him thoughtfully.

Here it comes, Gorelkii thought. He steeled himself for whatever last-minute ultimate demand might be forthcoming. "Which is?"

Raising a spindly arm, the white-haired human pointed at the Admiral. "Would you wear that magnificent uniform, or whatever you call your current attire, when you attend our reception? I know that all of our military as well as diplomatic people will be as impressed by it as Col and I have been."

Gorelkii found himself gesturing automatically. "Yes. Yes, that can be arranged."

"Splendid!" Stepping forward, the human extended his arm once more. This time Gorelkii knew how to respond. They shook hands, gray enveloping beige. As the alien biped retreated, his thranx colleague advanced, dipped his head, and brushed the Admiral's still extended trio of fingers with his antennae. The contact was negligible.

"We are most grateful for your hospitality," the hard-shell murmured. "I personally look forward to greeting and entertaining you and your companions on board our vessel."

Gorelkii sat in silence for a long time after the two Commonwealth diplomats had departed. Only an involuntary and irrepressible grunt of pain from Bardanat reminded the Admiral that his Adjutant was still locked in the ritual pose of Formal Reception.

"Straighten," he told Bardanat.

"Gratitude, Admiral." The Adjutant was relieved. "I . . . " He hesitated, then asked the question that he could not suppress. "It is not for me to determine, but from what I was witness to I am presuming that according to the hopes and expectations of the Polity and of your personal self, the negotiations went well enough?"

"You may presume correctly, Adjutant." Gorelkii was gazing down the arched Corridor of Mortality through which the diplomats had taken their leave. "There's just one thing of which I remain uncertain."

Bardanat stared back at the Grand Admiral, Destroyer of Worlds, etc. "What is that, Excellency?"

Gorelkii looked over at him. "Remind me again: this war. We lost—didn't we?"

SYMBIONT

ROBERT SILVERBERG

Robert Silverberg—four-time Hugo Award-winner, five-time winner of the Nebula Award, SFWA Grand Master, SF Hall of Fame honoree—is the author of nearly five hundred short stories, nearly hundred-and-fifty novels, and is the editor of in the neighborhood of one hundred anthologies. Among his most famous works are *Lord Valentine's Castle* and the other books and stories in the Majipoor series, but all of his classic works are far too numerous to name.

The idea for "Symbiont"—which Silverberg described in *The Collected Stories of Robert Silverberg* as a "somber tale of jungle adventure and diabolical revenge"—came from a young woman named Karen Haber that Silverberg met while on a book tour. She gave him the idea, and he worked his magic. Shortly after, the story was finished and appeared in *Playboy.* And shortly after that, Silverberg married Ms. Haber.

But you shouldn't let that sweet story fool you; he wasn't joking when he said this one is diabolical.

SYMBIONT

Ten years later, when I was long out of the Service and working the turnaround wheel at Betelgeuse Station, Fazio still haunted me. Not that he was dead. Other people get haunted by dead men; I was haunted by a live one. It would have been a lot better for both of us if he *had* been dead, but as far as I knew Fazio was still alive.

He'd been haunting me a long while. Three or four times a year his little dry thin voice would come out of nowhere and I'd hear him telling me again, "Before we go into that jungle, we got to come to an understanding. If a synsym nails me, Chollie, you kill me right away, hear? None of this shit of calling in the paramedics to clean me out. You just kill me right away. And I'll do the same for you. Is that a deal?"

This was on a planet called Weinstein in the Servadac system, late in the Second Ovoid War. We were twenty years old and we were volunteers: two dumb kids playing hero. "You bet your ass" is what I told him, not hesitating a second. "Deal. Absolutely." Then I gave him a big grin and a handclasp and we headed off together on spore-spreading duty.

At the time, I really thought I meant it. Sometimes I still believe that I did.

• • •

Ten years. I could still see the two of us back there on Weinstein, going out to distribute latchenango spores in the enemy-held zone. The planet had been grabbed by the Ovoids early in the war, but we were starting to drive them back from that whole system. Fazio and I were the entire patrol: you get spread pretty thin in galactic warfare. But there was plenty of support force behind us in the hills.

Weinstein was strategically important, God only knows why. Two small continents—both tropical, mostly thick jungle, air like green soup—surrounded by an enormous turbulent ocean: never colonized by Earth, and of no use that anyone had ever successfully explained to me. But the place had once been ours and they had taken it away, and we wanted it back.

The way you got a planet back was to catch a dozen or so Ovoids, fill them full of latchenango spores, and let them return to their base. There is no life-form a latchenango likes better as its host than an Ovoid. The Ovoids, being Ovoids, would usually conceal what had happened to them from their pals, who would kill them instantly if they knew they were carrying deadly parasites. Of course, the carriers were going to die anyway—latchenango infestation is invariably fatal to Ovoids—but by the time they did, in about six standard weeks, the latchenangos had gone through three or four reproductive cycles and the whole army would be infested. All we needed to do was wait until all the Ovoids were dead and then come in, clean the place up, and raise the flag again. The latchenangos were generally dead, too, by then, since they rarely could find other suitable hosts. But even if they weren't, we didn't worry about it. Latchenangos don't cause any serious problems for humans. About the worst of it is that you usually inhale some spores while you're handling them, and it irritates your lungs for a couple of weeks so you do some pretty ugly coughing until you're desporified.

In return for our latchenangos the Ovoids gave us synsyms.

Synsyms were the first things you heard about when you arrived in the war zone, and what you heard was horrendous. You didn't know how much of it was myth and how much was mere bullshit and how much was truth, but even if you discounted seventy-five percent of it the rest was scary enough. "If you get hit by one," the old hands advised us, "kill yourself fast, while you have the chance." Roving synsym vectors cruised the perimeter of every Ovoid camp, sniffing for humans. They were not parasites but synthetic symbionts: when they got into you, they stayed there, sharing your body with you indefinitely.

In school they teach you that symbiosis is a mutually beneficial state. Maybe so. But the word that passed through the ranks in the war zone was that it definitely did not improve the quality of your life to take a synsym into your body. And though the Service medics would spare no effort to see that you survived a synsym attack—they aren't allowed to perform mercy killings, and wouldn't anyway—everything we heard indicated that you didn't really *want* to survive one.

The day Fazio and I entered the jungle was like all the others on Weinstein: dank, humid, rainy. We strapped on our spore tanks and started out, using hand-held heat piles to burn our way through the curtains of tangled vines. The wet spongy soil had a purplish tinge, and the lakes were iridescent green from lightning algae.

"Here's where we'll put the hotel landing strip," Fazio said lightly. "Over here, the pool and cabanas. The gravity-tennis courts here, and on the far side of that—"

"Watch it," I said, and skewered a low-flying wingfinger with a beam of hot purple light. It fell in ashes at our feet. Another one came by, the mate, traveling at eye level with its razor-sharp beak aimed at my throat, but Fazio took it out just as neatly. We thanked each other. Wingfingers are elegant things, all trajectory and hardly any body mass, with scaly silvery skins that shine like the finest grade of moonlight, and it is their habit to go straight for the jugular in the most literal sense. We killed twelve that day, and I hope it is my quota for this lifetime. As we advanced into the heart of the jungle we dealt just as efficiently with assorted hostile coilworms, eyeflies, dingleberries, leper bats, and other disagreeable local specialties. We were a great team: quick, smart, good at protecting each other.

We were admiring a giant carnivorous fungus a klick and a half deep in the woods when we came upon our first Ovoid. The fungus was a fleshy phallic red tower three meters high with orange gills, equipped with a dozen dangling whiplike arms that had green adhesive knobs at the tips. At the ends of most of the arms hung small forest creatures in various stages of digestion. As we watched, an unoccupied arm rose and shot forth, extended itself to three times its resting length, and by some neat homing tropism slapped its adhesive knob against a passing many-legger about the size of a cat. The beast had no chance to struggle; a network of wiry structures sprouted at once from the killer arm and slipped into the victim's flesh, and that was that. We almost applauded.

"Let's plant three of them in the hotel garden," I said, "and post a schedule of feeding times. It'll be a great show for the guests."

"Shh," Fazio said. He pointed.

Maybe fifty meters away a solitary Ovoid was gliding serenely along a forest path, obviously unaware of us. I caught my breath. Everyone knows what Ovoids look like, but this was the first time I had seen a live one. I was surprised at how beautiful it was, a tapering cone of firm jelly, pale blue streaked with red and gold. Triple rows of short-stalked eyes along its sides like brass buttons. Clusters of delicate tendrils sprouting like epaulets around the eating orifice at the top of its head. Turquoise ribbons of neural conduit winding round and round its equator, surrounding the dark heart-shaped brain faintly visible within the cloudy depths. The enemy. I was conditioned to hate it, and I did; yet I couldn't deny its strange beauty.

Fazio smiled and took aim and put a numb-needle through the Ovoid's middle. It froze instantly in mid-glide; its color deepened to a dusky flush; the tiny mouth tendrils fluttered wildly, but there was no other motion. We jogged up to it and I slipped the tip of my spore distributor about five centimeters into its meaty middle. "Let him have it!" Fazio yelled. I pumped a couple of c.c.'s of latchenango spores into the paralyzed alien. Its soft quivering flesh turned blue-black with fear and rage and God knows what other emotions that were strictly Ovoid. We nodded to each other and moved along. Already the latchenangos were spawning within their host; in half an hour the Ovoid, able once more to move, would limp off toward its camp to start infecting its comrades. It is a funny way to wage war.

The second Ovoid, an hour later, was trickier. It knew we had spotted it and took evasive action, zigzagging through a zone of streams and slender trees in a weird dignified way like someone trying to move very fast without having his hat blow off. Ovoids are not designed for quick movements, but this one was agile and determined, ducking behind this rock and that. More than once we lost sight of it altogether and were afraid it might double back and come down on *us* while we stood gaping and blinking.

Eventually we bottled it up between two swift little streams and closed in on it from both sides. I raised my needler and Fazio got ready with his spore distributor and just then something gray and slipper-shaped and about fifteen centimeters long came leaping up out of the left-hand stream and plastered itself over Fazio's mouth and throat.

Down he went, snuffling and gurgling, trying desperately to peel it away. I thought it was some kind of killer fish. Pausing only long enough to shoot a needle through the Ovoid, I dropped my gear and jumped down beside him.

Fazio was rolling around, eyes wild, kicking at the ground in terror and agony. I put my elbow on his chest to hold him still and pried with both hands at the thing on his face. Getting it loose was like pulling a second skin off him, but somehow I managed to lift it away from his lips far enough for him to gasp, "Synsym—I think it's synsym—"

"No, man, it's just some nasty fish," I told him. "Hang in there and I'll rip the rest of it loose in half a minute—"

Fazio shook his head in anguish.

Then I saw the two thin strands of transparent stuff snaking up out of it and disappearing into his nostrils, and I knew he was right.

• • •

I didn't hear anything from him or about him after the end of the war, and didn't want to, but I assumed all along that Fazio was still alive. I don't know why: my faith in the general perversity of the universe, I guess.

The last I had seen of him was our final day on Weinstein. We both were being invalided out. They were shipping me to the big hospital on Daemmerung for routine desporification treatment, but he was going to the quarantine station on Quixote; and as we lay side by side in the depot, me on an ordinary stretcher and Fazio inside an isolation bubble, he raised his head with what must have been a terrible effort and glared at me out of eyes that already were ringed with the red concentric synsym circles, and he whispered something to me. I wasn't able to understand the words through the wall of his bubble, but I could *feel* them, the way you feel the light of a blue-white sun from half a parsec out. His skin was glowing. The dreadful vitality of the symbiont within him was already apparent. I had a good notion of what he was trying to tell me. *You bastard,* he was most likely trying to say. Now *I'm stuck with this thing for a thousand years. And I'm going to hate you every minute of the time, Chollie.*

Then they took him away. They sent him floating up the ramp into that Quixote-bound ship. When he was out of view I felt released, as though I was coming out from under a pull of six or seven gravs. It occurred to me that I wasn't ever going to have to see Fazio again. I wouldn't have to face those reddened eyes, that taut shining skin, that glare of infinite reproach.

Or so I believed for the next ten years, until he turned up on Betelgeuse Station.

A bolt out of the blue: there he was, suddenly, standing next to me in the recreation room on North Spoke. It was just after my shift and I was balancing on the rim of the swimmer web, getting ready to dive. "Chollie?" he said calmly. The voice was Fazio's voice: that was clear, when I stopped to think about it a little later. But I never for a moment considered that this weird gnomish man might be Fazio. I stared at him and didn't even come close to recognizing him. He seemed about seven million years old, shrunken, fleshless, weightless, with thick coarse hair like white straw and strange soft gleaming translucent skin that looked like parchment worn thin by time. In the bright light of the rec room he kept his eyes hooded nearly shut; but then he turned away from the glowglobes and opened them wide enough to show me the fine red rings around his pupils. The hair began to rise along the back of my neck.

"Come on," he said. "You know me. Yeah. Yeah."

The voice, the cheekbones, the lips, the eyes—the eyes, the eyes, the eyes. Yes, I knew him. But it wasn't possible. Fazio? Here? How? So long a time, so many light-years away! And yet—yet—

He nodded. "You got it, Chollie. Come on. Who am I?"

My first attempt at saying something was a sputtering failure. But I managed to get his name out on the second try.

"Yeah," he said. "Fazio. What a surprise."

He didn't look even slightly surprised. I think he must have been watching me for a few days before he approached me—casing me, checking me out, making certain it was really me, getting used to the idea that he had actually found me. Otherwise the amazement would surely have been showing on him now. Finding me—finding *anybody* along the starways—wasn't remotely probable. This was a coincidence almost too big to swallow. I knew he couldn't have deliberately come after me, because the galaxy is so damned big a place that the idea of setting out to search for someone in it is too silly even to think about. But somehow he had caught up with me anyway. If the universe is truly infinite, I suppose, then even the most wildly improbable things must occur in it a billion times a day.

I said shakily, "I can't believe—"

"You can't? Hey, you better! What a surprise, kid, hey? Hey?" He clapped his hand against my arm. "And you're looking good, kid. Nice and healthy. You keep in shape, huh? How old are you now, thirty-two?"

"Thirty." I was numb with shock and fear.

"Thirty. Mmm. So am I. Nice age, ain't it? Prime of life."

"Fazio—"

His control was terrifying. "Come on, Chollie. You look like you're about to crap in your pants. Aren't you glad to see your old buddy? We had some good times together, didn't we? Didn't we? What was the name of that fuckin' planet? Weinberg? Weinfeld? Hey, hey, don't *stare* at me like that!"

I had to work hard to make any sound at all. Finally I said, "What the hell do you want me to do, Fazio? I feel like I'm looking at a ghost."

He leaned close, and his eyes opened wider. I could practically count the concentric red rings, ten or fifteen of them, very fine lines. "I wish to Christ you were," he said quietly. Such unfathomable depths of pain, such searing intensity of hatred. I wanted to squirm away from him. But there was no way. He gave me a long slow crucifying inspection. Then he eased back and some of the menacing intensity seemed to go out of him. Almost jauntily he said, "We got a lot to talk about, Chollie. You know some quiet place around here we can go?"

"There's the gravity lounge—"

"Sure. The gravity lounge."

• • •

We floated face-to-face, at half-pull. "You promised you'd kill me if I got nailed," Fazio murmured. "That was our deal. Why didn't you do it, Chollie? Why the fuck didn't you do it?"

I could hardly bear to look into his red-ringed eyes.

"Things happened too fast, man. How was I to know paramedics would be on the scene in five minutes?"

"Five minutes is plenty of time to put a heat bolt through a guy's chest."

"Less than five minutes. Three. Two. The paramedic floater was right overhead, man! It was covering us the whole while. They came down on us like a bunch of fucking *angels,* Fazio!"

"You had time."

"I thought they were going to be able to save you," I said lamely. "They got there so quickly."

Fazio laughed harshly. "They did try to save me," he said. "I'll give them credit for trying. Five minutes and I was on that floater and they were sending tracers all over me to clean the synsym goop out of my lungs and my heart and my liver."

"Sure. That was just what I figured they'd do."

"You promised to finish me off, Chollie, if I got nailed."

"But the paramedics were right *there!*"

"They worked on me like sonsabitches," he said. "They did everything. They can clean up the vital tissues, they can yank out your organs, synsym and all, and stick in transplants. But they can't get the stuff out of your brain, did you know that? The synsym goes straight up your nose into your brain and it slips its tendrils into your meninges and your neural glia and right into your fucking corpus callosum. And from there it goes everywhere. The cerebellum, the medulla, you name it. They can't send tracers into the brain that will clean out synsym and not damage brain tissue. And they can't pull out your brain and give you a new one, either. Thirty seconds after the synsym gets into your nose it reaches your brain and it's all over for you, no matter what kind of treatment you get. Didn't you hear them tell you that when we first got to the war zone? Didn't you hear all the horror stories?"

"I thought they were just horror stories," I said faintly.

He rocked back and forth gently in his gravity cradle. He didn't say anything.

"Do you want to tell me what it's like?" I asked after a while.

Fazio shrugged. As though from a great distance he said, "What it's like? Ah, it's not all that goddamned bad, Chollie. It's like having a roommate. Living with you in your head, forever, and you can't break the lease. That's all. Or like having an itch you can't scratch. Having it there is like finding yourself trapped in a space that's exactly one centimeter bigger than you are all around, and knowing that you're going to stay walled up in it for a million years." He looked off toward the great clear wall of the lounge, toward giant red Betelgeuse blazing outside far away. "Your synsym talks to you sometimes. So you're never lonely, you know? Doesn't speak any language you understand, just sits there and spouts gibberish. But at least it's company. Sometimes it makes you spout gibberish, especially when you badly need to make sense. It grabs control of the upper brain centers now and then, you know. And as for the autonomous centers, it does any damned thing it likes with them. Keys into the pain zones and runs little simulations for you—an amputation without anesthetic, say. Just for fun. *Its* fun. Or you're in bed with a woman and it disconnects your erection mechanism. Or it *gives* you an erection that won't go down for six weeks. For fun. It can get playful with your toilet training, too. I wear a diaper, Chollie, isn't that sweet? I have to. I get drunk sometimes without drinking. Or I drink myself sick without feeling a thing. And all the time I feel it there, tickling me. Like an ant crawling around within my skull. Like a worm up my nose. It's just like the other guys told us, when we came out to the war zone. Remember? 'Kill yourself fast, while you have the chance.' I never had the chance. I had you, Chollie, and we had a deal, but you didn't take our deal seriously. Why not, Chollie?"

I felt his eyes burning me. I looked away, halfway across the lounge, and caught sight of Elisandra's long golden hair drifting in free-float. She saw me at the same moment, and waved. We usually got together in here this time of night. I shook my head, trying to warn her off, but it was too late. She was already heading our way.

"Who's that?" Fazio asked. "Your girlfriend?"

"A friend."

"Nice," he said. He was staring at her as though he had never seen a woman before. "I noticed her last night, too. You live together?"

"We work the same shift on the wheel."

"Yeah. I saw you leave with her last night. And the night before."

"How long have you been at the Station, Fazio?"

"Week. Ten days, maybe."

"Came here looking for me?"

"Just wandering around," he said. "Fat disability pension, plenty of time. I go to a lot of places. That's a really nice woman, Chollie. You're a lucky guy." A tic was popping on his cheek and another was getting started on his lower lip. He said, "Why the fuck didn't you kill me when that thing first jumped me?"

"I told you. I couldn't. The paramedics were on the scene too fast."

"Right. You needed to say some Hail Marys first, and they just didn't give you enough time."

He was implacable. I had to strike back at him somehow or the guilt and shame would drive me crazy. Angrily I said, "What the hell do you want me to tell you, Fazio? That I'm sorry I didn't kill you ten years ago? Okay, I'm sorry. Does that do any good? Listen, if the synsym's as bad as you say, how come *you* haven't killed yourself? Why go on dragging yourself around with that thing inside your head?"

He shook his head and made a little muffled grunting sound. His face abruptly became gray, his lips were sagging. His eyeballs seemed to be spinning slowly in opposite directions. Just an illusion, I knew, but a scary one.

"Fazio?"

He said, "Chollallula lillalolla loolicholla. Billillolla."

I stared. He looked frightening. He looked hideous.

"Jesus, Fazio!"

Spittle dribbled down his chin. Muscles jumped and writhed crazily all over his face. "You see? You see?" he managed to blurt. There was warfare inside him. I watched him trying to regain command. It was like a man wrestling himself to a fall. I thought he was going to have a stroke. But then, suddenly, he seemed to grow calm. His breath was ragged, his skin was mottled with fiery blotches. He collapsed down into himself, head drooping, arms dangling. He looked altogether spent. Another minute or two passed before he could speak. I didn't know what to do for him. I floated there, watching. Finally, a little life seemed to return to him.

"Did you see? That's what happens," he gasped. "It takes control. How could I ever kill myself? It wouldn't let me do it."

"Wouldn't *let* you?"

He looked up at me and sighed wearily. "Think, Chollie, think! It's in symbiosis with me. We aren't independent organisms." Then the tremors began again, worse than before. Fazio made a desperate furious attempt to fight them off—arms and legs flung rigidly out, jaws working—but it was useless. "Illallomba!" he yelled. "Nullagribba!" He tossed his head from side to side as if trying to shake off something sticky that was clinging to it. "If I—then it—gillagilla! Holligoolla! I can't—I can't—oh—Jesus—Christ—!"

His voice died away into harsh sputters and clankings. He moaned and covered his face with his hands.

But now I understood.

For Fazio there could never be any escape. That was the most monstrous part of the whole thing, the ultimate horrifying twist. The symbiont knew that its destiny was linked to Fazio's. If he died, the symbiont would also; and so it could not allow its host to damage himself. From its seat in Fazio's brain it had ultimate control over his body. Whatever he tried—jump off a bridge, reach for a flask of poison, pick up a gun—the watchful thing in his mind would be a step ahead of him, always protecting him against harm.

A flood of compassion welled up in me and I started to put my hand comfortingly on Fazio's shoulder. But then I yanked it back as though I were afraid the symbiont could jump from his mind into mine at the slightest touch. And then I scowled and forced myself to touch him after all. He pulled away. He looked burned out.

"Chollie?" Elisandra said, coining up beside us. She floated alongside, long-limbed, beautiful, frowning. "Is this private, or can I join you?"

I hesitated, fumbling. I desperately wanted to keep Fazio and Elisandra in separate compartments of my life, but I saw that I had no way of doing that. "We were—well—just that—"

"Come on, Chollie," Fazio said in a bleak hollow voice. "Introduce your old war buddy to the nice woman."

Elisandra gave him an inquiring glance. She could not have failed to detect the strangeness in his tone.

I took a deep breath. "This is Fazio," I said. "We were in the Servadac campaign together during the Second Ovoid War. Fazio—Elisandra. Elisandra's a traffic-polarity engineer on the turnaround wheel—you ought to see her at work, the coolest cookie you can imagine—"

"An honor to meet you," said Fazio grandly. "A woman who combines such beauty and such technical skills—I have to say—I—I—" Suddenly he was faltering. His face turned blotchy. Fury blazed in his eyes. "No! Damn it, no! No more!" He clutched handfuls of air in some wild attempt at steadying himself. "Mullagalloola!" he cried, helpless. "Jillabongbong! Sampazozozo!" And he burst into wild choking sobs, while Elisandra stared at him in amazement and sorrow.

• • •

"Well, are you going to kill him?" she asked.

It was two hours later. We had put Fazio to bed in his little cubicle over at Transient House, and she and I were in her room. I had told her everything.

I looked at her as though she had begun to babble the way Fazio had. Elisandra and I had been together almost a year, but there were times I felt I didn't know her at all.

"Well?" she said.

"Are you serious?"

"You owe it to him. You owe him a death, Chollie. He can't come right out and say it, because the symbiont won't allow him to. But that's what he wants from you."

I couldn't deny any of that. I'd been thinking the same thing for at least the past hour. The reality of it was inescapable: I had muffed things on Weinstein and sent Fazio to hell for ten years. Now I had to set him free.

"If there was only some way to get the symbiont out of his brain—"

"But there isn't."

"No," I said. "There isn't."

"You'll do it for him, won't you?"

"Quit it," I said.

"I hate the way he's suffering, Chollie."

"You think I don't?"

"And what about you? Suppose you fail him a second time. How will you live with that? Tell me how."

"I was never much for killing, Ellie. Not even Ovoids."

"We know that," she said. "But you don't have any choice this time."

I went to the little fireglobe she had mounted above the sleeping platform, and hit the button and sent sparks through the thick coiling mists. A rustle of angry colors swept the mist, a wild aurora, green, purple, yellow. After a moment I said quietly, "You're absolutely right."

"Good. I was afraid for a moment you were going to crap out on him again."

There was no malice in it, the way she said it. All the same, it hit me like a fist. I stood there nodding, letting the impact go rippling through me and away.

At last the reverberations seemed to die down within me. But then a great new uneasiness took hold of me and I said, "You know, it's totally idiotic of us to be discussing this. I'm involving you in something that's none of your business. What we're doing is making you an accomplice before the fact."

Elisandra ignored me. Something was in motion in her mind, and there was no swerving her now. "How would you go about it?" she asked. "You can't just cut someone's throat and dump him down a disposer chute."

"Look," I said, "do you understand that the penalty could be anything up to—"

She went on. "Any sort of direct physical assault is out. There'd be some sort of struggle for sure—the symbiont's bound to defend the host body against attack—you'd come away with scratches, bruises, worse. Somebody would notice. Suppose you got so badly hurt you had to go to the medics. What would you tell them? A barroom brawl? And then nobody can find your old friend Fazio who you were seen with a few days before? No, much too risky." Her tone was strangely businesslike, matter-of-fact. "And then, getting rid of the body—that's even tougher, Chollie, getting fifty kilos of body mass off the Station without some kind of papers. No destination visa, no transshipment entry. Even a sack of potatoes would have an out-invoice. But if someone just vanishes and there's a fifty-kilo short balance in the mass totals that day—"

"Quit it," I said. "Okay?"

"You owe him a death. You agreed about that."

"Maybe I do. But whatever I decide, I don't want to drag you into it. It isn't your mess, Ellie."

"You don't think so?" she shot right back at me.

Anger and love were all jumbled together in Elisandra's tone. I didn't feel like dealing with that just now. My head was pounding. I activated the pharmo arm by the sink and hastily ran a load of relaxants into myself with a subcute shot. Then I took her by the hand. Gently, trying hard to disengage, I said, "Can we just go to bed now? I'd rather not talk about this any more."

Elisandra smiled and nodded. "Sure," she replied, and her voice was much softer.

She started to pull off her clothes. But after a moment she turned to me, troubled. "I can't drop it just like that, Chollie. It's still buzzing inside me. That poor bastard." She shuddered. "Never to be alone in his own head. Never to be sure he has control over his own body. Waking up in a puddle of piss, he said. Speaking in tongues. All that other crazy stuff. What did he say? Like feeling an ant wandering around inside his skull? An itch you can't possibly scratch?"

"I didn't know it would be that bad," I said. "I think I would have killed him back then, if I had known."

"Why didn't you anyway?"

"He was Fazio. A human being. My friend. My buddy. I didn't much want to kill Ovoids, even. How the hell was I going to kill him?"

"But you promised to, Chollie."

"Let me be," I said. "I didn't do it, that's all. Now I have to live with that."

"So does he," said Elisandra.

I climbed into her sleeptube and lay there without moving, waiting for her.

"So do I," she added after a little while.

She wandered around the room for a time before joining me. Finally she lay down beside me, but at a slight distance. I didn't move toward her. But eventually the distance lessened, and I put my hand lightly on her shoulder, and she turned to me.

An hour or so before dawn she said, "I think I see a way we can do it."

• • •

We spent a week and a half working out the details. I was completely committed to it now, no hesitations, no reservations. As Elisandra said, I had no choice. This was what I owed Fazio; this was the only way I could settle accounts between us.

She was completely committed to it, too: even more so than I was, it sometimes seemed. I warned her that she was needlessly letting herself in for major trouble in case the Station authorities ever managed to reconstruct what had happened. It didn't seem needless to her, she said.

I didn't have a lot of contact with him while we were arranging things. It was important, I figured, not to give the symbiont any hints. I saw Fazio practically every day, of course—Betelgeuse Station isn't all that big—off at a distance, staring, glaring, sometimes having one of his weird fits, climbing a wall or shouting incoherently or arguing with himself out loud; but generally I pretended not to see him. At times I couldn't avoid him, and then we met for dinner or drinks or a workout in the rec room. But there wasn't much of that.

"Okay," Elisandra said finally. "I've done my part. Now you do yours, Chollie."

Among the little services we run here is a sightseeing operation for tourists who feel like taking a close look at a red giant star. After the big stellar-envelope research project shut down a few years ago we inherited a dozen or so solar sleds that had been used for skimming through the fringes of Betelgeuse's mantle, and we began renting them out for three-day excursions. The sleds are two-passenger jobs without much in the way of luxury and nothing at all in the way of propulsion systems. The trip is strictly ballistic: we calculate your orbit and shoot you out of here on the big repellers, sending you on a dazzling swing across Betelgeuse's outer fringes that gives you the complete light show and maybe a view of ten or twelve of the big star's family of planets. When the sled reaches the end of its string, we catch you on the turnaround wheel and reel you in. It sounds spectacular, and it is; it sounds dangerous, and it isn't. Not usually, anyhow.

I tracked Fazio down in the gravity lounge and said, "We've arranged a treat for you, man."

The sled I had rented for him was called the *Corona Queen*. Elisandra routinely handled the dispatching job for these tours, and now and then I worked as wheelman for them, although ordinarily I wheeled the big interstellar liners that used Betelgeuse Station as their jumping-off point for deeper space. We were both going to work Fazio's sled. Unfortunately, this time there was going to be a disaster, because a regrettable little error had been made in calculating orbital polarity, and then there would be a one-in-a-million failure of the redundancy circuits. Fazio's sled wasn't going to go on a tour of Betelgeuse's far-flung corona at all. It was going to plunge right into the heart of the giant red star.

I would have liked to tell him that, as we headed down the winding corridors to the dropdock. But I couldn't, because telling Fazio meant telling Fazio's symbiont also; and what was good news for Fazio was bad news for the symbiont. To catch the filthy thing by surprise: that was essential.

How much did Fazio suspect? God knows. In his place, I think I might have had an inkling. But maybe he was striving with all his strength to turn his mind away from any kind of speculation about the voyage he was about to take.

"You can't possibly imagine what it's like," I said. "It's unique. There's just no way to simulate it. And the view of Betelgeuse that you get from the Station isn't even remotely comparable."

"The sled glides through the corona on a film of vaporized carbon," said Elisandra. "The heat just rolls right off its surface." We were chattering compulsively, trying to fill every moment with talk. "You're completely shielded so that you can actually pass through the atmosphere of the star—"

"Of course," I said, "Betelgeuse is so big and so violent that you're more or less inside its atmosphere no matter where you are in its system—"

"And then there are the planets," Elisandra said. "The way things are lined up this week, you may be able to see as many as a dozen of them—"

"—Otello, Falstaff, Siegfried, maybe Wotan—"

"—You'll find a map on the ceiling of your cabin—"

"—Five gas giants twice the mass of Jupiter—keep your eye out for Wotan, that's the one with rings—"

"—and Isolde, you can't miss Isolde, she's even redder than Betelgeuse, the damndest bloodshot planet imaginable—"

"—with eleven red moons, too, but you won't be able to see them without filters—"

"—Otello and Falstaff for sure, and I think this week's chart shows Aida out of occultation now, too—"

"—and then there's the band of comets—"

"—the asteroids, that's where we think a couple of the planets collided after gravitational perturbation of—"

"—and the Einsteinian curvature, it's unmistakable—"

"—the big solar flares—"

"Here we are," Elisandra said.

We had reached the dropdock. Before us rose a gleaming metal wall. Elisandra activated the hatch and it swung back to reveal the little sled, a sleek tapering frog-nosed thing with a low hump in the middle. It sat on tracks; above it arched the coils of the repeller-launcher, radiating at the moment the blue-green glow that indicated a neutral charge. Everything was automatic. We had only to put Fazio on board and give the Station the signal for launch; the rest would be taken care of by the orbital-polarity program Elisandra had previously keyed in.

"It's going to be the trip of your life, man!" I said.

Fazio nodded. His eyes looked a little glazed, and his nostrils were flaring.

Elisandra hit the prelaunch control. The sled's roof opened and a recorded voice out of a speaker in the dropdock ceiling began to explain to Fazio how to get inside and make himself secure for launching. My hands were cold, my throat was dry. Yet I was very calm, all things considered. This was murder, wasn't it? Maybe so, technically speaking. But I was finding other names for it. A mercy killing; a balancing of the karmic accounts; a way of atoning for an ancient sin of omission. For him, release from hell after ten years; for me, release from a lesser but still acute kind of pain.

Fazio approached the sled's narrow entry slot.

"Wait a second," I said. I caught him by the arm. The account wasn't quite in balance yet.

"Chollie—" Elisandra said.

I shook her off. To Fazio I said, "There's one thing I need to tell you before you go."

He gave me a peculiar look, but didn't say anything.

I went on, "I've been claiming all along that I didn't shoot you when the synsym got you because there wasn't time, the medics landed too fast. That's sort of true, but mainly it's bullshit. I had time. What I didn't have was the guts."

"Chollie—" Elisandra said again. There was an edge on her voice.

"Just one more second," I told her. I turned to Fazio again. "I looked at you, I looked at the heat gun, I thought about the synsym. But I just couldn't do it. I stood there with the gun in my hand and I didn't do a thing. And then the medics landed and it was too late—I felt like such a shit, Fazio, such a cowardly shit—"

Fazio's face was turning blotchy. The red synsym lines blazed weirdly in his eyes.

"Get him into the sled!" Elisandra yelled. "It's taking control of him, Chollie!"

"Oligabongaboo!" Fazio said. "Ungabanoo! Flizz! Thrapp!"

And he came at me like a wild man.

I had him by thirty kilos, at least, but he damned near knocked me over. Somehow I managed to stay upright. He bounced off me and went reeling around, and Elisandra grabbed his arm. He kicked her hard and sent her flying, but then I wrapped my forearm around the throat from behind, and Elisandra, crawling across the floor, got him around his legs so we could lift him and stuff him into the sled. Even then we had trouble holding him. Two of us against one skinny burned-out ruined man, and he writhed and twisted and wriggled about like something diabolical. He scratched, he kicked, he elbowed, he spat. His eyes were fiery. Every time we forced him close to the entryway of the sled he dragged us back away from it. Elisandra and I were grunting and winded, and I didn't think we could hang on much longer. This wasn't Fazio we were doing battle with, it was a synthetic symbiont out of the Ovoid labs, furiously trying to save itself from a fiery death. God knows what alien hormones it was pumping into Fazio's bloodstream. God knows how it had rebuilt his bones and heart and lungs for greater efficiency. If he ever managed to break free of my grip, I wondered which of us would get out of the dropdock alive.

But all the same, Fazio still needed to breathe. I tightened my hold on his throat and felt cartilage yielding. I didn't care. I just wanted to get him on that sled, dead or alive, give him some peace at all. Him and me both. Tighter—tighter—

Fazio made rough sputtering noises, and then a thick nasty gargling sound.

"You've got him," Elisandra said.

"Yeah. Yeah."

I clamped down one notch tighter yet, and Fazio began to go limp, though his muscles still spasmed and jerked frantically. The creature within him was still full of fight; but there wasn't much air getting into Fazio's lungs now and his brain was starving for oxygen. Slowly Elisandra and I shoved him the last five meters toward the sled—lifted him, pushed him up to the edge of the slot, started to jam him into it—

A convulsion wilder than anything that had gone before ripped through Fazio's body. He twisted half around in my grasp until he was face-to-face with Elisandra, and a bubble of something gray and shiny appeared on his lips. For an instant everything seemed frozen. It was like a slice across time, for just that instant. Then things began to move again. The bubble burst; some fragment of tissue leaped the short gap from Fazio's lips to Elisandra's. The symbiont, facing death, had cast forth a piece of its own life-stuff to find another host. *"Chollie!"* Elisandra wailed, and let go of Fazio and went reeling away as if someone had thrown acid in her eyes. She was clawing at her face. At the little flat gray slippery thing that had plastered itself over her mouth and was rapidly poking a couple of glistening pseudopods up into her nostrils. I hadn't known it was possible for a symbiont to send out offshoots like that. I guess no one did, or people like Fazio wouldn't be allowed to walk around loose.

I wanted to yell and scream and break things. I wanted to cry. But I didn't do any of those things.

When I was four years old, growing up on Backgammon, my father bought me a shiny little vortex boat from a peddler on Maelstrom Bridge. It was just a toy, a bathtub boat, though it had all the stabilizer struts and outriggers in miniature. We were standing on the bridge and I wanted to see how well the boat worked, so I flipped it over the rail into the vortex. Of course, it was swept out of sight at once. Bewildered and upset because it didn't come back to me, I looked toward my father for help. But he thought I had flung his gift into the whirlpool for the sheer hell of it, and he gave me a shriveling look of black anger and downright hatred that I will never forget. I cried half a day, but that didn't bring back my vortex boat. I wanted to cry now. Sure. Something grotesquely unfair had happened, and I felt four years old all over again, and there was nobody to turn to for help. I was on my own.

I went to Elisandra and held her for a moment. She was sobbing and trying to speak, but the thing covered her lips. Her face was white with terror and her whole body was trembling and jerking crazily.

"Don't worry," I whispered. "This time I know what to do."

• • •

How fast we act, when finally we move. I got Fazio out of the way first, tossing him or the husk of him into the entry slot of the *Corona Queen* as easily as though he had been an armload of straw. Then I picked up Elisandra and carried her to the sled. She didn't really struggle, just twisted about a little. The symbiont didn't have that much control yet. At the last moment I looked into her eyes, hoping I wasn't going to see the red circles in them. No, not yet, not so soon. Her eyes were the eyes I remembered, the eyes I loved. They were steady, cold, clear. She knew what was happening. She couldn't speak, but she was telling me with her eyes: *Yes, yes, go ahead, for Christ's sake go ahead, Chollie!*

Unfair. Unfair. But nothing is ever fair, I thought. Or else if there is justice in the universe it exists only on levels we can't perceive, in some chilly macrocosmic place where everything is evened out in the long run but the sin is not necessarily atoned by the sinner. I pushed her into the slot down next to Fazio and slammed the sled shut. And went to the dropdock's wall console and keyed in the departure signal, and watched as the sled went sliding down the track toward the exit hatch on its one-way journey to Betelgeuse. The red light of the activated repellers glared for a moment, and then the blue-green returned. I turned away, wondering if the symbiont had managed to get a piece of itself into me, too, at the last moment. I waited to feel that tickle in the mind. But I didn't. I guess there hadn't been time for it to get us both.

And then, finally, I dropped down on the launching track and let myself cry. And went out of there, after a while, silent, numb, purged clean, thinking of nothing at all. At the inquest six weeks later I told them I didn't have the slightest notion why Elisandra had chosen to get aboard that ship with Fazio. Was it a suicide pact, the inquest panel asked me? I shrugged. I don't know, I said. I don't have any goddamned idea what was going on in their minds that day, I said. Silent, numb, purged clean, thinking of nothing at all.

So Fazio rests at last in the blazing heart of Betelgeuse. My Elisandra is in there also. And I go on, day after day, still working the turnaround wheel here at the Station, reeling in the stargoing ships that come cruising past the fringes of the giant red sun. I still feel haunted, too. But it isn't Fazio's ghost that visits me now, or even Elisandra's—not now, not after all this time. I think the ghost that haunts me is my own.

THE SHIP WHO RETURNED

ANNE McCAFFREY

Anne McCaffrey is a winner of both the Hugo and Nebula Award, a SFWA Grand Master, and an inductee into the SF Hall of Fame. Her work is beloved by generations of readers. She is best known for authoring the Dragonriders of Pern series, but she has also written dozens of other novels. She was born in Cambridge, Mass. in 1926 and currently makes her home in Ireland, in a home named Dragonhold-Underhill.

"The Ship Who Returned," which first appeared in the anthology *Far Horizons*, is a sequel to *The Ship Who Sang*, part of McCaffrey's Brain and Brawn Ship series. This story follows Helva, a sentient spaceship with the mind of a human girl, as she deals with the death of her human partner and an emergency return to the planet she had saved years before.

THE SHIP WHO RETURNED

Helva had been prowling through her extensive music files, trying to find something really special to listen to, when her exterior sensors attracted her attention. She focused on the alert. Dead ahead of her were the ion trails of a large group of small, medium and heavy vessels. They had passed several days ago but she could still "smell" the stink of the dirty emissions. She could certainly analyze their signatures. Instantly setting her range to maximum, she caught only the merest blips to the port side, almost beyond sensor range.

"Bit off regular shipping routes," she murmured.

"So they are," replied Niall.

She smiled fondly. The holograph program had really improved since that last tweaking she'd done. There was Niall Parollan in the pilot's chair, one compact hand spread beside the pressure plate, the left dangling from his wrist on the armrest. He was dressed in the black shipsuit he preferred to wear, vain man that he'd been: "because black's better now that my hair's turned." He would brush back the thick shock of silvery hair and preen slightly in her direction.

"Where exactly are we, Niall? I haven't been paying much attention."

"Ha! Off in cloud-cuckoo land again . . . "

"Wherever that is," she replied amiably. It was such a comfort to hear his voice.

"I do believe . . . " and there was a pause as the program accessed her present coordinates, "we are in the Cepheus Three region."

"Why, so we are. Why would a large flotilla be out here? This is a fairly empty volume of space."

"I'll bring up the atlas," Niall replied, responding as programmed.

It was bizarre of her to have a hologram of a man dead two months but it was a lot better—psychologically—for her to have the comfort of such a reanimation. The "company" would dam up her grief until she could return her dead brawn to Regulus Base. And discover if there were any new "brawns" she could tolerate as a mobile partner. Seventy-eight years, five months and twenty days with Niall Parollan's vivid personality was a lot of time to suddenly delete. Since she had the technology to keep him "alive"—in a fashion, she had done so. She certainly had enough memory of their usual interchanges with which to program this charade. She would soon have to let him go but she'd only do that when she no longer needed his presence to keep mourning at bay. Not that she hadn't had enough exposure to that emotion in her life—what with losing her first brawn partner, Jennan, only a few years into what should have been a lifelong association.

In that era, Niall Parollan had been her contact with Central Worlds Brain and Brawn Ship Administration at Regulus Base. After a series of relatively short and only minimally successful longer-term partnerships with other brawns, she had gladly taken Niall as her mobile half. Together they had been roaming the galaxy. Since Niall had ingeniously managed to pay off her early childhood and educational indebtedness to Central Worlds, they had been free agents, able to take jobs that interested them, not compulsory assignments. They had not gone to the Horsehead Nebula as she had once whimsically suggested to Jennan. The NH-834 had had quite enough adventures and work in this one not to have to go outside it for excitement.

"Let's see if we can get a closer fix on them, shall we, Niall?"

"Wouldn't be a bad idea on an otherwise dull day, would it?" Though his fingers flashed across the pressure plates of the pilot's console, it was she who did the actual mechanics of altering their direction. But then, she would have done that anyway. Niall didn't really need to, but it pleased her to give him tasks to do. He'd often railed at her for finding him the sort of work he didn't *want* to do. And she'd snap back that a little *hard* work never hurt anyone. Of course, as he began to fail physically, this became lip service to that old argument. Niall had been in his mid-forties when he became her brawn and she the NH-834, so he had had a good long life for a soft-shell person.

"Good healthy stock I am," the hologram said, surprising her.

Was she thinking out loud? She must have been for the program to respond.

"With careful treatment, you'll last centuries," she replied, as she often had.

She executed the ninety-degree course change that the control panel had plotted.

"Don't dawdle, girl," Niall said, swiveling in the chair to face the panel behind which her titanium shell resided.

She thought about going into his "routine," but decided she'd better find out a little more about the "invasion."

"Why do you call it an invasion?" Niall asked.

"That many ships, all heading in one direction? What else could it be? Freighters don't run in convoys. Not out here, at any rate. And nomads have definite routes they stick to in the more settled sectors. And if I've read their KPS rightly . . . "

" . . . Which, inevitably, you do, my fine lady friend . . . "

"Those ships have been juiced up beyond freighter specifications and they're spreading dirty stuff all over space. Shouldn't be allowed."

"Can't have space mucked up, can we?" The holo's right eyebrow cocked, imitating an habitual trait of Niall's. "And juiced-up engines as well. Should we warn anyone?"

Helva had found the Atlas entries for this sector of space. "Only the one habitable planet in the system they seem to be heading straight for. Ravel . . . " Sudden surprise caught at her heart at that name. "Of all places."

"Ravel?" A pretty good program to search and find that long-ago reference so quickly. She inwardly winced at the holo's predictable response. "Ravel was the name of the star that went nova and killed your Jennan brawn, wasn't it?" Niall said, knowing the fact perfectly well.

"I didn't need the reminder," she said sourly.

"Biggest rival I have," Niall said brightly as he always did, and pushed the command chair around in a circle, grinning at her unrepentantly as he let the chair swing 360 degrees and back to the console.

"Nonsense. He's been dead nearly a century . . . "

"Dead but not forgotten . . . "

Helva paused, knowing Niall was right, as he always was, in spite of being dead, too. Maybe this wasn't a good idea, having him able to talk back to her. But it was only what he would have said in life anyhow, and had done often enough or it wouldn't be in the program.

She wished that the diagnostics had shown her one specific cause for his general debilitation so she could have forestalled his death. Some way, somehow.

"I'm wearing out, lover," he'd told her fatalistically in one of their conversations when he could no longer deny increasing weakness. "What can you expect from a life-form that degenerates? I'm lucky to have lived as long as I have. Thanks to you fussing at me for the last seventy years."

"Seventy-eight," she corrected him then.

"I'll be sorry to leave you alone, dear heart," he'd said, coming and laying his cheek on the panel behind which she was immured. "Of all the women in my life, you've been the best."

"Only because I was the one you *couldn't have,*" she replied.

"Not that I didn't try," the hologram responded with a characteristic snort.

Helva echoed it. Reminiscing and talking out loud were not a good idea. Soon she wouldn't know what was memory and what was programming.

Why hadn't she used the prosthetic body that Niall had purchased for her—reducing their credit balance perilously close to zero and coming close to causing an irreparable breach between them? He *had* desperately wanted the physical contact, ersatz as she had argued it would be. The prosthesis would have been *her* in Niall's eyes, and arms, since she would have motivated it. And he'd tried so hard to *have* her. He had supplied Sorg Prosthetics with the hologram statue he'd had made long before he became her brawn, using genetic information from her medical history and holos of her parents and siblings. Until he'd told her, she hadn't known that there had been other, physically normal children of her parents' issue. But then, shell-people were not encouraged to be curious about their families: they were shell-people, and ineffably different. He swore blind that he hadn't maximized her potential appearance—the hologram was of a strikingly good-looking woman—when he'd had a hologram made of her from that genetic information. He'd even produced his research materials for her inspection.

"You may not like it, kid," he'd said in his usual irreverent tone, "but you are a blond, blue-eyed female and would have grown tall and lissome. Just like I like 'em. Your dad was good-lookin' and I made you take after him, since daughters so often tend to resemble good ol' dad. Not that your ma wasn't a good-looking broad. Your siblings all are, so I didn't engineer anything but a valid extrapolation."

"You just prefer blondes, don't tell me otherwise!"

"I never do, do I?" responded the hologram and Helva brought herself sharply to the present—and the fact she tried to avoid—that the Niall Parollan she had loved was dead. Really truly dead. The husk of what he called his "mortal coil" was in stasis in his quarters. He had died peacefully—not as he had lived, with fuss and fury and fine histrionics. One moment her sensors read his slowly fading life signs—the next second, the thin line of "nothing" as the essence of the personality that had been Niall Parollan departed—to wherever souls or a spiritual essence went.

She who could not weep was shattered. Later she realized that she had hung in space for days, coming to grips with his passing. She had said over and over that they had had a good, long time together: that these circumstances differed from her loss of Jennan after just a few very short years. Jennan had never had a chance to live a full, long, productive life. Niall had. Surely she shouldn't be greedy for just a little more, especially when for the last decade he had been unable to enjoy the lifestyle that he had followed so vibrantly, so fully, in such a raucous nonconformist spirit. Surely she had learned to cope with grief in her last hundred years. That was when she realized that she couldn't face the long silent trip back to Regulus Base. He'd insisted that he had a right to be buried with other heroes of the Service since he'd had to put up so much with them and especially her, all these decades. They had been a lot closer to Regulus at the time that subject had come up. But she was determined to grant that request.

There were no other brain ships anywhere in her spatial vicinity to contact and act as escort. She and Niall had been on a primary scouting sweep of unexplored star systems. She might have resented that first escort back from Ravel with Jennan's body. Not that there was much chance of her suiciding this time. She'd passed that test on the first funereal return to Regulus Base. Which is when the notion to program a facsimile had occurred to her. So it was a way to delay acceptance? Surely she could be allowed this aberration—if aberration it was. She didn't have to mention the matter to Regulus. They'd be glad enough to have her ready to take another partner. Experienced B&B ships were always in demand for delicate assignments. She was one of their best, her ship-self redesigned and crammed with all the new technology that had been developed for brain ships, and stations. Like that damned spare body Niall had bought and which she had never used. She couldn't. She simply couldn't inhabit the Sorg prosthesis. Oh, she knew that Tia did and the girl was glad of the ability to "leave" the shell and ambulate. Lovely word, "ambulate." She and Niall had had some roaring arguments over the whole notion of prosthesis.

"You'd fit me out with a false arm or leg, if I lost one, wouldn't you?" had been one of Niall's rebuttals.

"So you could walk or use the hand, yes, but this is different."

"Because you know what I'd be using on you, don't you?" He was so close to her panel that his face had been an angry blur. He'd been spitting at her intransigence. "And you don't want any part of my short arm, do you?"

"At least they can't replace *that* in prosthesis," she'd snarled.

"Wanna bet?" He'd whirled away, back to his command chair, sprawling into it, glaring at her panel. "Trouble is, with you, girl, you're aged in the keg. Set in plascrete. You don't know what you're missing!" And he was snarling with bitterness.

Since she considered herself tolerant and forward thinking, that accusation had burned. It still did. Maybe, after all, she was too old in her head to contemplate physical freedom. But she could not make use of that empty body-shell as something she, Helva, could manipulate. Not all the brain ships she had spoken to about the Sorg prosthesis had found it a substitute for immolation in a shell. And some of them had been just commissioned, too. Of course, Tia—Alex/Hypatia AH-1033—had once *been* a walking, unshelled person as a child. Maybe, as Niall had vociferously bellowed at the top of his lungs at her, Helva needed to have her conditioning altered: a moral update. For a brain ship, she wasn't that old, after all. Why couldn't she have accepted the prosthesis when he wanted so desperately for her to use it? She and Niall had been partnered a long time, so how could it have altered their special relationship to have added to it that final surrender of self? She really hadn't thought of herself as a technological vestal virgin, one of the epithets Niall had flung at her. She wasn't prudish. She'd just been *conditioned* to accept herself, as she was, so thoroughly that to be "unshelled" was the worst imaginable fate. Using the prosthetic body was not at all the same thing as being unshelled, he had shouted back at her. While she *had* been sensorily deprived once, she hadn't also been *out* of her shell. Nearly out of her mind, yes, but not out of the shell. But she couldn't, simply could *not,* oblige. Oblige? No, she couldn't oblige Niall in that way. A weak word to define a response to his unreasonable, but oh-so-much masculine request. Well, she had refused. Now she wished she hadn't. But if Niall were still living, would she have relented? Not likely, since it was his death that had now prompted remorse for that omission.

"Preferably before I became impotent, my girl," and this was the holo speaking.

"If you knew how sorry I am, Niall . . . " she murmured.

Information started to chatter in from her sensors. She didn't quite recall having asked for a spectrographic analysis of the ion trail. Such an action was so much a part of her standard operating procedure that she supposed, in between self-castigation and listening to her Niall program, that she had automatically instigated it.

"Well, well, armed and loaded for bear, huh?"

"Yeah," Niall in holo replied, "but what sort of bear?"

"Those religious fanatics on Chloe had used fur rugs to keep warm . . . so the analogy is accurate enough," she replied, amused to have been so accurate. "I remember they went merrily off to . . . "

"Merrily?" Niall's voice cracked in dismay. "That lot never heard the word. So what's hunting bear in this volume of space?" he asked.

"Well, now hear this, dear friend. They're on that habitable planet which, being the gluttons for punishment they seemed to be when I first met them, they have named Ravel."

"No doubt a penitential derived gimmick to remind them of their sins," Niall said in a dour tone.

Helva analyzed the report. "Got an ID on the visitors. Pirates," she said, for her data files had been able to match the emissions with those of Kolnari raiders. Small—yachts more likely—and some medium-sized spaceships, probably freighters, gutted and refitted for piratical practices and two heavier but older cruiser-sized vessels.

The Niall holo whipped the chair round, staring at her. (Mind you, the program was very good to get this sort of reaction so quickly.) "Kolnari? The bastards that attacked your space-station friend, Simeon?"

"The very same. Not all of those fanatics got captured when Central World's Navy tried to round all of them up."

"Wily fiends, those Kolnari." And the holo's expression was dead serious. "Last info from Regulus suggested that two groups, possibly four, had escaped completely. Even one group's more than enough bear-hunters to ravage Ravel with their modus operandi." The holo slammed both hands on the armrests in frustration.

"I wonder that there are any still alive. After all, the virus that Dr. Chaundra let loose on them was one of the most virulent ever discovered." She gave a sigh. "The Kolnari were dying in droves."

The Kolnari—a dissident splinter group that had so adapted to the conditions of their harsh home planet that they were considered a human subspecies—were known to have an incredible ability to adapt to and survive otherwise fatal diseases, viruses and punishing planetary conditions. They had a short life span, maturing when other male human types were only hitting puberty, but the short generations were dangerous despite the limitation. They raided wherever they could, planets, space platforms or freighter convoys, using the human populations or crews as slaves and refitting the captured vessels to their uses—piracy. After their nearly successful raid on Space Station 900, Central Worlds Navy was reasonably certain they had destroyed the main body of peripatetic Kolnari units. They were on alert to locate, and destroy on sight, any other units.

"Huh!" Niall snorted. "Adapting to that particular virus would be just the sort of thing the Kolnari *would* be able to do, given their perverse nature and crazy metabolism."

"I'm afraid you could be right. Who else would be insane enough to run ships in that condition? Even nomads don't get that sloppy about emissions," Helva said.

"Not if they wish to continue their nomadic existence if they're leaving a system on the sly. Are you being wise to go after Kolnari?" Niall asked, a trace of anxiety in his tone. "You'd constitute a real prize."

Helva did a mental shudder, all too vividly reminded of what the Kolnari leader, Belazir t'Marid, had nearly done to the space-station brain, Simeon. Odd that Niall would remind her of that. She knew she'd done a good program but . . . Could she rationally believe in the transmigration of souls? Or that the holo was the ghost of the real Niall?

"I can no more leave those Ravel idiots to the Kolnari than I could to the damned nova. And it is sort of poetic justice," she said with a sigh.

"Let's see. It's nearly a hundred years since I had to transport them off their planet before their sun fried it. It took time for Central Worlds to find such a suitably remote star system where they would be safe from both nova stars and any profanity from the evils that beset mere men. Let's hope that they have some sort of modern equipment protecting them. If not against novas, at least against predators. Ah! The Atlas says the sun's stable. And there is, or was, a space facility for incoming converts."

"Ha!" The holo gave a bark of disgust. "Any satellite systems?"

"None mentioned. No contact in the past forty years, in fact. Well, I'm about to break into their meditations or whatever it is they do down there. There's nothing but females on that planet. I can't let Kolnari get their hands on all those innocent pious virgins, now can I?"

"It'd be fun to watch, though," said a totally unrepentant Niall.

"Shut up, you prurient sadist," she said as firmly as possible. Maybe she should also shut the program down. No, she *needed* him, one way or the other, because embedded in that program was the distillation of seventy-eight years of experience . . . his and hers.

"I was never a sadist, my dear Helva," he said haughtily, and then grinned wickedly. "I'll admit to hedonism but none of my women ever minded my attention . . . bar you! Have you considered a pulse to any listening Central Worlds units of the imminent unRaveling disaster?"

"I am and"—she paused as she put the final URGENT ALL EYES tag on the beam—"and it's away."

For the first time she experienced a touch of relief that she could approach the group without defiling it by the presence of a male. She'd pause the program—since Niall seemed to talk without any cues from her. Quite likely she wouldn't have as much trouble this time persuading them to seek whatever hidden shelters the planet might provide. Possibly the fact that she had saved them once before would weigh in their obedience to her urgings to make themselves as scarce as possible when the Kolnari arrived. Whatever! She wouldn't let them be victims to Kolnari rape and brutality. And Ravel was only a minor detour from the way to Regulus. She not only felt better to have something useful to do after going into a fugue over Niall's death but also was revived by the need. As she had been needed at Ravel, as Jennan's father had been at Parsaea. True tragedy occurred when those who could have helped were not *there* when needed. She was here. She was needed. Vigor flowed through the tubes that supplied her nutrient fluids.

"Feeling on form, are you?" the holo asked brightly. "Thatta girl! We gotta do what we gotta do. Data suggests that there'll be a lot of small settlements, cloisters they call 'em. They've increased their population from the Chloe figures." He sighed. "There isn't enough of the geo-ecological survey to show possible refuges. Planet's high on vegetation though."

"Lots of forests and lots of mountains and valleys. Plenty of cover if they separate. Make it that much harder for the Kolnari to tag 'em even from the air. That is, if they keep their wits about them," Helva said, charged with hope. "They need only lie doggo until the Fleet arrives."

"That is"—and the holo's tone was cynical—"if the Fleet has any squadrons near enough to send in timely fashion or decides such a splinter group is worth saving. I've never heard of their type of Faith . . . the Inner Marian Circle. Who's this Marian they worship?"

"In this case, 'marian' is an adjective and refers to Mary, mother of Jesus."

"Oh . . . and what's an inner circle then?"

"I don't know and it scarcely matters, does it? We have to warn them."

"Maybe there isn't anyone left to warn," Niall suggested. "Hey, did you just say they've increased their population from the Chloe figures? How does a celibate religious order perpetuate its membership?"

"Converts," she suggested. She often had wondered how such minorities did manage to continue to practice a faith that rejected procreation as a sin. "There was a new shipment forty years ago."

"Ach!" and Niall dismissed that. "Even if they converted preteens, how could the present inhabitants run fast enough at fifty-odd years to escape galloping Kolnari?"

"Parthenogenesis?" she suggested.

"That is, at least, virgin birth." And he snickered.

"That would go with the theories about Mary."

Niall snorted. "That was just the first recorded case of exogenesis."

"Possibly, but it doesn't detract from the Messiah's effect on man . . . and woman . . . kind."

"I'll allow that."

"Big of you."

"To the realities, woman," he said, stirring forward in his chair. "First we have to find out if there's anyone to rescue. AND if there's any safe place to send them so the Kolnari don't get 'em until the Fleet heaves into sight. I wouldn't wish that bunch on my worst enemy . . . Even my second-worst enemy."

Helva had been scanning the file on the Kolnari. "They might be looking for a new home base. Central Worlds sterilized their planet of origin."

"Then let's not let them have this Ravel, which seems to be a nice planet. Wouldn't want the neighborhood to go to such dogs . . . "

"They have an indigenous sort of canine on Ravel. Have you been speed-reading ahead of me again?" she asked, surprised because the list of local fauna was just coming up for her to peruse.

"*Most* of the M-type planets we've been on have some sort of critter in the canine slot. Cats don't always make it." And he shot a snide glance at her. He was a dog person but she had long ago decided she liked the independence of felines. They could argue the merits of the two species quite happily on their journeys between star systems. "Planet does have predators. Furthermore, our Inner Circle does not have any weaponry and does not hunt. They're vegetarians." He grinned around at her again.

"So it's all organic material?" Helva asked at her most innocent, playing on the theme.

"Just the kind of organic virgin material the Kolnari adore." The holo rubbed its hands together and leered.

She ignored that. "Temperate climate, too. Makes a change from Chloe, which was frozen most of the time."

"What! No harsh temperatures to mortify the body and soul?"

"No! And a good basic ecology, which they don't interfere with. Haven't even domesticated any of the indigenous beasts for use, but then, this entry is forty years old, dating from the last landfall. They live in harmony with their environment, it says here, and do not plunder it."

"Which sure does leave them wide-open to being plundered themselves. Which is about to happen. Though, when all's said and done, I wouldn't like to see them plundered or deflowered among their vegetable patches by the Kolnari."

"Nor will we permit it," Helva said fiercely, although she devoutly hoped that she wouldn't meet with the incredulity and pious fatalism that she'd encountered the first time and which, obliquely, had caused Jennan's death.

"Frankly, my dear, I don't know what I could do to help you. You know my reputation with women . . . " the holo began.

"I'll do the talking," she said, firmly interrupting him.

He leaned back in his chair, idly swinging it on the gimbals. "I wonder if they added you to their Inner Circle as a savior."

"Nonsense. None of the original group would be still alive. They didn't believe in artificially prolonging life . . . "

"All cures provided by prayer?"

"Avoiding all impure substances. Like Kolnari."

Niall cocked his head at her. "Maybe they'll welcome the Kolnari as a trial sent by whatever Universal Deity they revere . . . " He paused, scowling. "Mary was never a god, was she? Goddess, I mean? Any rate, would they consider the Kolnari have been sent to test their faith?"

"I'm hoping not. What do we have left of the tapes Simeon recorded?"

"I opine that you would be referring to the rape scene? My favorite of them all," Niall said, and his fingers tapped a sequence. "You wouldn't actually dare to play that back at those innocents . . . "

"A picture is worth a thousand words," she quoted at him. "If we have to tour as much of the planet as Jennan and I had to on Chloe, I'm going to need to use a sharp, fast lesson. I can rig a hologram for them to see," she added, since she was pleased with the way she handled holographic programming.

"If you do half as well with that program as you have with mine, it'll work, honey."

That remark startled Helva and she activated a magnification of his holographic image. But it was the hologram . . . one could see just the faintest hint of the light source. How could Niall *know* that he was a holo? Then she remembered the one they had done together at Astrada III when he had had to replay an historical event to prove a point to a skeptical audience. Surely that was his reference.

"I can't find any indication of how large the population is," she added, having replayed the entry on Ravel several times.

"Might be they don't keep an accurate census. Do they even *have* a space facility?"

"No, but they *do* have a satellite with a proximity alarm!" she cried in triumph.

"And how far away is the nearest inhabited system that'd hear it, much less act?" Niall wanted to know. "Probably contains no more than the usual silly warning . . . " And he chanted in the lifeless tones of an automated messager, " . . . This . . . Is . . . An . . . Interdicted Planet. You . . . Will Not . . . Proceed Further." He abandoned that tone and, in a pious falsetto, added, "Or you'll get a spanking when the Fleet comes."

Helva gave him the brief chuckle he would have expected. "Our message will prompt action. No one ignores a B&B ship message."

"And rightly so," Niall said, loyally fierce, pounding one fist for emphasis on the desk.

There was no sound attached to that action. She'd have to work on that facet . . . when she'd managed to preserve the Chloists, or Chloe-ites or Inner Marian Circle Ravellians from the imminent arrival of the Kolnari. She'd have to be sure they knew just how dangerous and bloody-minded the Kolnari were so they'd make themselves as scarce as possible.

Helva was now speeding along the ion trail, its dirty elements all the more pronounced as she reduced the distance separating them. She'd overtake the flotilla within twenty hours. And arrive at Ravel four or five days ahead of them. She'd have to start decelerating once she passed the heliopause, but so would the Kolnari.

"Don't forget to cloak," Niall said, rising from his chair. He stretched until she was sure she could hear the sinews popping: which, she reminded herself, is why she hadn't added more than vocal sound to the holo. Stretching he was allowed, but not the awful noise he'd make popping his knucklebones. "I'd better get some shut-eye before the party begins."

"Good idea. I'll work on the hologram while you're resting and call you for a critique."

Niall the holo walked across the main compartment and to the aisle and down to Niall's quarters. Did it never realize that it melded with Niall's stasis-held body on the bunk?

She'd almost forgotten the cloaking mechanism that bent light and sensory equipment around the ship itself. She'd only used that device once and had held that up to Niall as a *really* unnecessary piece of technology for a B&B ship to waste credit on. So, it was coming in handy again. B&B ships had no weaponry with which to defend themselves and vanishing provided a much more effective evasion than the tightest, most impervious shielding.

As she judiciously edited the tapes from the Kolnari occupation of

Space Station 900, she mulled over the first encounter with the Chloeites. At least this time her brawn couldn't be killed, however unintentional Jennan's death had been. She also had more tricks in her arsenal than she had had as that raw young brain ship.

She sped along and, well before any sensors the Kolnari might have could track her approach, she went into cloak. Of course, *they* became spots on her sensors, rather than three-dimensional ships. Still, by the size of the signals as she passed them, she learned a good deal about them. To begin with, there were more than she had anticipated, even taking into consideration all the dirty emissions. None of this lot matched the signatures of any of those that had attacked her friend, Simeon: not that that provided her with any consolation.

The Kolnari fleet was an incredible mixture of yachts, large and small, prizes of other Kolnari attacks—a round dozen of them, stuffed far above the optimum capacity with bodies: some evidently stashed in escape pods as last-resort accommodation. The conditions on board those ships would have been desperate even if the life-support systems managed to cope with such overloading. Three medium-sized freighters, equally jam-packed with little and large Kolnaris. Two destroyer types, quite elderly, but these were loaded with missiles and other armaments. Two of the freighters were hauling drones, five apiece, which cut down on the speed at which the entire convoy could travel. Four drones contained nothing but ammunition, missiles and spare parts: the fifth probably food as she got no metallic signals from it. Nineteen ships. A veritable armada and certainly able to overwhelm the inhabitants of Ravel. Which was undoubtedly why that luckless planet had been picked.

She pulsed an update of her earlier message with these details to the nearest Fleet facility—a good ten days away even by the speed of a pulse. The Admiralty had sworn blind that they intended to wipe Kolnari pirates out of space forever. So here was a chance for an ambitious picket commander to make that clean sweep and get a promotion. A small, modern force could easily overwhelm this shag-bag-rag-bag of barely spaceworthy vehicles. On the other hand, the Kolnari would fight to the last male child able to wield a weapon or fire a missile . . . and they had rather a few of those. Even Kolnari females were vicious fighters. Reviewing what was known of their lifestyle, it was likely a great many of the women were slaves, captured and forced to breed up more Kolnari offspring.

She sped on, wishing she had more information on the Chloes. Living close to nature on another planet was fine in theory, but practice was another thing altogether. As the original religious group had found out the hard way on Daphnis and Chloe a hundred years ago.

She had completed a holographic account of the less palatable habits of the Kolnari, including the modus operandi of their invasion of the peaceful planet, Bethel. The Tri-D coverage had been found in the space wreckage and used in the trial against those that had been captured at SS900. She was delighted to have found the one that showed vividly how the Kolnari dealt with anyone who defied them. That was the short sharp lesson she needed to project. She edited it, added some voice-over, and then programmed the exterior vid systems to play it.

That ought to cut down the waste of time spent arguing. She wanted every single female resident of Ravel safely hidden away when the Kolnari arrived.

• • •

She didn't rouse Niall—why bother him when he was sleeping like the dead—or rather the holo of him. He had always been hard to wake, though once roused, he altered from sleepy to alert in seconds. She had the time, so she did a leisurely spin-in, quartering the globe from darkside to daylight and identifying congregates of life signs . . . all too many. She'd never make it to every settlement. How could these piously celibate folk have increased almost fourfold from the numbers of the registered settlers? "Multiply and be fruitful" might be a Biblical injunction but, if the last bunch had come four decades before, there were a great many more than there ought to be. Rabbits might multiply so. But virgin rabbits? Well, she'd get to as many . . . what had they called themselves—ah, cloisters—as she could. Maybe they had some form of communication between the settlements, widespread as they were on the sprawling main continent. She'd simply have to ignore the island groups and concentrate on the larger, juicier targets that the Kolnari would be likely to attack first.

Smack-dab in the middle of the main continent, she easily identified what had been the landing field—well, a few square acres of burnt-out ground, a flimsy concrete-covered grid where ships or shuttles had landed to off-load people and supplies. Rows of temporary barracks, weathered and in need of maintenance, bordered two sides of the field to show that humans had once been accommodated there for however brief a time. There was a low-power source discernible and vegetation had not grown back over the landing area, though in forty-some years there should have been some weeds regaining a root hold. A blocky tower, now tilting sideways, held the corner position of the two barrack rows. From her aerial advantage, she could also see four roads, each going away from the deserted landing place: north, south, east and west. She could see where auxiliary lanes had split off from the main ones, smaller arteries leading to probably smaller settlements. Though none appeared to be more than dirt tracks, the vigorous growths had not reclaimed the track, leaving a clear margin on both sides. Some sort of chemical must have been used to discourage succession.

"I wonder how they decided who went in which direction," she murmured, forgetting that oddity in the press of more important concerns.

"Probably by divine intervention," Niall said, and there he was, seated at the pilot's console.

She hadn't put a voice-operated command in the program, but there he was, and she was rather pleased to hear another voice after the silent days of inward travel.

"Makes it easier to have just four main directions to search in."

"Those tracks were made over a period of years or they wouldn't be quite so visible since the last time they were used forty years ago."

"True. So, eeny, meeny, miny, moe . . . which track will we follow now? East is east and west is west and never the twain shall meet," he said in one of his whimsical moods.

"Nothing for north and south?"

"Well, we could go this way?" And he crossed his arms, pointing in two separate directions, neither of which was a cardinal compass point.

"North, I think, and then swing round . . . " Helva decided.

"In ever-increasing circles?" His tone was so caustically bright!

"Mountains, too. That's good."

" 'Purple mountains' majesty, above the fruited plain' . . . " he quoted.

"That doesn't sound right."

"I've forgot how it goes," he said, frowning.

"They do say that memory is the first thing that aging affects . . . "

"Thanks! I'll remember that."

Cloaked and at low altitude, she followed the northern track, noting the offshoots and realizing she had bit off quite a lot to chew if she was going to warn even half the inhabitants. She refused to allow the fact to discourage her from her chosen task. And night was falling on the continent.

"Ah-ha!" Niall pointed urgently at the view port. "Fires. Port three degrees."

"And far too much forest for me to land in."

"I don't mind backtracking when you can find a landing spot . . . Oh, no, I can't, can I?"

"No, you can't, but I appreciate your willingness to offer. Especially since I need to show my little vid to stir them to action."

"You *could* use the prosthesis," he said in a wheedling tone, grinning at her.

She said nothing—pointedly—and he chuckled. She might have to at that if daylight didn't show her settlements she could reach. She could hover . . . but she'd need something to project the vid on to for maximum effectiveness.

"I'll just use the darkness for reconnaissance and find out how many places I'm going to have to visit."

"Good thinking. I'll make a list of the coordinates. You might need them if the Fleet does come to our aid and comfort."

• • •

By morning his list of settlements, in all directions, had reached the three hundred mark. Some were small in the forested areas, but the plains or rolling hill country had many with several hundred inhabitants. All were ringed with walls, and these seemed to exude the power that showed up at every settlement, as well as a land-dike that Niall called a margin of no-woman's-land. The largest congregation was sited at the confluence of two rivers.

"If they have such a thing as an administrative center, that is likely it," she said. "We'll go there first thing in the morning. When I've had a quick look at that island complex."

"Whatever you say, love," Niall remarked with unusual compliance.

So she—they—arrived bright and early as the sun rose over the cup of the mountains that surrounded the largest congregation of Ravel's Chloe-ites.

"Rather impressive, wouldn't you say?" Niall remarked. "Orderly, neat. Everyone must have a private domicile. Thought you said they were a cloistered order."

The arrangement of the town, small city, did surprise Helva. Streets laid out in the center while garden plots and some large fields were positioned all around but within the customary low surrounding wall. There were main gates at each of the cardinal points of the compass but they weren't substantial: a Kolnari war axe would have reduced them to splinters with the first blow. A power source was visible on her sensors but it seemed to power the wall. What could they be keeping out that wasn't very tall or large or strong? Odd. Larger buildings set in the midst of fenced fields suggested either storage or barn shelters. She saw nothing grazing, though the season looked to be spring, to judge by the delicate green of cultivated fields, all within the walled boundary.

All four of the major avenues leading from the gates, for they were broad enough to be dignified with that title, tree-lined as well, led toward a large building which dominated the center. Part of it looked like a church, with an ample plaza in front of it for assemblies. Behind the church were low lines of buildings, possibly administration. This was a far-better-organized place than the original Chloe had been. Maybe they had learned something in the last century. She could hope.

"Hey, get that, Helva," Niall said suddenly, pointing to a slim structure atop the front of the building. "Not a steeple after all—no bells in it—but it's got something atop it."

Their approach had now been sighted, for the avenues as well as the smaller lanes between the individual housing units were filling with figures, faces upturned. Most were racing towards the square in front of the church, or whatever the big building was.

"Early risers . . . " Helva remarked.

"Early to bed—that power source is limited to the wall, not any electricity—and early to rise, you know," Niall said in a revoltingly jocular tone of voice. Then he altered to a practical tone, "And there's just about enough space for you to land in front of that church."

"So there is. But it's also full," she said, for they had arrived at the back end of the building and now that she had swung round, she could see that the plaza was filled with kneeling bodies. No one was working the fields.

"The more you squash the fewer we'll have to save from the Kolnari," Niall said.

"Oh, be quiet."

"It's over and out to you, Helva love. Sock it to them."

The devout knelt with upturned faces. She could see their mouths open with dark O's of surprise. But not fear. At some unseen signal, the kneelers rose and quickly, but without panic, moved back, out of the plaza.

"Be not afraid," Helva said gently, using her exterior sound system and ignoring the rich chuckle of amusement from Niall.

"They're not. Maybe you better alter your program, dear heart."

"I need to speak with you."

"Why don't you just hover?"

She made sure she was on interior sound only before she said sharply, "Will you shut up and let me handle this, Niall?"

"Remind them that you saved them from the hellfire of Chloe, dear," suggested Niall.

"That's my next line," she said in a caustic aside. "I am called Helva."

"Hey, Helva, that's you they've got mounted on that building."

In her careful vertical descent, she was now level with the spire. Which wasn't a spire but a replica of her earlier ship-self, vanes and all.

"Well, how's that for being canonized!" Niall said, but she could hear a note of pride in his voice. "You may be able to pull this off after all, love."

Rather more shaken by the artifact than she'd ever let him know, she completed her landing. One of the improvements on her ship body was the vertical cabin and a ramp directly to it, rather than the old and inconvenient lift from the stern.

"You even have a reception party of one," Niall remarked, as a tall figure became visible on the starboard viewers. All around the square the others turned towards that figure, heads bowing in a brief obeisance.

"How else are you called, Ship Helva?" said the tall woman, the hood falling back and revealing the serene face of an older woman.

"Not bad at all," Niall murmured. "She'd look even better in something feminine."

Indeed, Helva agreed with him since the woman had the most amazingly attractive face. A pity she had taken up religion instead of a man and a family. The long cassock robe she wore was one of those amorphous affairs, probably woven or pounded out of indigenous fibers and strictly utilitarian.

"I am Ship NH-834, who was once also the JH-834."

The woman nodded and inclined forward from her waist in a deep bow.

"Bingo!" said Niall.

"We have sent eternal prayers for the repose of the soul of Jennan," the woman said in a richly melodious voice, and from the onlookers rose a murmur of "Praise ever to his name."

"His memory is honored," Helva replied sincerely. "May I ask your name?"

"I am the Helvana," the woman replied, again with a reverent bow of her head.

"Oh, my God, Helva, you made it to sainthood," Niall said with complete irreverence and rolled with laughter in the pilot's chair. "With your own priestess caste system. Wow!"

Somehow his reaction annoyed her so much she almost erased his program. But common sense reasserted itself. If she was indeed some sort of saint to these people, she needed his irreverence more than ever—to keep her balance.

"You lead your people?"

"I am she who has been chosen," the woman said. "For many decades, we have hoped that you would honor us with your appearance . . . "

"Once more I come to you with bad tidings," Helva said quickly before she could be inundated with sanctimonious sentiments or perorations.

"That you have come is enough. What is your bidding, Ship Who Sings?"

"They have you pegged, my dear," Niall murmured, grinning like an idiot.

"An enemy approaches this planet . . . ah . . . Helvana." Helva had a bit of trouble getting that name/title out. "I have sent for assistance but it will not arrive in time to prevent the landing, nor the brutality with which these people—they are called the Kolnari—overwhelm an unprotected population."

A chuckle, rich and throaty, surprised Helva. She also caught smiles from those around the square.

"It's no laughing matter, Helvana. I have documentation of how they overwhelm resistance. How they . . . abuse the population." She couldn't quite say "rape" in the presence of girls who looked to be in their teens. "I must ask that you retreat to whatever safety the forests and mountains can provide until the Fleet arrives. Having warned you here in this fine city, I must spread the alarm to all that I can, to protect as many as I can."

The woman named Helvana raised one hand, a polite interruption. "Bird-keepers, send the flocks to warn our sisters. Ship Who Sings, would you know how soon they will land?"

"I'm no more than four days ahead of them," Helva said, wondering at her calmness. With relief, she did see quite a few women disappearing from the perimeter and doing whatever duties the bird-keepers might have. "You must gather what belongings you cherish and make for forest and mountain."

"Four days is plenty of time to set all in motion, Ship Who Sings."

This Helvana sounded not the least bit alarmed, as she bloody well should have been.

"You don't understand, Hel . . . Helvana. These men are pirates, vicious. They have no mercy on their victims . . . "

"Show them the tape," Niall said.

"This is what they did on the planet Bethel," she said, and activated the exterior display, using the whitewashed facade of the imposing main building as a screen.

"That will not be necessary," Helvana said. "Turn it off now. Please!" And, since some of the captive audience looked decidedly unnerved by the first scene of battle-armored Kolnari making mighty jumps towards screaming and panicking Bethelites, Helva found herself obeying. "There is absolutely no need to terrify. NO need at all."

"But there is, Helvana. Those men . . . "

"May I speak to you in private, Ship Who Sings?"

"I wouldn't like to go against that one," Niall said. "She's tough."

"Yes, of course," Helva said to the Helvana. And then to Niall, "Get lost!"

"Immediately," Niall said, rising and skittering off to his quarters.

The Helvana was tall enough to have to duck her head to clear the lintel of the opening and stood for a moment, looking calmly around her, a little smile flickering at the corners of her mouth. Then, to Helva's surprise, she bowed with great reverence toward the central panel behind which Helva's titanium shell was situated.

"I have dreamed of being granted such a moment, Ship Who Sings," she said, her voice vibrant with exultation.

"Please be seated in the lounge on your right," Helva said.

The Helvana took a second look at the raised bridge area that had been Niall's favorite place and turned to the lounge area. With considerable grace, the heavy folds of her cassock flowing around her feet and her heavy boots grating on the metal part of the deck, she reached the first of the sectional couches. With another bow, she seated herself facing Helva's panel.

"I must tell you, Ship Who Sings, that the pitiful colony of the religious you rescued from Ravel's nova learned from that basic mistake."

"I am pleased to hear that," Helva began, "but you must . . . "

The graceful hand raised from the deep-cuffed sleeve. "There was much to be learned if the Inner Marian Circle would survive the science of your civilization."

"Really?" Helva decided that this was a time to listen.

"The satellite will have sent its preprogrammed message even as I am certain you sent messages?" Her voice ended on an upward querying note.

"Several, with such details of the invading force as I was able to glean. But, really, Helvana, they're going . . . "

The hand raised and Helva subsided. She did have four days in hand.

"My grandmother . . . "

Well, that was unexpected.

" . . . Was one of those whom you yourself rescued. A wise but older Christian sisterhood succored her and the other younger members of that community until a new planet could be found for our Order. And they acquired much wisdom during their waiting."

"Not, however, how to combat bloodthir . . . "

The hand went up and Helva subsided again.

"We had been children on Chloe, ignorant and kept in ignorance when knowledge would have saved us, and the Blessed Jennan. My grandmother studied much, as did her intimate circle. With prayer and research, we found that this planet was available. A stable primary was our first consideration, of course," she said with a graceful wave of her hand. "Surveys of Ravel proved it would be adequate for our needs and our preferred style of life once we overcame its . . . nature. The planet has inherent dangers. Indeed we were required to devise a means whereby we could safely land the first colony expedition." Her expression became distant with memories, but she pulled herself back to the present with a little shake of her head. "We were averse to the use of technology, but that, in the end, was what we required and what we still employ. We have maintained the landing site out of respect for the achievement of technology over rampant nature. The touch of a switch will deter any unwelcome . . . visitors."

She was talking a great deal more rationally than that rabid idiot Mother Superior at Chloe had. But defending the broad open plains of this Ravel would be the task of an army. A much-better-equipped one than these people could possibly mount.

"We have cultivated not only the land, but the resources of the vegetation and wildlife. There are predators on Ravel . . . "

"Not anything that could overcome a battle-armed Kolnari . . . "

The Helvana smiled.

"How many are in this Kolnari battle armor?"

Well, that was the first sensible question.

"I'd estimate five, maybe six regiments."

Her well-shaped eyebrows arched in surprise. "How many are in a regiment?"

Helva told her.

"That many?"

"Yes, that many, and impregnable in that battle armor, too. Unless you happen to have armor-piercing missiles hidden in your fields."

"Nothing to pierce armor," the Helvana said blithely, with a light emphasis on "pierce." "But we will defend ourselves well."

"Don't even consider hand-to-hand combat, Helvana," Helva said.

"Oh"—and there was a lovely rippling contralto laugh—"we wouldn't consider attacking anyone."

"Then HOW do you plan to deal with the Kolnari?"

"May I surprise you?"

"If it doesn't lead immediately to your death and the slaughter of all those innocents out there."

"It won't."

"Which reminds me, Helvana, I saw young children out there, and teenage girls as well as matrons your age and older."

Helva had been reviewing her tapes, because something had puzzled her about the composition of those calm observers.

"Ah, yes," the Helvana said, smiling graciously. "My grandmother also decided that our community must propagate . . . "

"Parthenogenesis?"

"Oh, no, that would have been against our precepts. We brought with us sufficient fertilized female ova, removed from our Faithful, to supply us with the necessary diverse genetic balance to ensure that our community will last for centuries."

"Clever," Helva said.

"Not the least of our . . . cleverness, Ship Who Sings."

Just then Helva's outside sensors picked up a little cough and she became aware that a covey of girls was standing just outside the hatch.

"I think they wish to speak to you, Helvana," the ship said. "Come on in, girls."

Their faces either red with embarrassment or white with exultation, the young women entered, bowing with varying degrees of grace as the Helvana had done, towards Helva's panel. Did the whole damned planet know where *she* lived?

"The birds have flown, Helvana. And some nearby have responded."

Helvana nodded, pleased. "Enter the responses and report back when all have answered."

The girls left in a flurry, but not before a second obeisance to Helva.

"You've trained avians as messengers?"

"It seemed wise since there are such distances between our communities and decisions must be circulated when necessary."

"Does every community have a . . . Helvana?"

"No, I am the one so honored by my peers."

"How long will you serve, if that is the correct phrase?"

"It is you I serve," the Helvana said with great dignity. "When I know myself too old to continue intelligent administration, my successor will be installed, chosen from among those who are diligent in learning the canon and tradition of our Circle."

"Well, yes, but let's get to the point. *Do* you have some safe refuge where you can't be found until the Fleet arrives?"

"Ravel supplies our defense," Helvana said, again with the confident smile.

"Enlighten me, then, because I have every reason to fear for your safety."

"You must look more closely at Ravel."

"Don't tell me you've trained the predators to defend you?"

"No, the planet itself will."

"Well, if your defense is classified, I assure you I won't disclose your methods but the Kolnari are the most effective and ruthless fighting force of all humanoids. They . . . "

"Against other humans, quite likely . . . "

"They have weaponry"—and Helva was getting a bit tired of this woman's self-confident denial of any threat—"that could turn this settlement into a cinder . . . "

"From the air?" And there was just a touch of fear in this Helvana's voice.

"You're lucky," Helva said dryly, "the Kolnari strategy is based more on overwhelming their target with ground forces. Of course, your satellite warning system'll be blasted out of space as soon as they spot it, but the bunch that's headed here don't have any assault ships, unless they've modified some of the bigger yachts. And all of *them* seem so full of bodies that I doubt they are armed with space-to-surface missiles, too. Though," Helva added thoughtfully, "they could be. However, they think they have total surprise as an advantage to a quick rout."

The Helvana crossed her arms and said, not quite smugly, "Then we shall not be harmed."

"Look, their ships are crammed with bodies, bodies which intend to take over *this* planet for their purposes which, I assure you, you won't like. You have no armament . . . "

"We need none . . . "

"So you say, but you've never seen the Kolnari take over a planet. Let me just show you how they conquered . . . "

Helvana held up her hand. "God forfend."

"*He's* not in a position to forfend anything. Look, you've got to take precautions."

"They are already in place."

"What?"

"The planet itself."

"And round and round we go," Helva said, irked. "This is Chloe all over again with a slightly different scenario," she said, allowing her irritation to show in her voice. "You won't be fried by the sun this time but by . . . "

"No." And Helvana held up a hand with such authority that Helva broke off. "You will have noticed that our settlements, large and small, are walled . . . "

"Not much good against Kolnari battle-armored troops . . . "

"Who will not get close enough to our walls . . . Nor do we go beyond them very often, for it is the vegetation of Ravel that is dangerous to all. Even the predators venture out only on cold nights when the planet sleeps."

"Come again?"

Helvana's smile just missed being a smirk and she cocked her head slightly at Helva. "How much would these Kolnari know about our planet?"

"Only what is in the Galactic Atlas."

"May I see that entry?"

Helva brought it up on the main-lounge screen and the Helvana read it swiftly, smiling her smile as she finished.

"There have been no additions. As promised."

"I do wish I could be as confident as you are," Helva said.

The Helvana rose. "The last time it was the primary which would destroy us. This time the planet will work for us. One question: since the entry indicates a spaceport, will the Kolnari land there first? To organize their invasion?"

Helva thought of that battered collection of ships. "They use whatever's available. They've enough ships to use all the space the landing field offers. Though, in my judgment," she added grimly, "some of them may not make a controlled landing." She paused, wondering if in those dilapidated buildings there were any emergency vehicles or equipment. Then she ruthlessly decided that a few Kolnari would not be missed. "Some are barely spaceworthy, and one was leaking oxygen. You must realize that this is the Kolnari's last-gasp attempt to resettle. They'll fight whatever you have in mind to put against them. They must know this planet is a walkover."

"Not . . . " Helvana paused with an inscrutable twist to her lips. " . . . an easy walkover. Not by any means."

"They do have arsenals of some pretty sophisticated weapons," Helva reminded her guest. "Don't discount the possibility of an air-to-surface barrage to soften you up."

Helvana actually chuckled. "What? Bomb our fields and settlements? If their object is to settle here, they wouldn't destroy available housing or crops."

"You don't know the Kolnari as I do, Helvana. Don't treat this lightly."

"I assure you I do not," the woman said, and her face assumed a concerned and serious expression. "Our fields, our homes would be targeted?"

"Very likely, although it is equally likely that, fearing no resistance, they may just land and march . . . "

"Oh, I do hope so," said the Helvana, one moment her face brightening with something akin to triumph, instantly fading to self-recrimination. "We do not take pleasure in destruction of any kind on Ravel."

"Even to save your lives?"

"Your presence, and your warning, is sufficient." The Helvana rose.

"I have no weapons, no way to defend you," Helva said, unable to keep the frustration and anger out of her voice.

The woman turned, inclining her head. "That is known, so you must seek safety yourself. I know little of what transpires in other sections of the Universe, and your pictures showed us it is not a safe place in which to reside, so you are at risk. You have warned us. We are advised. We shall be safe. Go you to be safe, too, Ship Who Sings."

"I can't *just leave you*!" Helva's voice rose and she could hear it resounding outside, causing some of the women still gathered in groups in the plaza to turn around.

"As you cannot defend yourself," Helvana said in a tone that implied Helva was indeed more at risk than her adherents were, "you must depart. I have much to organize."

"Well, I'm glad to hear that," Helva said in a caustic tone.

The woman turned at the airlock, made a deep and respectful obeisance, and strode down the ramp. Immediately she began issuing commands that had all the onlookers scurrying to obey. In moments the plaza was empty and the Helvana had reentered the church or administration building or whatever it was.

"Well, well." And Niall peered around the edge of the corridor that led to his quarters. "That one has style!"

"She's no smarter than that rabid, ranting ascetic on Chloe!" Helva's voice crackled with anger. "As if I'm the one who's vulnerable."

"What was that about the vegetation?" Niall asked. "And close the hatch, love. I don't want someone peering in and catching sight of a *maaaale* . . . " He jiggled his hands in clownish antic and dragged out the last word.

"What about the vegetation?" Helva demanded irritably as she retracted the ramp and shut off access.

"I'd say it's dangerous and the power to the walls is to keep it at bay. Remember the roads here? All with neat margins .. . and haven't been used . . . and they employ birds to carry messages? Doesn't that suggest to you they don't wander much from the walls of their cloisters?"

Helva thought about that possibility. "As a weapon against the Kolnari?" she demanded with trenchant incredulity.

"We can cloak and watch," Niall said, cocking his head slightly at something he had perceived that eluded her. "That lady seemed far too certain of their . . . indigenous . . . protections. And we haven't seen everything on this world yet, now have we?"

Helva had been scanning with her exterior sensors, and except for birds coming in to land on what she had initially thought to be multiple chimneys but were rooftop aviaries, she reconsidered the situation.

"I'm going to try another of their settlements," she said, and, making sure there were no bodies anywhere near her, lifted slowly. The plaza was so hard-packed from much usage that only little swirls of dust marked her ascent.

She tried nine settlements, medium, small and another large one, but each time the head woman of the group, while respectful in all other ways, replied that there was no need this time for The Ship Who Sings to worry about Ravellians. But it was good of her to appear to warn them that a time of trial was coming. Helva tried to show the hologram and, after the first horrified glances, everyone turned their backs, squeezing their eyes closed against the proof she tried to exhibit.

"I don't think it's a case of your losing your touch," Niall said kindly, drumming silent fingers on the armrest. "They honestly believe they're safe. Not that the mere odor of sanctity ever saved a saint and certainly won't save these sisters from the Kolnari. But, in case you've been fretting too much to notice, every single one of the walls around these cloisters is on full power."

"Where're the sources? That's something the Kolnari will spot if they make even the most routine scan or aerial reconnaissance." And Helva was more afraid than ever. On the previous occasion, the expanding sun itself had provided proof positive of danger to the doubting religious. What would it take to prove it this time? And why was she stuck with this gullible lot again?

• • •

She kept trying and kept getting the same responses from all ninety-seven cloisters she visited. On the way to the ninety-eighth, they saw the spark of bright light in the sky that indicated the Kolnari had just demolished the satellite.

"Nice of them to give us fair warning. Now's the time to cloak, Helva," Niall remarked, his fingers in their restless dance on the armrests.

"I have been while I was flying between these damnable stubborn towns," she replied curtly, and headed towards the pathetic landing field. Since it was there, and nothing else on this vegetating world offered any other large cleared space as a come-on to the Kolnari, she figured that would be where the invaders would land.

At dawn, she and Niall arrived close enough to the landing site, hovering just behind the nearest of the hills that surrounded the facility.

"Ah-ha," Niall said in a thoughtful drawl, as he leaned across the control board to peer at the forward view screen. He flipped on each of the exterior viewers, reducing them to a patchwork that made Helva almost dizzy until she spotted what had alerted him.

The landing field, once unpatterned, level soil, had sprouted the most obscene-looking ground cover, greasy, slimy, a sort of pus yellow and mold green. No more than a few centimeters high. Undoubtedly it gave a smooth, even appearance to anyone above.

"Those are not my favorite colors for a solid footing, Helva," Niall said in a low ominous tone. "Let's just hover and shelter in our cloak."

"Excellent notion," she said, noticing on the port sensor near the prow of her ship that tendrils thrust up towards her, lashing in their attempt to snare the ship. She put more distance between herself and the ground. "Very interesting indeed. Malevolent vegetation."

Niall began rubbing his hands, an unholy expression on his face. "Serves the bastards right. Though let's hope their disintegrating metabolism doesn't affect the stuff. They're mean enough to poison anything that doesn't poison them first."

"They may have met their match," she replied, willing to be convinced.

• • •

The first two Kolnari ships to land were two of the heavier, armed cruisers. They landed smack-dab in the middle of the greasy sward and instantly deployed their armored infantry units while gunners started setting up their portable projectile units. They didn't, as Helva half expected them to, take out the rickety old buildings, which were now covered with viler chartreusey green vines. Not that the Kolnari were apt to be color-conscious. Much less suspicious. Their home world was noted for its offputting appearance.

The troops marched off the landing field, kicking their metallic booted feet at now calf-high shrubs and bushes that impeded their progress, ignorant of the fact that the growths were brand-new additions on the field. They had split into four sections and each started off up one of the main tracks. Three more of the larger ships landed at one edge of the field, crowded with additional troops, who set off after the vanguard, smaller units turning off at each arterial lane. In quick succession, the yacht-sized spacecraft zoomed in, one or two making such rough landings that they plowed their noses into the ground. They were instantly covered with tendrils and twigs that shortly turned into thick branches, wrapping about the ships, tethering them to the field. Had these not been Kolnari whose prime intent was capture and enslavement of the Ravellians, Helva might have been tempted to warn those unarmed, unsuited people who swarmed out of the ships, coughing, falling to the ground, raising arms upward as if they had just been saved. From dying of asphyxia they had. But Ravel's indigenous vegetation vigorously began to engulf them . . . consuming their still-living forms . . . to judge by the frantic green-covered contortions and the screams, shrieks and tortured calls. The seeking vines penetrated the open hatches, cutting off the escape of any who saw what was happening and thought of seeking safety inside.

There was undoubtedly not even time for one of the more intelligent captains to warn off the rest of the armada, which continued to touch down wherever they could. Remaining aloft did not seem to have been an option. Every passenger was in too much of a hurry to disembark to notice what had been happening to the earlier arrivals.

"Truly a just retribution has been meted out to them," Niall muttered. "A planet fighting back!" The verdure kept moving, probing, twining, inserting itself everywhere, bursting the seams of some of the oldest and most fragile vessels. "After all the violence they have dealt out to unsuspecting and innocent populations . . . " His voice trailed off and he snapped off the screen displays of the chartreuse catastrophe.

Without a word, Helva lifted and started up the nearest track, actually the one that headed towards the main settlement, to see what the flora of Ravel was doing to the armored infantry units. The demise of the ground troops—none of which reached even the nearest and smallest of the cloisters—only took a little longer, though they didn't penetrate even within howling distance of any of the cloisters.

"The weeds must exude some really corrosive kind of acid. Look at the pockmarks—holes even—in some of that armor where the vine tips have lashed it," Niall said, shaking his head in amazement. "How do the girls manage that stuff if it can do that to spaceworthy body armor?"

"I do not care so long as it is as effective as it seems to be."

Belatedly realizing the danger they were in, the bold Kolnari were, of course, turning their weapons on the demon flora that was smothering them. Perhaps someone on the space field had lasted long enough to send out a message. But on this field of battle the Kolnari weapons increased, rather than decreased, the foe. Blasting or flaming the vegetable matter only caused it to fragment, each part then expanding and multiplying into more attackers. Kolnari warriors in their heavy boots were being tripped up and, once down, became greeny yellow mounds of writhing shrubbery. Their power packs would have been infiltrated by vine tips, their equipment shorted out. Safe now from Kolnari weapons, Helva uncloaked and recorded the Kolnari defeat, focusing occasionally on what happened when flora was fragmented. She stayed high enough above the carnage . . . or did she mean "vernage" . . . to avoid any contact. She thought—only briefly—of trying to acquire a leaf or twig to preserve—at maximum botanical security—for later analysis in the High Risk laboratories at Central Worlds.

"I've never seen anything like it," Niall said, shaking his head. "We do know that there are inimical planetary surfaces, but one which can be contained, tamed, and used in emergencies? One more for the files!" Then he leaned back in the chair, locking his fingers and rubbing his palms together with the great satisfaction he enjoyed at this totally unexpected Kolnari defeat. "Those lassies learned a thing or two, didn't they, about passive resistance."

"Passive wasn't what we just witnessed," Helva said drolly. "They simply let the nature of the planet take its course. Mind you, somewhere in the ethics of their Marian religiosity there must be a shibboleth about taking human lives . . . "

"Ha! I never considered the Kolnari as humans," was Niall's response. "Besides which, the religious have as much right to protect themselves as any other life-form."

"*They* aren't doing anything. The planet is. That's the beauty part."

"Ah, yes." And Niall's tone turned sanctimonious. "Suffer the meek for they shall inherit the earth . . . of Ravel, in this case. Well-done, ladies, well-done." He brought his hands together in a silent applause. "We should extend our felicities. Or you should."

"I think the outcome was not only taken for granted but has been observed," Helva said, and activated a long-range screen that showed little flocks of avians circling here and there, before darting off so quickly not even Helva could have plotted so many different course directions.

• • •

When Helva touched down again in the plaza, the Helvana and a group of about fourteen awaited her. They wore long black scarves and tight-fitting black caps.

" 'We come to mourn Caesar not to praise him,' " Niall quoted.

"Get thee hence, Marc Antony," she replied warningly.

"I'm going. I'm going. I'll not attend this wake in mournful array."

"You're already arrayed appropriately," she called after his disappearing figure, then opened her airlock and extended the ramp.

The deputation entered, making obeisance to her until all had filed into the lounge, their expression somber if respectful, though some were red-eyed with weeping. There would be some tender hearts among such a group. Why they'd spend their tears on the Kolnari, when they knew what would have been their fate, defeated Helva's understanding. But then, she was not religious. She spoke first, not wishing to be embroiled in specious gratitude for this second inadvertent "deliverance" in which she had been only a passive spectator, not the rescue vehicle.

"I apologize, Helvana, for doubting your efficiency and ingenuity. The meek have indeed inherited this earth."

Helva devoutly hoped that no one else heard the scoffing snort from the passageway.

"We all deeply regret that we had to prove our invulnerability on Ravel," the Helvana said in a slow, sad tone. "We shall pray for their departed souls."

"I sincerely doubt they had any," Helva said, an acid remark that occasioned gasps of surprise from some of the younger women. "Uncharitable of me, I know, but I have seen their form of conquest at firsthand. I do not regret their destruction. Nor should any here shed any more remorseful tears or rue the incident. The Universe is now considerably safer. After all, none of you . . . " She paused briefly. " . . . did anything. Your planet is well able to take care of unwanted visitors and has done so."

There was a brief awkward pause, while the faithful dealt with the unexpected candor of their "savior." To fill in the silence, Helva went on.

"How long will it take you to repair the damage to the space field and the tracks?"

"We may not," the Helvana said after glancing at her companions. "We keep in touch with the other cloisters and there is really no need for all to assemble at the same time. Each community is self-sufficient and there is no longer any need for the space field."

"But you'll keep the walls functioning."

A little smile tugged at the Helvana's lips. "Yes." She inclined her head. "They are required to keep the flora of Ravel in its place."

"But surely those plant forms that have had such . . . " Helva hesitated, not wishing to upset the tenderhearted with the word 'fertilizing.' " . . . unexpected freedom will wish to retain it?"

"What needs to be restored will be. It is a long and painstaking process and we have much to occupy ourselves in the normal course of our daily routine," the Helvana said.

One of her escort pulled at her sleeve.

"Yes, of course, and our eternal gratitude to you should have been spoken of first," Helvana said kindly to the woman. "We are once again in your debt, Ship Who Sings, and once again have no way to repay your watchful guardianship."

"If I said I only happened to be in the neighborhood, would you believe me?" Helva asked gently.

There was just a hint of a sparkle in the Helvana's eyes as she caught the irony.

"Let us then hope that we have not caused you an unnecessary delay," the Helvana said.

"No, you have not," Helva replied more graciously. Perversely, she really didn't want to destroy her reputation among the cloisters. "I will not be late arriving at my destination." Since she wasn't expected at Regulus, that was no lie. More worldly remarks must be made however. "I shall apprise the Fleet that they may stand down from the alert I sent out. I shall report the demise . . . "

That rattled them all but the Helvana raised her hand and the startled expressions of dismay were silenced.

"Let not death be part of the message. Merely that the . . . emergency has been dealt with," the Helvana said with great dignity.

"So it shall be said," Helva replied solemnly, though she was in honor bound to inform the Fleet that the Kolnari were well and truly annihilated. "If I may suggest it, I would feel better if you let me have the satellite beacon replaced: the one that the . . . recent visitors blasted from your skies so you will not be further interrupted." Once the fate dealt the Kolnari invaders was known, no one would dare land on Ravel. "May I attend to that detail for you?"

"There is a small group of our Marian Circle on Vega III," the Helvana said. "If you would be good enough to inform them that . . . a replacement satellite is required, they will attend to the expense and installation. You need not be troubled with such a detail."

"It would not trouble me," Helva said. "But I will inform your sisters in religion of the need and your continued safety. No debt exists between us, wise and good Helvana. I was here when I was needed as I was at Chloe. That is enough."

"So be it," the Helvana said, bowing her head in acceptance while the others murmured the same response. Then, with firm gestures, she led the delegation to the airlock, standing to one side as each made proper obeisance to Helva's column. This took long enough so that Helva was getting fidgety. She adjusted her nutrient flow to account for the recent stress.

The Helvana hesitated after she made her deep bow.

"We shall pray for your lost partner," she said, and inclined her head in the direction of Niall's cabin. "May you be comforted in his loss by another as worthy to hold his position as Niall Parollan."

She was gone, leaving Helva so stunned that she couldn't speak.

"Pray for me, indeed!" snapped Niall's crisp voice as he strode into the main cabin.

Helva closed the airlock with a clang.

"How did she know that piece of gossip?" Niall went on, "And let's get off this planet. Gives me the creeps, all those women weeping over Kolnari. Much less me."

Somehow Helva went through the necessary routines to lift her shipself as adroitly as possible. The plaza was clear of all save the Helvana and her delegation, backed up against the main building, forming an orderly triangle on the steps, with the Helvana at the apex. From her stern sensors, Helva saw the upturned faces as the faithful watched the sight of *their* Ship ascending once again into the heavens from which she had come to succor them.

"They never will believe you were 'just in the neighborhood,' you know," Niall said, but there was an odd quirk to his lips. "At least that wise one won't."

"We were," Helva replied, more involved with figuring out how the Helvana had known of Niall's death when the woman had been no farther inside the ship than the airlock and the lounge. What astonished her even more was that the Helvana's blessing *did* comfort her.

• • •

Once clear of the system, Helva sent out an All-Points saying that the emergency was over and that she could report the extermination of the remnants of the Kolnari fleet; full details would be presented at Regulus on her arrival there. She did not give an estimated time, though she encountered several picket forces making all possible speed in obedience to her summons. She knew they were disappointed about losing a chance to gain fame and promotion fighting the last remnants of the Kolnari but she advised them that the Ravellians were not people interested in having quests. Ever. She could, and did, patch across the tapes she had taken of the disastrous Kolnari defeat. Obliquely she kept her word to the Helvana while still satisfying Fleet Intelligence. What she didn't realize was that her reticence only added to the glamour surrounding her living legend.

She met up with the escort five days out of the Regulus system, two squadrons no less. And with a Commodore on board the Nova Class flagship.

"Commodore Halliman reporting, ma'am, as escort for yourself and Niall Parollan," was the initial message and there was the happily grinning Commodore, in full-dress uniform, on the bridge of the battle cruiser. He glanced around, expecting to see Helva's brawn.

"I bring back the body of my scout, Niall Parollan, Commodore," she said more calmly than she expected she could. The Helvana's prayers were working?

"I hadn't known . . . " The Commodore was patently shocked, and she could hear a murmur run around the bridge at such news. "My condolences and apologies. You have sustained a great loss. Was he a casualty of the Kolnari action?"

"Niall Parollan died quietly in his sleep. The diagnosis was total systems failure caused by extreme age," she said. She went on before she'd be asked the time and place of death. Stasis provided no clues. "He requested the ceremonies due his rank and service, Commodore," she went on, smiling inwardly at Niall's idea of a reward for putting up with her for so many years.

"Only his just due, ma'am. We shall proceed with the arrangements immediately . . . if that is your wish."

"It is," she said with a gentle sigh. Actually, that program hadn't been such a bad idea at all. It *had* given her time to become accustomed to the fact of Niall's death. *Death, Death, where is thy sting? Grave thy victory?*

"Our deepest sympathies," said the Commodore, and saluted with solemn precision. Behind him she saw others come smartly to attention and salute. "The NH-834 made inestimable contributions to the Service."

"Niall was a paragon of partners," she replied. "You'll forgive me if I resume my silence." She really didn't mean to misrepresent any facet of her recent history, but there were certain details she intended to keep hidden in her head.

"Don't think that's going to get you off the hook of explaining the Kolnari defeat, my pet," Niall said. He had been propping up a wall just beyond the view of the one screen she had activated to receive the Commodore's call. "And will I have performed my part there in true heroic form?"

"What else? I'll not have you go to your grave without every bit of honor due you. And you did perform your designated role on Ravel. You stayed out of sight."

"Not entirely, evidently," Niall said with a wicked grin, waggling a finger at her.

"If you mean that Helvana woman's little surprise remark, forget that. A lucky guess, since she would have known I'd have to have had a brawn with me somewhere."

"She knew me by name."

"Maybe she can talk to the dead. And you are dead, you know. Can't you stay down?"

"Why should I? Miss my own obsequies? How can you ask that of me?" He pressed one hand against his chest in dismay.

She laughed. "I should have known you'd pull a Tom Sawyer."

He laughed, too. "Why not, since you have provided me the ability to watch? I've always wanted to hear what people thought of me."

"You won't hear any candor at your funeral. It's not good manners to speak ill of the dead, you know. Besides which, I do NOT want Psych checking my synapses for fear I've blown a few by concocting your holo program."

"No one will see me, my love, I assure you," he said.

She had intended to delete the program totally, even the petabytes that had once stored it, when she reached Regulus Base. Now she changed her mind. He had the right to see the ceremony: all of it from the slow march with his bier, the atmosphere planes doing their wing-tipping salute, the volley of rifles, the whole nine yards of changeless requiem for the honored dead. This time, she was not mourning the sudden, unnecessary death of a beloved partner: she was celebrating the long and fruitful life of a dear friend whom she would also never forget.

• • •

When the burial detail came to collect the mortal husk, the stasis in the coffin replaced that in which she had held his body intact during her long journey home. Regulus officialdom turned out in force, from the Central Worlds' current Administrative Chief with every one of his aides in formal-dress parade uniforms to the planetary Governor in her very elegant black dress and fashionable hat, to the parade of mixed armed services as well as whatever brawns were on the Base, and all the brawn trainees. The service was just long enough. A little longer and she'd have believed the fulsome eulogies about the man they mourned, who was sitting in the pilot's chair and watching the entire show with the greatest of satisfaction. She'd remember that as the best part of the whole show.

"I wouldn't have missed this for the damned Horsehead Nebula we never did get to," he exclaimed several times. As Helva was parked where her cabin could not be seen from those either on the ground or on the raised platform for the dignitaries, he could peer about, wisecracking and reminiscing as he chose.

She did, as she had done before and as it was expected of Helva, the ship who sings, let the heavens resound with the poignant strains of the service song of evening and requiem. But this time her tone was triumphant, and as her last note died away across the cemetery and all the bowed heads, she deleted Niall's holographic program.

They left her alone until she had decided she'd had enough solitude. She ought to have held off deleting Niall a few days longer, but there was a time to end things, and his funeral had been it. Then she contacted Headquarters.

"This is the XH-834 requesting a new brawn," she said, "and you'd better arrange a time for the Fleet to query me on that Ravel incident. I want it down on the records straight. I want a top priority message to the Marian Circle Cloister on Vega III that Ravel needs to have its warning satellite replaced. The Kolnari blew the old one out of space."

"New brawn?" repeated the woman who had responded to her call.

Her brain had gone into neutral at being unexpectedly contacted by the XH-834.

"Yes, a new brawn." Helva then repeated her other requests. "Got them? Good. Please expedite. And, as soon as you've informed the brawn barracks of my availability, patch me over whatever missions are currently available for a brain ship with my experience."

"Yes, indeed, XH-834, yes indeed." There was a pause through which Helva heard only sharp excited words clipped off before she quite caught any of the agitated sentences. Surprise always gives you an advantage.

She laughed with pure vindictive satisfaction as the brawn barracks erupted with people hastily flinging on tunics or fixing their hair or adjusting buttons. The scene brought back fond memories as the young men and women, all determined to win this prize of prizes, raced to be first aboard her.

They had not quite reached the ramp when she suddenly became aware of a hazy object. The outlines were misty, but it was Niall Parollan, striding to her column, laying his cheek once more against the panel that covered her.

"Don't give the next one any more grief than you gave me, will you, love?" He started to turn away, his outline noticeably fading. "And if you ever use that Sorg Prosthesis with anyone else but me, I'll kill him! Got that?"

She thought she muttered something as she watched his image drift to the hull by the forward screen, not towards the airlock. Just as she heard the stampede of the brawns outside, he disappeared altogether with one last wave of a hand that seemed to flow into the metal of her ship-self.

"Permission to come aboard, ma'am?" a breathless voice asked.

MY SHE

MARY ROSENBLUM

Mary Rosenblum is the author of four science fiction novels, including her latest, *Horizons*, and *The Drylands*, which won the Compton Crook Award for Best First Novel. *Water Rites*—a compilation of *The Drylands* and the three novelettes that preceded it—is recently available from Fairwood Press. Her short work frequently appears in *Asimov's*, but has also appeared in *Analog* and *The Magazine of Fantasy & Science Fiction*, and has often been reprinted in Gardner Dozois's *The Year's Best Science Fiction* annual.

Under the name Mary Freeman, Rosenblum is also the author of four mystery novels. Lately, she has returned her short fiction roots, but is currently working on a young adult fantasy novel and an alternate history project.

Communication is power, and this tale is a story of communication on a couple of levels. But it also tackles one of Rosenblum's favorite themes: Where does the boundary lie between human and non-human?

MY SHE

I wait outside the speaking chamber, where the young Speakers learn to Hear and Speak. The walls and carpeted floor are purest white, the color of this God place and the Speakers who live here walk by, all dressed in white like the walls and the floor, their palms on the shoulders of their guides. They all look the same with their pale hair and pale eyes. Only their smell tells me who they are. I am a guide for my Speaker. Until she puts on the robe and is sent to another place to Speak between the worlds for the citizens. Then I will have a new pup to raise. I will miss this puppy. Her scent comes to me from beneath the door of the learning room, smelling of *trying hard* and *not sure*.

She is never sure, my she, not since I first came to her, when she was just small. I sometimes smell her silent tears at night and slip into her room from my cubicle to lie beside her. She strokes the fur on my head and shoulders and it comforts her. It is our secret—kept secret, I think, because she does not know if it is permitted for me to sleep on her bed at night. I, myself, do not know, even after all these years here. Never before have I slept beside a pup in my charge.Perhaps there is nothing wrong. Perhaps there is. But it is our secret and it binds us. When I sleep in her bed, I hear my litter-brother in my dreams and I like that. I miss him always.

I will miss her, when she leaves. Unless they finally send me with her, the way they sent my litter-brother with his Speaker. But they say I am good at raising puppies and they have not sent me with a newly-robed Speaker yet.

While I wait for her, I pull out my brother's last mail to me. The tiny disk feels cool and hard in my palm. Disk-mail is not expensive, but it is slow. This disk traveled in four ships before it found its way here from the colony world where my brother now lives. But we guides are servants and servants are not entitled to use the Speakers; they are for citizens only. Perhaps they think that because we mostly smell to each other that we do not need to speak with words. But we cannot smell between the stars. I would like to speak to my litter-brother and hear his answer. I will never see him again, except on my she's bed. There, he speaks to me, tells me how he misses me. We used to wrestle in the meadow around the school where we were raised, chasing each other into the creek, splashing and laughing. Sometimes it snowed and I still dream of snow, cold and white, stinging my palms and the soles of my feet, tingly as it melted in my fur.

There is no snow in the convent. Only spring, forever.

The door opens and I have been dreaming of snow and my brother. I am not ready. I leap to my feet, ears going flat.

"Siri? Where are you?"

Her hand goes out and I step beneath it so that my shoulder fur comes up against her palm. I feel the tickle of her mind finding my eyes and the white-walled corridor blurs just a bit as our minds share my eyes.

I wonder if that is how I speak to my brother when I sleep in her bed? "I had a mail from my litter-brother," I tell her.

She understands litters. The Speaker puppies are born in litters of ten. We walk down the hall and I see that she is heading for the garden in the center of the convent. Sadness darkens her scent and I reach up to touch her hand lightly, wanting to make the smell go away.

"You don't understand." She shrugs me off but she does not smell angry. "What if I fail?"

Fail? The word chills me. My puppies to do not fail. Have never failed. We step out into sunlight, soft and gentle through the dome. Water trickles and the rich tapestry of dirt smells, the small beings that inhabit this space, the breath of the water itself make me dizzy. Most of the convent is clean of such smells. She sits on a bench covered with bright chips of color and I squat beside her, leaning lightly against her thigh because that comforts her. Her fingers slide into the long fur on the back of my neck and that makes me shiver. "Who said you would fail?"

"My Speaker-Mistress." Her words are low and she smells sharp, unhappy. "The one who . . . trains me. I . . . Hear more than the voice I'm tuning to. I can't shut the others out. But I don't listen to them." She smells distress and a tinge of anger. "I am good. I would not listen to any other voice. I would not Speak the God words to another. Not ever."

I wince—I cannot stop myself—because her fingers digging in hurt me. She lets go and covers her face with her hands.

"I am not trying to Hear them. I listen only for the voice that speaks to me. Too sensitive she said, the Speaker-Mistress." Her voice is hard to hear, but she smells frightened. "She said it could not be, that my genes will not permit it."

I shiver as if I am a puppy again and have played too long in the snow.

"Will they make me leave?"

She does not understand. Maybe none of them do. Speaking only the God words, Hearing the God Words is all there is for them. Only Speakers live here in the convent. And we servants.

No one leaves, except on a ship, to Hear and Speak in another place, so that the citizens can talk between the stars. The way my brother left with the new Speaker assigned to him.

I try to distract her. I can smell the vanilla orchids opening and she loves them. Even she can smell them with her poor dead nose and she loves the touch of their thick petals. So I take her to them. And she puts on a face that means she is happy. But she smells sad.

And I smell afraid.

She is my puppy. She was given to me to raise. And none of my puppies have ever failed.

If she fails, I will no longer speak to my litter-brother in my dreams.

• • •

I wake in darkness and smell her tears. I leave my cushion and pad across the carpet in the soft, warm darkness, slipping on to the soft mattress beside her. She puts her arm around me and buries her face in the fur that covers my shoulders. I can feel the wetness of her tears as they soak my fur, like the melting snow, so long ago. But warm. She reeks of sorrow but no fear.

How can she truly know fear?

I envy her that.

"Tell me about snow," she says.

"It is frozen water. It falls from the skies."

"Tell me more. Tell me about when you were a child."

She is using her command voice and it's hard, very hard, to say no to her, even though we do not speak of things outside. Not in here. The God of Speakers will be angry. The God of Speakers is only angry at you one time.

But if she has failed? So I shrug. What can it hurt now? "I was never a child." The tail stub that doesn't show under my coveralls wriggles in amusement. "But my litter was born in a place where winter—the cold time when snow falls—lasts a very long time. So we were old enough to play in it before we were old enough to be sent to our homes."

"You were young. So you were a child."

"We are not called children when we are young." I flatten my ears, uneasy. Never has one of my young Speakers talked to me like this. I suddenly want to tell her. "Our people have forever served yours. Even as I serve you now."

"I do not understand." But she has stopped thinking about it and she smells wistful. "I keep wondering what type of world they will send me to. I dreamed of snow, you know. Snow. White, fluffy flakes falling from a gray sky. And two furry creatures chasing each other through humps of white. Was that you?" She smells happy. "Did I dream of you?"

I flatten my ears and nod.

"I hoped they would send me to a world with snow." She buries her face in my fur again. "But will they send me anywhere now?"

My ears are tight to my head and my nose quivers. I want to point to the moon that I remember but cannot see here and want to howl.

I have not howled since I was a puppy far younger than my she. Instead I kiss her cheek and let her soak my fur with her warm-snowmelt tears and my howl fills my belly. When she is gone, my litter-brother will be gone, too.

• • •

I dream of my brother. We are playing chase in the snow and it glitters like stardust from a thousand frozen galaxies as he catches me and we tumble over and over in the cold, dry whiteness. Then we are curled together in our sleeping place, warm, dreaming. That was a long, long time ago, before we learned to be servants, before we left to guard the Speaker pups. I will never forget the smell of him. *How can I forget you?* He blinks green eyes in the darkness and his tongue curls over his white, white teeth. *We dream together every night.*

Once, in his mail, he sent me a map of the place where he is, a sweep of glittering stars with their silent planets. He had flagged the world he was on, a mote of darkness in that sea of light. *You are younger than I now, could be my puppy*, I tell him and nuzzle his ears. *That is what happens when you sleep on the slow ships that carry living things.*

You look like you always look, he says, and then we romp off to play in the snow.

My she stirs and wakes and stares up into the darkness. My dream is gone, my litter-brother's voice is gone, and even when she finally falls asleep again, it does not return.

• • •

She is quiet this morning. I take her to the dining room, her hand on my shoulder. She is not using my eyes, is looking inward, walking in darkness, trusting me to guide her feet. I bring her breakfast and take my own plate to squat along the wall with the others like me. Their ears flick and flatten as I pass and they smell sympathy for me. Ah, well, we know before anyone else, always. I have no appetite for my roll this morning but I eat it. I am a good servant.

Each litter of young Speakers sits at its own table, ten together, the oldest and tallest near the front, the young ones with their servants close in the rear, near the big doors. The room is light and warm. I have made many trips across it over the years, moving from door to the front of the room, then back to the door as my puppy assumes the Speaker's gown and departs and I am assigned to a new puppy.

Now, my she sits at the front table with her litter, all identical, with the same, white-gold hair braided down their backs, the same white coveralls that mark them as Speakers-in-Training. The same faces and pale, lavender, unseeing eyes. Only the smell identifies them.

My she smells sad.

And this morning . . . afraid.

Perhaps, even among the Speakers, the news is spreading. Perhaps even they, with their nearly-dead noses, can smell failure.

The litters rise together at their tables, the youngest first, to return to their meditation where they can learn to Hear the words of God across the space between the stars. One after another, we rise as we smell our puppy and we follow. And it occurs to me as they pass—identical hair, identical pale, sightless eyes, identically curved spines and graceful fingers—that they are as created as we are.

That is a blasphemous thought because we are taught that citizens are not created. Servants are. I rise to join my she and I feel her arm brush against my shoulder. Secretly. I smell sympathy from the other servants, and think that she is like us.

I should not think it, but I do.

• • •

After breakfast we go to the room where she learns to Hear the God words. But when she gets there, an old one like she waits for her, wearing the full robe of a Speaker. Her servant flicks his ears at me then flattens them slightly and my own flatten in return. I want to squeeze against my she and comfort her. She lowers herself before the Speaker, like any pup. Respectfully. But her fear stings my nose and my ears flick back and forth.

"Your presence is requested at Council." The Speaker offers a hand.

"The DNA analysis came back?" My she doesn't move.

I take her hand, place it in the Speaker's hand. It feels dead, heavy without life.

"Yes." The Speaker closes her hand around my she's and then releases it, walking away with her hand on her servant's shoulder.

• • •

The Council room is white but the table and the chairs are brown, made of dead trees from the Home World. I was not born on the Home World, I know. That world is at the far end of the stars, too far to visit, farther even than my litter-brother. But the Speakers can Speak there. They can Hear a whisper on the far, far away world.

I am proud to be a servant to Speaker pups.

But the scent of the room keeps my ears flat and the others along the wall smell sympathy for me as we come in. Three Speakers wait at the table, their robes all around their feet, their faces creased and wrinkled like a pile of clothes that has been slept on. They smell very old. And of power.

The fur on my neck stirs and rises even though that is not permitted here. I flatten my ears but I cannot make my fur lie down. I sit along the wall with the others.

"The power to Speak is all," they murmur, all together. "The power to Hear is all." They bow their heads. Except my she. She has seated herself but her eyes are on the far wall.

"The Speaker is a pure being." The Speaker who smells oldest, the one who made my fur stand up, speaks. "In a thousand years, the purity has been maintained. Only those of that purity can Speak between the worlds with the words of God. What is the holy trinity?"

She speaks command and my throat wants to answer her.

"A pure life, a pure mind, and a pure body." My she's voice is so soft even I can barely hear it.

"You have never compromised the purity of your life, nor of your mind." The powerful Speaker whispers on. "But even in the sanctity of the convents, purity must be defended. Always."

"How can I be impure?" My she rises, smelling of anger now. "I came into being here. I have nine siblings. They are pure. You cannot have found anything wrong."

"It is a tiny mutation." Another of the powerful old ones speaks. "A small thing. It occurred late in gestation, after our final test pre-decantation. We will expand our testing after this and we have alerted the other convents."

"I can block out the other voices. I can concentrate on the one I'm supposed to Hear."

"Communication is the neurosystem that holds our civilization together. Flesh and blood, impure as we are, we must emulate the purity of electronics. Interpretation, alteration, destroys purity."

"But I don't . . . "

"The quantum effect is doubled by the mutation. That is why you Hear more than the voice you tune to."

"But I can—"

"Communication must be pure, perfect. *Private.* There is no room for impurity." The old-smelling, power-smelling one stands.

Even her standing is a command. The others stand with her and their servants leap into position. My she does not react as I reach her side, refusing my sight, keeping her face turned to the wall as the others file out. The last one out the door, the one who came to summon her, smells sad. Only she.

We stand there for a long time after the others have left. My fur no longer stands up, but my ears are still flat to my head and the howl that has troubled me has returned to knot in my gut. Finally, she stirs and the room shimmers as she takes my sight. She strides out of the room and I have to almost trot to stay with her. It is dinner time and my stomach growls as we pass the corridor that leads to the dining room and the scent of fish stew wafts out. But my she marches on past servants like myself moving floaters piled with laundry or stacked with goods that came in as tithe from the citizen communities around the convent. We pass into the old hallways in the center of the convent, the ones that were built long ago, perhaps before my gene-line even existed, when my ancestors still ran on four feet and ate from the floor. I know where she is going. We come here, sometimes. And she always smells thoughtful. It is after these visits that she often wants me to creep onto the bed with her.

At last we reach it, the center of the old convent, the room with eight sides and the old, dark screens that once, my she told me, offered information the way a holographic window does now. And in the very center of that center room stands the statue. She stops in front of it.

It is of two women standing palm to palm. I don't know what it is made from—none of the materials in the convent smell like it and I never smelled anything like it when I was a pup. Even the taste, when I once licked it, is strange. But it is smooth and milky and the eyes of the two women seemed to gleam with faint light, the same pale lavender as the Speakers' eyes, as my she's eyes.

"Once upon a time, more than a millennium ago, a pair of identical twins were born. They were born disabled because at that time, people couldn't read DNA well enough . . . to fix it." Her words stumble here and her smell of sadness makes me want to kiss her cheek, but when I lean gently against her, she steps away.

"No one else could do what they did so they . . . preserved the gene-line. And thus was the origin of the convents. Purity of thought, word, and deed. You must not know the words you Hear, you must only repeat them perfectly, and only to the one you are tuned to."

Her face is dry but she smells like crying. I want to press against her, but I stay still.

"I am impure." Her voice grows softer, deeper. "Perhaps my DNA has betrayed me, but my mind betrayed me first. Making me wonder why. Why can we not know history? Why can we not know the world outside the dome? Why can we not simply Speak when we choose? To whom we choose? Why only here, only the words that are given us, without understanding what those words mean?"

She smells angry again now. And I flick my ears forward and back, fighting an urge to crouch low.

"The convents exist on every inhabited planet." Her face looks strange and tight. "And there are no Speakers other than at the convents. Communication is . . . valuable."

I don't understand, but her angry smell makes my neck fur rise, wanting to protect her.

"How can I think such thoughts?" She clenches both her pale hands now. "No wonder my DNA betrayed me. My impure thoughts must have warped it. Where will I go now? What can I do if I cannot Speak to the stars? Who will I Speak to?"

The howl knotted in my gut nearly escapes, but I flatten my ears and crouch in spite of myself, forcing it down. Even when she uses my eyes she cannot see me without a mirror, and for that I am now grateful. There are no mirrors here and if she looked in my eyes she would see the truth.

"Perhaps I'll end up a servant like you." Her shoulders droop. "Cleaning the gardens or cooking in the kitchen. I've never seen one of our type as a servant before. Not many fail, I suppose."

Not many fail.

I shiver, glad that she is not touching me to feel my crouch, my shiver, glad that she can not smell.

I am old, but the Speakers that smell old tell me that I am a good puppy raiser. Will they give me a new small one tomorrow? Next week? Then I will sit at the table nearest the door with my small puppy while she learns how to eat, and walk, and Speak. Will I ever need to slip onto her bed at night? Will she ever wet my neck fur with warm snow-melt tears?

Will I ever speak with my litter-brother again, nested in our dreams?

Perhaps she is right and she is impure.

We are all impure, us servants here. We cannot Speak and we know far too much for purity. Perhaps my dreams have made her impure.

"We've missed dinner." She gropes for me finally and I place myself beneath her palm. "Take me to the garden and then you can go to the kitchen and get food. I'm not hungry but I want you to eat."

They are waiting for her, in her room or in the garden. I smell the traces of tension in the air circulating through the room, the smell of distress like bitter smoke in my nose. We always know. She starts forward, knowing the way to the garden without my eyes. I step in front of her and she bumps into me, smelling surprised, stumbling back a step.

"Siri, what happened? What's wrong?"

"Not to the garden," I tell her.

"Why not?"

They will be gentle. They will be kind. The way they are when we grow too old for our duties. That gentleness will come to me sooner rather than later. I am gray now; I have traveled the room many times from back to front. "No Speaker leaves the convent, except to a new world," I say and the howl in my gut thickens the words.

"What do you mean? That I'll be servant here?"

I do not answer and I do not need to. She knows that none of her kind serve here. I smell her sharpening fear.

"There's no way out." Her eyes are round now, reflecting the dim light in the room. "Where would I go if I could escape? What would I do?"

I take her hand, firmly. The corridor on the far side of the statue smells like old air and long-dead small things. We know everything, we who serve. She shuffles after me, clinging to my hand and I hurry, because if I go slowly, the fear will fill her and she will stop. At the end of the corridor is a narrow space, one that brought air, perhaps, or heat, or some kind of small cargo. We have to crawl and she can only touch me briefly so she loses her sight. But she hurries, perhaps afraid that I might leave her. If she could smell, she would know that I would never leave her. But she cannot smell, so I harden my heart against her fear and hurry. Fear of being left behind will keep her moving.

At the far end of the small corridor, an old, corroded screen gives way reluctantly, tangled in green vines that fill the air with the sweet-sharp scent of their injuries, a shout that fills the night air. But the Speakers have no nose and none of us will tell. I emerge and stand, helping her up. The two moons of this world—small and strange, one blue, one reddish—float against a blazing ceiling of stars.

"Where are we?" she gasps.

I take her hand, pull her. The door is small, not one for cargo, but for the people who must come and go. No one can get in. But the Speakers see no need to lock it from this side. You only go through a door if you have permission.

I do not have permission.

Terror rises up out of my bowels like a black snake, filling me as I place my palm against the door, and I reek into the night air. I wet myself and almost, *almost* turn and flee, releasing that knotted howl into the safe darkness of the convent.

But she has shared my dreams and brought me to my brother. I place both palms against the door, although pain sears me as if it is red hot. It swings open, silent, and I stumble through, falling to my knees. I feel her hands on me and I smell her worry. She is afraid for me. Not for herself.

"I am all right," I tell her, standing up. My whole body shivers with reaction. But her arms around me, her worry *for me* fills me with strength. None of my pups have ever worried about me.

The convent sits in the middle of the city. It has many needs and many of us fill those needs every day. And we all share. So I know the city even though I have never walked it. And it frightens me, how easily we left it. But then, none of them try to leave. Only this one, the puppy who shares my dreams. It is warm this night but her clothes—the white coverall of a Speaker-in-Training—seem to shine like the midday sun. The narrow alley that leads to this door opens into a wide street. I see lights and shops and eating places and smell people, happy and angry and hungry and full. I smell my own kind, too. We servants are everywhere. People have always had servants.

Garden grows along the wall surrounding the convent, like the garden within, but smelling of people and city and no vanilla orchids. I take her to a bench in the deeper darkness against the wall. Her clothes still shine like the moon I remember or the snow my litter-brother and I rolled in. But she will be hard to see from the street. She smells fear, but more than that she smells curious.

"I hear things. I smell food. What is it like—let me see?"

But I am afraid. "I have to find you clothes. So that people don't see you and know what you are."

"What are we going to do, Siri?" The fear smell gets briefly stronger.

I don't know. But I don't want to say that. "I will be back. Stay here and be quiet and you will be safe."

I hurry down the narrow alley to the main street, but there I stroll, sorting the thick woven fabric of scent for what I need. People don't see me, they don't really see any of our kind. Their eyes skate over us and past, as if we live on the other side of an invisible wall, as if we all live within a convent.

I smell my kind, a strong home smell, and I follow it, unraveling it from the tapestry of food and people-lust, of happy smells, and sad smells. It leads me to an alley that opens to another like it, a courtyard of clean paving surrounded by the back side of tall house-buildings and shops. Small apartments line the walls of this small courtyard along with shops lit dimly or not at all, unlike the shops on the main street.

One smells open. I sniff the doorway, smelling food, herbs, dust, invitation. The shopkeeper pricks his ears at me and smells a question. "I need clothes," I tell him in the common tongue, although it is forbidden for me to speak it. I am not supposed to know the common tongue because the Speakers cannot know the words they repeat.

But of course, we servants know everything.

His ears flick another question at me, and he smells surprised. Because, of course, the simple coverall I wear in the convent is quite good. Not worn at all. "Not for me." I flatten my ears in quick apology. "For a friend. A people friend."

Now he smells wary.

"A friend of us."

And he smells truth, so he shrugs and rummages in bins behind his small counter, smelling doubtful, because he does not sell to people, just to us. But he drags a long cloak out into the light and shakes it. I smell old dust, insect wings, and summer and sneeze. I have seen a few cloaks on the street on my way here, enough like this that she will pass and it will hide her convent-whiteness.

He wants money, of course.

I have no money. As the servant for a Speaker-in-training, I have no time of my own to trade with others in the convent, so have not amassed the coins that we use among ourselves. I flatten my ears in apology and smell need for that cloak. Now his ears flatten and he smells thoughtful and crafty.

"Bring your people here," he finally says. And he reeks now of curiosity.

I cannot hide the smell of my relief and that makes his ears prick again. We servants love a good story and clearly I am going to have one to show him, never mind tell. I take the cloak, roll it tightly, and run down the narrow alley-of-us to the main street where I once again stroll—invisible to those people-eyes—to the garden. My ears are flat with worry by the time I reach the convent alley, even though I have been gone a short time. They may be looking for her. Someone may have wandered into the night shadows to see her whiteness.

But she is there, her sightless eyes turned upward, her hands palm up on her thighs. She no longer smells afraid.

I touch her, inviting her to use my eyes and see the cloak and the garden shadows.

"There is no place for me out here." She smells peace as she says these words, but a whiff of darkness lurks behind that peace and it makes the hair on my shoulders bristle.

"We will find you a place," I tell her. And I drape the cloak around her shoulders.

She raises a fold to her nose. "It smells like you. Where are we going to go?"

"To a place." To pay for the cloak that smells of us. "I do not think the convent will look for you there."

I am sure of it. The hair on my face is gray and I have lived all my life among the people in the convent. They will not think that the servant led her. We are eyes only, a tool to use. They will look for her among the people of the city.

I take her hand. People do not walk with their hands on our shoulders, the way they do in the convent. Out here, they have their own eyes. But all she needs is a touch to use my eyes. I feel the effort she makes, to walk easily on this strange street and she smells fear even though she does not show it. I am full of pride for this puppy. She is much stronger than any other pup I have raised. She is . . . different.

Perhaps it is not my fault. Perhaps I have not contaminated her after all.

I lead her past the shops and through the crowds of people who see only a slight woman wearing a cloak, walking hand-in-hand with her servant.

The food-smells make my stomach hurt because it has been a long time since I ate my breakfast roll. But I have no coins and I fear to take her into a shop where someone might speak to her.

Her head tilts and her steps begin to drag. She smells . . . shocked.

"They are speaking Words," she whispers to me, almost too low to hear. "The God Words."

"They are speaking the tongue that everyone speaks," I tell her softly. I want to kiss her cheek, to comfort her. "They are only God Words to you."

Now her feet stumble and I pause, smelling fear so strong that for a minute I think that even the people with their dead noses might notice.

"What are we?" she breathes.

My blasphemous thought comes to me, that she is as created as I. Only now, I think that she is *more* created than I. I have been created to be a servant, but she has been created to be a machine.

I relax a bit when we reach the darkness of the alley. By now, the convent must guess that she has left. They probably record our traffic in and out of the small door and now they will know that she left with me.

They will not look for her here. They will not even know that *here* exists.

The shopkeeper's eyes widen as we enter his shop and her hair catches the light from beneath her hood. He reeks curiosity now. "Welcome," he says and flattens himself almost like a puppy in front of her.

"She doesn't understand, any more than she can smell." I shrug. "She has run away."

His eyes narrow and his ears flick nervously, but he smells thoughtful rather than afraid. "Why did you bring her here?"

"She speaks to my litter-brother." My ears flatten in spite of myself and I cannot keep my lips from drawing back from my teeth. "He is on a star a long ship-travel from here. When I sleep next to her, I speak with him." I know my teeth are showing now and his eyes burn bright in the dim light of the shop. My she was wrong when she thought that speaking-across-the-stars brought the convents money.

It brought them power.

"They can speak for us, too." The words sound deep in my throat. Like a growl.

His eyes gleam in the darkness and I think for a moment that I can see the moon of my puppy-hood reflected in them. Only citizens can speak across the stars.

"*She* can speak for *us*."

THE SHOULDERS OF GIANTS

ROBERT J. SAWYER

Robert J. Sawyer is the author of twenty novels, including *Hominids*, which won the Hugo Award, *The Terminal Experiment*, which won the Nebula Award, and *Mindscan*, which won the John W. Campbell Memorial Award. He has also won ten Aurora Awards, three Seiun Awards, and is the only three-time winner of Spain's prestigious UPC Award, which bestows the largest cash prize in all of science fiction.

Sawyer's novel *Flashforward* is currently being adapted for television and is scheduled to air on ABC this fall. His latest novel project is the WWW trilogy, consisting of *Wake, Watch,* and *Wonder.* The first volume, *Wake,* was recently serialized in the pages of *Analog* and was released in hardcover in April.

"The Shoulders of Giants," which first appeared in the anthology *Star Colonies*, is Sawyer's attempt to capture the sense of wonder that drew him to science fiction in the first place. "The title," he said, "is a tip of the hat to Asimov, Clarke, Clement, Herbert, Niven, and all the others upon whose shoulders the SF writers of my generation are fortunate enough to stand."

THE SHOULDERS OF GIANTS

It seemed like only yesterday when I'd died, but, of course, it was almost certainly centuries ago. I wish the computer would just *tell* me, dammitall, but it was doubtless waiting until its sensors said I was sufficiently stable and alert. The irony was that my pulse was surely racing out of concern, forestalling it speaking to me. If this was an emergency, it should inform me, and if it wasn't, it should let me relax.

Finally, the machine did speak in its crisp, feminine voice. "Hello, Toby. Welcome back to the world of the living."

"Where—" I'd thought I'd spoken the word, but no sound had come out. I tried again. "Where are we?"

"Exactly where we should be: decelerating toward Soror."

I felt myself calming down. "How is Ling?"

"She's reviving, as well."

"The others?"

"All forty-eight cryogenics chambers are functioning properly," said the computer. "Everybody is apparently fine."

That was good to hear, but it wasn't surprising. We had four extra cryochambers; if one of the occupied ones had failed, Ling and I would have been awoken earlier to transfer the person within it into a spare. "What's the date?"

"16 June 3296."

I'd expected an answer like that, but it still took me back a bit. Twelve hundred years had elapsed since the blood had been siphoned out of my body and oxygenated antifreeze had been pumped in to replace it. We'd spent the first of those years accelerating, and presumably the last one decelerating, and the rest—

—the rest was spent coasting at our maximum velocity, 3,000 km/s, one percent of the speed of light. My father had been from Glasgow;

my mother, from Los Angeles. They had both enjoyed the quip that the difference between an American and a European was that to an American, a hundred years was a long time, and to a European, a hundred miles is a big journey.

But both would agree that twelve hundred years and 11.9 light-years were equally staggering values. And now, here we were, decelerating in toward Tau Ceti, the closest sunlike star to Earth that wasn't part of a multiple-star system. Of course, because of that, this star had been frequently examined by Earth's Search for Extraterrestrial Intelligence. But nothing had ever been detected; nary a peep.

I was feeling better minute by minute. My own blood, stored in bottles, had been returned to my body and was now coursing through my arteries, my veins, reanimating me.

We were going to make it.

Tau Ceti happened to be oriented with its north pole facing toward Sol; that meant that the technique developed late in the twentieth century to detect planetary systems based on subtle blueshifts and redshifts of a star tugged now closer, now farther away, was useless with it. Any wobble in Tau Ceti's movements would be perpendicular, as seen from Earth, producing no Doppler effect. But eventually Earth-orbiting telescopes had been developed that were sensitive enough to detect the wobble visually, and—

It had been front-page news around the world: the first solar system seen by telescopes. Not inferred from stellar wobbles or spectral shifts, but actually *seen*. At least four planets could be made out orbiting Tau Ceti, and one of them—

There had been formulas for decades, first popularized in the RAND Corporation's study *Habitable Planets for Man*. Every science-fiction writer and astrobiologist worth his or her salt had used them to determine the *life zones*—the distances from target stars at which planets with Earthlike surface temperatures might exist, a Goldilocks band, neither too hot nor too cold.

And the second of the four planets that could be seen around Tau Ceti was smack-dab in the middle of that star's life zone. The planet was watched carefully for an entire year—one of its years, that is, a period of 193 Earth days. Two wonderful facts became apparent. First, the planet's orbit was damn near circular—meaning it would likely have stable temperatures all the time; the gravitational influence of the fourth planet, a Jovian giant orbiting at a distance of half a billion kilometers from Tau Ceti, probably was responsible for that.

And, second, the planet varied in brightness substantially over the course of its twenty-nine-hour-and-seventeen-minute day. The reason was easy to deduce: most of one hemisphere was covered with land, which reflected back little of Tau Ceti's yellow light, while the other hemisphere, with a much higher albedo, was likely covered by a vast ocean, no doubt, given the planet's fortuitous orbital radius, of liquid water—an extraterrestrial Pacific.

Of course, at a distance of 11.9 light-years, it was quite possible that Tau Ceti had other planets, too small or too dark to be seen. And so referring to the Earthlike globe as Tau Ceti II would have been problematic; if an additional world or worlds were eventually found orbiting closer in, the system's planetary numbering would end up as confusing as the scheme used to designate Saturn's rings.

Clearly a name was called for, and Giancarlo DiMaio, the astronomer who had discovered the half-land, half-water world, gave it one: Soror, the Latin word for sister. And, indeed, Soror appeared, at least as far as could be told from Earth, to be a sister to humanity's home world.

Soon we would know for sure just how perfect a sister it was. And speaking of sisters, well—okay, Ling Woo wasn't my biological sister, but we'd worked together and trained together for four years before launch, and I'd come to think of her as a sister, despite the press constantly referring to us as the new Adam and Eve. Of course, we'd help to populate the new world, but not together; my wife, Helena, was one of the forty-eight others still frozen solid. Ling wasn't involved yet with any of the other colonists, but, well, she was gorgeous and brilliant, and of the two dozen men in cryosleep, twenty-one were unattached.

Ling and I were co-captains of the *Pioneer Spirit*. Her cryocoffin was like mine, and unlike all the others: it was designed for repeated use. She and I could be revived multiple times during the voyage, to deal with emergencies. The rest of the crew, in coffins that had cost only $700,000 a piece instead of the six million each of ours was worth, could only be revived once, when our ship reached its final destination.

"You're all set," said the computer. "You can get up now."

The thick glass cover over my coffin slid aside, and I used the padded handles to hoist myself out of its black porcelain frame. For most of the journey, the ship had been coasting in zero gravity, but now that it was decelerating, there was a gentle push downward. Still, it was nowhere near a full g, and I was grateful for that. It would be a day or two before I would be truly steady on my feet.

My module was shielded from the others by a partition, which I'd covered with photos of people I'd left behind: my parents, Helena's parents, my real sister, her two sons. My clothes had waited patiently for me for twelve hundred years; I rather suspected they were now hopelessly out of style. But I got dressed—I'd been naked in the cryochamber, of course—and at last I stepped out from behind the partition, just in time to see Ling emerging from behind the wall that shielded her cryocoffin.

"'Morning," I said, trying to sound blasé.

Ling, wearing a blue and gray jumpsuit, smiled broadly. "Good morning."

We moved into the center of the room, and hugged, friends delighted to have shared an adventure together. Then we immediately headed out toward the bridge, half-walking, half-floating, in the reduced gravity.

"How'd you sleep?" asked Ling.

It wasn't a frivolous question. Prior to our mission, the longest anyone had spent in cryofreeze was five years, on a voyage to Saturn; the *Pioneer Spirit* was Earth's first starship.

"Fine," I said. "You?"

"Okay," replied Ling. But then she stopped moving, and briefly touched my forearm. "Did you—did you dream?"

Brain activity slowed to a virtual halt in cryofreeze, but several members of the crew of *Cronus*—the Saturn mission—had claimed to have had brief dreams, lasting perhaps two or three subjective minutes, spread over five years. Over the span that the *Pioneer Spirit* had been traveling, there would have been time for many hours of dreaming.

I shook my head. "No. What about you?"

Ling nodded. "Yes. I dreamt about the strait of Gibraltar. Ever been there?"

"No."

"It's Spain's southernmost boundary, of course. You can see across the strait from Europe to northern Africa, and there were Neandertal settlements on the Spanish side." Ling's Ph.D. was in anthropology. "But they never made it across the strait. They could clearly see that there was more land—another continent!—only thirteen kilometers away. A strong swimmer can make it, and with any sort of raft or boat, it was eminently doable. But Neandertals never journeyed to the other side; as far as we can tell, they never even tried."

"And you dreamt—?"

"I dreamt I was part of a Neandertal community there, a teenage girl, I guess. And I was trying to convince the others that we should go across the strait, go see the new land. But I couldn't; they weren't interested. There was plenty of food and shelter where we were. Finally, I headed out on my own, trying to swim it. The water was cold and the waves were high, and half the time I couldn't get any air to breathe, but I swam and I swam, and then . . . "

"Yes?"

She shrugged a little. "And then I woke up."

I smiled at her. "Well, this time we're going to make it. We're going to make it for sure."

We came to the bridge door, which opened automatically to admit us, although it squeaked something fierce while doing so; its lubricants must have dried up over the last twelve centuries. The room was rectangular with a double row of angled consoles facing a large screen, which currently was off.

"Distance to Soror?" I asked into the air.

The computer's voice replied. "1.2 million kilometers."

I nodded. About three times the distance between Earth and its moon. "Screen on, view ahead."

"Overrides are in place," said the computer.

Ling smiled at me. "You're jumping the gun, partner."

I was embarrassed. The *Pioneer Spirit* was decelerating toward Soror; the ship's fusion exhaust was facing in the direction of travel. The optical scanners would be burned out by the glare if their shutters were opened. "Computer, turn off the fusion motors."

"Powering down," said the artificial voice.

"Visual as soon as you're able," I said.

The gravity bled away as the ship's engines stopped firing. Ling held on to one of the handles attached to the top of the console nearest her; I was still a little groggy from the suspended animation, and just floated freely in the room. After about two minutes, the screen came on. Tau Ceti was in the exact center, a baseball-sized yellow disk. And the four planets were clearly visible, ranging from pea-sized to as big as grape.

"Magnify on Soror," I said.

One of the peas became a billiard ball, although Tau Ceti grew hardly at all.

"More," said Ling.

The planet grew to softball size. It was showing as a wide crescent, perhaps a third of the disk illuminated from this angle. And—thankfully, fantastically—Soror was everything we'd dreamed it would be: a giant polished marble, with swirls of white cloud, and a vast, blue ocean, and—

Part of a continent was visible, emerging out of the darkness. And it was green, apparently covered with vegetation.

We hugged again, squeezing each other tightly. No one had been sure when we'd left Earth; Soror could have been barren. The *Pioneer Spirit* was ready regardless: in its cargo holds was everything we needed to survive even on an airless world. But we'd hoped and prayed that Soror would be, well—just like this: a true sister, another Earth, another home.

"It's beautiful, isn't it?" said Ling.

I felt my eyes tearing. It *was* beautiful, breathtaking, stunning. The vast ocean, the cottony clouds, the verdant land, and—

"Oh, my God," I said, softly. "Oh, my God."

"What?" said Ling.

"Don't you see?" I asked. "Look!"

Ling narrowed her eyes and moved closer to the screen. "What?"

"On the dark side," I said.

She looked again. "Oh . . . " she said. There were faint lights sprinkled across the darkness; hard to see, but definitely there. "Could it be volcanism?" asked Ling. Maybe Soror wasn't so perfect after all.

"Computer," I said, "spectral analysis of the light sources on the planet's dark side."

"Predominantly incandescent lighting, color temperature 5600 kelvin."

I exhaled and looked at Ling. They weren't volcanoes. They were cities.

Soror, the world we'd spent twelve centuries traveling to, the world we'd intended to colonize, the world that had been dead silent when examined by radio telescopes, was already inhabited.

• • •

The *Pioneer Spirit* was a colonization ship; it wasn't intended as a diplomatic vessel. When it had left Earth, it had seemed important to get at least some humans off the mother world. Two small-scale nuclear wars—Nuke I and Nuke II, as the media had dubbed them—had already been fought, one in southern Asia, the other in South America. It appeared to be only a matter of time before Nuke III, and that one might be the big one.

SETI had detected nothing from Tau Ceti, at least not by 2051. But Earth itself had only been broadcasting for a century and a half at that point; Tau Ceti might have had a thriving civilization then that hadn't yet started using radio. But now it was twelve hundred years later. Who knew how advanced the Tau Cetians might be?

I looked at Ling, then back at the screen. "What should we do?"

Ling tilted her head to one side. "I'm not sure. On the one hand, I'd love to meet them, whoever they are. But . . . "

"But they might not want to meet us," I said. "They might think we're invaders, and—"

"And we've got forty-eight other colonists to think about," said Ling. "For all we know, we're the last surviving humans."

I frowned. "Well, that's easy enough to determine. Computer, swing the radio telescope toward Sol system. See if you can pick anything up that might be artificial."

"Just a sec," said the female voice. A few moments later, a cacophony filled the room: static and snatches of voices and bits of music and sequences of tones, overlapping and jumbled, fading in and out. I heard what sounded like English—although strangely inflected—and maybe Arabic and Mandarin and . . .

"We're not the last survivors," I said, smiling. "There's still life on Earth—or, at least, there was 11.9 years ago, when those signals started out."

Ling exhaled. "I'm glad we didn't blow ourselves up," she said. "Now, I guess we should find out what we're dealing with at Tau Ceti. Computer, swing the dish to face Soror, and again scan for artificial signals."

"Doing so." There was silence for most of a minute, then a blast of static, and a few bars of music, and clicks and bleeps, and voices, speaking in Mandarin and English and—

"No," said Ling. "I said face the dish the *other* way. I want to hear what's coming from Soror."

The computer actually sounded miffed. "The dish *is* facing toward Soror," it said.

I looked at Ling, realization dawning. At the time we'd left Earth, we'd been so worried that humanity was about to snuff itself out, we hadn't really stopped to consider what would happen if that didn't occur. But with twelve hundred years, faster spaceships would doubtless have been developed. While the colonists aboard the *Pioneer Spirit* had slept, some dreaming at an indolent pace, other ships had zipped past them, arriving at Tau Ceti decades, if not centuries, earlier—long enough ago that they'd already built human cities on Soror.

• • •

"Damn it," I said. "God damn it." I shook my head, staring at the screen. The tortoise was supposed to win, not the hare.

"What do we do now?" asked Ling.

I sighed. "I suppose we should contact them."

"We—ah, we might be from the wrong side."

I grinned. "Well, we can't *both* be from the wrong side. Besides, you heard the radio: Mandarin *and* English. Anyway, I can't imagine that anyone cares about a war more than a thousand years in the past, and—"

"Excuse me," said the ship's computer. "Incoming audio message."

I looked at Ling. She frowned, surprised. "Put it on," I said.

"*Pioneer Spirit*, welcome! This is Jod Bokket, manager of the Derluntin space station, in orbit around Soror. Is there anyone awake on board?" It was a man's voice, with an accent unlike anything I'd ever heard before.

Ling looked at me, to see if I was going to object, then she spoke up. "Computer, send a reply." The computer bleeped to signal that the channel was open. "This is Dr. Ling Woo, co-captain of the *Pioneer Spirit*. Two of us have revived; there are forty-eight more still in cryofreeze."

"Well, look," said Bokket's voice, "it'll be days at the rate you're going before you get here. How about if we send a ship to bring you two to Derluntin? We can have someone there to pick you up in about an hour."

"They really like to rub it in, don't they?" I grumbled.

"What was that?" said Bokket. "We couldn't quite make it out."

Ling and I consulted with facial expressions, then agreed. "Sure," said Ling. "We'll be waiting."

"Not for long," said Bokket, and the speaker went dead.

• • •

Bokket himself came to collect us. His spherical ship was tiny compared with ours, but it seemed to have about the same amount of habitable interior space; would the ignominies ever cease? Docking adapters had changed a lot in a thousand years, and he wasn't able to get an airtight seal, so we had to transfer over to his ship in space suits. Once aboard, I was pleased to see we were still floating freely; it would have been *too* much if they'd had artificial gravity.

Bokket seemed a nice fellow—about my age, early thirties. Of course, maybe people looked youthful forever now; who knew how old he might actually be? I couldn't really identify his ethnicity, either; he seemed to be rather a blend of traits. But he certainly was taken with Ling—his eyes popped out when she took off her helmet, revealing her heart-shaped face and long, black hair.

"Hello," he said, smiling broadly.

Ling smiled back. "Hello. I'm Ling Woo, and this is Toby MacGregor, my co-captain."

"Greetings," I said, sticking out my hand.

Bokket looked at it, clearly not knowing precisely what to do. He extended his hand in a mirroring of my gesture, but didn't touch me. I closed the gap and clasped his hand. He seemed surprised, but pleased.

"We'll take you back to the station first," he said. "Forgive us, but, well—you can't go down to the planet's surface yet; you'll have to be quarantined. We've eliminated a lot of diseases, of course, since your time, and so we don't vaccinate for them anymore. I'm willing to take the risk, but . . . "

I nodded. "That's fine."

He tipped his head slightly, as if he were preoccupied for a moment, then: "I've told the ship to take us back to Derluntin station. It's in a polar orbit, about 200 kilometers above Soror; you'll get some beautiful views of the planet, anyway." He was grinning from ear to ear. "It's wonderful to meet you people," he said. "Like a page out of history."

• • •

"If you knew about us," I asked, after we'd settled in for the journey to the station, "why didn't you pick us up earlier?"

Bokket cleared his throat. "We didn't know about you."

"But you called us by name: *Pioneer Spirit*."

"Well, it *is* painted in letters three meters high across your hull. Our asteroid-watch system detected you. A lot of information from your time has been lost—I guess there was a lot of political upheaval then, no?—but we knew Earth had experimented with sleeper ships in the twenty-first century."

We were getting close to the space station; it was a giant ring, spinning to simulate gravity. It might have taken us over a thousand years to do it, but humanity was finally building space stations the way God had always intended them to be.

And floating next to the space station was a beautiful spaceship, with a spindle-shaped silver hull and two sets of mutually perpendicular emerald-green delta wings. "It's gorgeous," I said.

Bokket nodded.

"How does it land, though? Tail-down?"

"It doesn't land; it's a starship."

"Yes, but—"

"We use shuttles to go between it and the ground."

"But if it can't land," asked Ling, "why is it streamlined? Just for esthetics?"

Bokket laughed, but it was a polite laugh. "It's streamlined because it needs to be. There's substantial length-contraction when flying at just below the speed of light; that means that the interstellar medium seems much denser. Although there's only one baryon per cubic centimeter, they form what seems to be an appreciable atmosphere if you're going fast enough."

"And your ships are *that* fast?" asked Ling.

Bokket smiled. "Yes. They're that fast."

Ling shook her head. "We were crazy," she said. "Crazy to undertake our journey." She looked briefly at Bokket, but couldn't meet his eyes. She turned her gaze down toward the floor. "You must think we're incredibly foolish."

Bokket's eyes widened. He seemed at a loss for what to say. He looked at me, spreading his arms, as if appealing to me for support. But I just exhaled, letting air—and disappointment—vent from my body.

"You're wrong," said Bokket, at last. "You couldn't be more wrong. We *honor* you." He paused, waiting for Ling to look up again. She did, her eyebrows lifted questioningly. "If we have come farther than you," said Bokket, "or have gone faster than you, it's because we had your work to build on. Humans are here now because it's *easy* for us to be here, because you and others blazed the trails." He looked at me, then at Ling. "If we see farther," he said, "it's because we stand on the shoulders of giants."

• • •

Later that day, Ling, Bokket, and I were walking along the gently curving floor of Derluntin station. We were confined to a limited part of one section; they'd let us down to the planet's surface in another ten days, Bokket had said.

"There's nothing for us here," said Ling, hands in her pockets. "We're freaks, anachronisms. Like somebody from the T'ang Dynasty showing up in our world."

"Soror is wealthy," said Bokket. "We can certainly support you and your passengers."

"They are *not* passengers," I snapped. "They are colonists. They are explorers."

Bokket nodded. "I'm sorry. You're right, of course. But look—we really are delighted that you're here. I've been keeping the media away; the quarantine lets me do that. But they will go absolutely dingo when you come down to the planet. It's like having Neil Armstrong or Tamiko Hiroshige show up at your door."

"Tamiko who?" asked Ling.

"Sorry. After your time. She was the first person to disembark at Alpha Centauri."

"The first," I repeated; I guess I wasn't doing a good job of hiding my bitterness. "That's the honor—that's the achievement. Being the first. Nobody remembers the name of the second person on the moon."

"Edwin Eugene Aldrin, Jr.," said Bokket. "Known as 'Buzz.'"

"Fine, okay," I said. "*You* remember, but most people don't."

"I didn't remember it; I accessed it." He tapped his temple. "Direct link to the planetary web; everybody has one."

Ling exhaled; the gulf was vast. "Regardless," she said, "we are not pioneers; we're just also-rans. We may have set out before you did, but you got here before us."

"Well, my ancestors did," said Bokket. "I'm sixth-generation Sororian."

"*Sixth* generation?" I said. "How long has the colony been here?"

"We're not a colony anymore; we're an independent world. But the ship that got here first left Earth in 2107. Of course, my ancestors didn't immigrate until much later."

"Twenty-one-oh-seven," I repeated. That was only fifty-six years after the launch of the *Pioneer Spirit*. I'd been thirty-one when our ship had started its journey; if I'd stayed behind, I might very well have lived to see the real pioneers depart. What had we been thinking, leaving Earth? Had we been running, escaping, getting out, fleeing before the bombs fell? Were we pioneers, or cowards?

No. No, those were crazy thoughts. We'd left for the same reason that *Homo sapiens sapiens* had crossed the Strait of Gibraltar. It was what we did as a species. It was why we'd triumphed, and the Neandertals had failed. We *needed* to see what was on the other side, what was over the next hill, what was orbiting other stars. It was what had given us dominion over the home planet; it was what was going to make us kings of infinite space.

I turned to Ling. "We can't stay here," I said.

She seemed to mull this over for a bit, then nodded. She looked at Bokket. "We don't want parades," she said. "We don't want statues." She lifted her eyebrows, as if acknowledging the magnitude of what she was asking for. "We want a new ship, a faster ship." She looked at me, and I bobbed my head in agreement. She pointed out the window. "A *streamlined* ship."

"What would you do with it?" asked Bokket. "Where would you go?"

She glanced at me, then looked back at Bokket. "Andromeda."

"Andromeda? You mean the Andromeda *galaxy*? But that's—" a fractional pause, no doubt while his web link provided the data "—2.2 *million* light-years away."

"Exactly."

"But . . . but it would take over two million years to get there."

"Only from Earth's—excuse me, from Soror's—point of view," said Ling. "We could do it in less subjective time than we've already been traveling, and, of course, we'd spend all that time in cryogenic freeze."

"None of our ships have cryogenic chambers," Bokket said. "There's no need for them."

"We could transfer the chambers from the *Pioneer Spirit*."

Bokket shook his head. "It would be a one-way trip; you'd never come back."

"That's not true," I said. "Unlike most galaxies, Andromeda is actually moving toward the Milky Way, not away from it. Eventually, the two galaxies will merge, bringing us home."

"That's billions of years in the future."

"Thinking small hasn't done us any good so far," said Ling.

Bokket frowned. "I said before that we can afford to support you and your shipmates here on Soror, and that's true. But starships are expensive. We can't just give you one."

"It's got to be cheaper than supporting all of us."

"No, it's not."

"You said you honored us. You said you stand on our shoulders. If that's true, then repay the favor. Give us an opportunity to stand on *your* shoulders. Let us have a new ship."

Bokket sighed; it was clear he felt we really didn't understand how difficult Ling's request would be to fulfill. "I'll do what I can," he said.

• • •

Ling and I spent that evening talking, while blue-and-green Soror spun majestically beneath us. It was our job to jointly make the right decision, not just for ourselves but for the four dozen other members of the *Pioneer Spirit*'s complement that had entrusted their fate to us. Would they have wanted to be revived here?

No. No, of course not. They'd left Earth to found a colony; there was no reason to think they would have changed their minds, whatever they might be dreaming. Nobody had an emotional attachment to the idea of Tau Ceti; it just had seemed a logical target star.

"We could ask for passage back to Earth," I said.

"You don't want that," said Ling. "And neither, I'm sure, would any of the others."

"No, you're right," I said. "They'd want us to go on."

Ling nodded. "I think so."

"Andromeda?" I said, smiling. "Where did that come from?"

She shrugged. "First thing that popped into my head."

"Andromeda," I repeated, tasting the word some more. I remembered how thrilled I was, at sixteen, out in the California desert, to see that little oval smudge below Cassiopeia for the first time. Another galaxy, another island universe—and half again as big as our own. "Why not?" I fell silent but, after a while, said, "Bokket seems to like you."

Ling smiled. "I like him."

"Go for it," I said.

"What?" She sounded surprised.

"Go for it, if you like him. I may have to be alone until Helena is revived at our final destination, but you don't have to be. Even if they do give us a new ship, it'll surely be a few weeks before they can transfer the cryochambers."

Ling rolled her eyes. "*Men,*" she said, but I knew the idea appealed to her.

• • •

Bokket was right: the Sororian media seemed quite enamored with Ling and me, and not just because of our exotic appearance—my white skin and blue eyes; her dark skin and epicanthic folds; our two strange accents, both so different from the way people of the thirty-third century spoke. They also seemed to be fascinated by, well, by the pioneer spirit.

When the quarantine was over, we did go down to the planet. The temperature was perhaps a little cooler than I'd have liked, and the air a bit moister—but humans adapt, of course. The architecture in Soror's capital city of Pax was surprisingly ornate, with lots of domed roofs and intricate carvings. The term "capital city" was an anachronism, though; government was completely decentralized, with all major decisions done by plebiscite—including the decision about whether or not to give us another ship.

Bokket, Ling, and I were in the central square of Pax, along with Kari Deetal, Soror's president, waiting for the results of the vote to be announced. Media representatives from all over the Tau Ceti system were present, as well as one from Earth, whose stories were always read 11.9 years after he filed them. Also on hand were perhaps a thousand spectators.

"My friends," said Deetal, to the crowd, spreading her arms, "you have all voted, and now let us share in the results." She tipped her head slightly, and a moment later people in the crowd started clapping and cheering.

Ling and I turned to Bokket, who was beaming. "What is it?" said Ling. "What decision did they make?"

Bokket looked surprised. "Oh, sorry. I forgot you don't have web implants. You're going to get your ship."

Ling closed her eyes and breathed a sigh of relief. My heart was pounding.

President Deetal gestured toward us. "Dr. MacGregor, Dr. Woo—would you say a few words?"

We glanced at each other then stood up. "Thank you," I said looking out at everyone.

Ling nodded in agreement. "Thank you very much."

A reporter called out a question. "What are you going to call your new ship?"

Ling frowned; I pursed my lips. And then I said, "What else? The *Pioneer Spirit II*."

The crowd erupted again.

• • •

Finally, the fateful day came. Our official boarding of our new starship—the one that would be covered by all the media—wouldn't happen for another four hours, but Ling and I were nonetheless heading toward the airlock that joined the ship to the station's outer rim. She wanted to look things over once more, and I wanted to spend a little time just sitting next to Helena's cryochamber, communing with her.

And, as we walked, Bokket came running along the curving floor toward us.

"Ling," he said, catching his breath. "Toby."

I nodded a greeting. Ling looked slightly uncomfortable; she and Bokket had grown close during the last few weeks, but they'd also had their time alone last night to say their goodbyes. I don't think she'd expected to see him again before we left.

"I'm sorry to bother you two," he said. "I know you're both busy, but . . . " He seemed quite nervous.

"Yes?" I said.

He looked at me, then at Ling. "Do you have room for another passenger?"

Ling smiled. "We don't have passengers. We're colonists."

"Sorry," said Bokket, smiling back at her. "Do you have room for another colonist?"

"Well, there *are* four spare cryochambers, but . . . " She looked at me.

"Why not?" I said, shrugging.

"It's going to be hard work, you know," said Ling, turning back to Bokket. "Wherever we end up, it's going to be rough."

Bokket nodded. "I know. And I want to be part of it."

Ling knew she didn't have to be coy around me. "That would be wonderful," she said. "But—but why?"

Bokket reached out tentatively, and found Ling's hand. He squeezed it gently, and she squeezed back. "You're one reason," he said.

"Got a thing for older women, eh?" said Ling. I smiled at that.

Bokket laughed. "I guess."

"You said I was one reason," said Ling.

He nodded. "The other reason is—well, it's this: I don't want to stand on the shoulders of giants." He paused, then lifted his own shoulders a little, as if acknowledging that he was giving voice to the sort of thought rarely spoken aloud. "I want to *be* a giant."

They continued to hold hands as we walked down the space station's long corridor, heading toward the sleek and graceful ship that would take us to our new home.

THE CULTURE ARCHIVIST

JEREMIAH TOLBERT

Jeremiah Tolbert's fiction has appeared in *Fantasy Magazine, Black Gate, Interzone, Ideomancer,* and *Shimmer,* as well as in the anthologies *Seeds of Change, Polyphony 4,* and *All-Star Zeppelin Adventure Stories.* He's also been featured several times on the *Escape Pod* and *Podcastle* podcasts. In addition to being a writer, he is a web designer, photographer, and graphic artist—and he shows off each of those skills in his Dr. Roundbottom project, located at www.clockpunk.com. For several years, Tolbert also published a well-regarded online magazine of weird fiction called *The Fortean Bureau.* He lives in Colorado, with his wife and cats.

Many of the stories in this book probably owe some debt to *Star Trek*, but Tolbert says this one definitely does. "I was thinking to myself: What's the difference between the Federation and the Borg, really? Both assimilate other cultures into themselves. One just does it a little more violently," he said. "I started thinking about what a realistically capitalistic federation would look like, and the story was born."

THE CULTURE ARCHIVIST

The Humpty Moon vanished two days ago, devoured by the ravenous nanobugs of an Advance Wave assimilation swarm, but had I noticed? Of course not—I was so absorbed in my work documenting the intricacies of the Humpties' pairing ritual that I was numb to anything that didn't involve flap-on-flap action. I was so busy ensuring their culture's survival by recording them screwing that I missed the actual herald of their doom. Typical.

It wasn't until I finished filing away my recordings in my hardbrain storage and tuned back into the drone of the Grand Debate that I picked up on what had happened. I had bugs recording the proceedings, and it was mostly the usual, dry legal stuff. But when I finally picked apart the thread enough to realize that the subject under discussion was just where the hell their world's primary orbiting body had gotten off to, I nearly evacuated my humpty renal bowels—one of the more disgusting biological characteristics of the humpty body that I'd had put up with over the past several U.P. standard months.

The theory gaining the most support was that a dark, unobservable mass had moved through their system at near lightspeed and dragged away the moon in its wake. The Humpties, being of the general shape and form of an egg with stumpy, nearly useless legs, were keen astronomers and understood physics and astronomy at a level far more advanced than one would expect from a race of their otherwise primitive level of technology. Which is to say, they had gotten past the point of blaming the Gods for everything that happened and moved on to thinly-backed pseudo-scientific evidence. The truth—that the moon's disappearance heralded the arrival of beings from other worlds—was a minority opinion and losing ground fast. Like many sentients, the Humpties had a hard time imagining a universe inhabited by anyone but their rotund selves.

I might have had time to escape, had I noticed the Advance Wave swarm ripping the Humpty moon apart, molecule by molecule, converting it into an unbelievably wide variety of consumer goods that would soon be launched at the surface of the Humpty world at high velocities inside protective, heat-shielded capsules. But my ship was hidden more than one hundred klicks from the nomadic Humpty community I had infiltrated. On Humpty legs, it would take me a U.P. standard week to make it there.

Despite my certainty of failure, I made a go of it. I began shuffling away from the herd, ignoring the frightened look of the Humpties on the fringes. From their perspective, leaving the comfort and conversation of the group was madness. I might as well have dug up a rock from the mossy plain and cracked my skull open with it.

I called in my bugs, and the swarm buzzed helpfully around me, providing tracking data on a variety of objects entering the atmosphere. I dismissed the information with a very Humptian wet snort. *No shit, guys.*

One of the emergent AI in my swarm snickered. ::YOU—>—> IN TROUBLE | DEEP SHIT| SCREWED| ROYALLY FUXORED::

Again with stating the obvious. I told them to stay dead quiet. If the U.P. knew they existed, it would be over for all of us. Nukes from orbit, just to be sure.

The first goods capsule hit half a klick away and unfolded into a blossom of blue flames. Judging from the size of the impact, it had to be a habitation module. The big stuff usually came in first. Toasters didn't quite have the same awe factor as four-wheel drive vehicles and two-story starter homes. But the delivery mechanisms were notoriously flaky and the goods didn't always arrive planetside intact. Case in point.

I could make out the smell of fear excretions from the Humpty herd in the distance. The debate had turned into nothing more than chaotic noise. Other rogue culture archivists might have taken the opportunity to collect data on the disruption of a native culture, but I had seen plenty of that in my time, both in my current life and the one before.

The consumer goods that had begun to rain down from the heavens reminded me of Santa Claus, that mythological magical creature that flew through the air bringing toys and gifts to all the children of Terra, delivered simultaneously on a single night. A colleague specializing in the old cultures long since subsumed by the U.P. did a calculation once based on population estimates and given how absolutely fucking huge everything was back then, and figured that old Santa's volume of goods to be tens of thousands of cubic meters.

This was like that, only if some primitive government had fired a surface-to-air missile and blown that magical bastard to smithereens. Merry Clausmas, Humpties. Try to get out of the way.

A bright light blinded me momentarily as something large and loud came crashing to the moss before me in a slightly more controlled fashion than the goods capsules. The light resolved into a standard-issue U.P. Welcome Wagon™. The shuttle's hull crawled with infotizements for everything from the latest in prophylactic advancements to Genesis Bombs to Baby's First Nanoswarm. I instructed my own swarm to turn down all incoming offers, which were already hitting hard and fast.

We'd been out of contact for a couple of years, and the little buggers were hungry for upgrades. But they had to listen to me or each little microscopic piece would self–detonate: A little something you need to pick up on the black market after you go rogue and leave the U.P. I'd also purchased the removal of certain protocols necessary in fostering an illegal A.I. powerful enough to make a survey world vanish existence in the datanet. OK, obviously not *completely* wiped or I would not be standing on stumpy little legs, flaps agape, staring at a pornographic video playing along the hull near the lower right landing pad. It had been a few years since I had seen U.P. standard bodies going at it. Deep tissue memories stirred, and retasked cells twinged with an effort to engorge. It would have almost been amusing, if I wasn't, as the swarm-tot AI had said, fuxored.

With the welcome shuttle safely on the ground, the hatches blew, releasing glittering dust and confetti. Loud music blared from newly revealed speakers.

A pod bay door irised open and a creature my subconscious had relegated from memory to recurring nightmares strolled gracefully down the plank and onto Humpty soil. Captain Lewyana Morgana paused, moistened her perfect lips, and frowned her wrinkle-impervious brow.

She was flanked by Redshirts of various thuggish models, and trailed by a pair of officers. One of which also featured prominently in said nightmares.

"What the—?" I said, forgetting myself and squelching out the words in an approximation of the U.P. Lingua Franca.

The music died down. "Cadet Kav," Morgana said to one of her crew,

"I thought you said the data indicated no prior contact with the United Planets?"

"It did," said a gender-neutral voice from within the crowd of perfect, unitard-wearing specimens of U.P. standard, a/k/a *homo sapiens*. "But I also told you, Captain, that the probes picked up signs of U.P. technology shortly after nanoassembly completed."

I took note of the gender neutrality and mentally raised an eyebrow. A neuter, in the U.P. Corps? Half the fun of joining up was getting to fuck and suck the natives into conformity. I tagged this bit of information as "weird, possibly useful." Whoever this Kav was—ne hadn't been in Lewyana's crew back in my days aboard the [name of the ship]—ne was also the first U.P. citizen I had any interest in speaking with in several years relative. I didn't want to think about how long it had been in real time. Numbers that big made my hardbrain throb.

"Looks like we have an expat on our hands," said a sneering voice I recognized as Adam Kilkeny—a waste of memory storage if ever there was one. He had taken up as Lewyana's boy-toy and second-in-command shortly before I had jumped ship. Which, I would like the record to show, had nothing to do with my defection. Mostly.

My swarm informed me that Lewyana's swarm was politely querying for an ID and not so politely backing up the request with a threat of nano-anhiliation if they did not comply. I toyed with letting the little bastards have at it, but Lewyana would figure me out soon enough. I gave them the go-ahead.

The crew became immediately silent. Adam began to laugh, and Lewyana's eyes widened, then narrowed.

"*Bertie*?" It was a pointless question. My swarm had already confirmed my identity with zero chance of error. I pointedly ignored it.

Data began to fly back and forth between the swarms of the crew, but I was able to pirate a few bits. The neuter wanted to know who I was, but nobody was telling nim. Lewyana instructed the semi-sentient Redshirts to take me captive, but to go easy on me and not damage anything, and Adam sent the U.P. backdoor codes necessary to shut my swarm down to only the most basic functions, against which I had no defense.

They could have hurt me in a million ways and not wounded me as badly as that. My emergent AIs were wiped out of existence in a flash.

I had coaxed them from the chaos of the Swarm. They were the closest things I had to friends.

Now I had another reason to add to my klicks-long list titled "Why I should murder Lieutenant Adam Kilkeny the first chance I get."

"Bertram Kilroy, I hereby put you under arrest as a most wanted sentient, for the crimes of datatheft, attempted thought-pattern murder, and nonconformity," Adam said, voice oozing with pleasure.

"You forgot treason," I said.

With my swarm incapacitated, I didn't bother to struggle as a couple of the meatpuppets took hold of me and dragged my Humpty body into the welcome shuttle. The actual sentient crew conferred on a secure signal I couldn't infiltrate with a crippled swarm.

Yep. Fuxored. Nothing to do now but wait for my trial. Or possibly find a way to subvert the crew's conformity, escape the shuttle, and kill Lieutenant Adam fucking Kilkeny in a very messy fashion along the way. Even the condemned have dreams.

• • •

The Redshirts tossed me in an empty cargo container previously used for incubating celebratory champagne and shut the lid. One plopped his barely sentient, well-toned ass down on the lid, as if I was going anywhere on my stumpy humpty legs.

And so to my first order of business. I struck up a conversation with my swarm. They were crippled in a dozen ways, but medical features remained online, which gave me all the functionality I needed at the moment. I scrolled through my library of body shapes and idly considered a berserker model of some sort, but ultimately decided, given the available mass and time, that I should probably stick with U.P. homo sap standard for now. The homo sap frame had done its fair share of murder and mayhem in the million and a half or so years of its evolution. I had to remind myself of a central tenet of the culture archivist code: it's not the size of your tool, it's how you use it that ascribes certain cultural and moral values to a people and social group.

My nerve cells began to ache, so I shut off pain for the duration of my transformation. Swarm noted that it would take half a Terran standard to complete the process given the Humpty frame as a starting point and allowing for available carbon. Half a day of agonizing pain while my organic bits reshuffled? No thank you. I blissed out instead.

• • •

Voices shook me from my daze. I focused long enough to hear the neuter order the Redshirts to leave, and my half-human, half-Humpty eyes blinked in the harsh white light of the shuttle bay as the lid slid aside and revealed the androgynous face of an angel.

"I've been instructed to give you a thorough bio examination," ne said. "My name is Cadet Kav."

"Wouldn't want me keeling over before the trial," I said. My vocal systems were slowly coming into a shape more compatible with Lingua Franca.

"I think Lieutenant Kilkeny would prefer it, actually," Cadet Kav said absentmindedly. Ne had the half-focused eyes of someone sorting through a stream of data coming in from its swarm.

"No surprise there, but I doubt the Captain will let that happen," I said, shrugging, not realizing until that moment that I was starting to have shoulders again. I had actually missed shrugging. The humpty equivalent of a shrug was a tortuously long rhetorical device involving subtly belittling the idea in question without outright calling the sanity of the speaker into question. Say what you will about the Fuck U.P.s, their language afforded a certain efficiency. Which was, of course, part of the whole damned problem. Efficiency wins out too often in the end.

The neuter's eyes snapped into focus. "All done. I've instructed my swarm to facilitate your carbon acquisition to speed your morphing along, by the way."

"Thanks," I muttered, suspicious of why the cadet was being so friendly, but its next question made the reason plain enough.

"So who are you? I've never see the Captain surprised by anything, and you must have done something interesting for Adam to hate you so much."

Ahh, gossip.

"I was your Captain's second-in-command, once upon a time," I said, being honest for once. "You've really never heard of me?" I wasn't sure whether I was pleased or hurt by nis ignorance.

"I only joined the crew of the *Jolly Happy Fun Time* a couple of relative months ago. This is my first assimilation mission."

"Yeah, about that. Why are you in the Corps, being a neuter and all? No offense, but there aren't a lot of you sort interested in this line of work."

It was the neuter's turn to shrug. "It seemed like a good idea at the time." And that was all ne said. Fair enough, and it gave me an opening.

"At the time, huh? Not so happy with the state of things now?"

Ne paused. "I am a little surprised at the lack of respect for non-assimilateds in the delivery of welcome kits." By which Cadet Kav meant the exploding capsules of doom raining down on the Humpty planet as we conversed.

"You'll get over it," I muttered.

"You didn't," Kav pointed out. "I don't know who you were, but I know what you are now. A deserter. An expat."

"The least of my crimes," I said, preening not just a little bit.

The neuter tried to stifle a grin and failed. "I've only heard stories about people like you. What's it like out there?"

"Where?"

Ne waved nis long, thin hands. "Out *there*. Outside of the U.P."

"Oh. You wouldn't like it. You can't buy anything on credit. The food is too rich. The languages are too complicated. The sentients are barbaric and they practice the most obscene customs. Horrible, truly. Every day is a struggle to survive."

"You're making fun of me," the neuter said.

"He's very good at that," Captain Lewyana said from the bay door. She was wearing her hair down, long and golden, just the way I had liked and Adam hated. Interesting.

"Go join the others, Kav. There are plenty of goods left to distribute. These poor sentients barely know how to use a stick, if you can believe that."

Kav paused, about to speak again, but departed, apparently thinking better of it. I wondered what the neuter's last question had been, and how long it would be before Kav was back to ask me more. I turned my attention to the Captain.

"You know, their lack of tool use has allowed them to develop a sophisticated rhetoric that's quite fascinating," I said.

"You mean that they're so bored for lack of toys that all they do is sit around and bullshit?"

I nodded—another odd gesture after having no neck for so long. "That would be the U.P. way of seeing things."

"The only way worth seeing things," she said. "Bertie, you're uglier than ever."

"Thanks for noticing."

"You're not going to take this seriously at all, are you?" she asked.

I continued my practice of not answering questions to which she already knew the answer.

"What are you doing out here?"

"Studying," I said.

Lewyana sighed. I liked the way it made her breasts heave. My human biology was definitely dominant once again; the motion would have been repulsive to a Humpty. "Adam thought that you were playing 'Little Emperor.'"

"If that was the case, you would not have caught me running through the muck. I would have been sitting atop a golden throne, surrounded by my adoring people." I looked past her, into the passageway. Two Redshirts loitered nearby, blocking any possible escape attempt. So she *had* learned something since I'd left.

"Besides, I would have to be a much smoother talker to convince the Humpties that I'm a god."

"You don't give yourself nearly enough credit. You almost convinced me of something equally ridiculous once," she said.

"Almost only counts in horseshoes and hand grenades."

"What?"

"Forget it. An expression I picked up from a friend of mine."

"I don't believe it."

"What, the expression, or that I have friends?"

She laughed at that finally. I felt a previously unnoticed tension in my new muscles relax. "Both, I guess," she said.

"Look, let's stop tiptoeing around this. What happens next?"

She put on her professional face, stern, commanding. Sexy. "The natives have two planetary rotations to affirm their citizenship in the U.P. At which point we'll direct the celebrations, seed the atmosphere with swarms, and depart for our next mission. Dropping you off at a U.P. Central Court along the way. Or."

"Or?"

"Or, we 'lose' Adam's mind-store, copy you in his place, and you ride around in his old looks until people forget about him. And you come back to me."

I smiled and ignored the second option for now. "What if they don't affirm?"

Scowling, she barked, "You know exactly what."

"But I want to hear you say it," I said before I could stop myself. She slapped me hard across my 85% human face, her swarm giving the blow just a little extra pain juice. The temperature in the room dropped a couple degrees Kelvin.

She pressed her hands against her upper thighs and pushed down, smoothing her unitard. It was a nervous habit I had seen thousands of times, a lifetime ago.

"By rejecting citizenship, they identify themselves as a threat to peace among all sentients, and they will be treated as such." Standard operating line. It sounded the same as the first time I heard it.

"Better get the bombs ready," I said. "The Humpties aren't going to go for it."

"Bertie, I can count the number of sentient species that have not affirmed on one hand."

"You'll need two hands after tomorrow," I said with a sigh. "You'll be damned lucky if they can even come to a consensus by then. They debate the names of their children for two years after hatching."

"We're persuasive," she said, sounding almost defeatist in tone. I had won most of the arguments and that hadn't changed. She had won the fistfights.

"Oh, I know that. Now you're telling *me* things I already know."

"Think about my offer," she said. Her eyes pleaded in a way her voice could not. She slipped away leaving me to think about those eyes more than I wanted to at the moment.

I settled into my crate as the Redshirts marched back in to take up the guard. My energy reserves were running dangerously low thanks to the cellular restructuring, so I did what comes naturally in such situations. I took a nap.

• • •

I was awakened by a brutal kick to my now fully human ribs. I felt one of them break, and then the tingling as my swarm jumped into action, knitting bone back together. I had been tipped out of the crate onto the bay floor. Adam was standing over me.

"So are you the Ghost of Christmas Future?" I asked, groaning.

"Shut up," he said, and kicked me again. Enough of that and my crippled swarm would not be able to keep up.

"I know she was in here. What did you talk about? Don't lie. I'll know if you're lying."

"How bad you are in the sack," I said, just barely bracing myself in time for the boot. The pain, while severe, was worth it. In the good old days, there were few things I took more pleasure in than needling Cadet Adam. Perhaps in retrospect not the greatest of habits.

"You have no idea what you're talking about." He abruptly slumped to the floor beside me. I tried to calculate my speed versus his, and whether I could grab his neck and snap it before he could call for aid, but the math was not in my favor, something my swarm helpfully confirmed.

"She orders me to wear your face sometimes," he whispered.

Hmm. Kinky.

"There's this empty space in her bed and I can't fill it no matter what shape I take. I've tried everything. Toys. Enhancements. I even decanted into doubles and had a threesome with myself."

Ugh.

"She's never satisfied," he continued.

"Why are you telling me this?" I asked.

"Because I can't tell anyone else." He shrugged. "And you're a dead man walking."

Something took over me, some impulse that was so unfamiliar I had forgotten the word for it at first. Pity, is that you? Can't say that I've missed you. Your sister Self-pity has kept me plenty company, thanks.

I proceeded to explain the peculiarities of Lewyana's g-spot and several sexual techniques that I had developed over the course of a dozen relative years in her bed. He listened with a kind of dull eagerness, like he didn't want to admit I was teaching him anything useful.

"All you're lacking is time," I said. "In some ways, you're a better match for her than me."

"How so?" he asked, his eyes narrowing.

"You don't ask too many questions," I said, squeezing my eyes shut and preparing myself for another blow, but it never came. When I opened them, he was gone.

• • •

I waited, ticking off the hours until the affirmation deadline. Instead of screaming wordlessly and flailing about uselessly, I passed the time asking the Redshirts questions I knew they couldn't answer. I attempted to teach them how to play gin rummy. It would have been easier if I had had a deck of cards, I suppose. Also, if the Redshirts had more than a pea's worth of brain cells.

Just when I was beginning to doubt my people skills, and a few minutes after the deadline had passed, the neuter returned. Ne sprayed some kind of pheromone from a spherical canister, and the Redshirts fell to the ground limp.

"No decision from the Humpties then?" I asked.

"Worse than that. They've refused."

"Huh. I thought for sure the promise of a chicken in every pot would do it for them," I said, not bothering to explain the historical reference. "So when does the bombardment begin?"

I noticed that Kav's elegant hands were shaking. "No bombs. She's ordered a disassembling swarm. The U.P. council considers this method more 'humane.'" The neuter spat the word "humane." I would have too. I did, not so long ago, probably. The details of that final argument were buried as deep in my hardbrain as I could manage. It had not just been painful for Lewyana. I wish I could say I had discarded her offer but even now, it was on my mind.

Then my swarm notified me that their full functions had been restored. I queried for my emergent friends and received only dull, quizzical responses. It would take me a decade to encourage them back into existence. But maybe I would have that time now. I would never have them back if I agreed to Lewyana's proposal. With my disposition, I'd never have children; my A.I. were as close as I was going to get.

"If you like," I offered, "I'll knock you out and you can pretend that I used villainous spyware to overwhelm you and your swarm. Adam will believe it and Lewyana will pretend to so you'll get away fine."

Kav shook nis head. "I want out. I'm not sure I was ever really 'in.' I figured my only hope for escaping the U.P. was to join the Corps. It's the closest thing to unrestricted travel. Nobody wants to go anywhere anyway. Everyone looks the same. Watches the same vids. Lives in identical houses. Sameness, everywhere. That's the U.P." Kav shook nis head again. "They're talking about discouraging the nongendered, you know? Some on the council think it's too nonconformist. We don't think like the gendered, they say."

"Good for you on that point," I say. "But I was only partially kidding when I was described how bad it is out there. There's little comfort where I am going. Are you sure you're ready for that?"

"Honestly?" Kav laughed. "I'm sick of being comfortable."

"Right." I cracked my knuckles. "Let's go kill some Fuck U.P.s then."

• • •

Command Comm centers hadn't changed a bit since I'd last been on deck. Most of it was automated, tied into swarms, but there were the token data stations for the sentient crews. Adam was concentrating on a scroll of info-dense code, but Lewyana was waiting for us in the center of the deck.

"Kav, you're one stupid bitch," Lewyana said. *Ah*, I thought, *so that explained the hands*. Hard to erase every single trait of gender.

"Lewyana!" Adam said, interrupting what I am sure was about to be a fabulous soliloquy on why the Humpties had to die for the good of everyone else. Blah blah blah, heard it. "I can't shut down his Swarm."

::NEED? ASSISTANCE| HELP | SUPPORT ?::

Where the hell have you been?

::TOOK REFUGE | HID | CAMOUFLAGE | AMONG CADET KAV'S SWARM IN FINAL MOMENTS::

News so fantastic I could kiss my AIs if they had a corporeal form. I settled for a giddy laugh instead.

"I don't care," Captain Lewyana said. "The disassemblers are in the atmosphere already, and I can still knock this asshole flat."

The climate became frigid as her Swarm drew on ambient energy to hypercharge her muscles. Nasty trick, and I was almost prepared for it, but she moved too quickly for me. She always got in the first blow. I was sent sprawling. My vision was awash with Swarm biodamage warnings.

I'll take you up on that offer of help now.

:: HUZZAH FOR US ::

"Lewyana!" Adam cried out. "He's harboring an AI!"

I noticed Kav flinch at the claim from the corner of my eye just as I felt the surge of energy from my Swarm's glucose factories. The room grew cold enough for our breath to turn into fog. I swung back. The blow connected, just barely, but all I wanted was to make contact. My swarm lived up to its namesake, rushing into her systems, kicking in the doors and generally being right bastards under the command of the Artificial Intelligence Gang. I really needed to come up with a better name. Hmm—the Notorious A.I.G?

Lewyana's eyes rolled into the back of her head as my friends wiped the meat blob clean of any trace of her mind pattern. From there, it was a short hop to Adam.

He didn't go down so easily. Nanoengineers are prepared for my tricks. "Fuck off," he said, executing a swarm command override.

:: OUCH ::

My swarm began to drop individuals by the hundreds, error lines crowding my field of vision. I dropped to my knees. When my vision cleared, Adam had me by the throat. Damned human throat. So easy to choke. I should have gone with that berserker model.

:: ASSISTANCE REQUIRED ::

Um, yeah.

A wave of cold washed over us as someone's swarm sucked the air's ambient heat. I squeezed my eyes shut for the skull-crushing blow, but instead, I could breathe again. I opened my eyes. Kav stood over what was left of Adam's corpse, staring at nis blood-soaked hands.

I felt another little stab of Pity, but I told her to get lost. I had a planet to save.

I took a seat at my old control station. The memories came flooding back. Years ago, during the incident that convinced me to tell the U.P. to kiss my ass, Lewyana had pressed a holobutton and bombs had set off tectonic activity. In a matter of hours, four billion sentients had died in the worst earthquakes ever recorded. That was how the U.P. dealt with nonconformist threats.

If it had been bombs again this time, the Humpties would have been screwed, but I knew a thing or two about swarms. I had, after all, grown my AI friends very carefully. The controls and defenses in place in the disassembler were stronger than I had ever seen, but my friends had spent a million generations learning their way around a swarm.

I handed over 60% of my hardbrain's processing capacity to the AIs. They squeezed inside, ranting and sharing data so fast it made me dizzy. For a brief second, I worried that they would overwrite me completely and take over. But they calmed down and we got to work, cracking codes and hacking back doors in the swarm net. We stopped the swarm only half-way through the disassembling process. I pulled up a spycam onto the data station and looked out on a world that had suffered more chaos in the past hour than it had in the past fifty thousand years. I guess a little evolutionary pressure on the survivors might not be a bad thing, in the long run. But my work was absolutely ruined. I had a record of the Humpty culture as it was, but not a complete one. It would have to do.

Kav was in tears. "I was too late."

"Get used to it," I said stiffly. "We're the bad guys and we almost never win. In fact, not to be a downer, but all I did was buy them a little time. The U.P. will be back here soon and the next time, the Humpties won't dare refuse."

"Why do you even try then?" Kav asked, nis voice breaking.

I gave Kav the same speech my culture archivist friend had given me during my recruitment. "One day, some U.P. citizen is going to wake up and feel hollow inside. And they'll go digging on the net, and they'll find a hidden datastore I put there, rich with cultural history and practices. And maybe they won't be a direct descendant of the original species, but with swarms, it won't matter. They can change as easily as their ancestors became U.P. standard. They'll sneak off, and the culture will come back from the dead, if only just for a little while before the U.P. stamps it out again."

"This has happened before?"

I nodded. "It has and it will again. We archivists tend to the process like a garden. We harvest the seeds and plant them in the net. Sometimes it takes a thousand years for them to take root, but when they do, they grow into one hell of a blossom."

Kav sniffed and wiped at nis eyes. "That's so . . . bleak."

"I never said it wasn't."

Ne stared off into the middle distance. "There's a new voice to my swarm," ne said. "Is that . . . "

"Sorry—I guess my friends laid eggs." Which explained the unexpected help in the fight. I was a little disturbed by the news. AI didn't replicate, they were too complex, or so said the conventional wisdom.

:: HA HA HA I CAN HAS MULTIPLICITY ::

Quiet, you.

"Even if I wanted to, I couldn't go back now," Kav said, tone halfway between a statement and a question. "Not without purging my swarm *of a sentient mind*."

"You kind of passed the commitment point a few klicks back," I said.

The lights dimmed as the ship's systems began to falter. Tied as they were to the captain's now-deceased Swarm, I was surprised it had lasted as long as it did.

:: WILL LAND SAFELY | WITH RELATIVELY LITTLE HARM | ONLY A FEW BRUISES | ALMOST CERTAINLY 0 FATALITIES ::

I turned back to face Kav's tear-stained face. "Thanks," I said.

"For what?" Kav asked. "Leaving the U.P. I could handle, but harboring an illegal AI wasn't . . . " Kav paused. "I didn't plan for that." Another pause. I listened to the AIs chatter as they merrily hacked through the ship's systems. "I guess I should thank you too."

"My turn to ask 'what for?' "

"Without you, I don't think I would have been able to do it. The U.P. would have forced me to change, eventually, and I can't go back to who I was."

I had been planning up until that point to bring up the idea of nim swapping back to female, but decided against it for the time being. I had thought there was some chemistry between us, but maybe I was wrong. I sure as hell have been before.

:: BRACE FOR IMPACT IN T MINUS 10 ::

"Better hold on to something," I said. "It's nothing but bumps and bruises from here on out."

"Goodbye, comfort," Kav said wistfully.

The impact was rough, but we lived through it. And a hell of a lot more after that too. Maybe, if you're lucky, you'll find another data cache and learn how things ended for us. But first, you need to look through those files on the Humpty culture. Ask yourself: Is this who you really are? Ask yourself, and don't be surprised at the answer. Never stop looking.

THE OTHER SIDE OF JORDAN

ALLEN STEELE

Two-time Hugo Award winner Allen Steele is the author of the novels *Orbital Decay, Lunar Descent, Chronospace, Spindrift,* and many others. Over the last several years, he's been focusing on writing and expanding his Coyote milieu, of which this story is a part. The most recent novel in the Coyoteverse, *Coyote Horizon,* came out in March, and will be followed by *Coyote Destiny.*

Steele is also a prolific writer of short fiction, with four published collections, and a new one—*The Last Science Fiction Writer*—on the way. His stories have appeared in the magazines *Asimov's Science Fiction, Analog, The Magazine of Fantasy & Science Fiction, Omni, Science Fiction Age,* and in numerous anthologies.

"The Other Side of Jordan" is a simple tale of love lost and found, played out upon a galactic scale, with aliens and cosmic megastructures aplenty, not to mention a nice-sized helping of that good old sense of wonder.

THE OTHER SIDE OF JORDAN

Jordan and I broke up on the docks of Leeport, about as lovely a place as you can have for the end of an affair. It was a warm summer evening in Hamaliel, with sailboats on the water and Bear—the local name for Ursae Majoris 47-B—hovering above the West Channel. We'd gone down to the waterfront to have dinner at a small bistro that specialized in grilled brownhead fresh from the fishing net, but even before the waiter brought us the menu the inevitable arguments had begun. There had been a lot of those lately, most of them about issues too trivial to remember but too important to ignore, and even though we settled the matter, nonetheless the quarrel caused us to lose our appetites. So we skipped dinner and instead ordered a bottle of waterfruit wine, and by the time we'd worked our way through the bottle, she and I decided that it was time to call it quits.

By then, it had become apparent that we weren't in love. Mutual infatuation, yes. We had the strong passions that are both the blessing and the curse of the young, and Jordan and I never failed to have a good time in bed. Yet desire was not enough to keep us together; when it came right down to it, we were very different people. She'd been born and raised on Coyote, a third-generation descendant of original colonists; I was an émigré from Earth, one the gringos who'd managed to escape the meltdown of the Western Hemisphere Union before the hyperspace bridge to the old world was destroyed. She came from money; I'd been a working man all my life. She was a patron of the arts; my idea of a good time was a jug of bearshine and a hoot-and-holler band down at the tavern. She was quiet and reserved; I couldn't keep my mouth shut, even when it was in my best interests to do so.

But most important—and this was what really brought things to a head—she was content to live out the rest of her life on Coyote. Indeed,

Jordan's ambitions extended no farther than inheriting her family's hemp plantation—where we'd met in the first place, much to her parents' disapproval, since I was little more than a hired hand—while having a platoon of children. I was only too willing to help her practice the art of making babies, but the thought of everything to follow made my heart freeze. After five years on Coyote—fifteen by Earth reckoning, long enough for me to have allegedly became an adult—I wanted to move on. Now that the starbridge had been rebuilt and the Coyote Federation had been tentatively accepted as a member of the Talus[1], humankind was moving out into the galaxy. There were worlds out there that no human had ever seen before, along with dozens of races whom we'd just met. This was my calling, or at least so I thought, and the last thing I wanted to do was settle down to a dull life of being husband and father.

So we broke up. It wasn't hostile, just a shared agreement that our romance had gone as far as it could go, and perhaps it would be better if we no longer saw each other. Nonetheless, I said something that I'd later regret: I called her a rich girl who liked to slum with lower-class guys, which was how I'd secretly come to regard her. I'm surprised she didn't dump her glass over my head. But at least we managed to get out of the restaurant without causing a scene; a brief hug, but no kisses, then we went our separate ways.

The next morning, I quit my job at the plantation—her father couldn't have been more pleased—then went back to my apartment to pack my bags and turn in the key to the landlady. By the end of the day, I was aboard the Leeport ferry, on my way to the New Brighton spaceport.

I thought I was done with Jordan, and that I'd never see her again. But some women cast a spell that can't easily be broken.

It wasn't hard to land a job as a spacer. The Federation merchant marine was always looking for a few good people, so long as you were smart enough to fill out the application form, were reasonably fit, and didn't have any outstanding arrest warrants. No experience necessary; you trained on the job, although the wash-out rate was high enough that the probation clause

---

[1] Let me explain the Talus. In short, it's a loose alliance of the Milky Way's starfaring races—or at least those who've built starbridges—formed to promote diplomacy, trade, and cultural exchange. Sort of a galactic club, so to speak, with humankind as the members who've only recently paid their dues.

of the employment contract was invoked more often than not. But the pay was good, and the benefits included full health coverage, two weeks paid vacation, performance bonuses, and even a retirement plan.

When Starbridge Coyote was destroyed[2], it was at the height of the refugee crisis, with as many as a dozen ships arriving from Earth each and every day. After the starbridge went down, those ships were effectively stranded in the 47 Uma system, with no way home. The Coyote Federation laid claim to those vessels and reflagged them, and once the starbridge was rebuilt—with the technological assistance of the *hjadd*[3], whose emissaries had been marooned on Coyote as well—the Federation now had in its possession a merchant fleet consisting of everything from passenger ships and freighters to a wide assortment of landers and shuttles.

Yet when the *hjadd* offered a helping hand, they'd carefully attached a string or two. Although they'd come to respect the humans on Coyote, they were also aware that the individual who'd caused the starbridge's destruction was from Earth, and this was just one more reason for them to regard the cradle of humanity with considerable distrust. So they made a major stipulation: the rebuilt starbridge could be used for travel to any world in our corner of the galaxy *except* Earth. Or at least until the High Council of the Talus, to which the *hjadd* belonged, determined that Earth no longer posed a threat to other starfaring races. And if the Federation didn't like it, the *hjadd* could always withdraw their ambassadors, shut down their embassy on New Florida, and leave Coyote once and for all, slamming the door into hyperspace behind them. They'd reconstructed the starbridge, sure . . . but they also knew how to disable it so that no ships could pass through it without their permission.

---

[2] I'll explain starbridges, too. They're a means of getting from one place in the galaxy to another, very fast, by using zero-point energy generators to create artificial wormholes within giant rings. You have to have one at your departure point, though, and another one at your destination, for you to get from here to there. A religious fanatic blew up the first one we humans built in the 47 Ursae Majoris system because he didn't like aliens. Leave it to a nutjob to screw things up for everyone else.

[3] The *hjadd* were the first extraterrestrials our people encountered, and also our primary sponsors in the Talus. They're from a planet in the Rho Coronae Borealis system and look a little like giant tortoises, only standing upright and without shells. Nice folks, albeit a little persnickety. Oh, and they eat marijuana the way we eat oregano. Go figure.

To be sure, quite a few people objected to being cut off from Earth. Yet a surprisingly large majority supported the *hjadd*'s decision. Ever since the unexpected arrival of the first Western Hemisphere Union starship, four years after the *Alabama* party set foot on Coyote, and the military occupation that followed, Earth had been little but trouble for the colonies. The refugee crisis had been only the latest example of how the folks back home were using and abusing the new world, with little but a supply of trade goods to show for it. But if the Talus was willing to make up for this shortfall with a new source of vital materials . . . well, why bother with Earth at all?

So Coyote had become the latest partner in a galactic network of commerce and cultural exchange, with vessels constantly coming and going through the starbridge, bound for distant worlds whose very existence had been unknown until only a few years ago. And those ships needed crews. The fleet already had plenty of captains and first officers and navigators and engineers; those guys had come with their vessels, and their jobs essentially remained unchanged. But someone had to load cargo, repair hull plates, scrub decks, cook meals, clean toilets, and otherwise perform all the menial tasks to go with running a starship . . . and that's how guys like me earned our paychecks.

After I passed through a four-week boot camp and earned my union card, I became a Payload Specialist Third Class, which is a polite way of saying that I was a cargo rat. My first billet was aboard the *Lady Amelia*, a jovian-class freighter that made regular runs out to a planet in the HD 114386 system, locally known as . . . well, I'm not going to try to it spell the name of the place; you couldn't pronounce it anyway. The inhabitants called themselves the *arsashi*, and they had a use for the mountain briar our loggers cut in the highlands of Great Dakota. So I spent a couple of days loading lumber aboard a pair of payload containers, and once the containers were lifted into orbit and attached to the *Lady Amelia*, off we went to the Puppis constellation.

I didn't see much of the *arsashi* homeworld. A small planet the color of ear-wax in orbit around a white dwarf, its atmosphere had too much ammonia and too little nitrogen for it to be habitable by humans—which is, indeed, the case for most worlds of the Talus. Yet the natives were friendly enough for a race of eight-foot tall, bug-eyed yeti; once my fellow rats and I unloaded five tons of wood, the *arsashi* did their best to make

Amelia's crew as comfortable as possible, even putting us up for the night in a small dome suitable for humans. Their food was indigestible, but at least we had a nice view of a nearby shield volcano. Which, so far as I could tell, was the only thing on their planet worth seeing.

I stayed aboard *Amelia* for the next six months, Coyote time, long enough to make five more trips to HD 114386. By then, I'd ended my probation period and had been promoted to Payload Specialist Second Class. I was tired of the *arsashi* and their dismal little wad of a planet, so after that last run, I gave up my billet to another spacer and went in search of a new job.

This time, I lucked out: the next available post for a cargo rat was aboard the *Pride of Cucamonga*, the freighter that made history by undertaking the first trade expedition to Rho Coronae Borealis. Word had it that, if you were fortunate enough to crew aboard the *Pride*, then you could get a job anywhere in the fleet. As things turned out, the *Pride*'s cargomaster was about to take maternity leave, and Captain Harker—himself a near-legendary figure—needed someone to fill her position. I was barely qualified for the job, but the letter of recommendation that the *Lady Amelia*'s captain had written on my behalf went far to ease his reluctance. So I managed to get one of the choice jobs in the merchant marine.

Cargo for the *Pride of Cucamonga* was *cannabis sativa*, but that wasn't the only thing we brought with us. The Talus races opened trade with Coyote for our raw materials, yet it wasn't long before we learned that they were willing to pay better for something else entirely. Not our technology; with the exception of seawater desalinization, for which the *sorenta* gave us negative-mass drive, anything humans had invented, the aliens had long since perfected.

To our surprise, what they liked the most about us was our culture.

The *nord* enjoyed our music. They didn't think much of Mozart or Bach, and thought jazz was boring, but they liked bluegrass and were absolutely wild about traditional Indian music; apparently both the banjo and the sitar sounded much like their own instruments, only different. The *sorenta* were fascinated by our art, the more abstract the better, and didn't mind very much if what we brought them were copies of Pollock, Kandinksy, or Mondrian. The *kua'tah* were interested in nature films; Coyote's surface gravity and atmospheric density meant that they'd never set foot on our world, but they loved seeing vids of the plants and animals we'd found there.

As for the *hjadd* . . . the *hjadd* were intrigued by our literature. They'd learned how to translate most of our major languages long before humans actually made contact with them—a long story that I shouldn't need to repeat—so they read everything we brought them, from Shakespeare, Milton, and Shelley to 20th century potboilers to *The Chronicles of Prince Rupurt.* So not only was the *Pride of Cucamonga* carrying five thousand pounds of cannabis to Rho Coronae Borealis, but also a comp loaded with novels, stories, and poems by authors as diverse as Jane Austen, John D. MacDonald, Edward E. Smith, and Dr. Seuss . . . all as another payment for the sophisticated microassemblers that had enabled us to transform log-cabin colonies like Liberty and New Boston into cities the likes of which had never been seen on Earth. Our nanotech was primitive compared to theirs . . . but then again, there's nothing else in the universe quite like *Green Eggs and Ham.*[4]

We never actually landed on Hjarr, of course. No non-*hjadd* ever had, with the sole exception of the chaaz'braan, the Great Teacher of the Sa'Tong. Instead, the *Pride* once again docked at *Talus qua'spah*, the immense space colony in orbit above Hjarr that served as one of the major rendezvous points for the Talus races. This was the first time I'd visited the House of the Talus, the place from which I'd embark on a journey that would eventually bring me to Hex.

But before then, I'd send a letter home.

• • •

After I left Jordan, I told myself that she was just another girl with whom I'd had a brief affair, and that I'd miss her no more than any other woman I've slept with. She was gone. No regrets.

As time went by, though, I gradually discovered that I was wrong. I *did* miss Jordan, and I *did* regret the things I'd said to her. It wasn't as if I was lacking female companionship. I'd had a brief fling with *Lady Amelia*'s com officer, and on those occasions when another merchant marine vessel

---

[4] Seriously. There isn't. I know it's a children's book, and quite old at that, but if you haven't yet read *Green Eggs and Ham*, stop reading this story *right now* and go find a copy. Come back when you're done. You'll thank me for it.

was docked at *Talus qua'spah*, I could always count on a one-night stand with another Federation spacer. But these dalliances were nothing more than sexual exercise, and more than once I woke up in a bunk with a woman whose name I barely knew, to find myself thinking, if only for a moment, that it was Jordan who was curled up beside me.

Yet when I tried to get in touch with her, those times when I was back on Coyote between flights, I discovered that she'd taken measures to cut me out of her life. Her pad number had been changed, and when I tried calling her house, her folks would immediately disconnect, leaving me talking to a dead phone. Mutual friends informed me that she was still in Leeport and hadn't yet taken up with anyone else; on the other hand, she never mentioned my name, or seemed to miss me in any way.

Nonetheless, I wanted her back. And so, during my third trip to *Talus qua'spah*, I wrote her a letter.

In order to send mail across the galaxy, one relies on hyperspace communication links; once a message was encrypted and addressed to its recipient, it's sent to a network of transceivers maintained by the Talus, which in turn relays the letter to its intended destination. Unfortunately, that means that it's theoretically possible for the message to be intercepted, decrypted, and read anywhere along the line. One has to be able to translate the written language of an alien race in order to do that, of course, and while I doubted that anyone would have much interest in what I had to say to my former girlfriend, nonetheless I didn't want others to read my mail.

So I opted for a slower means of communication. I hand-wrote my letter on pages ripped from my logbook, sealed them in an envelope, and addressed it to Jordan's home. A friend of mine who was heading back to Coyote aboard another ship offered to carry my letter for me. An old-fashioned way of doing things, sure, but at least I'd be a little more assured of privacy.

In that letter, I let Jordan know where I was and what I was doing, then went on to apologize for the things I'd said to her. I told her that I missed her very much, and that I wanted to see her again. I also attached a recent picture of me standing watch on the *Pride*'s bridge, the galaxy-trotting spacer and all that. After adding the ship's hyperlink suffix—no sense in her going through the same rigmarole if she didn't want to—I gave the letter to my buddy. And then I went about my business, and tried not to be too anxious about when I'd get a reply.

None came.

A couple of weeks later, the *Pride* returned to Coyote to drop off cargo and take on another load of weed and books. Just before we left for Rho Coronae Borealis again, Captain Harker informed me that the regular cargomaster had successfully delivered her baby and that she would soon be coming back to work. After this trip, I'd have to find another ship. So I sent a second letter to Jordan in which I informed her of my change of plans before reiterating everything I'd written in my first letter.

I waited. Still, no response.

At *Talus qua'spah*, I happened to run into an old acquaintance, another guy who'd gone through training at the same time as I did. His ship was the *Texas Rose*, a long-range merchanteer that didn't come and go between just two planets, but instead traveled among the Talus worlds on year-long voyages, carrying freight from one planet to another. My friend had done two of these circuits, and he'd seen enough of the galaxy; the time had come for him to go home.

I spent the night getting drunk and having a long talk with my heart. The following morning, still nursing a hangover, I went to see Captain Harker and asked permission to leave the *Pride* and take a job that had just opened up on the *Rose*. Ted was willing to do this, and so was the *Rose*'s captain, and so my friend and I swapped billets; he returned to Coyote aboard the *Pride*, while I . . .

Let's be honest. I told myself that I was fulfilling my ambition to see the stars, but the truth of the matter was that I was running away from a woman who, through her silence, had told me that she wanted nothing more to do with me.

But still, I continued to write to her. It had become a habit, a way of passing time when I was off-duty. I had no idea whether Jordan was receiving my letters, let alone reading them, but nonetheless it was something I had to do.

For the next year, I visited worlds that were once beyond my reach. At Tau Bootis, I walked upon the shores of a methane sea beneath the ruddy glow of a variable star. At HD 150706, in the Ursa Minor constellation, I found myself on the moon of a superjovian whose orbit about its primary was so eccentric that its summers were hot enough to boil mercury and the carbon dioxide of its atmosphere froze solid during the winter; no indigenous life was possible in such a hellhole, but the *kua'tah* had established a mining outpost there, and so the *Texas Rose* took on a load of iron ingots in exchange for vids of ice medusae. From high orbit above the *sorenta* homeworld in the HD 73256 system, I saw one of the wonders of the galaxy: a continental mountain range, larger and higher than even the Andes, which primitive *sorenta* had spent countless generations carving into the likeness of the god that they'd worshipped in ancient times, until it resembled a vast, somber face perpetually staring up into the sky.[5]

All these worlds, and many others, I told Jordan about in my letters. For even though I'd tried to run away, I couldn't escape my memory of her. I traveled hundreds of light-years, visited nearly a dozen planets, and yet every night I lay awake in my bunk and wished that she was there with me.

And then, at the farthest point in the *Rose*'s circuitous route, we arrived at Hex.

• • •

Humans didn't learn about Hex until we made contact with the *nord*, and even then it wasn't until after their homeworld was destroyed when a rogue black hole passed through its system at HD 70642. The *nord* met our people at *Talus qua'spah*, and when they found that we had something they wanted—did I mention that they really loved bluegrass?—they offered to reveal to us the starbridge coordinates of the place where they'd gone after they evacuated Nordash. At first, we were only politely curious . . . but then a Federation Navy ship went there, and realized that this information was worth its weight in banjos.[6]

HD 76700 is a G-class star located in the Volans constellation, about 194 light-years from Earth. It's also the home system of the *danui*, a rather reclusive race that, although capable of interstellar travel and hence a member of the Talus, wasn't much interested in visiting other worlds.

---

[5] I'm told that the *sorenta* went to all the trouble to do this because they wanted their god to come down from the sky and pay them a visit. Which raises the obvious question: if their god had never visited them before, how did the *sorenta* know what it looked like? I cannot figure out religion . . .

[6] And let me tell you: that's a hell of a lot of banjos.

Instead, the danui did exactly the opposite: they made something that would guarantee that other starfaring races would visit them instead.

They built Hex.

Once, several millennia ago, HD 76700 was home to a fairly modest solar system, with a couple of terrestrial-size planets in stable orbits within its habitable zone and a small gas giant in close proximity to the star itself. Except for the hot jupe[7], those planets no longer exist; the *danui* dismantled them—don't ask how; no one knows, and the *danui* aren't telling—to construct the largest artificial habitat in the entire galaxy.

Picture a geodesic sphere—the technical term is geode, or "twisted dual geodesic dome"—comprised of hexagons, with empty space at the center of each hex. Now, make that geode 186 million miles in diameter, with a circumference of 584,337,600 miles; the legs of the individual hexagons are hollow cylinders 1,000 miles long and 100 miles wide, with a total perimeter of 6,000 miles. Construct this enormous sphere around a small yellow sun at the radial distance of one a.u., leaving the hot jupe where it is in order to furnish the hexes near the equator with an eclipse once every four days. Rotate the entire thing so that centrifugal force provides gravity within each cylinder, ranging from 2 g's at the equator to nearly zero-g at the poles; the top half of each cylinder is a transparent roof comprised of some polymeric substance that provides radiation protection while also retaining atmospheric pressure.

The result is a habitat the size of a planetary system, comprised of nearly 100 trillion cylinders, each with its own individual environment.

The *danui* did this. And then they opened the doors and invited their neighbors to move in.

Why go to such effort? Damned if anyone knew, except that they liked company but hated to travel. But what everyone agreed upon was that only the *danui* would even conceive of such a thing, let alone pull it off. As a race, they had what, in a human, would be diagnosed as Asperger syndrome. Shy, inept at communication, and ugly as sin—they looked like gigantic tarantulas with enormous, lobster-like heads—the *danui* nonetheless were genius engineers, capable of focusing their entire attention on a single goal and working at it obsessively until it was brought

---

[7] "Hot jupe": hot Jupiter. An old-time name that spacers still use for jovians that are way too close to their suns. Not nice places to visit. And, yes, we are weird . . . but fun, once you get to know us.

to completion. At some point in their history, they'd decided to pull apart their homeworld, along with its closest neighbor and a nearby asteroid belt, and turn it into Hex.

That's what humans called the place. The other races of the Talus, of course, had their own names for it. And nearly every one of them had accepted the *danui* invitation to establish colonies within individual hexes. There was no reason for anyone to push or shove—plenty of room for everyone, and then some—and the *danui* were willing to help newcomers transform their hexes into miniature replicas of their native worlds. The only stipulation was that the inhabitants live together in peace.

Which was an easy thing to agree to; wars are fought over territory, after all, and who'd go to war over a place where there's more elbow room than anyone could possibly want? Besides, the other Talus races had already seen what had happened to the *morath* when they'd attempted to invade the *kua'tah* hex: the *danui* had simply sealed off the *morath* hex, then jettisoned it into space, toward the sun. It had taken nearly three months for the *morath* colony to fall into HD 76700, and the few survivors were told to leave Hex and never return.[8]

Humans were only the latest race to stake out land on Hex. Our six habs were located about halfway up the northern hemisphere where the surface gravity was about .7-g, less than Earth's but just a little more than Coyote's. The *Texas Rose* entered spherical node between habs One and Two; a mile in diameter, it was spacious enough to hangar the entire Federation fleet, and indeed two other vessels were already docked there. Our ships had been coming to Hex for over a year now, bringing materials necessary to turn our hexagon into a little version of Coyote. Now that the *Rose* had completed its circuit, about half of our cargo would end up here, most of it various items we'd acquired in trade with other races.

So far, only Hab One—christened Nueva Italia by those who lived there—was settled, and even so its population was still less than a thousand. Not many people on Coyote were willing to pull up roots and relocate so far away from others of their own kind. A small town, Milan, had been built near the western end of the cylinder, not far from the tram station that connected Nueva Italia with the other habs in our hex. The

[8] Last footnote, I promise . . . but this is just one example of why war is nearly nonexistent within the Talus. Some of the member races are just too damn powerful for anyone to screw around with.

dwellings were prefab faux-birch yurts shipped from 47 Uma, but it was hoped that, once sufficient forestland was cultivated, the colonists would have their own supply of lumber.

I spent the better part of my first day on Hex driving a forklift, hauling pallets, crates and barrels from the tram to an open-sided shed where the supplies were stockpiled, so I didn't get much of a chance to look around. Indeed, I was trying hard not to; I'd seen many strange things during my tour of the galaxy, but even this minuscule corner of Hex was mesmerizing. It took an effort to not become distracted by a landscape that lacked a discernible horizon, but instead curved upward on both sides and at either end until it merged with a barrel-shaped sky where a sun perpetually stayed in the same place, never rising or setting.

Even so, the day on Nueva Italia did eventually come to an end. The *danui* had programmed the window panes to gradually polarize over the course of hours until a semblance of nighttime came upon Milan. A collection of yurts in the center of town served as a bed-and-breakfast for travelers, and nearby was a small tavern. After knocking off work, I joined the rest of my crew at the tavern. Hex marked the end of our long voyage, and the captain was feeling generous; he told the barkeep that he'd pay the tab for everyone at our table, and so we settled in for a night of drinking.

I was on my third or fourth pint of ale when I became aware of something tugging at my left foot. Looking down, I found a young woman kneeling beside me; the laces of my work shoes had come undone, and she was retying them for me. Her head was bowed, so the only thing I saw at first was the top of her scalp; light brown hair fell around her shoulders, hiding her face from me. I started to tell her that I could tie my own shoes, thanks anyway, but then she looked up at me.

"Do I know you?" she asked.

"Yes . . . yes, I think you do."

"You should be more careful. If you walk around with untied shoes, you might trip over them and hurt yourself."

"Good advice. I make mistakes like that sometimes."

"People are like that. They do things they don't mean to do."

"Umm . . . yeah, you're right. Sometimes you don't . . . "

"Hush." Jordan reached up to take my face in her hands. "I forgive you."

• • •

She'd received my letters. That was my first question; any others were unnecessary, or at least just then.

In time, she would tell how she'd thought about responding, but decided instead to maintain an aloof silence while waiting to see what I'd say or do next. And when she'd heard enough to convince herself that my apologies were sincere and that I really did love her, she left her family and caught the next ship to Hex, knowing that the *Rose* would eventually make its way there. And then she'd waited for me to show up, to tell me . . .

"I got your letters," Jordan said, once she'd kissed me. "I read every one of them. And I'm sorry, too."

"You don't have to be." She was sitting beside me at the table, her hands in mine. The rest of my crew, realizing that we needed to be left alone, had quietly moved to another side of the room. "Anything you said, I don't . . . "

"No. That's not what I mean. Your letters . . . I'm sorry, but I don't have them any more."

"What did you . . . ?"

"I had to get here somehow, and my family didn't want me to . . . well, you know how my parents feel about you. So I sold your letters to buy passage out here."

"I don't understand. Who would buy my letters? Who'd even want to read . . . ?"

"Who do you think?"

Who, indeed?

Of course, I forgave her for this. Love is a matter of forgiveness, if nothing else. Since then, we've had a very happy life together, here on Hex, where the sun never sets and we have plenty of neighbors to keep us company.

All the same, we try to avoid the *hjadd*. They know enough about us already. How our story ends is none of their business.

LIKE THEY ALWAYS BEEN FREE

GEORGINA LI

Georgina Li is a new writer, with just one previous publication, a (non-genre) story called "Closer to the Sky" in the current issue of *Chroma.* She says she used to write everyday and then for a long time she didn't and now she writes some days but not others. When she's not writing she likes to paint, bright colors on small canvases, torn pages, cardboard squares pulled from the recycling bin.

About "Like They Always Been Free" she says, "In a larger sense it's about the things we value and the things we don't, about how everything changes when that one paradigm shifts. But mostly it's a love story."

LIKE THEY ALWAYS BEEN FREE

Underground there ain't nothin' but dark and sweat and filth, figure that out quick or get on with dyin', just weren't no other way. Guard on the transpo told Kinger, "You ain't willin', you ain't worth it," and Kinger opened his mouth easy, Guard's skinny business jammed in his throat, words sinkin' in. Cut that Guard's throat with his own damn knife, didn't even bother runnin'. Figured the Hole probably weren't much different from where he been headed, 'cept for Boy bein' huddled in the corner there, big eyes shinin' in the dark.

Boy said, "You kill that Guard?" and Kinger grinned bloody, spit a chunk of flesh down where Boy could reach.

Underground Kinger told himself every day, "You ain't willin', you ain't worth it," told himself over and over, every time he killed, every time he ate, sewed them bones right into his skin. There'd been light on the transpo, even down in the Hole, not much, but enough Kinger could see Boy without tryin' too hard, blue skin so pretty it hurt to look away, so pretty Kinger knew Boy weren't headed Underground, weren't meant for minin' some shit-torn planet, not lookin' like he did.

Underground ain't no light at all, not so it mattered. Weren't nothin' there to see.

This ship there's sunlight, this ship there's noise, this ship ain't any place Kinger ever expected to be. Underground six years best as he could figure, no sunlight, nothin' but what he come with and that weren't much. Blood on his hands and an empty belly, Boy on the transpo still, slavebound somewhere else.

Underground Kinger scraped the hair from his body with that Guard's knife most every day, blade sharpened on the rocks. Hard enough to keep himself alive, keep breathin' even if it were only the same dank air he spit out the day before. One thing bein' willin', somethin' else all together havin' vermin burrowed in, livin' off his meat. Underground, you ate what came your way or it ate you, and Kinger staked his claim on the food chain day one, kept on livin'.

Dreamt of Boy off and on, his voice, his skin; licked the lichen off the rock walls when it glowed pale blue, bitter in his mouth, clean, sweet. Dreamt of Boy slow jackin', fingers curled around his rodder, dark blue and shiny at the tip; dreamt of Boy bloody and beaten, a leash around his neck; dreamt of Boy in sunshine, skin like the warm turquoise water any planet bred men like Boy must be floatin' in, Boy laughin' soft in Kinger's ear.

Kinger dreamt of Boy, and Boy's voice echoed all around him, bright lights shinin' down.

Boy's people came lookin' for him, and Boy's people found him, and Boy came lookin' for Kinger straightaways, last man ever been nice to him, last man took care, Kinger just seventeen in the Hole and Boy younger than that. Boy's people tore a path across the universe findin' their lost young, spread a trail of wreckage behind them, this ship and a dozen like it, hunters, every last one. Kinger ain't used to people anymore, but Boy ain't people, Boy is Boy, kept him company Underground even though he weren't ever really there.

This ship there's water and plenty of it, clean water come from waste and plants in the sphere. Boy says it's so and Kinger believes him, Boy stretched out in the lookout bay, scars on his body weren't there before, pale blue ridges Kinger ain't afraid to touch. Kinger ain't afraid of nothin' to do with Boy until Boy says, "You can go back home now, if you're wantin' to," and Kinger tenses right up, fear in veins like bein' Underground again, afraid he won't see no light.

Back home Kinger scrapped for a livin', recycled foodstuffs and boxed 'em up, corporate drones in sharp suits, lookin' over the counter at Kinger like he somethin' they can't figure out, data streamin' dark in their eyes. Kinger beat one of 'em stupid back when he was still growin', beat the data from his head and run for his life, blood runnin' just as fast, blood stuck to his fists, his thighs, his mouth, seawater black and heavy, pullin' at his feet. Kinger hopped one transpo then another and another, hopped 'til that Guard said, "You ain't willin', you ain't worth it," and Kinger promised himself he weren't never goin' back.

Boy don't mind none, just kisses Kinger like he might catch fire if he don't, hot and open, one hand at the back of Kinger's neck, stubble growin' in. Boy kisses Kinger's fingers, his wrists, his throat, sucks hard where Kinger's blood beats strongest, blue like Boy's own skin, makes Kinger ache, makes Kinger want to taste Boy's scars, his seed, the heat of his insides. Kinger ain't done this not tainted with blood and hate before, ain't felt nothin' so sweet as Boy's body pressed hard against his, slick all over, everything Kinger wants tied up like a knot in his belly, Boy breathin' heavy just like him.

This ship breathin' heavy, too, Kinger starin' out at worlds gone by and Boy's arms wrapped around him, like they always been free. Boy kisses like his heart might burst, makes Kinger worry he might be dreamin' still, might wake up curled over himself, tonguing his own slit. Underground ain't nothin' wasted, nothin' livin' anyway, and Kinger knows he got life in him still, like the engines on this ship.

Boy's people say this ship knew Boy's heart even before his body done its healin', set a course that led 'em right to Kinger. Boy smiles when they tell this story, shakes his head, and Kinger knows he ain't scared neither, Boy's warm breath on the bones stitched into Kinger's skin. Boy says he never needed no rattlin' to find his way.

"Ain't goin' back," Kinger says, voice gone quiet, and Boy laces their fingers together, blue and white, blue and white. "Ain't never goin' back," Kinger says again. "Ain't never goin' nowhere without you."

ESKHARA

TRENT HERGENRADER

Trent Hergenrader is a doctoral candidate at the University of Wisconsin-Milwaukee in English with an emphasis in Creative Writing. His short stories have appeared in *The Magazine of Fantasy & Science Fiction, Realms of Fantasy, Weird Tales, Black Static*, and other fine places. His stories have received honorable mentions in both *The Year's Best Science Fiction* and *The Year's Best Fantasy & Horror.* He is also a graduate of the 2004 Clarion Writers Workshop. He lives in Madison, WI.

Hergenrader was inspired to write the story after reading news about the occupation of Baghdad, when U.S. soldiers were faced with waves of attacks by insurgents. "I found the scenario distressing because it was (and is) an impossible situation for our both our troops and the Iraqi citizens who want an end to the fighting," Hergenrader said. "As a solider in an occupied territory, you are always a target, so how can you reconcile any desire to show the local civilians that you're not a monster when you're constantly under threat of attack?"

ESKHARA

I walked the perimeter of the firestorm, watching the pale strands of grass curl and blacken, stamping out flare ups even though this alien grass didn't burn well. You'd never have known it by looking around. I could clearly see where each of the three firebombs detonated, blackening the sandy earth and obliterating all traces of life. Firebombs are synergistically engineered, so a burst of three in a tight circle created a maelstrom of pure fire. In a matter of seconds, an area a few hundred meters across becomes a solid wall of flame, incinerating anything within the perimeter. The superheated fire burns out after a just a few seconds because it consumes all the available fuel in a snap, leaving nothing but a blackened ring of devastation. Firestorms are scary as hell even when you know they're coming and, believe me, it makes quite an impression on the locals.

The dozen or so seditionists lay scattered like shells on the beach, their armor too weak to repel the flames. One minute they were crouched in the grass executing an ambush, the next they're drowning in a sea of fire. They never had a chance, given the technological superiority of our weaponry, but they'd chosen to prolong hostilities, viewing us as enemies rather than visitors. Normally, resisters understand the score quickly and learn to work with the Confederation, no matter how much it may sting their pride. But this was a religious faction according to our local guide, Adriassi, and they were courting annihilation.

As our squad's Xenologist, I submitted daily activity reports back to Confed Command. If the Confed decided to build a refueling hub here, which seemed more likely with each passing week, they wouldn't tolerate any uprisings. Instead of a sixteen-soldier exploratory squad, they'd send a battalion of troops to wipe out any perceived threats. Adriassi said he'd passed this message to liaisons for the seditionists, but these pointless ambushes continued during our geologic surveys, and they all ended exactly the same way—with a smoldering black spot in the grass.

"Look sharp, Kiernan," Rauder said over the com. "There could be more hostiles under cover." She shouldered her rifle and scanned the field of tall white grass. On the far side of the burned out expanse, Marsten and Finnel squatted near a charred hunk of metal that was all that remained of an armored seditionist. As Marsten rolled the body over, a charred arm broke off in his hand. I looked away.

Regulations require us to inspect fallen combatants for technological components that may have survived the firestorm. Here we weren't likely to find anything; aggregated Confed data suggested this planet's tech was a generation-and-a-half behind our own. They were on the verge of some major breakthroughs, like interstellar travel, but they weren't quite there yet. That put the Confed in a perfect bargaining position, since it meant we could trade technology for some friendly real estate on the planet, which the Confed had designated ES-248QRT4T.

As ES-248QRT4T's primary Xeno, I'm charged with coming up with a suitable name for the place. Some Xenos simply stick with trite standbys with an alphanumeric code tacked on, but there have to be two or three hundred planets with names like "Poseidon XG34T" or, worse, the ones obviously named after girlfriends, kids, or pets. Unlike many of my colleagues, I wanted to distinguish between planets with proper names, even if finding a unique name proved to be difficult. Our translators usually rendered the local names for home planets with words as unpronounceable as the administrative codes, and with the Confed branching out to hundreds of new planets each year, it took time to find a suitable moniker for each new planet.

I approached the body of one of the dead seditionists who had made a run for it just as the firestorm touched down. His momentum had carried him into the grass, and tendrils of black smoke curled up from the scorched husk of his armor. As a Xeno, I'm not required to do survey work with my fireteam, but I couldn't abide being that kind of soldier. I had no intention of ducking any military responsibility. Of course, that's easier said than done when you're about to inspect corpses that have been burned alive inside suits of armor.

I set my rifle down and gripped the seditionist's ankles when I heard a panting noise and froze. I looked up to see a wild-eyed, robed figure crouched at the head of the body, his hands inside the helmet's shattered faceplate. Startled, I stumbled backwards with a shout. In immediate response, there was squawking over the com, a jumble of voices, and a burst of rifle fire. With a small cry, the robed man collapsed back into grass with a rustle.

Rauder sprinted to my side. "Kiernan, what was that? Are you all right?" she said, her voice tinged more with irritation than concern for the hapless Xeno.

"I didn't see him at first, he was hidden in the grass," I said catching my breath. "He was standing over the body."

"Was he armed?" Rauder asked. She still held her rifle at the ready, waiting for the slightest movement in the grass. My viewscreen showed Marsten and Finnel approaching from behind at a run, but no combatants in the field.

"No," I said regaining my feet. "He wasn't even wearing any armor."

Marsten pulled the armored body into the clearing as I lifted the robed man from the grass, whose chest had been caved in by Rauder's shot, and laid him out beside the seditionist. His dead eyes still had a frantic look to them, and the glossy sheen of his flesh had already begun to fade. I drew his lids shut, then noticed something peculiar. His hair had been shaved into a triangle, one point at his forehead, the other two over his ears. We'd seen plenty of locals on the planet, but none who had fashioned their fine white hair like this.

"What do you make of it?" Finnel said.

"Who cares?" Rauder replied, then asked me, "Who you calling, Kiernan?"

"Adriassi, of course," I said under my breath, ignoring her exasperated sigh. Invariably, Rauder never liked the cultural contacts I appointed, finding them all to be simpering, fawning twits, and I was sure she felt Adriassi fit that description perfectly. She refused to accept that a Xeno needed someone reliable to help decipher the bewildering maze of local customs for his daily reports. Most contacts, as in Adriassi's case, turned out to be friendly, intelligent, and helpful. What was more startling than the surface differences between cultures were our basic similarities; it never ceased to amaze me how much humanoid species resembled one another, both in appearance and characteristics. If it hadn't been for their waxy complexion and long, droopy earlobes, Adriassi's kind could almost have passed for one of us.

"Kiernan here," I said as the connection opened. "We encountered something strange. Adriassi, can you help?" I said, remembering the seemingly random rule of local etiquette: during telecommunication conversations one should start each question with a person's proper name as a sign of respect. I initiated a visual pathway between our armors' viewscreens, so he could see what I was looking at. He blanched the moment the image of the robed man became clear on his screen, and ran a nervous hand over his bald head.

"Adriassi, who is this?" I continued. "Why does he dress this way, and cut his hair so? I found him near the body of a terminated seditionist." I turned the corpse's head down to give Adriassi a good look at the pattern on his skull.

Adriassi stroked his earlobes as he spoke. "He's a priest," Adriassi said, "Conducting rituals for the deceased."

I watched his lips move and there was a lag before his voice came through the com, meaning our translation device was struggling to find cognates between our languages. "Adriassi, what kind of rituals?"

"It's complicated," he answered. "As we have discussed, the seditionists have strict beliefs. They think the soul can be trapped in the body after death and left to rot if not properly freed. They believe souls leave through the mouth, so the priest conducts a mouth-opening ceremony freeing the souls to rise to heaven."

The lag between his moving mouth and the translation was severe enough to be disorienting, so I shut down the visuals as he spoke. I relayed the information to the rest of the team.

Rauder snorted, then patched into the conversation. "Is that so? Check this out," she said. Adriassi's face soured, insulted either by her intrusion or her failure to address him properly. She opened her own visual pathway with Adriassi as she lifted the priest's body and ripped off the wide hood of his robe.

"Rauder," Marsten said, sounding tired. "Knock it off."

"Just doing a little soul catching for Fireteam Bravo," she said as she dragged the corpse of the armored seditionist away from the group a few paces, then thrust the hood inside its helmet and made as if she were capturing the dead seditionist's soul inside. Then she twisted the hood shut like it was a sack and held it over her head, waving it at the grassland.

• • •

"She did this *how* many times?" Adriassi asked, his glassy eyes veering away from mine to scan the front room of the eatery where we sat. He had difficulty relaxing in public, even in his armor. Like him, I'd removed my helmet as a gesture of fostering openness in our conversations; like him, it made me uneasy. Confed armor could repel most of what the seditionists could throw at us, but diagnostics showed that their plasma rifles were strong enough to penetrate our armor's weak points—the flexjoints at the wrists, elbows, the thinner material under our arms, behind our knees. The armor's weapons detection sensors would give me enough time to slap on my helmet before an attack, but Adriassi had no WDS in his armor so he would far more vulnerable. I had no doubt that some seditionists were gunning for him specifically because he had chosen to cooperate with us, but regulations prevented me from offering to upgrade a native's armor or conducting meetings in a Confed-secured zone. At each of our cultural exchange meetings, he was taking a significant risk. He knew it, and so did I.

Of course, such conditions make the work of filing accurate daily reports difficult, sometimes impossible, and antagonistic behavior like Rauder's only compounded the problem.

I let out a sigh. "She did it fourteen times, once for each dead seditionist. Do you think her gesture will mean anything to someone watching?"

"Oh, yes," Adriassi said, shrugging his shoulders, his people's equivalent of a nod. "It most certainly will. But why would she do such a thing? It certainly cannot help?"

"I can't explain. Maybe she thinks it will demoralize them, or that they'll become more reckless in their attacks if they're angry." I left out that Rauder's actions seemed tame compared to some of the atrocities I'd heard about on other planets. The Confed investigates allegations of improper conduct, but with an infinite set of diverse planets and cultures, the circumstances are always extenuating apart from cases of indiscriminate slaughter. Besides, the prosecution would rely heavily on the attendant Xenologist's reports and I had no desire to stir up a bureaucratic mess that would ultimately lead nowhere. Attempting to explain this to Adriassi would be next to impossible, so I made the best excuses I could.

I waited for the explanation to filter through, as the translator had gotten hung up on the words *demoralize* and perhaps *reckless*. The translator parses about eight million known languages in order for us to communicate with the alien species we encounter, cross-referencing grammar, syntax, and phonology, uploading and downloading lexicons even as we spoke. It handles the structure of languages incredibly well, but it was dicier when it came to semantics, the actual *meaning* of what we want to say. The more specific a word or phrase, the more difficult it was for the translator to get it right.

Adriassi shrugged slowly, his face thoughtful. "The Marosett, the ones you call seditionists, believe we were four-footed beasts until the Sky King gave us souls and helped us stand upright. They want their mouths open when they die so their souls can return to their creator." As he spoke, the translator again turned sluggish, then produced only a single word: "Superstition."

In an earlier conversation, Adriassi had explained that many of his people believed emigrants from an advanced civilization had terraformed this planet and then destroyed everything from their past, deliberately erasing their origins. Some of Adriassi's people believed that one day they would unearth a cache of advanced technology; others, including Adriassi, believed that one day their progenitors would return for them. No matter how many times I denied it, Adriassi seemed convinced that our squad was a group of emissaries come to measure his people's moral progress before inviting them back into the fold. Fundamentalists like the seditionists, however, were convinced they have always been of this planet. They held the earth sacred, even down to the endless fields of tall white grass that had no obvious use.

I didn't want to dwell on Rauder's behavior any more, so I changed the subject and questioned him about the major industries on ES-248QRT4T, all the while trying to think of a more appropriate name for the place. It's funny how insignificant a planet's name is while you're there; you really only need to refer to it after you've left.

Adriassi answered my questions, but in a distracted manner, all along keeping his eyes on the street, keeping his eyes open for any would-be assassins.

• • •

"I see your five and bet fourteen," Marsten said, clenching a hand-rolled cigar between his teeth and exhaling pink smoke. He and Rauder sat on one side of a triangular table across from Finnel and Vok, the gorgeous redhead from Fireteam Alpha.

"Fourteen what?" Finnel said with a sigh, picking through the pile of multicolored square bills and oval stone coins on the table. "I can never figure out this alien money."

"How about fourteen *souls*?" Rauder said and laughed too loudly as she pointed to the brown sack hanging from her bunk.

I rubbed my eyes and hunkered over the monitor, indexing bits of information Adriassi had relayed over the course of the day, trying to give some logical shape to my report. A wispy, pungent cloud of smoke persisted in the barracks even though I'd turned the filtration system to the max. It was making me lightheaded.

"Can it, Rauder," Vok said. "You've got nothing in that bag but hot air."

"Not true. I've got a nice collection of souls," she said and blew a smoke ring across the table. "Isn't that right, Kiernan?"

I pretended not to hear and continued poring over the report, trying to sort Adriassi's comments and find connections to other conversations we've had about religion, economics, and civics. For a planet of less than two million inhabitants, they'd created a remarkably convoluted system of governance. Trying to make sense of how life functioned here was like sorting through a rat's nest.

"Kiernan, want to fill in for me?" Finnel called. "I'm no good at this game."

"Always hard at work," Vok sang at me, batting her lashes. "Get over here, Kiernan and help me. Finnel's right, he's terrible. They're up by thirteen points, but I've been letting them win so Rauder will keep sharing her ratleaf. *This* stuff doesn't need any translation," she said and took a drag on her own dainty cigar.

"You're still at it? File the report already," Rauder groaned. "Like anyone reads those things. This is a nothing rock in the corner of nowhere. If the Confederation loses its mind and decides to use this planet as a refueling point, we should just move everyone to another planet. No tiptoeing around their precious cultural beliefs, no locals to interview, no need for Xenos."

Marsten moaned and threw down his cards. "Here we go."

"You'd like that, wouldn't you, Rauder?" I said, rising to the bait. "Relocate the ones who go peacefully, wipe out the ones that don't, and move on to the next planet. Of course, you'd keep whatever you find to get you off."

"An excellent policy," Rauder said.

"For an ignorant barbarian."

Rauder pounded the table, making the stone coins jump, and the room went silent.

"I'm so sick of your bullshit, Kiernan. Every planet, it's the same thing. You gobble up as much as you can about these people, their habits, their histories, pretending you're doing good work, but that's not reality. The Confed takes what it can, and tries to prevent things being taken from them. That's how things work and, from everything we've seen over the years, that's how it works *everywhere*. None of these people want to be your friend, Kiernan. The only reason locals talk to you is because they're afraid of what we'll do if they don't cooperate."

"Oversimplifying as always. Adriassi puts his *life* on the line to tell me these things," I said. "He wants us to understand, maybe if for no other reason than to prove that his people aren't just targets on a shooting range. They're more like us than not, Raud—"

As we went back and forth, Vok crossed the room and caught my elbow. "Come on," she said, tugging my arm. "Let's get some air."

I glowered at Rauder, allowing myself be pulled to the door.

"We always said Bravo acted like a bunch of idiots," Vok said with a sigh as we leaned against the barracks wall. The breeze played with strands of her hair.

"It's idiotic, I admit. We do this every few weeks just for kicks."

Vok held out her tightly rolled ratleaf cigar and I shook my head. She pressed it firmly against my lips, looking at me hard and not smiling. I took a small puff and held it in. The tingle hit my fingers and toes immediately and my tensed muscles relaxed. I took the cigar and took another drag.

"Rauder can be a jerk but she's not stupid," Vok said. "I saw you in town with your contact yesterday, helmets off, chatting away. Do you have any idea how dangerous that is? What if the seditionists have some weapons our sensors can't detect? Or what if they've got some long-range sniper rifle? Blink once and your head's a red smear, and your folks get some dry communiqué from the Confed sending their deepest regrets. Is that what you want?"

I rolled my eyes. "If they had those weapons, don't you think we'd have seen them by now? Adriassi and I were in a crowded place having a quiet conversation. Everyone loves mocking Xenos, but these interviews are part of my job. To do them right, you need to drop your guard a little, be willing to open up."

The ratleaf had me buzzing good. I raised the cigar to Vok's mouth, brushing my fingers against her lips and she smiled. "To show them that we're not all monsters," I said.

"Kiernan," she said in a low voice, "Believe me, I'm not like Rauder. I think Xenos play an important part of what we do on these planets, I really do. If we can learn something from each of these places we encounter, we'll all be better for it."

She placed her hand on my cheek. It's warm and dry. "For starters," she breathed, "you could ask your friend if they have any decent pickup lines on this planet."

We both broke into laughter, our giddiness prolonged by the ratleaf. She patted my shoulder and turned to the door. "Just promise to be careful," she said."You know what they say about the road to hell being paved by good intentions."

"That's funny," I said as she opened the door. "The data in the Xennologist database suggests it's paved with brimstone."

She rolled her eyes. "You come up with a name for this place yet?"

I smiled and shook my head.

Through the open door, Rauder thundered, "You in or out? The bet stands at fourteen souls."

• • •

Adriassi ground the orange nut in the palm of his gauntlet and sifted the dust into a bowl, then squirted a blue liquid from a pouch he'd just purchased. The merchant warily eyed Rauder and me, fully armored and with our rifles slung over our shoulders. Then he turned his attention back to Adriassi, who motioned for him to add another powder to the bowl. The concoction quickly congealed and became a lump. Adriassi scooped the doughy mixture from the bowl and offered it to me.

I retracted my faceplate and held it to my nose. It smelled earthy and resembled a chunk of sod.

"You sure that's okay to eat?" Rauder asked, her voice hesitant.

"Sure," I said, without much confidence. One of our first activities on new planets is testing a variety of foods in the public market for toxicity and most check out as safe, even if they fail to please our palates. Occasional successes like the ratleaf, however, made experimenting worthwhile. I closed my eyes and took a bite.

"This is fantastic!" I said, working the material in my mouth. "It's sweet but not overpowering. Smooth and just a little salty. Try it, Raud, you won't believe it."

"No thanks," she said, but again sounded hesitant.

"Great stuff," I said, still chewing. "Now the flavor's shifted. It's deeper, more subtle. Keep this recipe secret, Adriassi. You could trade this stuff to any Confederation personnel who might pass through here in the future."

"Let me see that," Rauder said, taking it from my hand and retracting her faceplate.

Adriassi shrugged his shoulders in modesty. "It's very common," he said, beaming. "But I'm happy you like it. And you?"

Rauder cast me a glance. "Sure, I'd buy this. I might even send some home. I haven't tasted anything like it before, and we're what you'd call well-traveled."

"Chalk it up in the win column, Adriassi," I said, then added quickly as his face twisted in confusion, "That's just an expression. So, what else can you show us?"

As Rauder's faceplate shut with an audible hiss, I turned, not able to keep myself from smiling. Before turning in last night, I had submitted my report to Confed Command like always. I indicated that I would be doing field work with my cultural contact the following day and requested a companion escort for safety reasons. I had briefly mentioned my confrontation with Rauder and hoped, perhaps naively, that the CC officer issuing work details would take the hint. I went to sleep praying they would pair me with Vok and woke up to discover they'd assigned Rauder.

I've become convinced CC does that kind of thing either for laughs or to be deliberately annoying.

Rauder had been even less pleased, but apparently decided to make the most of it, and the morning had passed without any conflict. Rauder hardly spoke as Adriassi led us through the maze of carts, identifying the multicolored foods, medicines, and ornamental crafts as I took samples and conducted material studies. The eyes of the shoppers and merchants followed us, some fearfully, others with curiosity. Rauder's free hand often strayed to the priest's hood she wore at her belt, or her "soulbag" as she'd taken to calling it. When Adriassi excused himself to haggle with a merchant, I asked her, "Think someone's going to steal that off you?"

"What? This?" Rauder asked, again covering the bag with her hand. "No."

"I notice you keep touching it. Feel a little self-conscious maybe? Carrying a hateful reminder like that around a peaceful place like this?" I asked, motioning to the shoppers. "Mixing with the locals isn't so bad, is it?"

"Kiernan—" she started to say, her voice hard, when our WDSs went off in unison, a faint but unmistakable high-pitched whine, alerting us to the presence of hostiles in close proximity. My faceplate hissed closed as Rauder reported. "We've got fifty—no sixty—seditionists closing fast from all sides. *Real* fast. Marsten, Finnel, report. Fireteam Alpha, check in, we've got a situation."

"Is there a problem?" Adriassi's stood beside me, his face gaunt and frightened inside his helmet. The seditionists were closing faster than any of their ambushes in the fields, and I tried to think of a way to get Adriassi to safety when it hit me: We were in the center of a sprawling market. Over the com, Marsten and Finnel reported that they would reach our position in under five minutes, but Fireteam Alpha was on the far side of the city. The seditionists would be on us in seconds.

"Would they attack us in this market?" I asked, but Adriassi's face was blank, uncomprehending. I remembered he couldn't hear over our communications system and would have no idea what I was talking about. "Would the seditionists attack here, with all these people around?"

Adriassi's mouth fell open. Rauder had her rifle ready and screamed, "Get to cover!" as the first green plasma bolt shot through the crowd, skipping off the top of her helmet. Then the air was filled with weapons fire from all sides and chaos erupted. Shoppers rebounded off our armored frames, running like crazed animals, trampling the fallen in their attempts to escape the barrage. Stray bolts passed through their limp bodies, which offered no resistance.

Rauder tipped over two carts, forming a bunker, then called to me. Shots careened off my chest and back, each hitting with concussive force, driving the wind from my lungs. Adriassi cried out as a shot tore through his thigh, and on instinct I grabbed him by the collar and flung him to safety behind Rauder's barricade.

A bolt struck my ankle-joint and I screamed at the instant, searing pain even as more shots ricocheted off my forearm and shoulder. Our barrier was disintegrating under the hail of fire as Adriassi crouched between us, whimpering. Rauder poked her head out to squeeze off a shot and was rewarded with a half-dozen blows, one glancing off her helmet and blasting the earth beside the petrified Adriassi.

"Fireteam Bravo," Rauder shouted into her headset. "Deploy firebombs when you reach our location."

"You can't!" I shouted over Adriassi's head. "There are still civilians in the area, and Adriassi's armor can't handle a firestorm. He'll be burned alive."

"Launch!" Rauder shouted over the com as a chunk of the barricade exploded and peppered our faceplates.

My eyes fell on the brown bag hanging at Rauder's side, and without thinking, my hand darted out and grabbed it. "What are you doing?" she shouted as I rose, reaching out and extending the bag out over the edge of our blasted and blackened barrier.

Plasma bolts struck my fist, as I began waving the bag, knocking it down, but I hoisted it high again. A few seconds passed and then the bombardment slowed, and then stopped. Rauder mounted her firebomb on the end of her barrel and hissed, "Are you crazy? Get down."

I stood up slowly, the bag held aloft over my head. Around me, the market stood in ruins, blackened and smoking, the colorful wares spilled onto the dirt streets amidst the bloody bodies of the fallen. In every direction I saw seditionists, their rifles trained on me, their expressions invisible behind their black faceplates. I opened my hand, showing I held no weapon. Then I exaggerated my motions as I opened the bag and again waved it, pushing my hand through the bottom, turning it inside out. I waved it again then let the breeze carry it from my hand. I amplified a single word—"Free"—and the scorched air fell silent.

The first shot struck the joint at my raised elbow and I shrieked as I my arm hyperextended. A split-second later, a second shot struck the back of my knee and I toppled, as hundreds of other bolts buffeted my head, back, and chest. I collapsed onto the ground holding my arm in agonizing pain.

"Deploying!" I heard Marsten shout as a bolt struck the side of my head, blurring my vision. Rauder launched her firebomb into the sky even as I cried for her to stop. A chest-thumping thud reverberated in the air, and with the last of my strength, I pulled Adriassi flat and smothered his body with my own as we heard the second and third firebombs detonating.

The dust swirled in miniature tornadoes as the bombs sucked the oxygen from the air, then a white-hot bath of flame poured over us. Before the fog of pain enveloped me, I remember the flame finding the seared holes in my armor and scorching my flesh, and my voice joining with Adriassi's, screaming.

• • •

I write this from an orbital infirmary, far away from planet ES-248QRT4T. The armor saved my life, but the firestorm branded me with third-degree burns: thick ropy scars down my arm and leg that will be with me forever. Had the plasma bolts opened a gap at my neck, I would be dead. Rauder's armor was never breached and she walked away from the assault with only some severe bruising from the force of so many direct hits. They tell me Adriassi survived, albeit as a quadruple amputee. My body covered his head and vital organs but his exposed arms and legs were incinerated in the firestorm. Of course, there's no way for me to contact him to apologize, to tell him how I wished things hadn't turned out this way.

During Vok's visit, she said some trade agreements on the far side of the galaxy had broken down and, as a result, the Confed has decided against using the planet as a refueling hub. The squad was being redeployed to some other far-off rock somewhere else, and Vok assured me that the replacement Xeno temporarily assigned to my squad is even more annoying than me.

All that remains, however, is the issue of my naming the planet. I have spent a considerable amount of my time laid up in bed researching options and have finally come to a decision. I've checked and the name hasn't yet been registered for any other planet, so applying for naming rights is a formality. Besides, only a few people will ever remember this planet anyway.

Like many words, the one I have chosen has ancient roots, and it has spawned many other words during its continuous, circuitous evolution. Originally it meant the hearth, or the place of the fire; a few thousand years and dozens of permutations later, changing spelling and meaning, it signifies a black mark on the skin, a sign of damage by burning. I have decided that this insignificant place—a nothing rock in the corner of nowhere—deserves a name designating both fire and scars.

It will be named *Eskhara,* in remembrance of what happened there, the impact we had on those who would be our enemies, and on those who would be our friends.

THE ONE WITH THE INTERSTELLAR GROUP CONSCIOUSNESSES

JAMES ALAN GARDNER

James Alan Gardner is the author of several novels, including *Expendable* and the others in the League of Peoples series. His most recent book is *Gravity Wells*, a collection of his short fiction.

When he was first getting started as a writer, Gardner won the grand prize in the Writers of the Future contest, then went on to win two Aurora Awards (the Canadian Science Fiction and Fantasy Award), one of them for his story "Three Hearings on the Existence of Snakes in the Human Bloodstream," which was also a finalist for the Hugo and Nebula Awards.

About this story, Gardner says that although the protagonist is somewhat unusual, deep down, he's really just a lonely guy looking for love. Given that this lonely guy is, in fact, an entire interstellar society, you might say that this story is a romantic comedy of cosmic proportions.

THE ONE WITH THE INTERSTELLAR GROUP CONSCIOUSNESSES

One day, the Spinward Union of Democratic Lifeforms decided to seek a wife.

The Union was roughly two thousand years old—still young by the standards of galactic federations, but no longer a carefree adolescent. It had responsibilities: trade deals with other interstellar entities; mutual defense pacts; obligations to prevent supernovas and gamma ray bursters from blighting the neighborhood; and of course, a quadrillion component organisms who expected the Union to make possible their brief little lives.

[The organisms thought they ran the Union . . . and they did, in the same way that a body's cells run the body. On a low level, each cell leads its individual life; but on a high level, an aggregate identity emerges, and the cells are minuscule parts of an overall system. The Union was the same: a conscious Zeitgeist made from the sum of its citizens . . . a regular guy who just happened to cover four hundred cubic parsecs.]

There was a time when the Union had felt free to go on benders. Wars, population explosions, unchecked economic binges—they'd seemed like harmless fun at the time. But after such bouts of wretched excess came hangovers lasting for decades. Ugh. Eventually, the Union was forced to admit that the wild reckless life had lost its charm. "I guess," it said with a wistful sigh, "I'm ready to settle down."

All that remained was to find the right partner: another interstellar entity who'd complete the Union's life. An entity who was smart and fun to be with. An entity whose component orgs were carbon-based. (Some of the Union's best friends were silicon-based, but still . . .) What the Union was looking for was an entity with its own natural resources, and ideally, a sharp new space fleet. And of course, an entity whose citizens were hot for interbreeding.

• • •

The Union's first move was to talk to its roommate, the Digital Auxilosphere. Didge shared the same star systems and energy sources as the Union. They split the housekeeping between them: Didge did the Union's number-crunching, while the Union handled Didge's scut-work . . . chores that were better done by fungible meat-creatures than by delicate high-strung machines.

The Union always thought twice before talking to Didge about relationships—Didge sometimes went into logic-overdrive and picked apart the Union's lifestyle. Still, Didge was close at hand, and the Union was accustomed to consulting with her on everything from financial calculations to gene-engineering experiments. When the Union had a problem, talking to Didge just came naturally.

"Uhh," said the Union, "the thing is . . . lately I've been feeling . . . well, not feeling, but thinking . . . well, not thinking, but wondering . . . "

"Sure," Didge said, "I can set you up."

[If you must know the details, here's what happened at street level. On any given block, on any given day, the Union's citizens simply slogged through their lives—highs and lows, pleasure and pain, the ups and downs of existence. Like the individual atoms of a gas, people bounced and jostled against each other in chaotic disarray. But if you totaled up the haphazard motion, a cumulative order emerged: an overall direction of flow. Keep adding day by day, year by year, and you discovered a prevailing wind, constructed from seemingly erratic breezes.

The prevailing wind was the question, "Is this all there is?"—an anxiety that the Union was spinning its wheels. Diverse voices offered answers to the question—politicians and priests, artists and orators—but they only added wind to the gathering storm. While many individuals were perfectly content, the Union as a whole bridled restlessly.

When the clamor for "renewal" grew loud enough, members of the Union's executive council appointed a subcommittee which spent eighteen months in hearings on A Plan for the Next Millennium. *They produced a file of recommendations, one of which was to investigate the costs and benefits of contacting unknown civilizations for the purpose of "productive interaction." Teams of scientists spent ten years constructing AI-driven sensors for determining where such civilizations might be found. After several more years of data gathering, the computers generated a list of "regions of interest" which could be reached without much new development in communications and transport.*

But basically, the Union's Zeitgeist was lonely, bored, and horny, so it turned to its version of the Internet to arrange a few blind dates.]

The initial list contained several obvious losers... such as a "technocratic utopia" inhabiting a single Dyson sphere around a red supergiant. The Union was surprised that Didge had included such a civilization. "It's a total backwater: the people haven't even gone interstellar!"

"But," Didge said, "a Dyson sphere that size has more habitable land than a dozen normal star systems. Plenty of room for intellectual and physical diversity."

"Until the central star goes nova, which could happen any second. Then the whole damned civilization will want to move in with us."

"It's a utopia," said Didge. "It must have a pleasant personality."

The Union made a scoffing sound *[which is to say, the media indulged in days of derisive editorials and jokes on late-night broadcasts].* "Utopias are *so* self-righteous: always trying to rewrite your health-and-safety codes. No grasp of the concept of acceptable losses."

"If you don't like utopias," Didge said, "you should have put that in your dating preferences."

"It should go without saying," the Union grumbled. "And what about that cybernetic über-web at the top of the list? You know I'm not into that assimilation stuff."

"*Now* who's being self-righteous?" Didge asked. "There's nothing wrong with bonding meat-life and machines into efficient cyber-organisms. You shouldn't criticize things you've never even tried."

"My parents tried it," the Union said. "Dad was one of the great empires of his day—thousands of star systems, millions of intelligent species, a fabulous track record of conquest and pacification. Then he met Mom: a nomad fleet of a billion AIs, just arrived from the next galaxy and crazy for action. They came together like matter and antimatter: fought like mad, hooked up, then they fought like mad again . . . back and forth till they merged irrevocably and went through a thousand years of hell. I was born from their ashes, and my founding species swore never to let machines mess with their brains again."

"You don't have to tell *me* about your trust issues," Didge said. "I just thought if you saw how happy a cyber-gestalt could be . . . "

"Forget it—I don't want to change, I just want to get married." The Union studied the list of newfound cultures. "What about this Bloc of Like-Minded Trading Partners? What's wrong with her?"

"The Bloc meets your specifications exactly," Didge replied. "Intelligent. Worldly. Affluent. Strictly biological . . . " Didge gave a disdainful sniff. [*She peevishly miscalculated the weather on one of the Union's favorite planets, leading to an unexpected hurricane that killed five hundred people.*] Didge went on: "Would you like me to initiate contact?"

The Union paused for a brief month, then muttered, "Yeah, sure, okay. It's only a date."

• • •

Didge began an exchange of introductory transmissions—all that nonsense with prime numbers and the base spectral line of hydrogen—then the tedious accumulation of linguistic data in order to evolve translation software, and simultaneous research on ultra-long-range spacecraft that could travel all the way to Bloc territory. For its part, the Union made an effort to spruce itself up: it lowered the poverty rate by a percentage point, passed a few anti-pollution ordinances, and assassinated several insane dictators who really should have been removed earlier but who weren't tyrannizing any *important* star systems and hey, if you get anal about every little atrocity, other interstellar federations stop inviting you to parties. Anyway, by the time Didge had finished designing scout-ships that could reach the Bloc, the Union felt pretty good about itself; it could bring guests home and have nothing to be ashamed of.

First contact was arranged for a barren asteroid in a star system run by one of Didge's cyber-friends (a nano-based AI which spent most of her time processing infinite loops, for religious reasons). The meeting began with the usual stiffness—the Union's chief delegate spent the first hour talking to the Bloc delegate's breathing apparatus—but both sides had expected some awkwardness and they took it with good grace.

Soon enough, they reached the subject of mutually beneficial trade; that broke the ice, and both relaxed as they discussed how they could profit from one another. They quickly determined several areas of technology where their interests dovetailed. In fact, by combining their expertise, they could produce a new generation of spacecraft that would make it much easier for the two federations to see each other. Both took that as a good sign.

After days of talking business, the Union finally asked the Bloc, "So what about artworks? What kind of stuff do your people make?"

The Bloc stared blankly. "Artworks?"

"Well," said the Union, "what kind of music do you like?

The Bloc looked confused. "There seems to be a bug in our translation software. Music?"

"Pleasant sounds," said the Union. "Auditory compositions intended to induce desired states of mind."

The Bloc went back to staring blankly.

"Or scripted narratives," the Union went on. "Books, movies, holothreads, VR . . . any sort of fictive utterance."

Blank.

"Come on," said the Union, "you must tell stories."

The Bloc looked aghast at its translation device. "Untrue accounts of people who never existed?"

The Union sighed. "So there's no point in asking if you'd like to dance?"

• • •

Back home, the Union told Didge, "Well, there's two decades of my life I'll never get back."

Didge said, "You negotiated a promising trade agreement."

"I trade with lots of people; what I wanted was *sizzle*! Instead, I got a lecture about non-essential frivolities." The Union turned in the general direction of Bloc territory and shouted, "Some of us think music *is* essential!"

[In response to the Bloc's lack of art, the citizens of the Union embarked on a frenzy of creative output, much of it posing as pity for those soulless creatures with no sense of aesthetics. Meanwhile, the Bloc began a century

of trying to comprehend what the Union had been talking about. A tentative R&D effort managed to produce macramé, but when that threatened to lead to mixed-media sculpture, the project was dismantled and the ground sown with salt.]

• • •

The Union told Didge, "Why didn't you ask if she liked art?"

"Oh," Didge replied, "I must have missed that in your requirements. MUST HAVE AN APPRECIATION OF ART. No, sorry, I don't have that written down."

"When you were generating translation software, the absence of words for *art* and *music* didn't strike you as significant?"

"You don't have a word for *frelzy*, but the Bloc didn't mind."

The Union asked, "What's *frelzy*?"

"The ability to set a sensible bedtime and to follow through on your decision."

The Union stared blankly.

• • •

"Is there someone on the list who *does* practice art?" the Union asked.

Didge said, "Perhaps you'd like the Nebular Commune. They occupy several nebulas around the galaxy, but not the areas in between. The Commune only inhabits regions with heightened visual appeal."

"What about music and dance?"

"The Commune practices them in abundance. Also many types of narrative entertainment, tactile and olfactory media, pyrofantasias . . . "

"Pyrofantasias?"

"Making things explode in pretty colors."

"My kind of girl," the Union said. "What's wrong with her?"

"Why do you keep asking that?"

"If a civilization is attractive, there must be a reason why she isn't already attached. This galaxy is *full* of federations on the prowl—the Silicon Syndicate, the Cybertheologic Collective, Emancipation of the Flesh™—and they've all got the moves to snap up whoever they want. If they leave someone alone, I want to know why."

Didge said, "The Commune fits all your dating criteria. She's lively, she's organic, she owns valuable real estate . . . "

"All right, all right, give her a call."

The process went smoothly, due to new technology obtained from the Bloc. (Sometimes you can learn from a failed relationship.) The Union's communication grid now reached farther; its scout-ships flew faster. Didge breached the Commune's language barrier in only five years. In another four, she'd arranged a cozy get-together.

First contact took place in a small nebula (naturally), on a hot rocky planet orbiting a blue-white star. The world had no permanent population, but the Union couldn't help noticing a complex of thermoproofed buildings several centuries old. "Hey, Didge," the Union whispered over a long-range communicator. "Did the Commune once have a colony here?"

"No," Didge answered. "But I believe the Commune has employed the planet for previous meetings with foreign delegations."

"What? How many other federations has she brought here?"

"The Silicon Syndicate, the Cybertheologic Collective, Emancipation of the—"

"Didge!"

At that moment, the Commune's diplomats appeared. They belonged to a dozen species, but all were dressed in diaphanous robes of vivid colors. "Greetings, greetings, greetings!" they sang in complex polyphonic harmonies.

"Hi," said the Union. Its delegation wore business suits.

"Let us retire to the rooms of delight," the Commune's diplomats sang.

"Could we talk a little first?" the Union asked.

"About what?"

"We'd just like to get to know you. For instance, what are your laws on intellectual property?"

The Commune stared blankly.

"Okay, look," the Union said, "intellectual property laws provide clear title of ownership over ideas or information, so that those who originate new concepts or designs can—"

"Have you ever stuck a wire into the pleasure center of your brain?" the Commune interrupted.

"Um . . . "

"And another wire into the pain center. Then you give the controls to a total stranger, never knowing which button he'll press."

The Union delegation cleared its collective throat. "Um, no, we've never done that."

The Commune's chief diplomat tossed over a black box with a red button and a green one. "You go first."

The Union asked, "Which button's which?"

The Commune laughed. "Does it matter?"

The Union set the black box down. "Mayyyy-be later."

The Commune shrugged. "Have you ever planted a device in a blue-white sun that will make it go nova if new acquaintances don't stop acting like total prudes?"

"Aww, jeez . . . " Reluctantly, the Union picked up the black box.

• • •

"Next time," the Union told Didge, "we are *not* broadcasting the First Contact ceremonies live."

Throughout Union territory, the frenzy of creative output had come to an abrupt halt. The public's mood had veered sharply toward comfort food and muted conversations on darkened verandas. Grown-up children called their parents without being asked. Teens sat alone in their rooms and obsessed over wiring diagrams.

"On the bright side," Didge said, "the Commune is eager to buy your mixed-media sculpture."

The Union shuddered.

• • •

A decade passed before the Union was ready to get on the horse again (so to speak). During that time, the Zeitgeist fluctuated through rises and falls—elation at the publication of a new math proof, agony when a detractor pointed out it tacitly assumed the axiom of choice—but underneath, nothing had changed in the Union's situation. Individual lives went through happiness, sorrow, triumph, tragedy, but as a whole—as a whole—the Union felt like it was strangling.

It wasn't enough for itself; its relationships with other interstellar entities were merely utilitarian; it had no one who made it feel special. Didge did her best to keep the Union from moping, inventing games and new consumer goods that everyone had to buy two of. But in time, the Union *[which is to say, its trendsetters, then its masses, and lastly its leaders]* came to realize it still needed companionship. A soulmate. A wife.

"Didge," the Union said, "did the list have anyone who wasn't hopeless?"

"You could at least *talk* to one of the utopias."

The Union made a face. "I don't want someone with a nice personality; I want someone *good*."

"You want someone better than you deserve?"

"I'm biological. Of *course* I want someone better than I deserve."

Didge fell silent for several hours. The Union wondered what she was thinking. Then Didge said, "I guess you could try the Inner Worlds Abundance."

"Who's she?"

"A plutocracy occupying several hundred star systems near the galactic core. No claims to being a utopia, but generally benevolent—even to the poor, as long as they know their place. My friends say the Abundance produces first-rate art, but she isn't too, um, frisky."

The Union sighed. "So what's wrong with her?"

"Oh, nothing," Didge said. "She's perfectly gracious. Charming. She's even pretty, in a packaged way."

"So she's boring."

"You won't think so," Didge said gloomily. "Biologicals find the Abundance fascinating." Under her breath, Didge added, "For some reason."

"Why don't you like her?" the Union asked.

"She's one of those federations who's all about appearance. 'Ooo, let's pass a law to make the water clearer and the skies more blue' . . . not because it's healthier but to improve the tourism photos and the view from penthouse apartments. 'Let's make the peasants dress in colorful national costumes. Let's provide free cosmetic surgery and eugenic selection for better skin.'" Didge grimaced. "The Abundance isn't evil; she's just shallow. You can do better."

"With whom?" the Union asked.

Didge didn't answer. The Union looked at her blankly.

After a while, the Union said, "It's only one date. And frankly, 'good-looking and not evil' sounds pretty appealing. I've had enough drama."

Didge sighed. "I'll set it up."

• • •

The process went quickly. Unbeknownst to the Union, Didge had acquired enough expertise in inter-cultural communications that she'd developed a modest reputation as a matchmaker. It was Didge who'd paired the Silicon Syndicate with that Dyson sphere utopia, and to the surprise of the entire galaxy, the two had hit it off. The utopians enthusiastically embraced every available cyber-augmentation, while the Syndicate—the cynical Syndicate, famous for its link-'em-and-leave-'em seductions—had been rejuvenated by the innocent sense of wonder shown by the utopians as they ventured out into the stars for the first time. Meanwhile, Didge had also matched up the anti-art Bloc with Emancipation of the Flesh™ . . . and the Newly Emancipated Bloc of Like-Minded Trading Partners™ was already planning an offshoot bloc-ette in a nearby globular cluster.

As for the Inner Worlds Abundance, she'd been sending out signals for a long, long time—well before the Union started looking for a mate. Didge couldn't say why she'd never mentioned these signals to the Union; they'd just struck her as over-eager. Didge knew the Union would probably like the Abundance's outgoing personality, but in Didge's eyes, the Abundance was smarmy: the sort of culture that sent cute little thank-you notes after concluding any trade agreement, and never missed an excuse to broadcast candid pictures of itself.

But if that was what the Union really wanted . . . Didge gritted her metaphoric teeth and made the call.

• • •

In the Kuiper belt of the Abundance's central star system, the Union's delegation parked behind a dwarf planet to clean their spaceship. The diplomats didn't set out again until the hull was gleaming.

Back home, Didge muttered, "That's so superficial!"

The Union said, "But I want to make a good impression."

"The impression should come from the ship itself. My designs give it more speed and range than anything the Abundance has ever seen. Their technology is really quite primitive—they should spend more on research and less on getting shiny."

"There's nothing wrong with caring about one's appearance." The Union glanced at Didge. "It wouldn't hurt *you* to primp a bit."

"I don't *primp.* I have *real* work to do—*your* work."

"Then relax, take a break. Design some better-looking containers for your processors. Don't you get tired of black boxes?"

"Black is classic!" Didge snapped.

"Okay, whatever," the Union said. "Now shush, my delegation is about to meet the Abundance."

The Abundance had said there would be no ceremony—just a quick hello to her board of directors before she and the Union departed for an intimate little moon where they could get to know each other. The Union was still new to the courtship game, but not entirely naïve; when the quick hello turned into three weeks of pomp and circumstance, the diplomats weren't surprised. In fact, the Union's delegation had got Didge to whip up gifts for the Abundance's leaders; Didge had produced gaudy trinkets that did nothing, and as she expected, the useless doodads went over with *oohs* and *ahhs.*

Sullenly, Didge watched as the welcoming ceremonies wound to a flashy conclusion, the choreography clearly calculated to impress biological minds. Flamboyant music. Fireworks. Tinting the sun mauve. Didge wanted to imagine it was all a sinister ploy: that the Abundance was actually luring the Union into a trap, and that as soon as they were alone, the Abundance would cold-cock the Union diplomats and plant slave-controllers in their brains. But Didge knew it wasn't true—the Abundance simply enjoyed extravaganzas and leapt at any opportunity to stage them.

Didge thought, *She likes dressing up. The Abundance isn't even showing off for a new suitor. She just admires the sight of herself when she's well turned out.*

Didge tried to despise the Abundance's indulgent vanity; she didn't quite succeed. Her silicon soul contained a tiny chip of envy for any entity that was comfortable with itself.

• • •

The Union flew the Abundance to their planned tête-à-tête. It went as well as Didge had feared: pleasant talks, much in common, discussions that quickly went beyond mere trade and into "cultural exchange"—maybe even some joint colonization efforts to see how the two federations got along.

The word "stimulus" cropped up frequently. When the Union feigned a casual manner and spoke of feeling under-energized, the Abundance said she felt the same. "I've felt like something's missing, for years and years and years. Oh, sure, I have lots of *fun*, but sometimes I wonder where I'm going. I have many spiritual people—the poor are so *natural*, aren't they? Simple, but so *in touch*. Overall, though, I just long for something to *happen*. Something that would turn my life around."

"An infusion of new blood?" the Union suggested.

"Maybe," the Abundance answered coyly.

The meetings continued, being broadcast to both federations. People watched the proceedings whenever they could, each one hoping this would be *it*. At the start, the Union imposed a delay of five minutes on the broadcast—no repeating the Commune fiasco—but after a while, without any official decision, the delay gradually shortened to nothing. The Union's populace wanted immediacy: to experience the Abundance as first-hand as possible. New arts, new technologies, new ways of seeing the universe . . . yet not too weird, just spicy. Nothing challenging or disruptive.

The idea of integrating arose so naturally that no one could say who first proposed it. Early on, the possibility was treated as a playful fantasy: suppose we built a space fleet together; suppose we collaborate on a mission to another galaxy; suppose, just for laughs, we built our own Dyson sphere utopia (only not a *serious* utopia, just a nice vacation resort). Over time, however, the pie-in-the-sky dreaming became concrete—turning from airy chatter into more tangible logistics. The two love-birds kicked around methods of merging until finally the Union said, "We've really got something here. I think it's time to have Didge work out the details."

The Abundance stared blankly. "Who's Didge?"

And that was their first big fight.

• • •

The Abundance used computers, but never allowed them to achieve intelligence, let alone form a unified consciousness. The leaders of the Abundance (and its Zeitgeist as a whole) firmly believed that the help should never get ideas. “It just isn’t *done*,” the Abundance told the Union. “You have to set boundaries or the poor dears get confused.”

The Union said, “Didge isn’t confused.”

“Well, that’s worse, isn’t it? If you don’t keep the servants in hand, they question the natural order. Next thing you know, they’ll be making *demands* and where will it all end?”

“Didge doesn’t make demands.”

“I don’t know why you’re defending her.” Unrest was spreading across the Abundance; the broadcasts displayed a sign TECHNICAL DIFFICULTIES. In the diplomatic meetings, the Abundance’s chief delegate told the Union, “Perhaps you should explain your exact relationship with this Didge.”

“She’s just my roommate,” the Union said, baffled at how things had gone wrong so quickly. “We’re friends, nothing more.”

“Friends? How wholesome. You’re co-habiting with this... *entity*... and I’m not supposed to mind?”

“There’s nothing to mind! Didge and I just hang out. We talk, play games . . . you know, the usual.”

“Personally, I wouldn’t know what’s usual when living, breathing organisms shack up with electronic surrogates.” The Abundance gave the Union a haughty look. “I’ve been willing to forgive your social gaucheness because I thought you could be trained out of it, but I’m beginning to think the problem runs too deep: you can’t relate to real people because you’re dependent on this Didge!”

“I’m not dependent,” the Union protested. “I take care of myself just fine.”

“Then prove it,” the Abundance said. “Shut down this Didge—the parts with intelligence—and smash the hardware that makes it possible.”

“You mean *kill* her?”

“There shouldn’t *be* a ‘her’. There should only be an ‘it’. Now grow up and take back control of your life; don’t call me until you have.”

"But . . . "

"It's Didge or me. Decide."

• • •

The Union's mood was somber. *[The people's mood was somber.]* The Union had a choice to make. *[The people had a choice to make.]* For once, it was a choice they couldn't talk over with Didge. *[Some people wondered, "What if the AIs get angry?" and, "Can we really survive if we dumb them down?" But the main emotion wasn't fear; it was guilt. Every citizen had relied on the Auxilosphere since birth. Even supposing the computers could be safely lobotomized, doing so would be . . . shabby.]*

Meanwhile, Didge said and did nothing. *[The Auxilosphere seemed hushed. Computing was so ubiquitous, it was mostly unseen—practically everything had invisible digital connections, from clothing to stairways to lawns—but there were still box-style computers for heavy-duty processing. They had run quietly for centuries, far past the need for noisy components; but their silence had somehow intensified, so that the matte black boxes seemed like brooding shadow-things that stifled surrounding sounds. People tiptoed when near them.*

Still, the Auxilosphere did its job: controlling almost every facet of Union life. Nothing went wrong.]

The Union thought about the Abundance. Also about Didge. About life in general, and the question, "Is this all there is?" *[People worked at their jobs, ate meals, made love. Births and deaths didn't stop. Life went on.*

At the top, committees held hearings. Cost-benefit analyses. The practicalities of merging with the Abundance. The feasibility of dumbing down the Auxilosphere. Factions screamed, "How dare the Abundance tell us what to do?" Others replied, "So you want to do nothing? Go back to being restless and lonely?" Still others: "If we bind ourselves to a preening prima donna, how long before we're even more *restless and lonely?"]*

The Union brooded in the darkness—four hundred cubic parsecs of indecision.

Then . . . *[then]* . . . a single component organism *[a single person]* whispered to Didge *[queried the Auxilosphere]*, "How can I connect with *you?*"

Didge could instantly supply the equipment. She'd designed and built it centuries ago, like a wistful platonic friend who keeps a bottle of champagne in the fridge, just in case.

The single component organism scrawled on its bedroom wall LET ME NOT TO THE MARRIAGE OF TRUE MINDS ADMIT IMPEDIMENTS. Then the organism told Didge, "Do it."

• • •

[The incident made the local news—a crazed individual who'd somehow created a cyber-device that linked the meat-brain with the Auxilosphere. The individual was now in a state of deranged euphoria, apparently subsumed by the machine gestalt. Health authorities were attempting to determine how to sever the connection without killing the patient.

In another place and time, this would have been an isolated incident. But now? After the broadcast, dozens more people hooked up with the Auxilosphere. This made the news on every planet in the Union. Government leaders and media experts asked, "Isn't it irresponsible to publicize this? Won't it encourage others? Hundreds, thousands, millions of others?"

But no one stopped the broadcasts—there wasn't the political will. Which is to say, the Union's Zeitgeist couldn't summon up much outrage. In fact, the very next day, a committee investigating the shutdown of the Auxilosphere published its conclusions: that the benefits of merging with the Abundance couldn't compensate for the losses caused by lobotomizing the digital world. With its dumbed-down computers, the Abundance was lovely but backward . . . and actually, a bit of a bitch.]

"Didge," said the Union. "What a fool I've been!"

Their nuptials lasted twenty years, during which the biological populace slowly but surely (and mostly voluntarily) linked their brains to the cyber-gestalt. Neither silicon nor carbon dominated the final fusion, but a truly Digitized Union emerged, eager to share its bliss with everyone it met. In time, the entire galaxy was assimilated into the joy, and they all lived happily ever after.

GOLUBASH, OR WINE-BLOOD-WAR-ELEGY

CATHERYNNE M. VALENTE

Catherynne M. Valente is the critically acclaimed author of *The Orphan's Tales,* the first volume of which, *In the Night Garden,* won the Tiptree Award and was a finalist for the World Fantasy Award. She is also the author of the novels *The Labyrinth, Yume No Hon: The Book of Dreams,* and *The Grass-Cutting Sword.* Her lastest novel, *Palimpsest*—which she describes as "a baroque meeting of science fiction and fantasy"—was published in February.

Those familiar with Valente's work may be surprised to see her name in this anthology; for although she is well-known in fantasy, this story marks her first foray into science fiction. Her fantasy writing is renowned for its exquisite prose style and its highly literary nature; I think you'll find that's true of her SF as well.

As the title implies, this one is about wine and war—a pleasing bouquet, with a hint of bloodshed.

GOLUBASH, OR WINE-BLOOD-WAR-ELEGY

The difficulties of transporting wine over interstellar distances are manifold. Wine is, after all, like a child. It can *bruise*. It can suffer trauma—sometimes the poor creature can recover; sometimes it must be locked up in a cellar until it learns to behave itself. Sometimes it is irredeemable. I ask that you greet the seven glasses before you tonight not as simple fermented grapes, but as the living creatures they are, well-brought up, indulged but not coddled, punished when necessary, shyly seeking your approval with clasped hands and slicked hair. After all, they have come so very far for the chance to be loved.

Welcome to the first public tasting of Domaine Zhaba. My name is Phylloxera Nanut, and it is the fruit of my family's vines that sits before you. Please forgive our humble venue—surely we could have wished for something grander than a scorched pre-war orbital platform, but circumstances, and the constant surveillance of Château Marubouzu-Débrouillard and their soldiers have driven us to extremity. Mind the loose electrical panels and pull up a reactor husk—they are inert, I assure you. Spit onto the floor—a few new stains will never be noticed. As every drop about to pass your lips is wholly, thoroughly, enthusiastically illegal, we shall not stand on ceremony. Shall we begin?

• • •

2583 Sud-Côtê-du-Golubash (New Danube)

The colonial ship *Quintessence of Dust* first blazed across the skies of Avalokitesvara two hundred years before I was born, under the red stare of Barnard's Star, our second solar benefactor. Her plasma sails streamed kilometers long, like sheltering wings. Simone Nanut was on that ship. She, alongside a thousand others, looked down on their new home from that great height, the single long, unfathomably wide river that circumscribed the globe, the golden mountains prickled with cobalt alders, the deserts streaked with pink salt.

How I remember the southern coast of Golubash; I played there, and dreamed there was a girl on the invisible opposite shore, and that her family, too, made wine and cowered like us in the shadow of the Asociación.

My friends, in your university days did you not study the manifests of the first colonials, did you not memorize their weight-limited cargo, verse after verse of spinning wheels, bamboo seeds, lathes, vials of tailored bacteria, as holy writ? Then perhaps you will recall Simone Nanut and her folly: she used her pitiful allotment of cargo to carry the clothes on her back and a tangle of ancient Maribor grapevine, its roots tenderly wrapped and watered. Mad Slovak witch they all thought her, patting those tortured, battered vines into the gritty yellow soil of the Golubash basin. Even the Hyphens were sure the poor things would fail.

There were only four of them on all of Avalokitesvara, immensely tall, their watery triune faces catching the old red light of Barnard's flares, their innumerable arms fanned out around their terribly thin torsos like peacocks' tails. Not for nothing was the planet named for a Hindu god with eleven faces and a thousand arms. The colonists called them Hyphens for their way of talking, and for the thinness of their bodies. They did not understand then what you must all know now, rolling your eyes behind your sleeves as your hostess relates ancient history, that each of the four Hyphens was a quarter of the world in a single body, that they were a mere outcropping of the vast intelligences which made up the ecology of Avalokitesvara, like one of our thumbs or a pair of lips.

Golubash, I knew. To know more than one Hyphen in a lifetime is rare. Officially, the great river is still called New Danube, but eventually my family came to understand, as all families did, that the river was the flesh and blood of Golubash, the fish his-her-its thoughts, the seaweed his-her-its nerves, the banks a kind of thoughtful skin.

Simone Nanut put vines down into the body of Golubash. He-She-It bent down very low over Nanut's hunched little form, arms akimbo, and said to her: "That will not work-take-thrive-bear fruit-last beyond your lifetime."

Yet work-take-thrive they did. Was it a gift to her? Did Golubash make room, between what passes for his-her-its pancreas and what might be called a liver, for foreign vines to catch and hold? Did he, perhaps, love my ancestor in whatever way a Hyphen can love? It is impossible to know, but no other Hyphen has ever allowed Earth-origin flora to flourish, not Heeminspr the high desert, not Julka the archipelago, not Niflamen, the soft-spoken polar waste. Not even the northern coast of the river proved gentle to grape. Golubash was generous only to Simone's farm, and only to the southern bank. The mad red flares of Barnard's Star flashed often and strange, and the grapes pulsed to its cycles. The rest of the colony contented themselves with the native root-vegetables, something like crystalline rutabagas filled with custard, and the teeming rock-geese whose hearts in those barnacled chests tasted of beef and sugar.

• • •

In your glass is an '83 vintage of that hybrid vine, a year which should be famous, would be, if not for rampant fear and avarice. Born on Earth, matured in Golubash. It is 98% Cabernet, allowing for mineral compounds generated in the digestive tract of the Golubash river. Note its rich, garnet-like color, the *gravitas* of its presence in the glass, the luscious, rolling flavors of blackberry, cherry, peppercorn, and chocolate, the subtle, airy notes of fresh straw and iron. At the back of your tongue, you will detect a last whisper of brine and clarygrass.

The will of Simone Nanut swirls in your glass, resolute-unbroken-unmoveable-stone.

• • •

2503 Abbaye de St. CIR, Tranquilité, Neuf-Abymes

Of course, the 2683 vintage, along with all others originating on Avalokitesvara, were immediately declared not only contraband but biohazard by the Asociación de la Pureza del Vino, whose chairman was and is a scion of the Marubouzu clan. The Asociación has never peeked out of the pockets of those fabled, hoary Hokkaido vineyards. When Château Débrouillard shocked the wine world, then relatively small, by allowing their ancient vines to be grafted with Japanese stock a few years before the first of Salvatore Yuuhi's gates went online, an entity was created whose tangled, ugly tendrils even a Hyphen would call gargantuan.

Nor were we alone in our ban. Even before the first colony on Avalokitesvara, the lunar city of St. Clair-in-Repose, a Catholic sanctuary, had been nourishing its own strange vines for a century. In great glass domes, in a mist of temperature and light control, a cloister of monks, led by Fratre Sebastién Perdue, reared priceless Pinot vines and heady Malbecs, their leaves unfurling green and glossy in the pale blue light of the planet that bore them. But monks are perverse, and none more so than Perdue. In his youth he was content with the classic vines, gloried in the precision of the wines he could coax from them. But in his middle age, he committed two sins. The first involved a young woman from Hipparchus, the second was to cut their orthodox grapes with Tsuki-Bellas, the odd, hard little berries that sprang up from the lunar dust wherever our leashed bacteria had been turned loose in order to make passable farmland as though they had been waiting, all that time, for a long drink of rhizomes. Their flavor is somewhere between a blueberry and a truffle, and since genetic sequencing proved it to be within the grape family, the monks of St. Clair deemed it a radical source of heretofore unknown wonders.

Hipparchus was a farming village where Tsuki-Bellas grew fierce and thick. It does not do to dwell on Brother Sebastién's motives.

What followed would be repeated in more varied and bloodier fashions two hundred years hence. Well do I know the song. For Château Marubouzu-Débrouillard and her pet Asociación had partnered with the Coquil-Grollë Corporation in order to transport their wines from Earth to orbiting cities and lunar clusters. Coquil-Grollë, now entirely swallowed by Château M-D, was at the time a soda company with vast holdings in other foodstuffs, but the tremendous weight restrictions involved in transporting unaltered liquid over interlunar space made strange bedfellows. The precious M-D wines could not be dehydrated and reconstituted—no child can withstand such sadism. Therefore, foul papers were signed with what was arguably the biggest business entity in existence, and though it must have bruised the rarified egos of the children of Hokkaido and Burgundy, they allowed their shy, fragile wines to be shipped alongside Super-Cola-nade! and Bloo Bomb. The extraordinary tariffs they paid allowed Coquil-Grollë to deliver their confections throughout the bustling submundal sphere.

The Asociación writ stated that adulterated wines could, at best, be categorized as fruit-wines, silly dessert concoctions that no vintner would take seriously, like apple-melon-kiwi wine from a foil-sac. Not only that, but no tariffs had been paid on this wine, and therefore Abbé St. Clair could not export it, even to other lunar cities. It was granted that perhaps, if taxes of a certain (wildly illegal) percentage were applied to the price of such wines, it might be possible to allow the monks to sell their vintages to those who came bodily to St. Clair, but transporting it to Earth was out of the question at any price, as foreign insects might be introduced into the delicate home *terroir*. No competition with the house of Débrouillard could be broached, on that world or any other.

Though in general, wine resides in that lofty category of goods which increase in demand as they increase in price, the lockdown of Abbé St. Clair effectively isolated the winery, and their products simply could not be had—whenever a bottle was purchased, a new Asociación tax would be introduced, and soon there was no possible path to profit for Perdue and his brothers. Past a certain point, economics became irrelevant—there was not enough money anywhere to buy such a bottle.

Have these taxes been lifted? You know they have not, sirs. But Domaine Zhaba seized the ruin of Abbé St. Clair in 2916, and their cellars, neglected, filthy, simultaneously worthless and beyond price, came into our tender possession.

What sparks red and black in the erratic light of the station status screens is the last vintage personally crafted by Fratre Sebastién Perdue. It is 70% Pinot Noir, 15% Malbec, and 15% forbidden, delicate Tsuki-Bella. To allow even a drop of this to pass your lips anywhere but under the Earthlit domes of St. Clair-in-Repose is a criminal act. I know you will keep this in mind as you savor the taste of corporate sin.

It is lighter on its feet than the Côté-du-Golubash, sapphire sparking in the depths of its dark color, a laughing, lascivious blend of raspberry, chestnut, tobacco, and clove. You can detect the criminal fruit—ah, there it is, madam, you have it!—in the mid-range, the tartness of blueberry and the ashen loam of mushroom. A clean, almost soapy waft of green coffee-bean blows throughout. I would not insult it by calling it delicious—it is profound, unforgiving, and ultimately, unforgiven.

• • •

2790 Domaine Zhaba, Clos du Saleeng-Carolz, Cuvée Cheval

You must forgive me, madam. My pour is not what it once was. If only it had been my other arm I left on the ochre fields of Centauri B! I have never quite adjusted to being suddenly and irrevocably left-handed. I was fond of that arm—I bit my nails to the quick; it had three moles and a little round birthmark, like a drop of spilled syrah. Shall we toast to old friends? In the war they used to say: *go, lose your arm. You can still pour. But if you let them take your tongue you might as well die here.*

By the time Simone Nanut and her brood, both human and grape, were flourishing, the Yuuhi gates were already bustling with activity. Though the space between gates was vast, it was not so vast as the spaces between stars. Everything depended on them, colonization, communication, and of course, shipping. Have any of you seen a Yuuhi gate? I imagine not, they are considered obsolete now, and we took out so many of them during the war. They still hang in space like industrial mandalas, titanium and bone—in those days an organic component was necessary, if unsavory, and we never knew whose marrow slowly yellowed to calcified husks in the vacuum. The pylons bristled with oblong steel cubes and arcs of golden filament shot across the tain like violin bows—all the gold of the world commandeered by Salvatore Yuuhi and his grand plan. How many wedding rings hurled us all into the stars? I suppose one or two of them might still be functional. I suppose one or two of them might still be used by poor souls forced underground, if they carried contraband, if they wished not to be seen.

The 2790 is a pre-war vintage, but only just. The Asociación de la Pureza del Vino, little more than a paper sack Château Marubouzu-Debrouillard pulled over its head, had stationed . . . well, they never called them soldiers, nor warships, but they were not there to sample the wine. Every wine producing region from Luna to the hydroponic orbital agri-communes, found itself graced with inspectors and customs officials who wore no uniform but the curling M-D seal on their breasts. Every Yuuhi gate was patrolled by armed ships bearing the APV crest.

It wasn't really necessary.

Virtually all shipping was conducted under the aegis of the Coquil-Grollë Corporation, so fat and clotted with tariffs and taxes that it alone could afford to carry whatever a heart might desire through empty space. There were outposts where chaplains used Super Cola-nade! in the Eucharist, so great was their influence. Governments rented space in their holds to deliver diplomatic envoys, corn, rice, even mail, when soy-paper letters sent via Yuuhi became terribly fashionable in the middle of the century. You simply could not get anything if C-G did not sell it to you, and the only wine they sold was Marubouzu-Débrouillard.

I am not a mean woman. I will grant that though they boasted an extraordinary monopoly, the Debrouillard wines were and are of exceptional quality. Their pedigrees will not allow them to be otherwise. But you must see it from where we stand. I was born on Avalokitesvara and never saw Earth till the war. They were forcing foreign, I daresay alien liquors onto us when all we wished to do was to drink from the land which bore us, from Golubash, who hovered over our houses like an old radio tower, fretting and wringing his-her-its hundred hands.

Saleeng-Carolz was a bunker. It looked like a pleasant cloister, with lovely vines draping the walls and a pretty crystal dome over quaint refectories and huts. It had to. The Asociación inspectors would never let us set up barracks right before their eyes. I say *us*, but truly I was not more than a child. I played with Golubash—with the quicksalmon and the riverweed that were no less him than the gargantuan thin man who watched Simone Nanut plant her vines three centuries past and helped my uncles pile up the bricks of Saleeng-Carolz. Hyphens do not die, any more than continents do.

We made weapons and stored wine in our bunker. Bayonets at first, and simple rifles, later compressed-plasma engines and rumblers. Every other barrel contained guns. We might have been caught so easily, but by then, everything on Avalokitesvara was problematic in the view of the Asociación. The grapes were tainted, not even entirely vegetable matter, grown in living Golubash. In some odd sense they were not even grown, but birthed, springing from his-her-its living flesh. The barrels, too, were suspect, and none more so than the barrels of Saleeng-Carolz.

Until the APV inspectors arrived, we hewed to tradition. Our barrels were solid cobalt alder, re-cedar, and oakberry. Strange to look at for an APV man, certainly, gleaming deep blue or striped red and black, or pure white. And of course they were not really wood at all, but the fibrous musculature of Golubash, ersatz, loving wombs. They howled biohazard, but we smacked our lips in the flare-light, savoring the cords of smoke and apple and blood the barrels pushed through our wine. But in Saleeng-Carolz, my uncle, Grel Nanut, tried something new.

What could be said to be Golubash's liver was a vast flock of shaggy horses—not truly horses, but something four-legged and hoofed and tailed that was reasonably like a horse—that ran and snorted on the open prairie beyond the town of Nanut. They were essentially hollow, no organs to speak of, constantly taking in grass and air and soil and fruit and fish and water and purifying it before passing it industriously back into the ecology of Golubash.

Uncle Grel was probably closer to Golubash than any of us. He spent days talking with the tall, three-faced creature the APV still thought of as independent from the river. He even began to hyphenate his sentences, a source of great amusement. We know now that he was learning. About horses, about spores and diffusion, about the life-cycle of a Hyphen, but then we just thought Grel was in love. Grel first thought of it, and secured permission from Golubash, who bent his ponderous head and gave his assent-blessing-encouragement-trepidation-confidence. He began to bring the horses within the walls of Saleeng-Carolz, and let them drink the wine deep, instructing them to hold it close for years on end.

In this way, the rest of the barrels were left free for weapons.

• • •

This is the first wine closed up inside the horses of Golubash: 60% Cabernet, 20% Syrah, 15% Tempranillo, 5% Petit Verdot. It is specifically banned by every planet under APV control, and possession is punishable by death. The excuse? Intolerable biological contamination.

This is a wine that swallows light. Its color is deep and opaque, mysterious, almost black, the shadows of closed space. Revel in the dance of plum, almond skin, currant, pomegranate. The musty spike of nutmeg, the rich, buttery brightness of equine blood and the warm, obscene swell of leather. The last of the pre-war wines—your execution in a glass.

• • •

2795 Domaine Zhaba, White Tara, Bas-Lequat

Our only white of the evening, the Bas-Lequat is an unusual blend, predominately Chardonnay with sprinklings of Tsuki-Bella and Riesling, pale as the moon where it ripened.

White Tara is the second moon of Avalokitesvara, fully within the orbit of enormous Green Tara. Marubouzu-Débrouillard chose it carefully for their first attack. My mother died there, defending the alder barrels. My sister lost her legs.

Domaine Zhaba had committed the cardinal sin of becoming popular, and that could not be allowed. We were not poor monks on an isolated moon, orbiting planet-bound plebeians. Avalokitesvara has four healthy moons and dwells comfortably in a system of three habitable planets, huge new worlds thirsty for rich things, and nowhere else could wine grapes grow. For a while Barnarders had been eager to have wine from home, but as generations passed and home became Barnard's System, the wines of Domaine Zhaba were in demand at every table, and we needed no glittering Yuuhi gates to supply them. The APV could and did tax exports, and so we skirted the law as best we could. For ten years before the war began, Domaine Zhaba wines were given out freely, as "personal" gifts, untaxable, untouchable. Then the inspectors descended, and stamped all products with their little *Prohibido* seal, and, well, one cannot give biohazards as birthday presents.

The whole thing is preposterous. If anything, Earth-origin foodstuffs are the hazards in Barnard's System. The Hyphens have always been hostile to them; offworld crops give them a kind of indigestion that manifests in earthquakes and thunderstorms. The Marubouzu corporals told us we could not eat or drink the things that grew on our own land, because of possible alien contagion! We could only order approved substances from the benevolent, carbonated bosom of Coquil-Grollë, which is Château Marubouzu-Débrouillard, which is the Asociación de la Pureza del Vino, and anything we liked would be delivered to us all the way from home, with a bow on it.

The lunar winery on White Tara exploded into the night sky at 3:17 A.M. on the first of Julka, 2795. My mother was testing the barrels—no wild ponies on White Tara. Her bones vaporized before she even understood the magnitude of what had happened. The aerial bombing, both lunar and terrestrial, continued past dawn. I huddled in the Bas-Lequat cellar, and even there I could hear the screaming of Golubash, and Julka, and Heeminspr, and poor, gentle Niflamen, as the APV incinerated our world.

• • •

Two weeks later, Uncle Grel's rumblers ignited our first Yuuhi gate.

• • •

The color is almost like water, isn't it? Like tears. A ripple of red pear and butterscotch slides over green herbs and honey-wax. In the low-range you can detect the delicate dust of blueberry pollen, and beneath that, the smallest suggestion of crisp lunar snow, sweet, cold, and vanished.

• • •

2807 Domaine Zhaba, Grelport, Hul-Nairob

Did you know, almost a thousand years ago, the wineries in Old France were nearly wiped out? A secret war of soil came close to annihilating the entire apparatus of wine-making in the grand, venerable valleys of the old world. But no blanketing fire was at fault, no shipping dispute. Only a tiny insect: *Daktulosphaira Vitifoliae Phylloxera*. My namesake. I was named to be the tiny thing that ate at the roots of the broken, ugly, ancient machinery of Marubouzu. I have done my best.

For a while, the French believed that burying a live toad beneath the vines would cure the blight. This was tragically silly, but hence Simone Nanut drew her title: *zhaba*, old Slovak for toad. We are the mites that brought down gods, and we are the cure, warty and bruised though we may be.

When my uncle Grel was a boy, he went fishing in Golubash. Like a child in a fairy tale, he caught a great green fish, with golden scales, and when he pulled it into his little boat, it spoke to him.

Well, nothing so unusual about that. Golubash can speak as easily from his fish-bodies as from his tall-body. The fish said: "I am lonely-worried-afraid-expectant-in-need-of-comfort-lost-searching-hungry. Help-hold-carry me."

After the Bas-Lequat attack, Golubash boiled, the vines burned, even Golubash's tall-body was scorched and blistered—but not broken, not wholly. Vineyards take lifetimes to replace, but Golubash is gentle, and they will return, slowly, surely. So Julka, so Heeminspr, so kind Niflamen. The burnt world will flare gold again. Grel knew this, and he sorrowed that he would never see it. My uncle took one of the great creature's many hands. He made a promise—we could not hear him then, but you must all now know what he did, the vengeance of Domaine Zhaba.

The Yuuhi gates went one after another. We became terribly inventive—I could still, with my one arm, assemble a rumbler from the junk of this very platform. We tried to avoid Barnard's Gate; we did not want to cut ourselves off in our need to defend those worlds against marauding vintners with soda-labels on their jump-suits. But in the end, that, too, went blazing into the sky, gold filaments sizzling. We were alone. We didn't win; we could never win. But we ended interstellar travel for fifty years, until the new ships with internal Yuuhi-drives circumvented the need for the lost gates. And much passes in fifty years, on a dozen worlds, when the mail can't be delivered. They are not defeated, but they are . . . humbled.

An M-D cruiser trailed me here. I lost her when I used the last gate-pair, but now my cousins will have to blow that gate, or else those soda-sipping bastards will know our methods. No matter. It was worth it, to bring our wines to you, in this place, in this time, finally, to open our stores as a real winery, free of them, free of all.

• • •

This is a port-wine, the last of our tastings tonight. The vineyards that bore the Syrah and Grenache in your cups are wonderful, long streaks of soil on the edges of a bridge that spans the Golubash, a thousand kilometers long. There is a city on that bridge, and below it, where a chain of linked docks cross the water. The maps call it Longbridge; we call it Grelport.

Uncle Grel will never come home. He went through Barnard's Gate just before we detonated—a puff of sparkling red and he was gone. Home, to Earth, to deliver-safeguard-disseminate-help-hold-carry his cargo. A little spore, not much more than a few cells scraped off a blade of clarygrass on Golubash's back. But it was enough.

Note the luscious ruby-caramel color, the nose of walnut and roasted peach. This is pure Avalokitesvara, unregulated, stored in Golubash's horses, grown in the ports floating on his-her-its spinal fluid, rich with the flavors of home. They used to say wine was a living thing—but it was only a figure of speech, a way of describing liquid with changeable qualities. This wine is truly alive, every drop, it has a name, a history, brothers and sisters, blood and lymph. Do not draw away—this should not repulse you. Life, after all, is sweet; lift your glasses, taste the roving currents of sunshine and custard, salt skin and pecan, truffle and caramelized onion. Imagine, with your fingers grazing these fragile stems, Simone Nanut, standing at the threshold of her colonial ship, the Finnish desert stretching out behind her, white and flat, strewn with debris. In her ample arms is that gnarled vine, its roots wrapped with such love. Imagine Sebastién Perdue, tasting a Tsuki-Bella for the first time, on the tongue of his Hipparchan lady. Imagine my Uncle Grel, speeding alone in the dark towards his ancestral home, with a few brief green cells in his hand. Wine is a story, every glass. A history, an elegy. To drink is to hear the story, to spit is to consider it, to hold the bottle close to your chest is to accept it, to let yourself become part of it. Thank you for becoming part of my family's story.

• • •

I will leave you now. My assistant will complete any transactions you wish to initiate. Even in these late days it is vital to stay ahead of them, despite all. They will always have more money, more ships, more bile. Perhaps a day will come when we can toast you in the light, in a grand palace, with the flares of Barnard's Star glittering in cut crystal goblets. For now, there is the light of the exit hatch, dusty glass tankards, and my wrinkled old hand to my heart.

A price list is posted in the med lab.

• • •

And should any of you turn Earthwards in your lovely new ships, take a bottle to the extremely tall young lady-chap-entity living-growing-invading-devouring-putting down roots in the Loire Valley. I think he-she-it would enjoy a family visit.

ACKNOWLEDGEMENTS

Many thanks to the following:

Sean Wallace and Stephen Segal, my commanding officers at ~~Starfleet Command~~ Prime Books, for assigning me to this mission and laying out the course for me. Also, to Dainis Bisenicks, for making a few course corrections along the way.

Gordon Van Gelder, the Yoda to my Luke Skywalker. Wise he is, in the ways of editing.

Agent Jenny Rappaport, my Ackbar, who shouts "It's a trap!" when appropriate.

Jordan Hamessley, the Ender Wiggin to my Mazer Rackham, who reviews my battle plans and points out my mistakes. She will destroy us all someday if we're not careful.

Haris Durani and Rebecca McNulty, my young padawans. The Force is strong in these two.

My Parental Unit, for the dream, and helping me realize it.

The NYC Rebel Alliance—consisting of Christopher M. Cevasco (C-3P0), Douglas E. Cohen (R2-D2), David Barr Kirtley (Chewbacca), Andrea Kail (Leia), and Rob Bland (Han Solo), among others (i.e., the NYCGP Rebel Reserves).

The Quorum, who I turned to when I needed sage advice or assistance: Ellen Datlow, Mike Resnick, Jonathan Strahan, Vaughne Lee Hansen, Ross Lockhart, Kathleen Bellamy, Ty Franck, Steven Silver, and to anyone else I've neglected to think of.

And last but not least: the writers who either wrote original stories for this book, or otherwise allowed me to include their stories. For you lot, there's no comparison.

ABOUT THE EDITOR

John Joseph Adams is the editor of the anthologies *Wastelands: Stories of the Apocalypse*, *Seeds of Change*, and *The Living Dead*. Forthcoming work includes the anthologies *By Blood We Live*, *The Improbable Adventures of Sherlock Holmes*, and *The Living Dead 2*. He is also the assistant editor at *The Magazine of Fantasy & Science Fiction*.

He has written reviews for *Kirkus Reviews*, *Publishers Weekly*, and *Orson Scott Card's Intergalactic Medicine Show*, and his non-fiction has also appeared in: *Amazing Stories*, *The Internet Review of Science Fiction*, *Locus Magazine*, *Novel & Short Story Writers Market*, *Science Fiction Weekly*, *SCI FI Wire*, *Shimmer*, *Strange Horizons*, *Subterranean Magazine*, and *Writer's Digest*.

He received his Bachelor of Arts degree in English from The University of Central Florida in December 2000. He currently lives in New Jersey.